A

GRL

LIKE

YOU

A GIRL LIKE YOU

Cari Scribner

CIRCUIT BREAKER BOOKS

Circuit Breaker Books LLC
Portland, OR
www.circuitbreakerbooks.com

This is a work of fiction. Names, characters, businesses, places, events, locales, and incidents are either the products of the author's imagination or used in a fictitious manner. Any resemblance to actual persons, living or dead, or actual events is purely coincidental.

Clothespin illustraion by nikolam/stock.adobe.com

Book design by Vinnie Kinsella

ISBN: 978-1-953639-00-4
eISBN: 978-1-953639-01-1

LCCN: 2020921848

For My Sydney

1

"Lucky Strike" had a photo of a bowling alley in his dating profile. I hadn't been bowling for years, not since the kids were little, but I'd heard it was good exercise. After exchanging several messages making small talk, we agreed to meet at High Roller Lanes.

Strike, aka Louie, was waiting outside the doors, a zippered vinyl bag in each hand, when I pulled in. He was wearing a brown-and-gold striped bowling shirt and yelling my name, as if I hadn't already seen him.

"Jessica! Yo, Jess!"

Well, at least he's friendly. And it would be nice to play with a pro, not with the kids who threw gutter balls, then cried.

"Jessica?" He was still yelling, and for a moment I worried he was hard of hearing and I would have to shout back.

"Yup, that's me. I heard you calling when I was parking, Louie."

"Wanted to make sure you saw me."

It would be hard to miss him. He had packed at least fifty more pounds on the already large frame he'd shown in his photos and in real life he had a greased-back, Elvis-style pompadour. He pushed the door open with his shoulder and sailed through, leaving me to hold the door for myself before it shut in my face.

OK. Maybe just overly eager to get onto the lanes.

"It's $20 for two games, so you pay for one and I'll get the other," Louie said generously.

"What about renting shoes?"

"Got my own right here." He held up the smaller bag. "And my lucky ball."

I suppressed a laugh.

I traded my sneaks for scuffed bowling shoes and followed Louie, who was nearly skipping, to our lane.

"OK, well, let me just get warmed up."

He cracked his knuckles and did some side bends at the waist. Then as I watched in amazement, he bent over and touched his toes to stretch the back of his legs and rotated his neck, which also cracked.

"How's that going for you?" I asked.

"One second," Louie said, massaging his own shoulders, then briefly running in place. "OK, ready. I'll go first."

I sat down in the orange booth, a front row seat, thinking maybe I'd learn something from him. "Go for it."

He picked up his purple bowling ball that looked so shiny I wondered if he'd polished it.

And then he began to shuffle. Literally shuffle, from where I was sitting all the way out to the lane, already swinging his ball with his right arm.

OK. Maybe bowling form had changed since I'd last played.

But when he got to the line to make his throw, instead of making one more swing and propelling it toward the pins, he just dropped it, making a really loud noise that interrupted the man on the next lane.

The ball took an interminable time to roll down to the pins, eventually reaching a near halt and knocking down two pins. Two.

"Well, I got gypped on that one. Should have been a straight shot, but it had a wicked right hook."

OK.

He took his second shot, knocking down two more pins.

"Jesus!" Louie was clearly pissed. "Guess I'm off my game today."

He came back and glumly sat down.

I got up with my not-so-shiny pink ball and tried to use good form, throwing with surprising force, knocking down half the pins, leaving room for what might be a spare on the next roll.

"You got lucky on that one," Louie hollered.

Relaxing my shoulders, I took a shot that curved directly where I wanted it, taking down the remaining pins. Spare!

Louie glared from his seat.

"Lucky again."

He did another shuffle throw, taking down three pins, followed by a gutter ball.

"Where's the bar?" he growled.

He stormed away, not even asking if I wanted a drink.

I threw a 4 pin, then knocked down 3, narrowly missing a spare. Then I waited.

When my kids were little, I'd taken them bowling many times, but the only part they liked was choosing a bowling ball, always too large for their tiny handspans. Ian would carry his ball halfway down the alley, then drop it with a thud and try to kick it toward the pins. Madison threw hers so hard it would end up in the adjacent lane. After a few more attempts, I lured them off the lanes with quarters for a machine that dispensed rainbow hair ties and plastic orange motorcycles, because no kid wanted gumballs anymore.

It occurred to me that Louie might have run, leaving the bowling alley and me in his dust.

Eventually he showed up with a half-empty plastic cup of beer, and foam on his upper lip.

He took another shuffling shot. Threw a 2 pin.

"Goddammit!" he said, still too loud.

After his second shot, a gutter, he drained his beer and went back to the bar for another, this time also bringing back a soft pretzel drenched in cheese sauce.

Screw him, I thought.

I bowled my best game ever, scoring 150. Louie: 79. Actually, I was surprised his score was that high.

By then he'd had three beers, the pretzel, and a slice of pizza with bacon. He used the men's room almost every time I shot, as if he couldn't bear to watch.

"Well, that's that," I said when the game ended.

"Yeah, that's it," Louie said. "My shoulder's been bothering me, so I didn't play like I normally do."

Neither of us mentioned the second game we'd paid for.

I exchanged my shoes and headed for the door.

"We'll have to do something different next time," Louie said.

Thankfully, he was holding his two bags, so there was no chance of a hug.

"I think we're done, but it was nice meeting you."

"OK," Louie said, shuffling off to his car.

Note to self: Next time I feel the urge to bowl, go with the kids.

How had I gotten to this awkward stage in my life? The only way to tell this story is to go back and start at the beginning.

2

BRYAN AND I TOOK TURNS CRYING AS WE WENT THROUGH OUR CLOSET, then his dresser drawers and his shoe pile. We tried to stay calm as we sorted out his summer clothes, the ones he would take when he moved south.

He was looking for his golf shoes, which had never reappeared after we moved into the house three years earlier. I hoped there would be plenty of sunny golfing days for him in North Carolina. Our marriage was over, but I wished him a better life after he went south.

Bryan's daughter, Cassie, who's twenty-four, and toddler-age son, Ben, lived in Wilmington. Every month, Bry made the twelve-hour trip south to visit them, leaving after dinner and driving through the night. While he was in North Carolina, he'd text me pictures of himself with Ben on the beach, jumping waves in his little blue surfer swimsuit. He made sand sculptures of giant turtles, pirates having elaborate sword-fights, sunfish. Bryan was teaching Ben how to throw a Frisbee. He would carry Ben past the short, spitting waves and stand facing the surf, while Cassie took photos of them in silhouette. She had the pictures made into a collage that Bryan kept on our dining room wall.

There were times we had talked about moving to Wilmington together. For me, it was speculation, wishful thinking about how great it would be to live near the beach. For Bryan, I began to realize, it had become almost a necessity to flee New York winters and be closer to his family.

"Guess you won't need these," I said, tossing his thermal long johns into the donate pile.

It was my turn to cry.

We stood in the bedroom near the half-empty closet and he pulled me to his chest. We held on to each other for what felt, more than anything, like we were saying I love you, and goodbye.

3

I KNEW THAT ONE WORD, A SINGLE WORD, "STAY," WOULD HALT THE course of the runaway train. Stay.

It had been months since Bryan and I agreed we were both miserable in the marriage, that the many, many ways we'd tried to fix it hadn't done any good at all. I'd actually made a pro/con list, and the only thing on the pro side was that I loved him. We genuinely loved each other. We just didn't love the life we had together.

We wanted to keep things normal, just for a little while, maybe until the start of spring. It was February in New York; who knew when spring would arrive. Sometimes it was early April, other years the end of May.

That night, we went to the home goods store and bought black and white bath towels and a rose-scented candle for the coffee table. He wanted to go to the mall and look at jeans because he thought they were on sale. I went with him, and he bought two pairs for $30—a great deal, really.

That night, we curled up so far away from one another in bed that my arm dangled off the side. I couldn't bear to see Bryan, the way he slept with his hands under his face like he was praying, how he kicked at the covers when his feet got too warm, quietly mumbled on occasion, as if trying to tell me something in his sleep.

My five-year-old little Yorkie, Penny, small and confused, lay between Bryan and me in the wide, king-sized bed. Her sleeping spot was usually at our feet so Bryan and I could reach for each other. But it had been a long time since either of us moved closer to the other in bed.

We had been together since right after my first divorce. I hate the way people refer to it as getting "remarried," announcing to the world you failed the first time around. We'd been married three years; two of them were really good. My first husband, Adam, was my college sweetheart. I'd met Bryan right after Adam left. I never really took the time to pause and reflect on the good sense of stringing one relationship into another. More than once, the word "rebound" came to mind.

Bryan and I had some very good times and some very bad ones, but in the end, it was time for it to be done.

I realized it was time to tell my kids what was going on between Bryan and me.

"So, I hope you're all right with this... I don't want to upset you, but Bryan and I are separating," I told my daughter, Madison, who's twenty-five, the next morning when she came over for scrambled eggs. She had her own apartment ten minutes away, but dropped by for things like breakfast, laundry, and long debates about the meaning of life.

"Yeah, well better that than stay unhappy—morose, really," Madison said, opening a box of raisins.

"You could tell things weren't right?"

"I know you, Mombo," Maddy said, staring me down with her pretty green eyes and expertly applied black eyeliner. "It's been like the plague around here since Christmas."

So I hadn't done such a good job of making things seem normal.

"You think Ian will be OK?"

My son Ian was twenty-one and lived with Bryan and me.

"Ian's pretty tough, and it can't possibly be as bad as when Dad left."

"Yeah, I was worried about that," I said, looking around for Penny, because everything felt better when she was on my lap. At night, before we fell asleep, I always thanked her for saving my life every day.

"But still, Ian knows things haven't been good for a while, too. I'll talk to him if you want," Madison offered.

"It's OK, Madd, I'll tell him."

Madison and Ian had always been close. Before he was born, she practiced putting a diaper on her Baby Alive doll, helped me set up the crib that had once been hers, went to the obstetrician with Adam and me to see the ultrasound live on the screen.

Ian had been sucking on his toes in one of the sonograms, something that delighted her.

The day he was born, Maddy was the first visitor.

"Is this really Ian?" she'd asked, looking at the little swaddled lump of a red-faced newborn. "Does he know how to play?"

Madison was a little mother to Ian, holding him in the tub so I could wash his little hairless head, pushing his stroller, feeding him

Gerber strained apples and pears. When he got old enough to play, he pushed around her Barbie Doll Malibu, built castles with Legos for her Rapunzel doll, and cooked by her side in the Betty Crocker play kitchen.

"Don't stare at my brother," Maddy used to tell people in line at the grocery store who were admiring Ian. "He belongs to me."

For his fourth birthday, Ian asked for a Ken doll to play with her Barbies. One year for Christmas when he was five, Ian got his sister a silver ring and asked her to marry him.

I was so lucky to have kids like my son and daughter, blessings I counted every day.

Now I was giving up someone I loved.

I called to Penny, but she was standing right next to my ankle where I couldn't see her.

"How about you, sweetie? You surprised by the news?"

Penny tilted her head the way dogs do when they're listening intently. Then she came over and scratched at my leg to be picked up.

"At least I'll always have you," I said into her warm shoulder.

"You'll always have all of us," Madison said, lobbing a raisin at me. "And you must have a plan. You always have a plan."

4

BRYAN AND I DUG TO THE BOTTOM OF HIS CLOSET TO SORT, SEPARATING the heavy clothes he'd worn to get through frigid New York winters. The wool L.L.Bean sweaters went in the donate pile, which quickly became a mountain. I folded the cotton-lined jeans, flannel shirts, and zip-up fleece jackets—things that were once on his Christmas list—and even the thick cabled socks I'd found at the Army-Navy store three months before, the ones with the reinforced toes.

Truth was, Bryan was cold from October to April—most of the year, really—in the fickle New York weather. His favorite thing was a heavy, hooded robe that I got online when he turned fifty-six. He wore it tightly belted, hood up, in a way that made him look like a boxer headed for the ring. I used to hum the *Rocky* theme and he would shadow box, back in the days when things were fun.

I had waited months, all winter, for things to change, for us to get out of the rut we'd settled into, Bryan on the couch and me at my computer writing blogs and website copy for insurance companies, warehouse-sized home stores, and anyone else who would hire me. It was freelance work that brought in enough money to pay the mortgage; Bryan paid the rest of the household expenses.

Bry increasingly hated upstate New York winters, the long stretches of unforgiving wind, snow, boulder-like and crusty, turning black from the exhaust from cars and impossible to scrape off the driveway and sidewalk out front. New York winters sting your face and make you run cursing to your car. You wonder why in hell you choose to live in New York, until beloved spring arrives, followed by summer, making you forget the evil, unbreakable winter.

We'd tried, both of us, to get him through the winters with some enjoyment. He'd become a stellar snowman-builder. We got his and hers snowshoes and tramped around the backyard. But his fingers and toes lost sensation quickly, and I ended up being the one looping around the willow tree out back, wearing down a path in the newly fallen snow.

Bryan had those hand warmers you crack to release heat in every one of his pockets and inside his boots and gloves. He wore cotton-lined jeans, two T-shirts, a button-down flannel, and always had shoes or slippers on his feet. He swaddled himself in fleece blankets when he was on the couch, which had become more and more frequently. We constantly argued about how high to turn up the thermostat.

We also argued about things far more serious, especially his very dark winter mood swings. It was something that frayed holes in the fabric of our marriage. Bryan didn't seem to listen to or care about anything I came up with that could possibly help.

"Why don't you talk to a doctor?" I asked him one Sunday afternoon while he was huddled on the couch.

"A doctor? What kind of doctor?" he answered without opening his eyes.

"Well, not a psychologist really, maybe a specialist that prescribes meds...?"

Bryan opened his eyes. "You think I haven't thought of that, or tried it?"

"What do you mean?" I sat down at the end of the couch and he reflexively moved his feet away from me.

"Yeah, I saw docs, more than one. One said Seasonal Adjustment Disorder. Another said social anxiety. Another said I was fucking bipolar. Every one of them had their own ideas."

I was startled by his anger. "So, what did they say?"

Bryan sat up, kicking the blanket off his legs impatiently. "Listen, Jessica, I tried a bunch of antidepressants, mood stabilizers, anything they could throw at me. I took shit for more than a year."

It was silent in the living room. Even Pen, who had been watching us in wonder about his raised voice, hunched down in her dog bed.

"What happened?" I asked.

"They made me jittery or exhausted, dry-mouthed and afraid to leave my house, my palms were sweaty, my heart raced, and worst of all, I couldn't get it up for sex." He put his head in his hands, covering his face.

"Well, there are some new ones out there—"

"Stop it! Just give it a break! Stop trying to fix me like I'm one of your kids." With that, he got to his feet and stormed out of the living room.

I leaned back on the couch pillows, my hand on my chest, feeling like I'd been talking to a stranger.

But I was also angry. In all our talks about his moods, why hadn't he told me he'd gone for help? When was this? Years before I'd met him? Months? What else didn't I know? And how dare he use my kids in an argument against me? That, to me, was the greatest cruelty.

As I thought back to the months before, I realized I'd done a lot of cajoling, cheering, joking, anything to try and get Bryan to respond. I'd run out of ideas—and worse, I had no plan whatsoever.

5

"I'M NOT HAPPY," I SAID ONE NIGHT AFTER WORK WHILE HE WAS COOKING chicken.

Bryan didn't turn around. The oil was splattering on the stove; he had it on too high.

"Are you happy?" I asked.

"As happy as anyone, I guess," he said.

"Is that good enough?"

"What are you saying, Jess? That you're not happy with our life? With me?"

"I don't know what I'm saying. Are you saying you're happy?"

Bryan turned down the heat on the chicken, came over and put his arms around me. His gray scruff scraped my chin. He'd grown the beard to try and keep his face warm. I wasn't crazy about it but if it helped, I didn't care.

"What else can we do to make it better?" he asked.

I breathed in the smell of his shirt, a mixture of mountain fresh dryer sheets and the paprika he was sprinkling on the chicken.

We used to cook together, tossing pasta around, simmering sauce, trying but never managing to master braising beef or baking pumpkin scones, covering the kitchen and ourselves in flour and corn starch and pepper. We always planned to take gourmet cooking lessons but never got around to it.

Bryan used to be up for anything: a spontaneous game of mini-golf at 10:00 at night, shopping for Halloween decorations even in September, or choosing the perfect blue paint for the bathroom from among dozens of swatches. We once went to an all-night discount store for shovels because we'd bent ours trying to dig out our cars from the enormous snowbanks the plows had made.

I was always reminded of my childhood in New York in the wintertime. My older sister Katrina and I would bundle in so many layers we could barely move our arms, and only our eyes and noses showed. Weekends, we'd be up early to get suited up and head outdoors to meet our neighborhood friends. We built tunnels in snowbanks, dug up chunks of crusty snow and called it pizza, stamped out dirty words with our boots in fresh snow in a field where our parents would never see. We'd stayed out until our mom hollered for dinnertime, our cheeks stinging and flushed when we went inside. Our mother always made us take off our boots and lay them on the radiator even though they had no chance of drying out because we scarfed down tomato soup and grilled cheese so we could get back outside. Nighttime came early in the winter; the sun set around 4:30 p.m. and we reluctantly returned home, every layer of our winter clothes wet. Katrina even wore a hole in the knees of her snow pants and got a brand-new pair for Christmas, something I resented to this day because I had to wear my old crappy ones until they were the length of capris.

When I was growing up, a local rec field was flooded every year and turned into a makeshift ice rink. The ice was always choppy and caused lots of falls, but we didn't care. I had to wear my sister's hand-me-down skates and my mother always asked me if I could wiggle my toes to keep them warm. We pretended to be figure skaters, doing shaky figure 8s, or speed skaters with our shoulders hunched down, racing each other. Katrina, two years older, always beat me. I remember crying so hard when I lost the races that she bought me hot chocolate from the refreshment stand for 25 cents. It badly burned my tongue, but I didn't care.

I liked New York winters, the howling winds and flurries giving a perfect excuse to bundle under cozy comforters and read. I'd never had a fireplace but hoped one day to buy a house with a large one in the family room. Despite the burned tongue of childhood, hot chocolate was a staple in the wintertime.

Winters in New York were something I never considered living without. I'd raised my kids on snowmen and snow tubes and sleds and hot chicken soup to warm up a winter chill. The seasons were part of my everyday life, like the sun rising in the east and setting in the west—part of who I was.

But it was something Bryan had never experienced, my love of New York, and no matter how many snowball fights we'd had and snowmen we'd built, there was no enjoyment in winter for him and never would be.

6

I'D MET MY FIRST HUSBAND, ADAM, IN A PHOTOGRAPHY CLASS AT COLLEGE. His photos were so good the teacher used them as examples for the rest of us, who, like me, produced grainy images more gray than black or white.

He took one of the most classic photos I've ever seen that summer, or any summer since, of a Grateful Dead fan wrapped in an American flag on his way to an outdoor concert in the rain.

I ruffled the fur on a stuffed teddy bear and titled it a "bad bear day."

"When are we getting married?" Adam had asked on our third date.

We were twenty-two; our love was relentless, voracious, so real it was palpable. We had one of those outrageous four-tier wedding cakes with pink cascading frosting flowers, topped with a plastic bride and groom with dark hair—they were supposed to be us. The ruffled train on my dress trailed all the way down the aisle. We danced to "Wind Beneath My Wings," singing the lyrics to each other. In all the pictures, in every single shot of us, we look so freaking happy I swear there is sunlight shining from behind our eyes. We were shimmering. I remember how my face hurt from all the smiling.

* * *

Maddy and Ian were both planned for and loved at first sight. Adam was still a great photographer and took beautiful shots of the kids that he framed and gave me for Christmas.

We'd been utterly clueless with Maddy, wishing she had been sent home with an instruction manual when we left the hospital.

At least six times, we were convinced Maddy's cough was croup. We called our pediatrician's answering service to leave frantic messages, then sat with her in a steamed-up bathroom, the shower running hot water. It cleared out all our nasal passages and calmed her cough, which of course never was croup.

Once, when she was a toddler, Madd sneezed and a string of spaghetti came out of her nose, something she had for dinner hours earlier. We chided ourselves for not noticing she had snorted some of her pasta, but she showed no signs of suffering from the stray strand of spaghetti.

I saved every one of her baby teeth, documented her first steps and words and waving bye-bye, in a journal for posterity. I taped a lock of blonde hair from her first haircut, during which I cried as they trimmed only the ends of her hair, leaving it long like mine.

Ian came along when Maddy was four. His first smile was for his sister. We used to put Ian in his baby seat and gather around him, all of us, admiring him like a Christmas present, the best gift we'd ever received. Ian thrived from all the attention.

Adam had been a hands-on father in the beginning—changing diapers, cleaning up baby food flung to the floor, coaching Ian to say his sister's name. He'd come up with the great idea of floating a handful of Cheerios in the toilet and telling Ian to aim for them with his pee, a game that had him potty trained within a week.

We got a Big Wheel with an extra seat on the back and Madd rode it around the kitchen, Ian belted safely in the back, blowing kisses at us every time they circled. I carried Ian to walk Maddy to the bus stop for kindergarten and he looked for her everywhere while she was gone.

When he was barely two, he was waving and yelling goodbye to his sister, and when her bus came at the end of the school day, he would run from the front porch where we were waiting and throw himself into her outstretched arms.

I had a busy freelance writing business, writing ad copy and editing textbooks and college catalogs until my eyesight blurred. As time went on, Adam began to focus more on his job selling medical equipment across a wide area of the Northeast, a job that required quite a bit of travel. I relished the role of primary caregiver for the kids. Adam took care of all the household finances; I was never interested in anything beyond balancing a checkbook.

Adam spent most Saturday afternoons out in his Ford truck taking landscape photos: trees with branches extended like arms, the sun slanting through leaves just before sunset, a peach pit he found on a sidewalk. His work was as beautiful as when we'd met.

We lived in a modest middle-class neighborhood where all the children were growing up together. We had birthday and Easter parties for the kids, making so many cupcakes I still feel sick at the thought of buttercream frosting. The kids did their own Halloween parade around the cul-de-sac, ending up at our house for pizza for the kids and hot toddies for the adults.

How had the years flown by so quickly? I volunteered at the elementary school, putting on a witch costume for Halloween and helping kids bob for apples in third grade, filling balloons with water for kids to toss at each other outside on field day in middle school. I chaperoned trips to Mystic Seaport, the Bronx Zoo, and the Boston Aquarium, my kids never seeming to be embarrassed being seen with their mother. We still had a magnet shaped like a shark's tooth, from the aquarium gift shop, on the fridge.

Adam had given Maddy extra money to buy a plush polar bear at the zoo, something she still slept with. While he listened to their stories at the dinner table, he disappeared afterwards to go onto his computer. Working at the computer had become his favorite pastime.

Every year as they grew older, I wished like hell I could freeze them in time and keep them young. They were my favorite people in all the world.

But as hard as I tried to hold on to them, the years slid away.

Time was going too fast for me to keep up.

7

WE WERE, THE FOUR OF US, A COHESIVE FAMILY, HAPPY CHILDREN, ADULTS who were partners and had fallen into a groove of parenting. It worked. For a long time, it worked. I never imagined it breaking.

Unless he was at the gym, Adam was always home after work. Sometimes he missed dinner when he went out Saturdays to take photos, but I knew he was doing something he loved.

As time went, the years so fleeting, Adam's interaction with us changed. He started to seem robotic, as if he were there in person but not giving any thought or taking any interest in anything around him, with the kids or in our life.

It took me a while to even notice.

The kids were teenagers and had their own soccer schedules, band practice, and meet-ups with friends. I taxied them around until they got their driver's licenses. Maddy passed the first time, but Ian had to take it twice because he was so chatty with the instructor, he missed a right turn. He'd been friendly and outgoing all his life. I credited his sister's mothering for this.

One year when Ian got the highest grade at a science fair for making a replica of a beehive to warn people of nest desertion, Adam had been at work. But when he got home, Ian was waiting by the door to tell his dad. Adam had congratulated him heartily, and together they made a wooden frame for his certificate.

As the kids grew into their older teens and went out at night with friends or to part-time jobs, I found myself alone. It felt like I no longer had a partner in my life. I had a sinking sense that Adam and I had grown irreparably apart in the years we'd focused on earning a living and raising the kids. Could we ever become close again?

The last time we'd had sex, we were both tired and probably relieved when it was over. My sexual appetite was always greater than Adam's, but we'd made it work over the years, even if I had to resort to rubbing out an orgasm by myself. We'd watched porn, but the camera shots bothered Adam's sense of artistry, so we switched to looking at Tumblr photos that were still graphic but far more tastefully done.

But Adam spent increasing amounts of time in the fourth bedroom we'd turned into his office space. I could hear him clicking away on the keyboard, but when I asked him about it, he'd said he was just searching the web for sports updates or looking at the work of various photographers.

I posted notices for freelance work on Craig's and got a steady stream of clients, which kept me occupied evenings when Adam was upstairs. One night, when he was working late, I couldn't shake the sense that something was going on. I went into his home office and tried to sign onto his desktop computer. It was password protected.

I did what I do every time I need help: I called my best friend Eddie.

I'd met Eddie in high school art class. I was a lowly freshman and he was a senior. He was a brilliant sculptor/painter/illustrator. I had an interest in everything but talent in none. One day back in high school, I was nearly crying over a ceramic spoon holder I'd made for my mother's stove but which exploded in the kiln.

"Air bubbles," said Eddie. "You gotta really work the clay."

He showed me how and my next project—a paperweight in the shape of a turtle—survived the deadly kiln. We sat together in art class from then on, and some of his magic rubbed off on me. I managed to pull a B in class, which kept my GPA up despite my lousy math grades.

I could always count on Eddie to be by my side during all my triumphs and disappointments. This time, it didn't feel like anything good was coming.

"I don't want to sugarcoat this, so I won't," Eddie said in his usual candid manner. "Could there be another woman?"

Of course I had considered that. Adam was still great-looking; the gray at his temples only made him look more distinguished. He went to the gym, was a great listener, wore suits and jeans equally well. I was sure I wasn't the only woman to find him sexy.

"Can't you break into his computer?" Eddie asked.

"What is this, *Mission Impossible*? How exactly would I break in? Like cracking some code?"

"Do you know his password?"

I didn't. In fact, I'd been surprised he'd used a password to sign on. If he was catching up on news and sports, why was he so guarded?

"It'll be OK," Eddie said. "It can't be that bad."

8

Turned out, it was not only that bad, it was worse.

On a Saturday morning in March, when the first buds were appearing on the flowering cherry tree, I was writing at the kitchen table when I heard the screech of brakes like someone was slamming on them to stop. When I went to the window, I saw Adam, with an enormous smile on his face, climbing down from the driver's seat of a camper as long as two dumpsters, jutting out from the end of our driveway and into the road.

I went outside in wonder.

"Well, what do you think?" Adam asked, actually patting the thing affectionately. "She's a beauty, isn't she?"

All I could think was that he'd rented the RV for a trip à la the Chevy Chase vacation movies. But he hadn't even talked about a trip like that.

"Nice," I said, trying to keep my voice even. "What's it for? Planning a vacation?"

"A vacation of a lifetime," Adam said, using his sleeve to shine the door handle. "She's ours."

"Ours? I don't understand—where's your truck?"

"Sold it to buy this beauty."

I sat down hard on the front lawn, trying to take it all in. Sold his truck. Stashed money. Bought a camper. Without me even knowing?

"You're kidding, right?"

"Jess, I'm serious. Thought we'd take weekend trips, all of us together. And there's more good news: the company expanded my territory across New England all the way up to Maine. So, I'll be on the road more—sorry about that part—but I figured instead of hotels, I'd take the RV and stay at campgrounds."

I tried to make sense of his words. But I couldn't get past his statement that we'd all go camping on weekends.

The kids were too busy with their own lives and wouldn't give up a weekend with their friends to go away with us. And my idea of going away for the weekend was watching the sunset from the balcony of a little B&B.

Sure, we'd been camping when the kids were young, hauling out a tent big enough for the four of us, portable grill, sleeping bags, a bag of marinated chicken, water sandals, towels, marshmallows, even lights to string on trees near our site.

But there were too many bugs for Ian, and Madison swore she heard coyotes in the woods. The kids tramped dirt inside the tent, the batteries ran out in the lights, we burned the chicken. Our site seemed to be at least half a mile to the nearest bathroom, and the kids drank so much soda we had to take them there every hour. Even I had to admit the black flies were bad.

There was a moment, after the kids crawled dirty-footed into their sleeping bags, when Adam and I sat out by the dwindling fire looking at the stars in what seemed like the biggest sky we'd ever seen. We held hands and talked about having a third child, which wasn't in the cards. Later on, we zipped our sleeping bags together and cuddled in a way we hadn't the time to in many months.

We vowed to get a sitter for the kids and go camping as a couple, but we'd never found the time. We thought about taking the kids again, but after the buggy/coyote-sounds trip, the kids didn't want to go again.

Now here it was, this clunky, ugly thing on our driveway.

"Home away from home!" Adam said.

"Doesn't look like home to me," I said at last. "Doesn't look like a way to vacation, either."

Adam came over and sat next to me. The neighbor across the street came out to look at the abomination in our driveway. I pretended I didn't see him staring until he went back inside, only to peer out at us from his living room windows.

OK, it wasn't rusty or in bad condition, but it was huge and dreadfully out of place in our cul-de-sac.

"OK, well, I've been saving up my bonuses for a couple of years."

A couple of years? Without me knowing? What the hell?

"I've been looking at campers and planning trips for months."

So that was it. That was what he'd been doing sneakily up in the office. Not looking at porn. Not looking around on dating sites. Researching his next life at campgrounds.

"Figured we could make some spending money selling a lot of our stuff that we won't need—you know, big garage sale. We won't need many belongings, living in this beauty."

I closed my eyes, imagining putting price stickers on my beige sofa, wicker rocking chairs from the front porch—hell, even my extra bath towels and blankets, because how would they ever be stored in a thing that clearly had no linen closet? Maybe hang a clothesline and display most of our clothes for a couple bucks per piece: the black sequined cocktail dress I still couldn't zip, the matching stilettos, more pairs of leggings and sneaks than I cared to count, my favorite Fair Isle sweater, my wedding dress.

Adam climbed back into the RV and sat proudly behind the wheel. "What do you think?" he said proudly. "Wanna take a pic for Facebook?"

I did not want to. All I wanted to do was go back into the house and pretend it never happened, rub my eyes, open them, and find the driveway empty.

Adam kept talking about having a big New England adventure. But something was ringing in my ears: the realization that he didn't want our life, our lovely, full life, anymore. I couldn't imagine him thinking I would take to the road with him, leaving behind everything we'd built there. It was our life he rejected, and also me. Adam's plan to live in the RV and travel was nearly as shocking and hurtful as if there'd been another woman.

What he was telling me was this: he wanted a different life, a life that wouldn't include me. Had he honestly thought I'd jump at the idea of living in a home that was never in the same place more than a couple nights? That we'd pick up part-time jobs along the way to buy more hot dogs and canned beans to cook over a fire? Wash our sleeping bags in laundromats and dry them on the roof? There were so many things I'd hate about living on the road, I stopped listing them in my mind and shut down, not even close to being able to take in all that was happening, how our lives had changed in under an hour.

"Give it some time," Adam said soothingly. "The travel bug will bite you soon enough."

Waiting for that bug to bite me, Adam parked the camper out back beneath the maple tree, spending nights outside by a fire he made in a makeshift pit he'd built from cinder blocks and cement.

Ian went out some nights to sit with his father. But Adam seemed just as content being alone in the dark by the glow of the fire. He played Bob Marley songs and got into the habit of wearing a wide-brimmed straw hat. He grew a beard, although he had to keep it neatly shaved for work. I hadn't noticed how gray he was until the beard grew out.

We barely spoke that summer, living in our separate quarters like neighbors more than anything else. Many nights I'd stand with the lights off in our bedroom, now my bedroom, and watch him from the window.

On a Sunday in mid-August, I walked out back where Adam was sitting against a backdrop of tree silhouettes and fireflies, having a Sam Adams. He was barefoot, wearing cargo shorts and an Eddie Bauer T-shirt I'd given him many birthdays before. Now it was faded at the collar, but the well-worn clothes suited him.

"Hey," he said, clearly delighted to see me.

"We have to talk," I said, pulling up a blue canvas seat.

Adam sighed. "Nothing good ever comes after those words."

"What are we doing here?" I said, twisting the ends of my hair. "This is crazy, living apart just because you're having a midlife crisis."

Adam sighed again, this time heavily. He took off his straw hat and turned it around in his hands. "This is something I have to do," he said quietly. "I feel trapped here. I'm suffocating. It's what I need to do."

Bob Marley was singing about everything being all right. The glow of the distant fireflies dimmed. From inside the house, I could hear Madd laughing with some friends.

"So, this is how it ends, after all these years?" I managed to say.

"This is how it ends," he said, his voice echoing with finality.

THE LOSS SET IN WITH INDESCRIBABLE FORCE A MONTH LATER WHEN Adam packed up and left for his new solo life. I had to drag myself out of bed, and when I did, everything felt wrong.

I had three fender-benders in two weeks.

More than once, I sat in my car at a stop sign waiting for the light to change.

I took acid control tablets four at a time when the instructions said take two.

I pumped gas and then drove away with the gas cap on the roof of my car, went to the local auto parts store and bought a new one. The next week, I did it again. When I went sheepishly to see the auto guys, they told me they were going to order an extra cap to save for the next time I came in. It could have been funny, but it wasn't.

I took a fall on the front steps and bounced on my shoulder down two stairs to the sidewalk, breaking three ribs horizontally. For days I couldn't raise my right arm, reach out, or pick anything up. Coughing and sneezing brought piercing pain. I waited to puncture a lung. Truth: I almost wanted to get worse so I could retreat to a hospital bed, wear a nightgown, and be served painkillers and lime Jell-O by kindly nurses.

I cried when I ran out of conditioner. I cried at the supermarket when they didn't have unsalted rice cakes. I cried when Ian left for high school, because I didn't want to be alone. I cried until I ran out of Kleenex and had to wipe my nose on an old washcloth. I cried into Penny's fur until it was matted.

I ordered immune support and mood-boosting vitamins on Amazon, then forgot to take them. I drank new age cold remedy tea that didn't stop my nose from running like a hose when I cried. But I had kids to take care of and a household to run as a single mother. I didn't have the option to take to my bed.

I tried hard to form a plan but came up empty. The best I could do was to get up every morning and be there for the kids. Get them up and ready for school. Make their lunch, find something for dinner besides scrambled eggs, wrestle with math homework, listen to their stories, remind them to turn out the lights and go to sleep. Tell them their dad loved them but needed to get away for a while, as if the separation weren't permanent.

Adam kept in touch with Ian and Maddy. I had to give him credit for that. He called Ian every night, which meant so much to our son. Maddy talked to Adam less frequently. Like me, she took it hard that he wanted to live in a camper, traveling the country, rather than in our home that stayed in one place.

Divorce papers came in the mail seven weeks after Adam left, from a small town in Ohio.

He must have paid all the legal fees. All I had to do was sign and return the papers in the self-addressed, stamped envelope. Such a small, innocuous way to end a marriage, but when I brought the envelope to the post office to mail, I clung to it as if I couldn't let go. I tried to breathe with the razors I felt crisscrossing the place where my heart once was.

The Adam years were over.

It was six months later that Bryan and I stumbled upon each other, literally, in a restaurant in Ashton where I'd gone with Eddie to watch a live band play.

I was inching my way to the bar for a dirty martini for Eddie and a vodka cranberry for myself when a cute guy suddenly turned with a draft beer in each hand, and even as he tried to balance the mugs, they sloshed all over the front of my white T-shirt. Well, it wasn't really mine; I'd borrowed it from Maddy because I had no cool bar clothes.

It was a wet T-shirt contest gone very wrong.

"I'm so sorry, let me help—"

"It's OK," I said, even though it wasn't.

"Here," he said, shrugging off his jean jacket. "Take this."

"No, I can't—"

"I don't want you to have to leave before the band comes on," he said, tipping his head a little to the side, as if trying to figure out whether he'd seen me before.

"Well, all right." I put it on, and it covered the beer stains.

"I'm Bryan," he said, extending his hand.

"Jessica."

"I'm sorry again for the way we met, but I'm glad we did."

We found a quieter corner of the bar where we could talk without yelling. Eddie gave me a discreet thumbs-up before heading out.

When he left, I still had the jacket in my closet. Never did give it back.

Bryan was the opposite of Adam—wiry, about 5' 10" to Adam's 6' 3" with a flat stomach and muscular arms that flexed in the snug black T-shirts he wore. He was also completely bald, but it suited him. He shaved his head, which looked great because it was perfectly symmetrical. Adam loved to talk and make people laugh but Bryan was quieter, an intent listener, following every word I said.

Bryan had a tattoo of Batman that he'd designed himself, spanning the space between his shoulder blades. He was a gifted artist. He could sketch cartoons, paint modern acrylics on huge canvases with wide swaths of red and blue and yellow, sculpt garden gnomes by hand. He was working on a clay chess set and every playing piece was perfect.

I loved to watch him work, so focused on the small details of his project that he didn't notice anything going on around him, blue eyes intent on what he was creating, his long fingers sketching or painting or molding.

Bryan made his own Halloween costumes. Once they were done, he was completely unrecognizable. He made a latex face piece so closely resembling The Joker in *Batman* that it was startling. Another year he was Penguin from the DC comics, with a wide padded belly, webbed feet, and beak. OK, so he was also a bit of a comic book geek.

We loved to go out the weekend before Halloween to bars in Ashton because he always won the contest for the most original costume. It wasn't enough for me to wear Halloween-themed clothes one day a year, so I'd developed a somewhat obsessive habit of buying leggings online with Halloween themes and wearing them throughout the year. I scoured internet consignment and secondhand sites and amassed an impressive collection of leggings with mummies, dueling pirates, skulls and roses, witches stirring cauldrons, and dancing skeletons. My favorites were black with goth green Frankenstein faces. Or maybe the vampires with fanged teeth. Or the Day of the Dead sugar skulls. It depended on my mood.

Bryan was patient, while I always felt rushed. He took his time with everything.

We got married, partly on a whim, eight months after we met, in a small ceremony with a few friends and my kids, followed by pasta and meatballs at our favorite Italian place.

Time flew while we were having fun.

Bryan and I accumulated layers of memories during our three years together. We loved all the holidays and celebrated every single one to the hilt. In March there was a big St. Patrick's Day parade in downtown Ashton, something we looked forward to all year. We scoured the internet for Irish apparel, choosing a green fedora and stick-on orange eyebrows, moustache, and sideburns for Bry. I wore a green beanie with an orange pom-pom and long fake orange braids hanging down my back. We wore every green thing we had in our wardrobes, right down to green socks. Bryan told me I should buy a green bra; it would be festive, and also sexy to him, but when I was too busy and never got around to it, he ordered one online—a push-up bra with shamrocks over the nipples. He asked me to wear it other times of the year because he liked it so much.

We'd lined up early on State Street, joining enormous crowds of people toasting the holiday, many of them already slurring their words at noon. We sang along to "Irish Eyes are Smiling," hooted for the dancing leprechauns, felt the thunder of bagpipes in our chests as rows of musicians marched by. Street vendors sold Irish flags, long green horns that made strange moose call noises, streamers, balloons, and huge blow-up shamrocks. The parade marchers threw out chocolate coins wrapped in gold foil to the kids, who scurried into the street to scoop them up and stash them in their pockets.

The weather on St. Patrick's Day in upstate New York was always unpredictable. One year it was so balmy we were sweaty in green hoodies. Another year the wind chill was so bad we had to leave halfway through because Bryan couldn't stand the cold. As we drove away, we could still hear the sound of bagpipes from the Interstate.

We walked Penny, who pulled at her leash to greet strangers, on a familiar route that wound past the ice cream stand, down to the antique shop, and through a church parking lot. Penny was the perfect companion dog, tail wagging furiously when she saw something interesting.

Penny was my first dog. My parents didn't allow pets outside of cages or glass bowls. My sister and I had our share of neon tetras, guinea pigs, and hamsters. I waited until my kids were old enough to help with a pet, but from the moment I got her, she was mine in the way a third child might have been. Despite her small, compact, eight-pound body, Penny bravely took on winter, trying to climb snowbanks, standing on three legs to warm up one paw, then switching. There was a small wooden table on the back porch she liked to stand on to keep all her paws from freezing. I had a dozen brightly colored fleece jackets for Pen that zipped her up snugly and kept her warm as she sat outside and watched me shovel.

Shoveling is hard work. Especially after the snowplow piles icy clumps at the end of the driveway. When I was young and had to help shovel, I used to push the heavy snow out into the middle of the road and leave it there, until our neighbor complained because it all ended up in his driveway. But shoveling is a hell of a good workout, and right where I needed it, twisting at the waist and throwing a shovelful up to a rapidly rising snowbank. Besides, Ian took care of the deep white stuff with a snow blower, so all I had to do was clear the sidewalk.

But as the seasons progressed, winter increasingly took its toll on Bryan, sapping his energy and making him miserable to the point where he answered questions with grunts and head-shaking. He was thin and never seemed to put on weight, a fact that always irked me because I put on a pound when I ate an Oreo, but his lanky build gave him less insulation.

He abandoned his art projects; the chess pieces collected dust and he put his painted canvases in the back of a closet. One of the garden gnomes lost its little clay hat and Bry told me to just throw it away because he didn't have the energy or desire to make a new one.

Bryan worked ten-hour days at the silk-screening shop where he screened designs on shirts, banners, garden flags, and just about anything else needing a logo. He'd been there for eight years and the work had become monotonous—and worse, grueling. I knew this. But I always thought I could snap him out of his deepening despair. Turned out, I couldn't.

I'd even suggested marriage counseling, but after his experience with doctors prescribing meds that didn't help, Bryan refused to consider it.

"I don't know what to do," I said into Bryan's shoulder while his chicken sizzled. "I feel like we've tried everything and we're running out of ideas."

THAT MARCH, WHEN WINTER REFUSED TO LET GO, I'D RUN OUT OF IDEAS to reconnect with Bryan. And so I knew it was time. Time for lingerie.

Not that I didn't have anything sexy. There was the St. Patrick's Day bra with the shamrocks barely covering my nipples. A little skimpy Santa chemise. Somewhere in the back of my underwear drawer was a stretchy black thong. Truth was, Bryan and I hadn't really cared about the wrappings; we were always in a hurry to get to the good parts. He was lithe and limber and adventurous in bed, which thrilled me after years of uninspired, vanilla marital sex.

I spent more than an hour shopping Amazon for racy, uncomplicated lingerie that I would be able to slip out of seductively, or at least without losing my balance and falling over.

Anything with a garter belt was out of the question, because it highlighted the exact part of me I wanted to underplay: my upper thighs.

There were hundreds of pleather bodysuits and over-the-knee platform boots, most accessorized with a whip. Not interested. I had no desire to dominate a man. If I were ever in a dom/sub relationship, I knew I would be the one submitting.

Crotchless panties? Pass. Role-play outfits? I considered a Little Red Riding Hood costume that was actually kind of hot. But it would barely cover my ass, another part of my body I hoped not to spotlight.

I finally went with a black lace peek-a-boo bra that exposed my greatest asset: my boobs. I threw in a pair of boy shorts I hoped would have enough spandex to suck in my stomach. I clicked the order button, hoping I wouldn't look ridiculous and also hoping the lingerie wouldn't stay on for very long once Bryan and I got our hands on each other.

The next Friday night, I made grilled chicken salad for dinner, hoping Bryan wouldn't hunker down on the couch with a fleece blanket and turn on Netflix.

"Here you go," I said, bringing a bottle of Moscato to the dinner table. "I got wine!"

"Why are you acting so strange?"

"Strange?" I was slightly offended, and the peek-a-boo bra had turned out to be extremely itchy, especially under a turtleneck. I was seriously concerned about breaking out in hives.

"I don't mean strange, just…giddy," Bryan said, holding out his wine-glass to be filled.

After we finished eating, Bryan helped load the plates into the dish-washer, then headed to the living room.

I took a deep breath. How to be seductive? How to be serious at the same time? Giddy, I felt pretty certain, wasn't sexy.

As predicted, Bryan was huddled beneath the blanket with little sheep carousing in a field.

I picked up a corner of the blanket and slid in next to him.

He put his arm around me. Good sign. And yawned. Bad sign.

I kicked myself for not planning ahead and wearing a cardigan that I could slowly unbutton instead of a turtleneck I'd have to struggle with to get out of. But something had to be done, and it had to happen before Bryan nodded off, which was about forty-five seconds. I got off the couch and gamely pulled the turtleneck off over my head. There I was, itchy black bra with my nipples exposed, and vampire leggings.

"Wow," Bryan said, visibly stunned. "What is that?"

Either he didn't recognize my boobs, or he'd never seen a bra with-out cups. I considered grabbing the turtleneck to cover up, but before I could, Bryan was off the couch and leading me to the bedroom.

Success.

I quickly unbuttoned his flannel shirt, then fumbled with the zipper of his jeans, which were snug over his erection. It had been a long time since I'd been that turned on. Pulling his jeans off, I got on my knees to take him in my mouth.

"Wait," he said, pulling me up. "I want to see. Show me what else you have on."

At the last minute, I'd left the boy shorts on the floor and gone with nothing on under my leggings. When I sat on the edge of the bed and began peeling them off, Bryan was the one on the floor ready to use his tongue.

But as soon as he opened my legs and touched me, it happened. I broke out nervous laughter, which I can tell you is a serious mood-breaker.

"Let's try again," I said, reaching back to unhook the bra.

"Leave it on," Bryan said, pulling my hands away.

I loved to be told what to do. And with that, I was wet and ready. I wanted to just skip the foreplay, but Bryan wanted to make a night of it. He ran his hands across my breasts, fingering the black lace, which unfortunately made it itchier. I fought the urge to scratch and wished he'd let me take the damn thing off and just lie there naked. Bryan ducked his head to lick my nipples, and this time thankfully I didn't laugh, but moaned instead. He loved to use his tongue, and I was the lucky recipient.

But I didn't want to just lie there and make him do all the work.

I pushed him down on the bed next to me, effectively putting the brakes on everything he was trying to do. Well, that was a wrong move. Time to rethink. I decided to throw caution to the wind and get into a good, sweet 69, but there was the usual dilemma: his ass in the air or mine? Neither was an attractive option, which is why I rarely initiated the position.

Woman on top, I decided after deliberating for a moment.

Lying next to Bryan, both of us naked except for the one wearing the itchy bra, I realized to accomplish this somewhat gracefully, I would have to turn in the other direction in the bed and swing my leg over his chest. The turning went fine. The swinging, not so good.

"Shit, Jess," Bryan said, sitting up after I kicked him in the nose.

"Is it bleeding?" I grabbed the box of Kleenex and held one up to his face.

"I don't need that," he said, waving it away. "No. It's not bleeding. It's fine."

"How many fingers am I holding up?" I said, trying to inject a little humor.

"Let's just try and pick up where we left off."

Sweet talk, that wasn't, but I was determined to have a memorable roll in the hay. We started kissing again; this time I stayed put and didn't try anything fancy that required rolling all over the bed. Bryan stroked my hair, which I always loved, and ran a row of kisses down my neck to my shoulders, making me shiver.

It was good, I told myself. We were back in the saddle again. But when Bryan reached down and fingered me, he stopped and sat up.

"What are you doing?" I asked, leaving my legs open for him to play.

"I think we need some lube. You're kind of dry."

"What are you talking about?" I asked indignantly. I reached down and touched myself and realized he was right. I was the Sahara Desert.

"I don't understand," I sputtered. "I was soaked a minute ago."

"Don't women dry up after menopause?" Bryan said, tilting his head to one side in a way I took as mocking.

"I'm in perimenopause, for your information, and it's probably just because we haven't had sex in a while." I didn't mean to sound sarcastic, but the menopause thing really pissed me off.

The room fell silent.

"I'm tired anyway," Bryan said quietly, pulling on pajama pants he'd left on the floor that morning.

I took the bra off in the bathroom, wadded it up and tossed it into the trash.

So much for lingerie.

Then I looked for calamine lotion to put on the rash that had formed. The left side was worse, a raggedy circle of hives around the space over my heart.

12

Despite the thwarted sex, we'd gamely continued to work hard on our marriage that winter. Wednesday night was date night, going out to horror movies (his choice) or rom-coms (mine) then out to try a new restaurant. We'd had chunks of chicken tossed on our plates at a Japanese place, dunked cubes of bread into cheese at a fondue eatery, enjoyed spicy Indian food until the gas hit us hours later.

We got up and made waffles together Saturday mornings with this great double waffle maker I got on Amazon. Bry wore his Rocky robe while he warmed his cold hands on a coffee mug.

I ordered him one of those lights that were supposed to mimic the sun to help people with seasonal depression. He said it gave him headaches, so I put it next to the peace lily, which thrived under its warm glow.

We played Monopoly and Clue. Sometimes Ian joined in, even though he said he was too old for board games.

I couldn't sleep many nights when Bryan went to sleep with the heated blanket on its highest setting. Instead, I got up and sat at the kitchen table with a mug of orange spice tea. I needed a clear mind to think about what I could and would do.

When the kids were middle-school age, they'd come home with various middle-school problems: a friend who snubbed them, a moody teacher, failing to score the game point in gym volleyball.

I tried hard not to solve the kids' problems for them.

"So, what's your plan?" I'd asked instead. "You always have a plan."

I'd run out of plans to make my marriage to Bryan work.

"Maybe it would help to get a new job and work less hours. I can look for one," Bryan said at last.

We'd been through all that before. I'd emailed Bry job openings, critiqued his résumé, helped write cover letters, quizzed him on common interview questions, picked out a nice dress shirt and tie. But he'd never gotten around to applying for other jobs.

"You don't want to change jobs," I said in the kitchen as he cooked.

"No, I don't, but I'll try to find something else," he sighed. "I don't know where I'd find one. At my age I can't exactly start over."

"Your chicken is burning," I said, pulling away.

"Jess, what do you want me to say?"

I counted the seconds clicking by on the kitchen clock. Click. Click. Click.

"I don't think there's anything to say." I started to cry.

"So that's it? Just like that, we're done?" His voice had an angry edge like the time I'd tried to talk to him about antidepressants.

I cried harder.

Bryan came to me, putting his arms around me and shushing me.

"You think I should move out, then?" His voice was back under control.

"Where would you go?" I pulled away to look at his face.

"South, to be with Cassie and Ben," he said with the conviction of someone knowing, at last, where they belong.

GETTING DIVORCED THE SECOND TIME TOOK MORE THAN RETURNING postage-paid paperwork.

I told Bryan I would find a lawyer and get the papers drafted. I'd gotten the names of four attorneys online. Two of them never called me back for the free consultation. One told me over the phone it would take six months and a $2,500 retainer to finalize the divorce. The fourth gave me an appointment to talk at her office. I arrived to find a handwritten sign on the door of the lawyer's office: *Please don't let the cats out.*

I stood for a moment before going in, careful not to let any cats escape through the glass door and pad down the hallway. I stared at the saltwater fish tank and wondered if the turquoise and yellow fish drove the cats batty. I saw toys and cat beds, but no actual cats.

"Jessica Gabriel?" The lawyer was wearing khakis and a red fleece pullover with a snowflake dangling off the zipper. It was the end of winter, but her office was chilly. I followed her out of the reception area into her office, where there were files piled on the desk and stacks of yellow legal pads with notes scrawled in pencil.

"Jesus, this place is a shit show," she said, laughing at herself.

She had to move things around to make space to work on her desk, but once she sat down, she made the kind of eye contact where you either trust them or think they're trying to pull one over on you. I liked her instantly.

"So you're divorcing," she said simply. "I'm sorry."

"Thank you."

"How many years together?"

"Four—well, three years married."

"Any kids?"

"No, the children—well, they're adults now—belong to me. They're mine." I felt like we were divvying up communal property. "Their father left to travel, ah, cross country, but he's still in the picture, sort of."

I had no idea why I was giving her the story of my life. She nodded as if she understood, or cared, which I'm sure she didn't.

"And the house?"

"Also mine." I tried not to fidget.

A cat appeared out of nowhere and rubbed against my leg.

"Now, you know New York is an equal distribution state. Under the law, he is entitled to half the assets, including the house." She tapped her pencil on her desk.

"Yes, but he's willing to sign off on it."

"Good. Other assets?"

"I've split the bank account with him," I said.

What little money we'd saved over the three years amounted to about $5,000 for each of us.

"Debts? Cars?"

"Just the mortgage, and we each have our own car."

"Well," she said, leaning down to scoop up yet another cat. "This is an easy one. All we need is a basic agreement and the court to uphold it."

"My husband—ex—is hoping to leave for North Carolina in two weeks...."

"Good for him! That won't be an issue," she said confidently, scratching behind the cat's ear. "I'll have the papers drafted and ready for him to sign in ten days."

I couldn't believe it could be that easy to dissolve a marriage. Like antacid tablets dropped into a glass of water. Plop plop, fizz fizz.

As I left, two different cats tried to follow me out, but I was too quick for them, closing the door firmly behind me. When I looked back, one of the tabbies was leaning her paws up against the glass as if trying to stop me from going, to take it all back and try to make it right again.

14

TWO WEEKS LATER, BRYAN LOADED UP HIS SUV, FILLED TO CAPACITY with boxes and bins and garment bags, his bike rack and off-road bike on the back.

I'd left the house to drive around. Anything to not be there when he left.

"On my way," he texted. "I'll let you know when I get there."

It was March, a late spring. People call it the mud month because all it does is rain right into April. Some years the rain uncovered hidden blooms in the front garden and along the backshed—sprouts of greenery that would bring purple and pink tulips and bright yellow daffodils.

Not the year Bryan left. That year, winter held on tight.

I worried about everything, not the least of which was money.

I'd been earning enough money to cover the mortgage by freelance writing web copy, SEO landing pages, e-blasts and newsletters for local businesses: dry cleaners, auto shops, solar panel companies, florists. I had also been lucky to get referrals for new clients. Those first terrible days after Bry left, I couldn't even open my computer, much less finish an assignment. My concentration was shot.

It was like having Adam and Bryan both leaving me at the same time. I hadn't been able to fall under the crushing weight of grief when Adam took off. I'd gotten busy with the kids and taking care of the house and all the small details that kept my mind busy and my feet moving forward. I exhausted myself to the point where I couldn't even think straight, much less feel the heaviness of what I'd lost.

This time, after Bryan left, I took to my bed.

Madison came every day and sat near my pillow.

"God it's hot in here," she said, waving her hand around. "What are you even wearing under all these blankets?"

"Pajamas," I said, my voice muffled by the heavy blankets pulled over my head, even though I was boiling hot.

"Your Ben & Jerry's tie-dye, and those ratty high school sweatpants?"

"They're not from high school, they're from college."

"Well, you can't just lie there."

"Watch me."

"I'm sure this is all normal, but you can't keep this up much longer," Madison said. "What's your plan, anyway? You always have a plan."

"Not this time."

"Now you're being dramatic."

"Look at this," I said, thrusting my arm out from under the covers. I had red, itchy, inflamed spots running from my wrist up to my elbow, like poison ivy, but I hadn't been outside for three days.

"It's probably heat rash from these damn blankets. Are you even drinking water?"

What Madison failed to understand was that I didn't care if I dehydrated and shriveled up. I didn't care about living in pajamas or not showering or even the fact that Penny needed a bath, since she'd been huddled under the covers next to me, never leaving my side.

"Honestly, I can't believe you're still in bed. So, what's your plan?"

I felt like a fool. I was lost. I needed Bryan. What had I been thinking?

What I hadn't known was that being with someone means there's a person who cares what you're doing, how you feel, what you need, at least most of the time. There's a person frequently within reach. You can go check in with them, sit by them, put your arms around them. There's a person to listen and maybe even help solve problems. They give a shit about your day.

All of this brought flashbacks of Adam, to the good times when the kids were little: parent-teacher conferences, the games of Yahtzee and Monopoly, taking them to the drive-ins knowing they'd fall asleep before intermission.

I'd overcome the sense that I was responsible for Adam taking off, knowing logically it wasn't my fault he wanted to be somewhere else, have a different life than the one we'd built. But the parallel circumstances of being alone were wildly painful. Adam had taken to the road, and so had Bryan.

After Adam, I'd moved on and forged a new life with Bryan. I'd had it, that new life, and I sent him away. In his black SUV with a bike on the back.

After Bryan left, I had to sit in my own head and figure out how I felt, and how to even begin to feel better. It was a kind of loneliness I'd never known before. It had all happened so fast, that damn cat lady lawyer made the paperwork appear so quickly—voilà! You're divorced! Free to go your separate ways! Godspeed!

I remembered the day in the kitchen with the chicken frying, how much sense it made then for us to separate, how clear it had been that Bryan belonged in the sun with his family, how amicable we'd been, how we congratulated ourselves for being adults and handling it all so well.

I wasn't prepared to fall to my knees when I found one of his T-shirts at the bottom of the laundry basket. I lined up all the bottles of hot sauce, salsa, and cranberry mayo in the fridge front and center to make myself believe he was still there (he was big on condiments), hugged his pillow at night until it no longer smelled like him, kept the one lone flip-flop I found in the closet in a drawer in my nightstand, because I couldn't bear to throw it out.

Grief, as it turned out, wasn't linear. It was more like one step forward, two steps back. Or up and down. A fucking roller coaster.

I wasn't prepared for that kind of sorrow.

I wasn't prepared to be that alone.

I had needed Bryan to recover from Adam. Now they were both gone. Now what?

15

Madison did what she felt she had to do: she called Eddie to get me out of bed.

Eddie had stayed by my side through my first divorce, listening to me lament, drying my tears, stopping me after two glasses of wine. He'd pointed out all the positive things to being single: freedom, not having to answer to anyone, parenting the way I wanted, using the whole bed to sleep, filling the fridge with Chobani and apples and bags of pre-washed spinach. He was there for me in the way a best friend always seems to be.

"OK, it's time to rise and shine, Sleeping Beauty," Eddie announced, coming into my bedroom and throwing open the room-darkening shades.

"Tired," I mumbled.

"You've been in bed all day, missy," he announced. "I think someone's being a little bit diva here."

"Leave me be," I said, pulling the blanket over my face.

"Well this may cheer you, Ms. Shopaholic," Eddie held up a brown box from Amazon. "You should be earning cash back with all the things you buy. Have you considered therapy?"

"If you're trying to make me laugh, it's not working."

"Let's see what we've got here," Eddie said, pulling off the tape and opening the box. "Ah, here's something practical. A steamer? This for rice? Didn't you buy one a few months ago?"

"It's a facial steamer." I pushed the covers off to look. "You steam open your pores and your moisturizer sinks in better. It's like an at-home facial."

"Oh, now that's something I could get into," Eddie said, pulling out the directions. "We could save a lot of money at the day spa."

Eddie and I took a trip to the spa every couple of months for a Swedish massage, mineral bath, and manicure. We'd done facials a few times and his gentleman's facial left his skin buffed and glowing. Mine gave me rosacea on my cheeks.

"Facials really aren't for people with sensitive skin," the twenty-year-old esthetician had told me afterwards.

"Get out of bed and we'll steam open our pores," Eddie said when I refused to budge. "In twenty minutes, you'll look like new."

"I don't care how I look. I'll probably just return it."

Eddie chuckled. "You'll make Amazon regret their generous return policy. I bet you send back half the stuff you order."

"Not half," I said indignantly. "I keep lots of stuff—the striped mittens, the kitchen towels with the roosters on them, that roller thing for sore feet."

Penny bounded over to Eddie, wagging furiously. She nudged his hand and he scratched behind her ears.

"Traitor," I told my dog.

"Let me remind you that I didn't grieve this much when Matthew left me," Eddie said, pulling my covers right off the bed.

"You weren't with Matt three years."

Eddie sighed. "Well, it felt like forever." He sat down and rubbed my leg.

"Yeah, but then you met Don, and now you're happily married, damn you."

"I had my share of heartache before Donny. You helped me get through it, just like I'm going to get you out of this little slump of yours."

I turned away from Eddie and curled up. "You don't understand."

"Honey, I understand fine. Do I need to remind you of the bad times? The pro and con list?"

I grunted in response.

"Picture last winter," Eddie said. "Bryan came home from work and collapsed on the couch, where he ate dinner and then went to bed at 9."

"He worked ten hours a day; he was tired," I said.

"You stopped communicating altogether, you stopped having sex—"

I groaned. "I regret telling you that."

"Sweetie, you tell me everything. That's what I'm here for. Besides, it keeps me entertained."

I grunted again.

"Seriously, babe," Eddie said, brushing the hair out of my face. "You can do this. You survived Adam. You can survive anything."

Maybe he was right. Probably not, but perhaps.

"Now come on, up you go. I brought your favorite."

"Chai tea?"

"Bucket of spaghetti."

"For breakfast?"

"Sweetie, it's 5:00 in the afternoon."

"Meatballs?"

"What do you think I am, a rookie? Of course, meatballs, but you don't get any until you take a shower. Your hair is doing a thing all its own, and it ain't pretty, my dear. Sort of a cross between Cruella De Vil and Broom Hilda."

I didn't care how I looked, but the spaghetti sounded good, so I sat up and swung my legs over the side of the bed, feeling lightheaded.

"Someday this will all be a blip in the road," Eddie said, holding out a hand to help me up.

"I suppose you're going to tell me to give it time?" I said, grabbing my black-cat leggings and heading to the bathroom.

"I don't know if it's true what they say about time healing everything that hurts," Eddie said. "But it's the only thing we can think of to say, even if it's utter and complete bullshit."

16

"IT'S RAINED A LOT SINCE I'VE BEEN DOWN HERE," BRYAN TEXTED FROM North Carolina. "But that's OK, because at least it's not freezing cold."

Bryan had found a one-bedroom apartment less than ten miles from his Cassie and Ben. He said it was small but all he needed for furniture was a bed, a couch, and a kitchen table with two chairs. Beyond that, he was starting over.

"There's so much stuff I need that I never thought of," he texted. "Like a trash can, a frying pan and a broom. Do you think you could ship down my Blu-ray player? I want to watch the *Batman* movies with Ben. Can you believe he's never seen them?"

What I couldn't believe was that he sounded like the old Bry, the one who went to Halloween festivals and parades and always beat me in mini-golf.

He needed his Blu-ray player, and I needed him, especially now that he sounded like his old self. I would send Bry anything he needed. No, I would drive down and deliver them. I could leave now and be there by sunrise. I realized, for the first time, that if Bryan had moved across town, we'd never stay separated. I'd be at his doorstep when he got home from work every day.

The only thing keeping us apart was the 1,800 miles between us.

But I couldn't tell Bryan this. I couldn't tell him how much I cried, or keep him up on family news, like about Ian's project on the Egyptian empire, or that there was so much lint in the dryer vent it almost caught fire. I couldn't tell him how I'd lain in bed the days after he left, because I didn't want him to feel responsible.

Instead, I asked if he was eating.

"Mostly eggs," he texted me. "Scrambled, hard-boiled, you name it. I still can't poach an egg the way you do."

Sometimes you have to leave behind the ones you love, he'd told me.

And sometimes you have to send them away.

Bryan had three solid leads on jobs, and I was hopeful one of them would pan out. He'd be more settled then. In the texts, Bry still called me "honey," and "sweetie," because that's who we were to one another, maybe forever. We didn't use emojis, because it would always be the crying face.

"Do you see a lot of Cassie and Ben?" I asked.

"I get to take Ben when Cass works on weekends. I'm also looking for some new projects to start in between job interviews."

I'd imagined Bryan holding Ben's hands and swinging him over the low waves at Wrightsville Beach, digging in the sand for crabs barely larger than spiders. Cooking burgers on the grill. Riding his bike.

A couple days later, after three glasses of wine, I did the unavoidable: I drunk-texted Bry.

"How's it going?"

He texted back immediately.

"Pretty good. I've had second interviews but no offers."

"The right thing will come along," I texted, sipping more wine and looking down at Penny, who was tilting her head to one side the way she did when she was studying me.

"How are you doing? How're the kids?"

"They're good, busy, Ian is finishing up spring semester. Maddy started a new job as an assistant in a doctor's office while she decides what to do with her life."

"Still not quite sure what to do with that sociology degree, huh?"

"Nope."

"So, how are you?"

I felt the tears sting my eyes and my heart lurch.

My fingers were poised to text that I was fine, I was good, I was busy. But I couldn't type those words.

"Not great," I texted, breaking our silent rule to not tell each other when we were having a bad moment. "I cry a lot."

"Yeah, I cried on the drive down here."

"Did we do the right thing? I think maybe I want to take it back," I texted, looking for Kleenex.

"It's too late, Jess, you know that. We can't go back."

"I miss you," I said hiccupping. "I miss you every day."

"Me too. But we did the only thing we could think of to get happy," Bry texted. "We'll both be better. Just takes time."

There was that fucking saying again about time healing things. Time moved like a snail from one lonely day to another, and it didn't seem like anything was getting any better.

"I love you," I texted, blowing my nose on a napkin.

"I love you, Jess. Even when I don't text, know that I miss you," was his last message for the night.

I fought myself to resist texting him again.

I wanted to message him about the good times, the adventures, like our trip to Salem, Mass, known as the "witch city" for Halloween when we'd dressed up for the Witch's Ball in a fancy hotel believed to be haunted.

We went as a Day of the Dead wedding couple. I found a hoop-skirted wedding dress at a thrift shop and Bry bleached out an old suit. I got a Marie Antoinette wig, snowy white, that stood up six inches from the top of my head. I hot-glued lace around the spokes of an umbrella and spray-painted it white. Bryan made a top hat out of an old brimmed fedora and heavy-duty cardboard.

The B&B we found was just a short walk to Derby Square, a cobbled street blocked off to traffic, where vendors sold everything from feathered and sequined witch's hats to skull-topped walking sticks to caramel popcorn. Street performers posed for photos and $1 tips: two parents and their daughter sat on a wicker chaise dressed as The Addams Family, looking eerily like Gomez, Morticia, and Wednesday. A green-faced Frankenstein, complete with nuts and bolts stuck to his neck, clomped around in black platform shoes, holding out his arms and pretending to chase people down. A trio of friends dressed as mice with pointy noses, long tails, and dark sunglasses: "three blind mice."

"We gotta try some of these next year," Bry said, taking pics with his cell and tipping all the street performers.

Halloween morning, we couldn't get ready soon enough. We powdered our faces and arms with theatrical make-up until we looked ghost-like. Then Bryan drew the iconic sugar skull patterns around our faces, filing them in with bright pink, green and yellow paint. I needed Spanx to fit into the wedding dress, but once it was on, it gave me an hourglass shape Bryan said was sexy.

We walked all around Salem that day, from the harbor with the tall sailing ships to the street lined with gift shops, tarot card readers, and psychics, then down to the sweet shop for multi-colored candy corn and solid chocolate witches and warlocks.

When we danced at the Witch's Ball, I felt like Cinderella's odd cousin.

Afterwards, crowds of costumed kids and adults spilled into the streets. Many people stopped us to ask if they could pose with us for pictures. Bry said we should start taking tips.

We stayed out till dawn, finally collapsing in bed, still white with powder.

"Best night ever," Bryan decreed.

We'd vacationed on Cape Cod, Myrtle Beach, Orlando, and Lake Placid. On every getaway, although I missed my kids and dog, the only person I wanted to be with was Bryan.

In many ways, that was still true.

Penny nudged my arm to be picked up.

"Thank you, sweetie," I said. I held Penny up on my shoulder the way I used to burp the babies after a bottle. She tucked her warm nose into my neck.

"You save my life every day."

We settled down to sleep, side by side.

17

A MONTH AFTER BRYAN MOVED SOUTH, IT WAS MORE THAN URGENT TO look at my finances. Because I hate math intensely, I made Ian sit down with me to write up a household budget: mortgage, utilities, groceries, cable, car loan, garbage collection.

I decided to cut out online shopping and entertainment entirely. I hoped I could break my Amazon addiction, which seemed necessary, to gauge by the fact I had a collection of a dozen pairs of Halloween leggings. As for movies, that's what Netflix was for.

When he printed out the spreadsheet, I felt sick as I looked at the columns of numbers.

"Wow, grim," Ian said, putting his arm around my shoulders.

"At least I have good credit," I said.

"Let's check Credit Karma," Ian said, already Googling it on his cell. "Yup, your score is 820, that's excellent. But you do seem to be lacking cash."

It was clear: The freelance work wasn't cutting it: I needed a full-time job, and I needed it fast.

We'd had to sell the suburban house where the kids had grown up, and afterwards, the three of us had moved 11 miles north to Meredia, a small, historic town that billed itself as the "Welcome Home Town." Eddie had lived in Meredia for ten years since his marriage to Donny and always said I'd like small-town living. I wanted to be out of the suburbs. I invested the equity from the sale of the home we'd had with Adam into the Meredia house. It was an older home but was exactly what the kids and I needed. My bedroom was on the first floor with my own bathroom, the kitchen, and the laundry room. Upstairs there were two good-sized bedrooms, a smallish office space, and a second bathroom. It gave Ian his own space; I rarely went up there.

The move into the town was a short one, but still required boxing up our belongings accumulated over fifteen years.

There were many things I had to part with, each of them difficult to give up: the light-up Santa that stood on our porch at least a dozen Christmases in a row; the kids' report cards starting in first grade; the Halloween punch bowl set with skull-shaped cups; the blender we never used because the idea of kale smoothies sounded better than they'd turned out to be. Ian sold the train set that he'd set up only once or twice, then lost interest. Madison donated half the clothes in her closet.

But there were many things I refused to part with. The bin of Dr. Seuss books, well-worn from bedtime story reading. Their baby books with locks from their first haircuts, their handprints, their kindergarten school photos. Ditto for Penny's puppy memento box with her first collar, a teething bone, and a little pair of suede boots we thought she might leave on in the snow but instead nudged off with her nose the minute we put them on. I also had a lock from Pen-Pen's first grooming.

I kept the haunted houses in our Halloween village set that flickered purple lights and made scary cackling witch noises when plugged in. The long-stemmed wine glasses, a wedding gift, still in the box because we were afraid we'd break them. An extraordinary painting of red and blue birds on a tree branch, a gift from Eddie for our 10th anniversary. Every ceramic project the kids had ever made in art class: the sleeping dog, the ladybug, the crooked vase, and Ian's pride and joy, an orange sneaker. There was the foil shamrock that had earned Ian first prize in art class, the bookmark made from a clothespin with a pom-pom face, the bunny with droopy ears made from a faded pink washcloth, the contorted witch face from a dried-out apple.

Adam had needed nothing in the camper. He said he didn't have room for any of the Father's Day cards strewn with glue, the macaroni necklaces Ian had made in kindergarten and surprised us with by giving them to his dad. He didn't want my favorite online purchases: the Calphalon pots and frying pans, the Keurig, the toaster oven, the waffle maker. As for the queen-sized comforter, plum with gold thread, that we'd bought two winters before, he left that with me also. He took a dish drainer and a few towels and some silverware, but not much more.

The divorce agreement included a small stipend for Ian, since Maddy was living on her own. I could easily have taken Adam to court to force him to pay more child support, but I didn't even know if he would have any money, and taking him to court would cost more legal fees and bring more stress to both of us. It was over, he was gone, there was nothing more to say.

There was a community bulletin board downtown in the town that I passed when I walked Penny, with municipal job openings—all of them terribly dull—but all with good benefits like health insurance, retirement accounts, and vacation days. After a few weeks, I saw a notice for an assistant clerk's job in the Meredia Town Hall, a brick building downtown on the same block as the post office and library.

"Don't you think you can do better, Mombo?" Mad asked, as I tried on a black pencil skirt and jacket for the interview, both of which were significantly tighter than they had been the last time I wore them.

"My clothes?"

"The job."

"It's a two-minute commute," I told her, wrestling with a red blouse that refused to drape across the waist of my skirt to hide my tummy pooch. "You guys are on dad's health insurance, but I'm up a creek. One good twisted ankle and I'll be in debt for years."

"You'll still do the freelance, right?" Maddy got up off the bed to help me with the blouse.

"Absolutely. Can you French braid my hair? I don't want to fuss with it."

With my hair in place, I was ready.

There were two people at the interview, bouncing questions back and forth so frequently that I wasn't sure who I should look at when I answered. The clerk I would be assisting was a man named Joe, who had been in the job eleven years and clearly made himself at home. He wore polyester tan pants and a dress shirt with the first three buttons undone. His forehead had a constant sheen of sweat that he mopped with a yellowed handkerchief he kept tucked in his shirt pocket. There were donuts on the conference table that I didn't touch; he ate four of the jelly-filled during the forty-minute interview.

I liked the town official, Linda. She was a small, birdlike woman who rolled her eyes at me while Joe crammed donuts into his mouth.

Job duties included answering phones and greeting people when they came in with questions or to pay bills. There was some filing, processing of vouchers and payments, and maintaining a database of water and sewer customers. I focused on what I imagined would be the positive parts of the job: being the face of the town, meeting new people, helping residents with questions and problems about their homes and property.

"What would you say are your greatest strengths and weaknesses?" Linda asked brightly.

Hmm. Good parenting skills? I make a killer guacamole? Amateur dog trainer?

"Um, I think I'm a good communicator; I can deal with people even when I'm under stress." I shifted in my seat.

"Oh, this isn't a high-stress job," Linda said, waving her hand as if brushing away a spiderweb. "And weaknesses?"

"Well, truth be told, math isn't a strong point," I said, kicking myself for choosing to share that particular tidbit.

"You won't be doing any trig here," she laughed. "That's why we have computers to do the work for us."

"Great," I said, enormously relieved.

"How long you lived here?" Joe broke in, a dribble of strawberry jelly stuck to his chin.

"Just over three years. But my friend has lived here for ten years."

"Newcomers, both of ya," Joe grunted. "I been here all my life. Parents used to own Benson's corner store. Remember that?"

"I'm sorry, I don't."

"Closed twenty-three years ago."

No shit, I thought. No wonder it wasn't familiar to me.

I had been worried there would be a typing test, but my skills were pretty good from freelance writing under deadlines. Ditto for my spelling and punctuation. It was even a personal pet peeve of mine when people were sloppy with English, as in "I ain't got none," or "do to the fact."

"Well I hope you don't mind tight quarters, because the assistant clerk's desk is right over there." Linda pointed to a low counter with two desks behind it, side by side, maybe four feet apart.

"Yeah, and you don't gotta go far for the john," Joe said. "It's the door right there." He gestured to a partly opened door just beyond the desks.

"Ladies or men's?"

Joe snorted. "Unisex, as they say."

I shuddered inwardly, trying to remind myself about the good parts of the job: an OK salary, great benefits, a commute that would allow me to get into work on time even after hitting the snooze button. The hours, 8:30 a.m. to 4:00 p.m., were also fine by me, as a non-morning person.

"Don't be expecting donuts every day," Joe said. "Unless you bring 'em!" He laughed at his own joke. "But there's a coffee pot in the back. Pitch in $5 a week and you can be part of the club."

I was glad I wouldn't be facing donuts every morning, because my affinity for glazed would add significantly to my muffin top. I wondered how two people could have a coffee club.

"We'll let you know in a day or two," Linda said, standing up and holding out her hand.

When I turned to Joe to shake his hand, he thumped me on the back the way you'd do if someone was choking, and said, "Good luck, Ms. Jessica."

Linda called the next day with a job offer. I took the kids and Eddie out for Mexican to celebrate. We toasted with margaritas in salted glasses and stuffed ourselves with black bean quesadillas.

18

Judging by Joe's appearance at the interview, there was no office dress code, but Frankenstein leggings were out of the question. I settled on the basic black skirt, white blouse, and pink cardigan for my first day. I scrubbed off my navy-blue nail polish and used a neutral shade of pink.

Before I left, I knelt down and covered Penny's face with kisses, like always.

"I'll be right back. I love you," I told her as I left. I looked through the window and saw her lie down, staring intently at the door. I always felt bad leaving her to lie on the kitchen floor while I was gone, waiting for me to come home.

"Come on back," Joe called out as the heavy front door of Town Hall banged behind me.

It was my first view of the desks behind the counter. Joe's desk was an abomination, cluttered with stacks of papers, three stained coffee cups, a big yellow happy face stress ball, a crumb-covered desk calendar, a photo of someone playing baseball, and what appeared to be a bag of doggie treats.

"Here's your desk and your inbox," Joe said, pointing to an overflowing three-shelved plastic unit very close to tipping over from the weight.

I could immediately see why Joe was so sweaty; it had to be 80 degrees in the office. I took off my sweater and hung it on the back of my chair. The chair at my desk was a small-backed stenographer's seat. Joe's was a high-backed black pleather chair with arms.

The front door of the office slammed, making me jump. Three older men in nearly identical flannel shirts came right up to the counter. The shorter one was leading a dog on a leash. An actual dog. Inside the office.

The three of them, even the dog, stood looking me up and down.

"This the new gal?" asked the one with the comb-over and mustard-colored tie.

Joe grunted in return, some sort of noncommittal reply.

I went back around the counter and held out my hand. "Jessica Gabriel."

"Wesley Scranton," the man grinned, revealing a couple of missing teeth. "Call me Wes."

"Lucky Salvadore, but I ain't lucky, so I go by Sal," said the man with the dog. "Pleased to meet ya, missy. This here is Beef Jerky."

"Beef Jerky?"

"Yeah, watch this," Sal leaned down and scratched behind the dog's ear, which made him squirm all over and shake his back leg furiously.

"See? He gets all jerky."

OK.

"Good boy, go ahead and say hi to the little lady here."

Beef Jerky reared up on and planted his two front paws smack on my skirt.

"Watch it there, Jerky," Sal said mildly. "Give the lady some space."

The dog didn't budge. We just stood that way, the dog and I, in some strange balancing act, until Jerky became bored and got down.

"Paulie," said the third guy, going around the counter in a way that made it clear he was at home in the office.

Paulie headed for the coffee pot in the back corner of the office, where three cups sat upside down on the counter. "Anybody bring donuts? Donut holes? Danish? Bagels?"

"I told her it was her turn," Joe said, motioning at me. "Apparently she didn't get the memo."

I laughed uncertainly, completely unsure if they were kidding or not.

"They have some great pastries at Brew Coffee on the corner," Wes said dreamily.

The guys filled their mugs, then settled down at the conference table. Sal took the leash off Jerky, who bounded into a chair by the window to bark at pigeons on the roofs of the stately brick buildings downtown.

Within minutes, Wes's head dropped to his chin. I could have sworn he'd fallen asleep.

"What's the weatherman say about this afternoon? Rain or shine?" Paulie asked no one in particular.

"I heard rain," Sal said, blowing the steam on his coffee.

"Nah, I think it's supposed to clear up," Paulie said.

"Aw, somebody wake up Wes," Joe said.

"WES!" Paulie and Sal shouted in unison, startling both Wes and me.

"He's got that sleeping sickness—you know, nardolepsy," Joe explained.

"Narcolepsy?" I said.

"Yeah, something like that." Joe scowled at me.

"Good thing they don't let him drive the school bus no more," Paulie said thoughtfully, sipping from his mug.

Seriously??

"You better get started," Joe said, pointing to a stack of papers piled in a box. "These are tax payments. All you have to do is input them on the spreadsheet on your Excel file, go into the account and make sure they paid the right amount, then reconcile it for the bank deposit."

"Excel? Reconcile?"

"Yeah, add up all the payments and cross reference them with the spreadsheet. K?"

Turned out, the job was all math.

My job, that is. Joe's job seemed to be mostly entertaining Sal, Wes, and Paulie. And Beef Jerky.

The phone rang nonstop, interrupting my stressful attempts to balance the spreadsheets. We were supposed to share phone duties, but when it rang, Joe ignored it and kept up his conversation with his friends about lawn mowers and the height of the blades and whether watering was a total waste of time and money.

"I'm calling about my tax bill," a resident said when I picked up the phone.

"How can I help you?" I knew squat about tax bills. All I knew was that I paid mine once a year.

"Why is it so damn high? Don't you know I'm on a fixed income? I can't possibly pay this."

I put the woman on hold.

"What should I tell this woman who can't pay her taxes?" I asked Joe.

Sal guffawed. "Tell her to be happy they ain't higher."

I looked at Joe for help.

"Tell her to write a letter to the town supervisor," he said, pulling out a backscratcher that looked like a hand and shoving it down the back of his shirt. "That's assuming she knows how to write."

I fielded complaints about leaves from neighboring trees blowing onto people's driveways, gophers trapped under sheds, how to dispose of old appliances, and even if there was a good Japanese restaurant in town. Someone actually called about their too-hot breakfast tea at Brew Coffee. Another wanted to know how to find the best handyman with low rates.

One old lady wanted us to send someone out to fix her leaky sink; another had lost her cat. An old man called because there was a torn-up green couch outside across the street where kids sat at night to smoke.

"It's the ugliest damn couch you ever seen," he told me. "Can't stand looking at it another day."

Joe somehow managed to eavesdrop on every phone call while simultaneously listening to his friends grouse about how deep the potholes were on Emmett Lane, and yelling at Wes every few minutes to wake the hell up.

"Well, I hear Stan the Man's Plumbing is good," I told a resident who sounded elderly.

"Ya can't recommend any company!" Joe hollered at me while I was still on the phone. "That's showing favoritism."

"I'm sorry, but it seems I can't make recommendations," I told the woman apologetically.

I took another call from someone who needed a trash removal company.

"I can't give out any names," I told him.

"Well then, what am I supposed to do?" He sounded genuinely out of ideas as to what to do.

"Have you looked at your neighbor's garbage bins?"

"That's still recommending a business!" Joe busted out. "What did I tell you about that?" He waited for an answer.

"Not to do it?"

"That's right, chicky, don't do it."

There was a round of laughter from the peanut gallery.

Other people called about what to do with their old TVs, where could they get a marriage license/library card/register their dog/ how to read their water meter/where was their water meter/could I go out to their house and help them find their meter.

And this was all before lunch.

At 1:00, Joe released me for my half-hour lunch break. Thankful for the three-minute commute, I drove home and found Penny sleeping in the same spot on the kitchen floor, still waiting for me.

I scooped her up and held her in my arms while I ate peanut butter toast over the sink to avoid dropping crumbs.

"I don't know how I'm going to do this," I told Penny. "I'm as tired as Wes."

19

"So, I signed us up for some spring classes," Eddie announced one night over wonton soup.

"What, now? Told you I'm not making any more jewelry. That beaded necklace debacle still haunts me."

"Yeah, you sucked at that," Eddie said thoughtfully. "We really should have started you out slow—some earrings, or maybe a brooch."

"No more jewelry, Eddie."

"OK, no jewelry. We're going to try some cooking classes," he said, rubbing his hands together briskly. "How do you feel about meatless burgers?"

"Blech."

"Try to keep an open mind, honey," he said. "It's not exactly healthy to live on a bucket of pasta and meatballs all your life."

"What's a burger without meat? Is it even a burger?"

Eddie pulled out the continuing education catalog from the local high school. Over the years, besides the ill-fated jewelry class, we'd taken Mahjong, Pickle Ball, Tai Chi and Finding Your Animal Spirit, in which, interestingly, we'd both turned out to have the spirit of a fox.

Eddie had gotten on a financial planning kick one year and we sat through "You Never Think About It, But You Need Life Insurance," "Estate Planning: Not Just for the Wealthy," and my personal favorite, "Steering Through the Winding Road of Retirement."

This time, he was going to make me cook.

"Meatless burgers made from lentils, quinoa and kale, and black beans," he read off. "They're bursting with garlic, gluten-free and aromatic. And if that's not enough, we get to take some home with free Kaiser rolls."

"Sounds pretty good," I said, reaching for another egg roll, suddenly hungry again. "What else?"

"Winey Chicken."

"What?"

"You know, chicken marsala and chicken piccata with white wine. And no, they probably don't let you drink the wine during class."

"What fun is that?"

Thursday night's meatless burger class was in the high school cooking lab, which we used to call Home and Careers. Walking the long, dim school hallways with Eddie made me feel fifteen all over again, from the scuffed linoleum floor to the scratched yellow lockers.

"I remember when I was a confused freshman wandering around looking for the B-wing," I told Eddie. "I had a map drawn on the back of my hand, which I thought was a pretty smart idea, but then it smudged, and I had to resort to asking other people for directions. They all sent me the wrong way. I was late to every class."

"Yeah, when I was there, we loved to make it hard on newbies," Eddie laughed. "I remember Laura Voss coming into English lit crying because she had gotten turned around and ended up finding our room just before the bell rang and class ended."

"Laura cried all the time. She cried in earth science when we had to gut a worm. She cried in gym when a dodge ball barely swiped her leg. She was just a crier."

"Wonder what ever happened to her? Anyway, here we are," Eddie said, opening the door for me.

Clustered around the stoves were four twentysomething couples either holding hands or with their arms around each other. The guys were wearing black jeans and the women had cat eyeglasses and braids in their hair. These were the trendy kids in high school, all grown up.

I looked at Eddie. He raised his eyebrows and shrugged. "Free Kaiser rolls," he mouthed.

The cooking teacher, wearing violet yoga pants, handed out written instructions.

"Any questions, just holler," she said, sitting back down at a table and pulling out her cell phone.

I pulled my hair back into a ponytail and rolled up my sleeves. Ten minutes later, we were all up to our elbows in lentils, quinoa, and black beans. Eddie's patties came out symmetrical and held together. Mine were lopsided and more square than round, but they were hefty and looked like a good meal. It was messy work, and I was glad I wasn't in my own kitchen. The mush clung to my hands and fingers, even when I tried scraping them back into the bowl.

"How'd you get yours so perfect?"

"They're a work of art, aren't they?" Eddie said, admiring his own patties.

But symmetry didn't matter when the instructor put down her phone and fired up a frying pan. She cooked a batch of meatless burgers while the others set out the promised Kaiser buns and ketchup. The room quickly carried the aroma of homemade dinner, something my house rarely smelled like anymore with the kids grown up. Dinner for me was usually oatmeal or eggs.

I'd cooked when the kids were younger, and we'd gather for family dinners in the dining room. Meatless lasagna and chicken chili were the favorites. We had a no cell phone rule that everyone respected, which meant the kids had to tell us about their school day or eat in quiet boredom—or worse, listen to their parents talk. Family dinners disappeared as Adam and I became distant. He would often take his plate into his office to work; the kids were on the run, and food was often grabbed from the small kitchen table or taken to go.

At the night class, Eddie and I and the cool-kid couples wolfed down our meatless burgers in record time. Even the yoga-pants teacher had one. We were officially stuffed. It was like the story of Jesus with the bread and fish: amazingly, there were leftover meatless burgers and rolls, even after we'd eaten so many. We happily divvied them up to take home.

"Don't forget to fill out the class survey," the teacher said. "Please give me five stars; I'm in grad school and need the extra money. One class gave me, like, two stars and I need to get my average up."

It was the most she had said the entire night.

I checked off five stars and added a smiley face for the hell of it.

"Would have been better if she had actually instructed," Eddie said as we walked to the parking lot.

Winey chicken class was the following Tuesday. When we parked and went into the high school, I looked up at the clock over the front desk out of habit to see if I would be late for class.

"I love the leggings," Eddie told me. "Always been a big fan of were-wolves howling at the moon."

"Thanks."

He held the door open for me when we got to the cooking room. Inside were six nearly indistinguishable grandmothers, from their cardigan sweaters buttoned all the way up, to their eyeglasses hanging from gold chains around their necks, to their odd choice of coral lipstick.

One of the grandmothers broke away from the group to introduce herself as the cooking instructor.

"Welcome to winey chicken!"

The grandmas had all planned ahead and brought aprons, all of them ruffled, one of them decorated with rolling pins, one with cherry pies.

Already clustered in a circle around the butcher-block island, the grandmothers were doing prep work. One was pounding chicken cutlets in a way that made me think she had come to the class angry. Another was daintily slicing paper-thin mushrooms.

"Those right there are restaurant quality," the instructor said.

The mushroom-cutter beamed.

"So, let's start with marsala, an especially dry white wine," the instructor said.

Eddie and I looked at each other. Far from wine experts, we nonetheless knew the difference between sweet marsala and a dry white.

OK.

"So, everyone get to a stove station and heat up your frying pans," she said.

We moved to the stoves and turned on the gas flames.

"If you can't control your temperature, turn it off and start over," the teacher said.

I looked at Eddie and we both shrugged. The room soon smelled of sizzling chicken

"By the way, don't open any of the cupboards with a sticky note on them," the instructor said.

The grandmothers, Eddie, and I all nodded without saying a word. She was the teacher, after all.

"It's because they may have mice in them," she added.

Our jaws dropped in unison. We looked around and saw several of the cupboards had neon yellow Post-Its on them.

"She's kidding, right?" I asked Eddie.

He shrugged again. "Don't know, but don't touch them anyway."

I had no plans to.

As we were cooking, the teacher went around to the closed cupboard doors, knocked on them lightly, then pulled out more Post-Its to stick on. Soon, most of the cupboards were contraband.

The chicken marsala came out beautifully, although maybe a little dry because the one grandma had pounded the cutlets until they were nearly transparent.

"I've set the table, so let's eat," the instructor said.

"Thought it was take-home," I whispered to Eddie.

"I think we get to keep the leftovers."

We sat at the round table with the grandmothers, picking up our forks to dig in.

The instructor clapped her hands, startling all of us. "Not before we say grace," she said sternly.

We dutifully recited the Lord's Prayer before eating.

Our plates were barely empty when the teacher jumped up, clapping her hands again. "Clean-up time!"

The grandma with the cherry pie apron raised her hand as if she were still in school. "What about the white wine chicken?"

"Oh, dearie, no time for that tonight."

We looked at the clock. We were exactly one hour into the two-hour class. But we followed directions and washed the pans and dishes. None of us were going to touch the cupboards, so we left everything in the drying racks.

"Here are your leftovers!"

The instructor handed out Tupperware containers. What? We'd devoured every bit of the chicken marsala.

I opened the corner of the Tupperware to look inside. There were more chicken cutlets, marinating in wine, completely frozen. It was the chicken piccata preparation, never to be cooked in this very strange night class.

"Well, it was more entertaining than watching you break things in jewelry class," Eddie said as we walked to his car.

"Think it was dementia?"

Eddie shrugged. "Maybe she drank the leftover wine."

"You think there were mice in those cabinets?"

"Honestly, I really don't want to know."

20

My cell rang as I was getting ready for bed. I was instantly awake, because the kids and I rarely used cell phones to make actual calls. We always texted. Even Penny raised her head from the bed pillow curiously.

"Hello?"

"Jess."

It was Bryan. His voice sounded so clear he might have been in the next room. "Bry?"

"Yeah, it's me."

"What's wrong?" I looked down at my slippered feet.

"Nothing. Just wanted to hear your voice."

"OK. Good. Well, here I am."

"What's doin' with you?" he asked.

"Well, I started that new job."

"That's right. How's it going?"

"Like a three-ring circus. The work is complicated and I need to concentrate, which is hard because of the three old guys who've made the office their home. Yesterday they had a twenty-minute discussion about what breed of dog one of them has."

"What is it?" Bry laughed.

"A mutt! And he brings the dog to the office every day."

"Isn't there some kind of dog rule to keep them outside?"

"There don't seem to be any rules there," I sighed.

"So are you gonna bring Penny to work?"

"Are you kidding? Their dog is so big, Pen could ride on its back. He could trample her!"

"Sounds like a doggone mess."

We both laughed.

"Tell me about Ben."

"He's amazing, Jess. He's fearless; he runs straight for the ocean, doesn't even care if the waves could knock him over while we all chase him, which makes him run even faster. He dips his fries in grape jelly and hates all the same veggies as me."

"Carrots? Peas? Everything but corn?" I knew Bry's picky eating habits by heart.

"Yup. All of the above."

We were silent for a moment, neither of us wanting to hang up or be the first to say goodbye.

"Well for now I'll just say good night," he said, as if he knew what I was thinking.

"Good night, Bry. Talk soon."

I settled back down next to Penny, nuzzling her neck, and even though she was sleeping, she moved her warm back closer to me.

I pictured Bryan in his little apartment with a table and chairs and Blu-ray player watching DC Comics movies with Ben. I missed him. Maybe we'd been wrong to separate and divorce.

Then I thought about him in the last, long, terrible months of our marriage, spending most of his time on the couch, wrapped in a blanket because he was always cold. It had been the right thing, even though it hurt on so many levels. He was getting better, and I was—well, keeping busy.

21

ONE MORNING IN MAY I REALIZED MY BEDROOM WAS EXACTLY THE SAME as it had been for the three years I was married to Bryan. I looked around the bedroom at the dark navy comforter, the nautical striped curtains, the dresser top where I still piled clothes. It was time for an overhaul.

I spent more than an hour and over $200 at Home Space, lugging shopping bags home and dropping them on my bed.

I cleaned until every surface of my bedroom shined. I vacuumed, then got down on my hands and knees to use carpet cleaner on tiny, barely visible spots on the rug. I folded all the clothes on my dresser to put in the chest of drawers that had been Bryan's.

I hesitated in front of it, running my fingers over the wood. I remembered the shock I felt when I found all the drawers empty, the sick feeling when I opened his sock drawer and found nothing but a few runaway nickels and dimes. I'd helped Bryan pack; why would I be stunned by the emptiness?

Taking a deep breath, I opened the top drawer, where he'd kept his boxers. A black pen without a cap rolled toward me. In the back of the drawer was a rolled-up piece of paper. When I smoothed it out, I saw a grocery list in Bryan's handwriting. I held it for a few moments, then put it back in the drawer.

I filled the dresser with my clothes, taking up an entire drawer for Halloween leggings, then took all the shoes tossed in the bottom of my closet and lined them up inside the third drawer, congratulating myself for my creative use of space.

But when I opened the bottom drawer, I drew in a sharp breath. There was a white T-shirt with a Day of the Dead skull on the front. It was so neatly folded that it looked as though Bryan had left it there for me. I broke down then, holding the shirt to my face, using it to wipe my tears.

After a while, I composed myself enough to unpack my shopping bags and put on the new comforter, seafoam green with violets scattered like they'd been blown by wind. It was oversized on the bed, but I liked it that way.

I fluffed the light-purple ruffled pillows and set them against the headboard. I'd bought candles in squat little jars that I put on my bed stand and both dressers, arranged the purple and yellow flowers in the green vase, put the jewelry tossed on my dresser top into a little china bowl.

The last thing I did was carefully refold Bryan's T-shirt, and tuck it under the bed pillows.

"Come on," I said to Penny, who had been watching with wonder, as if she'd never seen me clean before.

"We're done for now," I told her, and the room too.

22

ONE PROBLEM WITH THE TOWN JOB, EVEN WITH THE AMUSING GERIATRIC atmosphere, was the amount of time I spent sitting on my ever-expanding ass. I got only half an hour lunch and could barely squeeze in a short walk through the downtown business district while still having enough time to eat something.

I'd become an expert at making meatless burgers and kept a good supply in the freezer. I brought them most days for lunch. But the Kaiser rolls weren't exactly helping diminish my midsection, a muffin top that spilled over skirts that had once been loose at the waist. Even the elastic waistbands of my leggings were snug, something I ignored as long as possible.

It was time for drastic measures. It was time for the Y.

The Meridia Y was just ten minutes from my house. I went one Friday after work, circling the crowded parking lot for a good space. Ironic, because I needed exercise, but I didn't want to park too far from the gym's front doors.

I had a Pillsbury canvas bag I'd gotten for free after earning points for buying twenty-five tubs of cookie dough from Madison to fund a class trip. It seemed to work well as a gym bag to carry my sneaks, an old T-shirt of Ian's, and my sweatpants.

The silver-haired man at the front desk looked up as I went in. His nametag said Marvin and boasted a sticker of a man flexing his biceps.

"New member?"

"How did you know?"

Marvin didn't answer, and that made me more nervous than I already was. Maybe I should have gotten an actual gym bag.

"Single membership?"

Again, how did he know that?

"Yeah, single," I said, trying to sound casual instead of defensive.

"How often are you planning to come, twice a week? We recommend five or six visits to recapture fitness levels."

I was wearing a heavy coat, but clearly, he could see I needed to restore fitness rather than maintain. I was starting to feel the urge to tell him I was in the wrong place and bolt back to my car.

"Does it matter how often you come? For a single membership?" I brushed my hair out of my face, wishing I'd tied it back.

"No, no," Marvin said, briskly tapping the computer keys. "Just giving you some pointers."

OK. Well keep those tips to yourself, mister, I thought. Then again, he was in excellent shape and must be pushing seventy. Clearly he had recaptured his fitness, or maybe never lost it in the first place.

I handed over my credit card for a one-year membership. There was a four-week trial period during which you could cancel, no questions asked. In other words, you could give up and slink away and no one would make you admit to your failure.

"Is there a weekly weigh-in?" I said, attempting to joke with Marvin.

"There's a scale in every locker room," he said. "Don't weigh yourself every time you come; there will be ups and downs, and we don't want you to get discouraged."

Discouraged? I was a middle-aged woman with a Dough Boy bag in a gym for the first time since 1997 when I took a Mommy & Me tumbling class with Madison. I'd been told I had to recapture my fitness by someone twenty years older than me named Marvin.

I straightened my shoulders and pulled up the Pillsbury bag that had slid down my arm.

"Is there a tour?"

"Locker room's that way," Marvin said, pointing left. "Track is upstairs, you can see the pool and exercise room behind me. Trainers can help you out in there. Good luck!"

He could tell I needed it.

In the locker room, there were about a dozen women of all ages and all sizes in various stages of nudity undressing. On a bench near the orange lockers, a woman who was completely naked sat rubbing lotion on her arms. In front of a mirror by the sinks, an older woman was blow-drying her hair, also nude.

In high school, all the girls were required to shower after gym. It was widely rumored that the female gym teachers looked into the shower stalls to make sure we were naked and wet, not standing in there with our gym clothes on. I had been a "late bloomer," as my mother always said, and spent much of my freshman year terrified of a gym coach peeking behind the shower curtain. That, and aging, had resulted in what was apparently a higher level of modesty than most women's—clearly something I needed to work on overcoming.

I took my Pillsbury bag into a bathroom stall for a quick change in the Y women's locker room before heading down the hall to the equipment room. There was '90s music piped in, but most people were wearing headphones. I didn't have any portable music. At home, I listened to a stereo/radio.

People were stair-climbing, furiously pedaling, not just running but downright sprinting on treadmills, and in the back of the room, guys with oversized muscles were using weight machines I'd never seen before. A woman with wide rubber bands on her ankles was walking sideways down the middle of the room. Two teenagers were doing yoga stretches on an exercise mat, and a man whose upper body was comprised entirely of muscle was doing chin-ups. In front of the room, two guys with Y T-shirts who apparently worked there were standing behind a red counter, texting.

There were women of all ages in all stages of restoring their fitness, all of them wearing black capris and bright spandex tops with crisscrossed straps on the back that showed their sports bras underneath. Oh, come on. A dress code at the gym? I was literally the only woman wearing sweats, and other than the men, the only one with a baggy T-shirt. Thank God I'd decided against the spiderweb leggings, and my sneakers were fairly new.

I started with the treadmill, which was at least somewhat familiar. Once I got on and pushed "go," it jerked forward, picking up speed right away, so fast I stumbled. For a moment, I thought I might slide right off the back of it.

I looked around to see if anyone had noticed.

Nope. Everyone was in their own plugged-in world; no one was making eye contact. Wasn't the gym supposed to be a place to meet people? How exactly would that be done? All I could think of was to fling off a treadmill at their feet, disrupting their own machine.

Overestimating my own level of fitness, I bumped up the treadmill to a slight incline, walking briskly and wishing I hadn't tied my sneaks so tight. Twelve minutes later I was sweaty, breathless, and certain I'd already developed blisters on my heels. I hit the button to see how many calories I'd burned, certain it would be enough to share a bucket of spaghetti with Ian back home. The monitor said I'd burned 68 calories. Certain it was broken, I hit more buttons, but they only gave me more dismal news about my average speed and distance.

Wearily, I climbed off the treadmill and headed back to the locker room, wishing I'd brought soap and a towel to shower.

I had a long way to go, but every hope of recapturing some semblance of fitness.

23

It was time for me to learn how to manage small household tasks when Ian wasn't around to help. I started with pounding a nail into my bedroom wall to hang a new framed print of children in old-fashioned swimsuits, collecting shells at low tide. I was proud of myself for not hammering my thumb, and for hanging the print straight. I stood back to admire my work.

In the middle of the night, a large crashing noise startled Penny and me awake. I turned on my bedside lamp and stared at the wall where the print had been hanging when I went to bed.

Turns out, you need to find a stud in the wall before you nail something up.

I got up and looked behind the dresser. The nail had pulled loose from the wall, the print had slid down smashing the plastic outlet cover into small, sharp pieces. Somehow, the glass frame hadn't broken, and it was still standing straight on the floor behind the dresser.

I used two nails the next day to hang it, but had to ask Ian to put in a new plastic outlet cover.

"How did you manage this, again?" he asked in disbelief.

"Just fix it, smart ass."

Next on the list was letting the gas out of the snow blower to store it until next winter. I went out to the shed and pulled open the wooden door. Inside, it looked like funnel winds had blown through. There were snow shovels on top of beach chairs, boxes of rock salt to melt ice, a tangled badminton net, broken sleds, abandoned bags of topsoil, two tipped-over bicycles, and the boxed spiral light-up trees we put out at Christmas.

Tucked into one corner was a small green pail that Bryan used to water a strawberry plant he'd tried to grow, but the rabbits beat him to the berries. Inside was a plastic toy shovel like ones used to make sandcastles. I put them on a shelf in front of the shed. I liked to imagine Bryan using them with Ben at the beach.

Way in the back, I could see the lawnmower and the snow blower, half-hidden by plastic blue tarps we once used in the garden to try to eliminate weeds. I climbed over the piles, kicking aside the deflated wheelbarrow tire, the garden hose we never remembered we had and kept buying new ones, butterfly nets the kids hadn't used in fifteen years, a bocce set, and anything else that got in my way. When I finally reached the back, I grabbed the snow blower handle and wrenched it, banging my elbow on the wall of the shed.

"Shit, shit, shit!"

It took me five minutes to pull the red snow blower out of the chaos that was our shed and onto the driveway. Then all there was to do was start it and let the engine run out of gas.

I pulled the starter cord. Nothing. Pulled harder. A short, half-hearted wheeze came from the engine. About six pulls later, my shoulder muscles were screaming. Note to self: start arm work at the Y.

But I was determined not to let the snow blower win. My last pull felt half-assed, but the motor caught and roared. I did a little victory dance.

And then the toilet started running water continuously.

I put on my oldest leggings—faded witches on brooms—still tight around the waist because I had yet to recapture my fitness, went into the bathroom and jiggled the toilet handle.

Nothing.

I washed my hands and went to my laptop to Google "how to fix a leaky toilet." Seemed simple enough. Back in the bathroom, I took the lid off the toilet and jiggled the chain holding the rubber stopper controlling the water. Then I held it up for a minute. I thought it would help to see if the toilet refilled with the stopper up, so I flushed. It took about a minute for the toilet to fill and overflow all over the floor, bathmat, and my sneakers.

Penny stuck her nose around the corner of the doorway.

"You don't want to come in here," I said, grabbing some bath towels and throwing them down on the biggest puddles.

Penny stepped in with her front paws, then quickly retreated.

I knew I had no other choice: it was time to talk to the experts. I asked the men for help the next day at work.

"Never jiggle the handle!" Wes scolded me as if I were a child. "That just makes it worse."

"And definitely never flush," echoed Paulie. "You're just asking for an overflow."

"Did you pull the chain on the float arm?" Sal asked patiently.

After some unsuccessful attempts to teach me the working mechanisms of a toilet, Wes pulled out a Brew Coffee napkin and drew a diagram of the parts under the lid.

"Ya gotta empty it first," Sal said.

"She doesn't have to empty it. She can stick her hand in the back of the toilet—it's clean water," Paulie suggested.

"For god's sake, she doesn't want to be up to her arm in cold toilet water!" Wes argued on my behalf.

The three men finally agreed the best first step was turning the shut-off valve clockwise and draining the toilet.

"Then pry up the flapper."

"What's the flapper?" I asked.

When they were done laughing at my lack of toilet parts knowledge, Wes drew a round rubber seal on the napkin to illustrate. "Flapper problems, that's what'll get ya."

Paulie nodded in agreement.

"Chain's probably too long," Wes said thoughtfully. "Gotta shorten it so the flapper closes in time."

"Ya know, you can waste a good 200 gallons of water a day letting your toilet run," Sal said helpfully. "Haven't you been keeping an eye on your own water bill? You're a smart girl; surprised you never noticed till now."

* * *

I followed their directions that night, draining the toilet, checking the flapper to find the chain really was actually too long. I got out the wire cutters I used to make Christmas wreaths and clipped it slightly shorter. Voilà. The sound of running water in the tank had stopped, and the guys hadn't even had to make a house call to help me.

I thanked the guys with cinnamon raisin bagels the next day at work—substantially less costly than a plumber's bill, with a hefty boost to my confidence as an added side benefit.

24

BESIDES EDDIE AND MY SMALL DOG, MY BEST FRIEND WAS A PRECOCIOUS little girl named Lily, who was six and lived down the street. My house was at the end of the sidewalk, and Lily was allowed to ride her bike or push her baby doll stroller only on the sidewalk, so she always ended up at my front porch.

If I wasn't outside, Lily rang the bell and asked if Penny could go out to play. Sometimes, Lily's mother let her scooter up the sidewalk to my house after dusk to visit, just for a few minutes. I spent many weeknights outside with Penny, rocking in my wicker chair, watching cars go by.

"So, Bryan's gone?" Lily asked one warm evening in June.

"Yeah, he's...gone. Lives in the south, near the beach now."

Lily considered this for a minute. "I'd rather stay here and live with you and Penny."

"Thanks, kid," I said, ruffling her curly hair.

"You're welcome," she said, smoothing her hair. "You sad about him going to live near the beach?"

I smiled. Leave it to a kid to cut to the chase.

"I was pretty sad, but I'm getting better."

"Good for you," Lily said, then proceeded to tell me about a yellow and pink butterfly she'd seen in her backyard that landed on her trampoline.

* * *

"I like your nail polish," I told Lily one night, looking at her sparkly toenails.

"Thanks, my grandpa did them," she said, flexing her flip-flopped feet. "Then he let me paint his big toe only. He said he had to take it off before my dad saw."

"Your grandpa's a smart man."

"I know."

One summer afternoon, Lily settled herself on my front steps and emptied out her backpack.

"Grace is hungry, and I didn't have time to feed her before her walk," she explained, pointing to the doll with the tousled blonde ponytails. "So, I have to make her food now."

She set out a plate and pulled out a jar of bright blue Play-Doh, which she flattened between her palms, then cut into strips with a plastic knife.

"What are you making?"

"Fries."

Then she sat the doll on a small pink play toilet that made a real flushing sound when she pressed the lever.

I waited to see how Lily would feed Play-Doh fries to little Grace—who I'd never noticed had an open mouth—and to learn why she sat on the potty when eating. Lily carefully spoon-fed the doll, then picked her up and thumped on her head, causing the Play-Doh to eject from the doll's bottom, where there was also an opening, right into the toilet bowl.

"Your turn," she said, handing over the baby spoon.

"Why are your fingers blue?" Ian asked later that night.

"I was helping Lily make French fries."

"I'm not even going to ask."

* * *

Along with being an excellent mama to her dolls, Lily was a born gymnast. Part monkey, she balanced her small feet sideways on a tiny ledge outside our kitchen window, which I left open that summer like a drive-through restaurant. She showed up a few times a week, poking her little head into our kitchen, which made Penny stand on her hind legs and try to reach her.

Lily told me she sometimes came to our kitchen window and was disappointed when she found no one home. I put green sidewalk chalk on the ledge and told her to leave me messages. When she tapped on the window and no one answered, she wrote her name in the large, painstakingly formed letters of a kindergartner. Every few days I changed chalk colors to see if she noticed.

She always did.

Another day Lily drew a welcome mat with yellow chalk in front of the porch steps.

"This is so people will come see you," she told me.

"You're the only company I need, kid," I said, thinking how much she reminded me of Madison when she was little.

"Everyone gets lonely and wants visitors," Lily said sagely. "Even you."

She was right, of course. I'd reached the point of intense loneliness.

25

"So there's this new dating site," Eddie said, Penny on his lap, while I cleaned up the kitchen after dinner a month later.

"What?"

"It's where you look at profiles and message anyone you might be interested in."

"I know what a dating site is," I said, scrubbing at the baked-on lasagna in the dish. "Why would you think I'd want to do that?"

"Honey, you've got to get out of the house sometime."

I loaded silverware in the dishwasher. "I get out of the house. Every day I go to my fabulous new office clerk job. I file papers. I run mail through the meter. I type up meeting minutes. I listen to the Three Stooges debate which county has the best-tasting water."

"Yes, I know, work a monkey could do; you've told me many times."

"It's worse than monkey work," I said. "Someone called me today to ask if they could raise chickens in their backyard."

"Can they?" Eddie asked.

"Only if they have a very large lot," I sighed.

"Well, a crap job is all the more reason to get out and have some fun."

"No thanks," I said, hanging up the dishtowel.

"So, it's called Go Fish," Eddie said, opening my laptop.

"Well see, right off the bat, that's a stupid name," I sat down at the table with him anyway.

"I think it's rather clever. And besides, it's free."

"Free?"

"Yes, little miss budgeter, free."

I pulled my chair over as Eddie put on his glasses and logged onto the site. There was a graphic of a couple sitting on a dock with fishing poles in water full of cartoon hearts.

"See, right there, that's so dumb. Maddy's on Tinder—why don't I just try that, if you're gonna force me to put myself out there?"

"How do I put this diplomatically?" Eddie pursed his lips. "That's for kids, and the last time you dated, phones had cords."

"Thanks for the diplomacy."

"Shush. OK, let's write your profile. Age?"

"Forty-nine," I said with assurance.

"Seriously? You're going to subtract eight years from your age?"

"You think I should go with forty-five?" I asked hopefully.

"Let's just go with forty-nine, then," Eddie said.

"Are you saying I couldn't pass for forty-five?"

"I'm not saying that, sweet pea. Tell you what, I'll give you an extra inch on the height and say 5'5"."

"It doesn't ask weight, does it? I'm not saying my weight. God, even I don't want to know my weight; I've successfully avoided the scale at the Y."

"Calm down... it does ask your body shape: athletic, average, couple extra pounds, or BBW?"

"Oh my God, don't you dare put down a couple extra pounds," I howled. "Even though that's technically what I am."

"Average it is."

We clicked through a list of questions:

Is religion important to you?

"I should say yes, right? I'm Lutheran."

"When was the last time you were in church?"

"OK, no," I said.

"Would you describe yourself as spiritual?"

"Yes, that's a definite yes," I said confidently.

"What kind of music do you like?"

"I don't know what to say—everything but that loud, obnoxious post-hardcore punk crap Ian listens to."

"Variety," Eddie said, typing. "Are politics important to you?"

"Should I say yes? I should say yes, right?"

"You should tell the truth," Eddie said.

"OK, well, in election years yes; other times not as much as I should be."

"What's your profession?"

"Oh, shit, does it really ask that? I'm a clerk...no, wait, put down writer."

Eddie raised his eyebrows.

"I write," I said indignantly.

"OK, now to the good stuff," Eddie said. "How would you describe yourself in one word?"

"Mom."

Eddie shook his head.

"How about 'dog lover?' Men like dogs, right?"

Eddie sighed. "That's two words, and the idea here is to be enticing."

"Writer?"

Eddie rubbed his eyes. "How about 'adventurer?'"

"Yeah, well, then they'll think I like to do things, you know, adventurous. I don't think walking around the block with Penny makes me an adventurer."

"Wait, I know, there is a word that describes you—let me think," Eddie drummed his fingers on the table. "Means you like smart people."

"I have no idea."

"Well, thankfully, you don't have to be smart to love smart people," Eddie said. "Let me Google it."

I got up to pour wine.

"That's it! Sapiophile: a person who is sexually attracted to highly intelligent people!"

"Hmm."

"What do you mean, hmm?" Eddie said, accepting his wine glass.

"I mean, won't people have to Google it to know what it means?"

"The smart people you're trying to attract will know what it means, silly."

"If you say so," I said uncertainly.

"I do. Now, what are you looking for? Casual dating, LTR, or someone to marry?"

"What the hell's a LTR?"

Eddie sighed and took a deep drink of his wine. "Long-term relationship, dear. Are you looking for that?"

"I don't know."

"Babe, you gotta know what you want before you go looking."

"That was incredibly philosophical. Hold on while I call Hallmark."

"Ha ha ha," Eddie said.

"I guess casual dating."

"Nope."

"That's not what I'm looking for?"

"That means you're looking to hook up," Eddie said patiently. "You know, DTF?"

"What the hell is that?"

"Let's just say if a guy asks if you are DTF, tell him no immediately."

"What is it?"

Eddie sighed. "It means down to, and then the F-word."

"Well, that's interesting."

Eddie shrugged. "Everybody's DTF at some point. Except you, that is," he looked at me over the top of his glasses.

"Maybe I am DTF," I defended myself. "After all the boring sex I've had, maybe I want to try new things."

"You said the sex was good with Bryan, missy."

"Not at the end," I sighed. "It was nonexistent. So now I'm ready. Bring it."

"Good for you, Little Miss Frisky. You are free to go explore."

"Thank you."

"Just don't do anything you don't want to do."

"What does that mean?"

Eddie sighed. "Don't let anyone talk you into anything. Go with your gut."

"I plan to. And also go with other body parts a bit further south."

"What has gotten into you?"

"Like you said, I'm free to do what I like. Maybe it's time to let my hair down."

"As long as you keep your wits about you."

We both drank from our wine glasses.

"And also prepare to be ghosted," Eddie said. "A lot."

"Ghosted?"

"It's when someone messages you for a while—or even meets you—then disappears. Poof! And you have no idea what happened."

"God, that sounds terrible!"

"You think that's bad, wait until you've been 'mosted,'" Eddie continued.

"Explain, please."

"It's a new phenom where you go out on several dates and are led to believe you're the most wonderful person in the world, that you're everything they've been looking for, and then—"

"Then they run? Ugh, that's even worse. I would never 'most' someone."

"Never say never, Jess."

I got up and poured some pretzels into a bowl.

"Hey, can I put in there 'looking for someone with good grammar'?"

Eddie took off his glasses and rubbed his eyes. "What are you talking about, Jess?"

"You know how I am about spelling and grammar…I just don't want texts from a guy that mixes up there, their, and they're."

"No one likes a grammar snob, sweetie."

"Fair enough." I scowled at him.

"Now, let's pick a good profile name."

"I'm assuming we don't use our own."

"Right, chicky. And don't ask to use 'Mom of 2' or 'Dog lover,' because those aren't even remotely interesting," Eddie said, furrowing his brow.

"Hey, I'm interesting," I defended myself.

"Of course you are," he said, patting my hand. "But a profile name is like a billboard; people have to notice it."

"Hmm," I deliberated.

"Too bad you don't have an outdoor hobby, we could use 'Loves to Skate,' or 'Camping Fun.'"

We sat in silence.

"How about your zodiac sign—what is it?" Eddie asked.

"Aries."

"Let's go with that. You need to make it clear you're a woman, so Aries Girl, and you run the words together so it's AriesGirl."

"Yeah, I can go with that," I sighed.

Eddie snapped his fingers. "I've got it! A way to make it sound sexy: AriesGurl."

"If you think that works…."

"It works," he said, clapping his hands together. "What are we going to do about photos?"

"No photos! All I have are bad ones! I haven't had a good picture taken in ten years! More than that! The last good photo was Christmas 1999 because half of me was hidden behind the tree."

"Then it's time to get some new ones. Go find something sexy to wear."

"All I have is leggings," I said, thoughtfully. "I may have a V-neck T-shirt...."

"We're going to need more wine," Eddie said, rubbing his temples.

26

Despite all his protests, Ian joined Tinder. Maddy was on Bumble, so it was official: we were, all three of us, unmarried and on dating sites.

"So should we take bets to see who meets The One first?" Madison said one night in early August when we were having a bucket of spaghetti for dinner at my house.

"What the hell's The One?'" Ian asked, using his fork to poke around in the white cardboard bucket.

"You know, The One." Maddy took a long drink from her water glass. "And stop picking out all the meatballs, Ian. Mom, he's hogging the meatballs!"

"There are a bunch on the bottom; I ordered extra," I said calmly. "Let's get back to The One."

"The One is the person you're meant to be with, your soulmate, your perfect match," she said.

Ian snorted. "You're kidding, right, Madd?"

"Laugh all you want." She pretended to look offended. "But I think there's genuinely someone for everybody. You just have to find each other."

I slurped up a string of spaghetti, pondering this. The One?

I'd grown up on Cinderella and Snow White fairy tales, without question believing there was a prince out there for me. I never really got behind the idea of being saved by that prince, because I was always quite certain I could save myself, but that wildly romantic notion of having a soulmate? I'd bought into it big time.

For much of my adult life, Adam had been The One for what I'd believed was forever. After that, Bryan had been The One for a period of time. Maybe I'd maxed out on meeting the ones I was meant to be with.

"I see you feeding Penny pasta," I said to Ian. "She's going to get fat."

Ian shrugged. "She looks cute with a little bit of pudge."

"I wish someone would say that about me," I sighed.

The doorbell rang, and Penny charged at it like a bull.

"Lily, this late?" Madd asked.

"Nah, FedEx," Ian said. "Mom's shopping addiction has taken on a whole new level."

"Hey, I send a lot of stuff back," I defended myself.

I brought in the Amazon box and stuck it in a corner.

"Go ahead, Mom. You don't have to wait to open it."

Truth be told, I didn't want the kids to see me open the jade roller to de-puff undereye bags, the mini teapot shaped like Humpty Dumpty, or the set of three garden gnomes with little plaid hats.

"It's fine, I'll wait," I said. "Now, where were we?"

"So, no one believes there's someone out there for them?" Madison pushed her plate away and sat back in her chair.

"It's a bit of a stretch, don't you think? It's a big weight to carry around, thinking you have to be perfect for someone else," Ian said.

"No one has to be perfect. They just need to be better people when they're together," Maddy said. "What do you think, Mombo?"

"My days of believing in a prince out there for me are long gone," I said, picking up the empty bucket and carrying it to the trash. "But yeah, I do think there are people put in our paths that are good for us. You just have to be ready."

I bent down and scrubbed at Penny's chin to get off the bits of spaghetti sauce off her little face as she tried to bite at the dishcloth.

"So what's the verdict?" I asked the kids.

"I say wait for The One," Madison said. "Work is so busy, people coming and going all day long. Someone wonderful could walk in and start up a conversation any time; you never know!"

I envied her confidence and wished I had the same.

"It could happen in your office too, Mombo."

"Somehow, I don't picture Mr. Right just walking in the door to pay his sewer bill," I sighed. "How about you, Ian?"

"My plan is to cycle through as many women as possible while looking for The One," Ian said, laughing when I shot him a look of horror. "Kidding. But I can't just wait around for that one woman to come along."

"So what's your plan?" I asked him. "You always have a plan."

"Try to ignore how superficial the sites are and connect with someone genuine," Ian said.

It sounded like a plan.

27

By September, I had established an exercise routine.

Sort of. I went to the gym two or three days a week after work and once on weekends. Had I regained my fitness level? Nah. Overcome the locker-room modesty? Nope.

But I was proud of the fact that Marvin knew who I was now at the Y, greeting me by name when I went in. That made me almost a regular.

I walked fast on the treadmill at a slight incline, but found I sweated more on the stationary bikes. Each machine had a monitor that flashed units in bright red lights: miles completed, heart rate, calories burned. I brought in a hand towel to cover up the monitor, because it did me no good to know I'd only walked .08 miles, burned eleven calories and had the heart rate of a camel.

I didn't bring headphones like most of the crowd; instead, I watched the 6 o'clock news. I got accustomed to the '90s music and caught myself humming along to Madonna songs. I was chasing that runner's high, but so far, the best part of working out was being done and going home.

My goal was to recapture my fitness to the level where I could muster up the guts to even approach the locker room scale. At no time did I put bands on my ankles and walk sideways across the room. Nor did I yell out the number of miles I'd done like a small group of sprinters were in the habit of doing.

One night I was reaching the end of a long haul on the bike, sweat sticking my bangs to my forehead, nearly breathless, when a tall man with sculpted calf muscles walked by me, stopped, and pointed to his chest.

We were wearing the exact same T-shirt. Mine was an old St. Patrick's Day Marathon shirt of Ian's from six years before, with the name of the race emblazoned on the chest over a leaping leprechaun. Calf man's was the same, maybe a little more broken-in.

Among the sea of T-shirts in the workout room, most were athletic labels, making it even more odd to be wearing the same one as anyone else. Of course, he was a man and I was still the only woman who didn't wear sports bras and spandex, but that's another story.

Matching shirts had to be a sign something was meant to happen!

"What are the chances of this?" he said, settling into the bike next to me.

"Slim to none."

"Right?"

I knew having the same shirts had to be a sign.

"Did you run the race?" he asked.

"What? Oh, no, this is my son's shirt. I borrowed it," I overexplained.

I discreetly slowed my pace to stop panting. What to say?

"I'm Brant," he said.

"Jessica," I said, holding out my hand. Good Lord! Who shakes hands at a gym? And how did I not notice how clammy and wet my hand was before offering it to Brant Beautiful Calves?

Gamely, he shook hands with me.

"You come here often?" I wanted to kick myself, but both feet were on the bike. I was resorting to 1970s bar pick-up lines. WTF?

"It varies from day to day. Now that I'm retired, I can go anytime."

Retired? Hmm. He didn't look a day over forty-five. The only wrinkles he had were completely adorable smile lines around his green eyes.

"Lucky you," I said, attempting to brush my bangs back, but my sweat was like super glue. I thought about mopping my face with the hand towel, but there was an off chance I still had mascara on, and I didn't want to smear it all over.

From the back of the room, someone dropped a heavy weight onto the floor, a thudding sound that always made me jump. Marvin strolled in to chat with the personal trainers in the front of the room. I waved, but he didn't see me, so I pretended I was just fixing my ponytail.

Cathy's Kitchen was on the screen nearest me. She was making a bacon, potato, and cheese frittata that looked amazing and also a zillion calories per forkful. I looked away, as if watching Cathy would make me look too into food.

I brushed my sweaty forehead with the back of my hand and stealthily wiped it on the hand towel. I could tell by the fire in my calf muscles

I'd been on the bike at least 45 minutes, but hell if I was quitting now. I was determined to ride it out with Brant.

"What do you do?" Brant was outpacing me like crazy but still able to carry on a conversation.

"I work for the Town of Meredia."

"Downtown? I run there some mornings and stop for coffee."

"Brew Coffee?"

"That's the place."

Good god, he could know the Three Stooges!

We pedaled in silence for a minute. Maybe the shirt thing wasn't a sign. But Brew Coffee had to be.

"How do you stay busy?" I meant, aside from the marathon training.

"Gardening, mostly. I have some beautiful apple and fig trees. Ever had a fresh fig, right off a branch?"

"I've had Fig Newtons."

Brant tipped his head back and laughed, so I did too. "I like to show the grandkids how to grow their own fruit; they like the getting-dirty part."

Grandkids? Retired? Clearly, I had to rethink my vision of what today's grandfathers look like. I pictured Brant in an orchard of trees (did they look like apple trees? I had no idea) picking figs with several blond grandkids, all with green eyes like his. In my mind, the sunset made the whole scene look like a Sonoma Valley wine country commercial.

We pedaled in silence for a few minutes. I was glad for the chance to catch my breath.

"You have kids?" Brant asked, showing no signs of sweat.

"Two, both in their twenties."

"Nice."

"Yeah," I said. "My kids are both single. We're all single, actually. Single and ready to mingle."

I turned my face to the wall clock so he couldn't see my red face after sharing that unnecessary info.

Without warning, Brant was done biking, and incredibly, I was still breathing. He climbed off and stretched his calves again in a way that made me almost drool.

"Nice talking with you, Jess," he said, smiling.

"You too."

He turned to walk back to the weights area.

"Hey!" I called out before I could stop myself.

Brant turned back.

"It might be nice to talk sometime when we're not both sweating," I said. "Maybe Brew Coffee sometime?"

He hesitated and I immediately wished to take back the invitation, pluck it right out of the space between us.

"I'm really not dating right now. Nothing against you. I'm just not into it."

"Oh, sure, I understand. Dating is a pain."

I tried to manage a laugh, but it came out like a guffaw.

"See you around," he said.

I focused on the TV while Brant headed to the back of the room to use the weight machines. He was a cross trainer. Of course.

I immediately took my towel and wiped down my sweaty forehead, mopping at my forehead and eyes. To hell with the mascara. The monitor was flashing my stats, and they were amazing: I'd burned 390 calories! A personal record.

My legs were on fire when I got off the bike, but I straightened my shoulders and walked briskly toward the door. No slumping out for me, even if I'd been turned down for coffee. It was only coffee. Not like I'd offered him sex. Although maybe I would have.

"Lookin' good!" someone called.

It was Marvin, at the front counter in the exercise room.

I looked around.

"Yeah, you, Jess!"

I gave him a wave. I didn't have a date for Brew Coffee, but I had confidence, and I was on my way to regaining my fitness.

A man coming in held the door for me and I sailed through, feeling stronger. Feeling strong.

28

On a Saturday morning, I was using clothespins to hang my black-cat leggings on a rack to air dry, because one heated dryer cycle would make them capris. Penny was by my feet snoozing.

"Well, not to brag, but I just hit the 100 mark," Ian announced from the living room.

"A hundred what?"

"A hundred mutual likes," he said, coming into the laundry room to show me his phone.

"So, 100 women like you and you like them back. That's your dating pool."

I was a little envious.

"It's my profile pics, Mom," he said.

"What's so great about your photos?"

"Well, for starters, I took my shirt off—"

"What are you suggesting, Ian? That I show some skin?"

"Of course not," Ian said. He took an end of a blanket I was trying to fold by myself. Together, we made it into a perfect square. "But I do think it's time to think about putting up a full-body pic—with all your clothes on, obviously."

"That's exactly what I'm trying to avoid."

"Why?" Ian grabbed a handful of loose socks and helped me start sorting.

"Well, for one, I don't want to attract the type of guy who won't message a woman with just headshots," I pulled at a sock, glued to a towel with static. "Two, I'm going to the gym but still not feeling so great about how I look, so why would I want to preserve this moment in time with pictures?"

I had gained at least five pounds since Bryan had moved out, maybe closer to eight pounds. The muffin top was impossible to ignore. OK, ten pounds. I did not know exactly because I still hadn't recaptured my fitness enough to even think about approaching the scale at the Y locker room.

"What the hell?" Ian said, trying to help me sort the socks. "Why do socks never match? How can you stand doing this?"

"Everyone knows the dryer eats them," I said, taking the socks from him and piling them into a laundry basket.

"Think about that full-body shot," he said, running back upstairs.

A week later, Ian was messaging Hannah, mutual thumbs-up on Tinder. Her picture showed a pretty blonde, and she described herself as petite. She even showed a little skin in a beach pic. Intrigued, Ian asked her out to a movie date. Then the cold feet set in.

"Why are you so reluctant to go?" Madison said, handing him sneakers to wear instead of the Adidas sandals he had on.

"I don't know. It's just so much easier to text than to meet in person. I don't know."

"Ah, yes, the fear of putting yourself out there and risk getting hurt," Madison said, shaking her head.

"Like you don't have that problem?" Ian said.

"Not saying that," Madd said. "I give you credit for going out. Me and Mom, we'd rather hide at home."

"Hey!" I said. "Speak for yourself!"

"When's the last date you had, Mom?"

"1980."

Ian left early for the movie theater where he was meeting Hannah, while Madison and I sat down to argue over Netflix.

Ian texted me an hour later: "I've been catfished."

"What? What is that?"

"Catfished, when someone pretends to be someone else so they can reel in a date."

"Like an alias?"

"No, they post a picture that isn't even them!"

"Oh no…Hannah isn't that cute girl?"

"Mom, she said she was 5'3". She's as tall as me and built like a football player."

"I'm sorry, Ian. Is she at least nice?"

"The movie hasn't even started, and she asked me to hold her hand. Her friend dropped her off, so now I have to drive her home! What if she tries to kiss me?"

"You don't have to kiss her."

"She's as big as me, Mom, she could force it. She could be a female linebacker."

"Just leave the car running and say good night. Don't even hug her."

"Was that Ian?" Madison said, peeling an orange over a bowl on the couch, pausing the movie. "What's wrong?"

"He said he's been catfished...."

"That little bitch!"

I held out my hand out to Maddy for a wedge of orange and tossed it into my mouth.

Twenty minutes later, Ian texted me again. "It's getting worse."

"Are you texting during the movie? You know you're not supposed to do that," I said.

"I'm out in the lobby. Do you think it's OK if I leave?"

"Oh geez, Ian, I don't know."

"She put her hand on my leg and squeezed it!"

Madison was leaning over my shoulder to read Ian's texts.

"Tell him it's OK to run, Mom," Madison said heatedly. "Hannah, if that's even her real name, deliberately misled him. Tell him to run."

"If it's that bad, then yes, go ahead, but tell her you're leaving," I texted Ian.

Five minutes later, another text from Ian.

"I did it. I ran to my car. I mean I literally ran through the parking lot and drove away, as if she was chasing me."

"Did you let her know?"

"Yeah, I texted her that my sister needed a ride."

"OK, then don't worry about it. She misled you."

Madison nudged me in the ribs with her elbow, "Hey! That's what I said. Tell him I said that!"

"Are you on your way home?" I texted Ian.

"Yes, and I'm going off Tinder and never meeting anyone again."

"Now you're being dramatic."

"I'm serious. See you soon. Love you."

"Love you too."

SOME DAYS AT WORK WHEN JOE CAMPED OUT WITH HIS CRONIES AT THE conference table, I had a chance to check my messages on Go Fish or do a quick search to see who was online. Just about every guy's profile on Fish had a picture of a motorcycle, a selfie in swim shorts, an enormous-mouthed bass, or worse, a hunting rifle.

The men on the site had snappy profile names, like Talk2Me, BestYet2B, Dr.FeelGood, and PlsTryAgain.

I didn't exactly hit the ground running. I just hit the ground.

I looked at dozens of thumbnail shots and read profiles until they all sounded alike.

OK, they *did* all sound alike, but my point is I couldn't make up my mind about any of them.

It wasn't as easy as I'd thought. There wasn't any sunlight shining out of anyone's eyes. No one had a stamp on their forehead saying, "Come get me, Jessica." Worse still, none of the men came with warnings that said "insincere," "hookups only," or "I will break your heart."

When I got home, Penny stood on my lap with her two front paws on the table, looking at the computer screen, clearly confused.

"Help me find a good one," I said.

It was frustrating, complicated, time-consuming, and thrilling, all at once. And so began my long-term relationship with the dating site called Go Fish.

Within a couple days, I had set some ground rules.

"I don't want to be seen online on a Saturday night," I told Ian.

"Why not?"

"Because I'll look desperate."

"But they're online too."

"Exactly. I don't want to look as desperate as they are."

"But you want to date them."

"So far, no."

"You make no sense, Mom."

"I know."

Another ground rule: No contact with any guy who mentioned sex in their user name (sorry BigMikePorn and SitOnMe). Yes, I wanted sex—oh boy, did I want it—but not with someone obviously trolling for the best lay.

I had new discoveries about online dating.

"So, some guy messaged me to have drinks tonight," I told Ian.

"On a Sunday night?" Ian asked. "Don't you have to work tomorrow?"

"Yeah, so I'm supposed to meet him at nine."

"Oh god, you're kidding. You're not going. Don't go."

"Why not?"

"Because you'll never meet the right person on a Sunday night," he said with complete assurance.

* * *

"So this guy asked me to 'come cuddle.' Is that code?" I asked Maddy.

"Code? No, it's pretty blatant. It's a booty call. Also, stay away from anyone who asks you to 'watch Netflix and chill.'"

"OK, good to know. The way this is going, I may never have sex again."

"That's what we all say, Mombo."

* * *

"I messaged a man with a lobster on his head," I told her another day.

"You would yell at me if I did that!" Madd hollered.

"Probably, but at this point, I don't care."

"Why are you changing your standards based on how you feel?" Her eyes turned darker with sympathy.

Damnit. She was right. Again.

* * *

"Would you consider spanking to be good therapy?" I asked Madd over iced tea another day.

"What?"

"This guy wrote he's looking for spank therapy in his profile."

"Is he the spanker, or the spankee?"

"I'm thinking the spanker…."

Madison shuddered. "Sounds like he wants to take out his aggression on a woman's ass."

"Yeah, and it says OTK with hand…what's that?"

We Googled it.

"Over the knee," Madison said, showing little surprise. "With his hand. Charming."

"Well, that paints quite a picture."

"Next," Maddy said.

* * *

Looking at photos was free, but the upgrade, nearly overwhelmingly enticing, let me see who was online, who had looked at my profile or read a message I'd sent.

Madd and I both agreed that this option opened the door for a greater sense of humiliation.

"When I send a message, and he looks at my pics, then doesn't reply, it's a double rejection," I complained to Maddy.

"They don't even know you, Mom. What does it matter?"

"You know it matters, honey."

"Yeah, I do."

* * *

The later it got on Friday and Saturday nights, the lower I went on the list of who I would chat with. I went from my A-list guys to my B-list after midnight. Yes, the man doing the chicken dance was weird, but he was looking pretty good by 1:00 a.m. Ditto the guy with the barbecue tongs burning hotdogs. One guy used his wedding photo in his profile. I even broke my rule and replied to Tall2Ride, because maybe he was just tall and rode a motorcycle? Sunday mornings carried messages hinting of desperation after the guys spent Saturday night alone.

"Hey AriesGurl, want to meet for brunch?" TrueGentleman messaged me. "I'll buy you a mimosa."

"I already ate oatmeal," I replied honestly.

* * *

Over and over, I made the mistake of sharing too much info.

"Mom," Ian scolded. "You do not tell a guy you're making scrambled eggs on a Friday night!"

"But I was!"

"Yes, that's what's wrong with this picture!" he laughed. "Friday is a date night!"

"Not for me," I sighed.

* * *

"By the way, Dad says hi," Ian said casually one morning when he came downstairs.

"Uh-huh," I said, concentrating on smoothing the hair on Penny's back with a soft brush.

Ian talked to Adam all the time; I knew this and I was glad about it. I knew Ian turned to his father for advice and kept him in the loop about his life. Adam also planned his stops near the town so Ian could meet up with him and camp out. Also good.

Where I drew the line was sending chipper messages to Adam through Ian, something like "How's life on the road?" or "Did ya need any more silverware?" Not going to happen.

I thought about the night by Adam's camper when we decided to go our separate ways, literally. Bob Marley's lyrics were true—everything was all right, even though it was impossible to predict what might come next.

30

A MESSAGE CAME ACROSS FISH AROUND 5:00 ON A HOPELESSLY DULL Tuesday six weeks after I'd joined the site, from a guy whose profile name was MBAMan. His photo showed him lounging in an outdoor chair with a small dog curled around his shoulders like one of those neck pillows you use on airplanes.

MBA listed the usual testosterone-fueled hobbies: hiking in the rain, snowmobiling on the thin ice of lakes in winter, parasailing, jumping off rocks and snowshoeing uphill, but his profile was different: he was looking for friends, possibly not putting pressure on finding "the one." Also, he lived about five minutes from my house. Also, it was a Tuesday night.

"Let's go for a drink, AriesGurl. I think it would be good for both of us," messaged MBA, aka Michael.

I liked his confidence.

"How's 7:00?"

"Sounds good," Michael replied.

I quickly took my second shower of the day, then approached my closet with trepidation.

I knew what I wanted. I wanted to look self-assured, sultry, and maybe even a little sassy.

There was absolutely nothing I owned that would accomplish this.

I tore through my closet, flinging so many outfits on the bed that I buried Penny. Finally, I settled for a black peplum top, leggings with flowers instead of vampires, and Converse sneaks, with my hair in a ponytail, which hopefully didn't portray me as matronly, lonely, or overly hopeful.

I picked Nick's Tavern as a meeting place, a pub just out of town, blessedly dim and not known for any particular food specials, so the likelihood of people at the bar tearing into wings and bleu cheese was low. I have a thing about watching people eat wings. It's a phobia, really. I can't stand the whole process: the dunking in sauce, the slobbering at the chicken, the inevitable pile of discarded bones, the greasy hands. Yuck. No thanks.

Ian thought I was crazy to be meeting a man I barely knew.

"Did you get his last name?" he asked.

"No, but I'll text you from the bar's bathroom," I told him, checking my teeth for lipstick. "And Nick's is like six minutes away. You could get there really fast to save me if I need it."

"Remember, you can run if you want to. Don't be afraid to run," Ian said worriedly. "And next time, ask him to take a picture holding the day's newspaper so you know he's real."

"Thanks for the tip, honey," I said.

"Good luck, Mom," Ian said, looking just as nervous as I felt.

My palms felt clammy on the steering wheel, and when I got to the pub, I turned off the engine and sat there until my breathing calmed down. Then I realized there were windows overlooking the lot, and it was possible Michael could see me sitting in my car, so I bolted, slamming my door on the seatbelt.

"Shit, shit shit," I said, reopening the car door and fixing the belt.

I saw Michael at a corner table, watching the door so closely that he looked almost too hopeful, which was strangely comforting. I knew his face immediately—the deep-set gray eyes and strong chin—but since he'd been wearing a baseball cap in his pics, I didn't recognize the bald head.

Bryan is bald, I told myself. Bald is the new coiffure.

We hugged awkwardly, Michael bending way down in slow motion as I tried to recall if his profile said he was 6 feet or taller. Must be taller.

"What are you drinking tonight?"

Madison had coached me on what to order so there was no risk of getting drunk: Midori, ginger ale and vermouth, or even a wine spritzer with club soda—anything but plain soda, she said, but when I opened my mouth, I blurted out, "Ginger ale, on the rocks."

Over my childish soda (with ice) and his draft beer, Michael led the conversation.

"What do you do, Jess?"

"Well, I just started a new day job at town hall, but I write at night. Ad copy, actually."

"For who?"

"Insurance companies, a hardwood floor business, a couple of build-ers," I said, wishing it sounded more interesting. "And you?"

"Have my MBA, obviously."

"Yeah, I kind of figured that out."

"I'm an accountant for a small family business."

"Nice," I said.

"What kind of food do you like?" he asked next.

"American? I mean, Mexican? How about you?"

"I consider myself an adventurous eater," Michael said, sitting up taller.

"Like, eel, fungus, and bugs?" I asked.

"I'm sure I've had all three of them," Michael smiled. "Fungus would probably be the lowest on that list. What's your favorite food?"

"Shrimp. Oh, and chocolate."

"But never chocolate shrimp?"

Just as I was starting to relax, the #1 dreaded question came along, the question I knew I should have prepared for, but hadn't.

"What do you like to do?"

I knew what I should say, hike, bike, parasail, run uphill in the rain, lift weights, but instead this is what came out of my mouth: "Hang out with my kids and dog, Penny."

"Ah. What kind of dog?"

"Yorkie."

"How old?"

"Five."

"Nice. My pug is just a puppy."

"Yeah, saw her in the photo—really cute."

"It's a him."

That pretty much covered the topic of pets.

Michael took a deep drink of his beer. I worried he was trying to finish it so he could leave. A man brushed by Michael, jostling his beer a bit, and Michael gave him a dirty look.

"This place is too crowded."

It was a Tuesday night; the bar was barely half-full.

I had a terrible thought that Michael was going to suggest we go someplace quieter, like his car, or worse, his house, but instead, he went to the bar, coming back with another beer and a glass of red wine.

"Thought you might like an adult beverage," he said, sliding the wine glass toward me, his eyes glinting in the light over the table.

"Thank you." I took a sip.

The #2 dreaded question came next: "So what are you looking for?" Michael said, wiping the film off his beer glass, then smoothing the pockets of his camo cargo shorts.

"Oh, you know," I said.

It was clear from his face that he didn't know; he expected an actual answer.

"Friends, I guess, I mean, people, someone to do things with, so that I don't spend every night at my dining room table, working." I looked over Michael's shoulder to avoid eye contact. There was a party going on in the small banquet room, with a huge sheet cake covered in blue flowers, and a bunch of red helium balloons.

"I understand," Michael said quietly. "I get lonely too."

I looked at Michael closely. My heart rate went into overdrive.

My wine glass was empty. Michael ushered me out the door, his hand on the small of my back. "Where are you parked?"

"Way down there." I pointed to the only car in the lot with the interior lights on. Shit! I hadn't closed the door hard enough.

"Not the one with the lights on?" Michael said.

"I'm sorry, it is."

"Don't be sorry. Let's see if it starts."

I trudged in my sneakers to my car, thoroughly shamed. Climbing in, I turned the key, grateful beyond words when it started right away.

"I'm good," I turned to Michael.

He was already bending over in that slo-mo way, and I was thinking, *Thank God his head didn't hit the roof*, when he kissed me.

I hadn't been kissed in months. I'd forgotten how nice it was.

31

MICHAEL AND I IMMEDIATELY BECAME THE KIND OF PEOPLE WHO TEXT good morning as soon as we woke up, even though neither of us was a morning person.

He was a great texter.

"I dreamed about your long hair last night," he texted. "My hands got hopelessly tangled in it, and it was soft and smelled like rain."

I had dreamed that I was out of dog food. Michael seemed very sweet.

"You surprised me," I texted, the morning after our drink at Nick's.

"You didn't think you'd meet anyone you like at Fish?"

"No, in the parking lot."

"Ah, the kiss. Maybe we should do it again."

Not only was he a great kisser, but Michael's grammar/spelling was impeccable.

"When's your lunch hour?" he texted around noon.

"Right now, but I only get half an hour."

Michael worked about ten minutes away from the town office.

"I get an hour," he texted back.

"Jerk."

"Don't be a hater. One of these days, I will drive up there and meet you for your half-hour lunch at First Rate Deli."

I smiled at my phone.

"What's wrong with you?" Joe asked pointedly. "You got that spreadsheet ready for me?"

"Maybe she needs some fresh air," Paulie said over the sound of Wes snoring at the conference table. He looked over his reading glasses at me. "If we all pitch in a couple bucks, think you could be a good gal and run down to Spot for a half dozen of them cinnamon scones?"

I got up and went just for the sake of getting away from them for ten minutes.

After work, I logged into Fish to show Maddy Michael's picture.

"Eh, he's cute, but what does he look like without the hat on?" Madison said, examining the ends of her hair for splits.

"Well, he's bald," I said.

"Looks a little bit like a tall Bryan to me," Madd said, shrugging.

That night, as Penny snored at my feet, I stayed up texting Michael.

"So, I have to tell you, I searched for tall men with master's degrees, and you came up, but I was too afraid to message you."

"Why?"

"I thought you'd be too smart for me."

"OK, well, check that worry off your list. Anything else you wanta tell me?"

"There is something, but it's stupid."

"Tell me."

"At Nick's, we had a moment."

"I don't remember a specific moment," Michael texted. "But I know I liked you enough to kiss you. What was the moment?"

"Well, when we were looking at each other at one point, I got butterflies." OK, so the butterflies were mostly out of nervousness, but still, it was true.

"That's not stupid. That's sweet."

"I'm getting sleepy. This is a late night for me," I texted. It was 10:40 p.m.

"Don't go to bed yet. Tell me more about your life. Do you like your job?"

"Not really," I texted. "It's very technical, and I keep getting interrupted by the Three Stooges, these old guys who don't seem to have a home to go to. I get overwhelmed and go home with a headache, completely drained."

"You need to relax, Jess. Ever smoke pot? It's the best thing for stress."

Okaaaay. I would have never pegged Michael for a pothead. All right, maybe not a pothead, and most likely no one used that term anymore. Stoner?

"I don't smoke," I texted Michael reluctantly.

"Well, don't rule it out. I think you'd like it."

"Maybe."

"It even makes orgasms better. And you never drink? You had only one glass of wine the other night."

Hold on a minute—had he said "better orgasms"?

"There's one more thing," Michael texted. "I tend to be more dominant."

"Dominant?"

"Yeah, dominant in bed."

Now he had my full attention. I had to admit, it was a longtime fantasy of mine to be told what to do while having sex, to hand over control to a man I trusted. I didn't want pain or anything done in a harmful way, but a dominant lover? That I could get into.

We said good night, but I couldn't sleep. I'd told Eddie I was open to new experiences in bed. Maybe this was the perfect opportunity.

I texted Madison and told her the latest about Michael, my sort-of, maybe boyfriend.

"Lots of people smoke, Mom," she texted back right away. "It's a lifestyle choice. Just tell him you don't. Unless you want to?" Smiley face emoji.

I'd smoked plenty of pot. OK, I'd smoked a little pot. At least a half dozen times in high school, standing around a keg of Miller Lite with friends at an outdoor fire, lighting up and passing it around. I'd gotten the buzz, the cotton mouth, the paranoia, the raging hunger that resulted in inhaling half a bag of Fritos.

I hadn't smoked since. For a minute, I thought about getting high with Michael, maybe getting silly, maybe having extraordinary sex...did pot really improve sex?

If there was any chance it did, I was more than ready to give it a try.

32

MICHAEL AND I MET FOR GYROS SATURDAY AFTERNOON, FOUR DAYS AFTER our first date. Like everything else in town, it was within walking distance.

It was September. The days felt like summer, but the crisp nights had made the leaves begin to change, bursting forth with breathtaking crimson, gold, and orange.

The Mediterranean waiter was a cutie with green eyes and thick, slicked back hair. We each had the lunch special, a $7.50 platter with hummus, cucumber sauce, pita, and little piles of spring mix. When the bill came, Michael left it on the table untouched, until I got out my wallet.

"Let's see, your half was $9," Michael said, studying the bill.

"All I have is a twenty."

"Forget it. I'll pay this time; you can pick up the next tab. Where's that waiter?"

As we walked back to my house, I slipped my hand into his. "Do you want to sit on the porch awhile?" I asked casually, as if I hadn't made a pitcher of iced tea (with actual lemon slices floating on the top), scrubbed the bathroom, yelled at Ian for leaving the living room a mess, and fluffed all the pillows on my bed, in case I gave him a tour.

"Can't today—rain check," Michael said.

"Really?" I couldn't hide my disappointment.

"Yeah, I gotta go buy some hardy mums to plant before a frost," he said, starting to lean down to me. "Guess I can't surprise you this time."

It was a nice kiss on the sidewalk under the bright sun where all my neighbors could see, some of whom probably didn't yet know that Bryan was gone. A very public kiss. Ian was sitting on the front porch with Penny, but I believed the kiss was out of his sight.

"How was the date?" Ian smiled widely.

"Actually, really good," I said, patting Pen. "Did you bring her water out? It's really hot today."

"Right there, mother to all dogs," Ian said, pointing to a little bowl of water.

"I'm just going to take her inside," I said, holding out my arms to her.

"Looked like some great chemistry there," Ian called before I went inside.

Would the teasing of the mom never cease?

"How'd it go with the plants?" I texted Michael later. After a few minutes, I tried again. "Did you get the mums or something else?" I kicked myself for the stupid question, but I needed to hear back from him. It was suddenly really, really important for me to know what Michael was up to.

No reply.

He might be getting stoned and listening to music, or sitting on his own porch, but not knowing made me feel left out, as if he was having a good time and I was waiting around.

Which, unfortunately, I was.

Penny and I both had trouble sleeping, fighting for space on my side of the bed.

Sunday, I logged onto Fish to look at Michael's photos again. The little green clock next to his profile showed he'd been online for five hours. Five hours?!

I took Penny for a long walk around town. Too long, in fact. After half an hour she gave up and plopped down on the sidewalk. I scooped her up, my little lump of love, and carried her home.

"You're acting like an old lady," I told her, burying my face into her fur.

I had peanut butter on English muffins for dinner. And also three cheese sticks. And the rest of the Chex Mix Ian hadn't finished. And some braided pretzels.

Then I brushed my teeth and flossed and vowed not to eat again that night.

"I hope next time we can have iced tea on my porch, like an old couple," I texted him after dinner.

"We'll play it by ear."

What the hell did that mean?

I opened the pretzel bag again. I kept busy the rest of the night, trying to concentrate on a freelance job writing web copy for Benson's

Builders and not having much luck. Then I made a critical error. I had two glasses of Moscato. I swore I wouldn't text him again, but after I turned out my light and climbed into bed, the wine really kicked in.

"Are you awake?" I texted Michael.

"Yeah," he replied. "What's up?"

"Tell me a secret."

My cell screen stayed blank for several minutes. The equivalent of dead air time.

"I don't think this is how it works," he texted at last.

"What do you mean?"

"I don't think you ask people to tell you personal things."

"I was really just kidding," I texted, trying to backpedal.

What about his pot-smoking revelation? And being dominant in bed? Hadn't he said he wanted to share secrets?

"Look, I'm beginning to think you're not a good match for me."

I was dumbstruck. My stomach lurched—not in a good way this time. I had no idea what to do, so I did nothing.

A few minutes later, he texted again: "I can see you're much more interested in me than I am in you, and I don't like that."

"What?"

"I'm an adventurer, I'm a pleasure-seeker, a mover and shaker."

I thought of myself the same way now. I was seeking pleasure, although I hadn't actually found any yet.

"I'm used to people wanting to be around me," he texted. "It's not surprising that you want to, but you're coming on a little strong."

I remembered the man at the bar who barely touched Michael's arm but pissed him off anyway. How the half-full bar seemed crowded to him.

"OK. You attract people. That's cool."

"It's freaking great. I could be out with a different woman every night if I wanted to be."

Hmm. Was he stoned? Was this what pot did these days—turn people into assholes?

"Why tell me this? I don't understand."

"I don't know how to be clearer," Michael replied. "Listen, I have to go—good luck to you in your search, Jessica. Don't text me anymore, and I'll do the same."

I dialed Maddy's cell immediately, reaching for Kleenex.

"You were looking at the gyro waiter when you went to lunch!" Madison yelled at me. "You weren't even into Michael!"

"He was special," I cried, snuffling into the tissue. "He understood me like no one else has in a long time."

"Now you're being dramatic."

"He was smart and funny and attentive," I sobbed. "He was a really good texter!"

"He was a tall Bryan. Nothing more."

"I really liked him."

"He's dirt under your shoe, Mombo. Scrape him off."

For a week, I re-read all Michael's messages until Madd made me delete them. Then I bought a half-gallon of chocolate peanut butter ice cream, eating it out of the carton five nights in a row, wondering how good the sex might have been with a joint and confident, mean Michael.

33

"I HAVE NEWS," BRYAN TEXTED ON A SUNDAY MORNING NEARLY SEVEN months after he'd left.

"You got a job?" I was excited for him.

"I met someone."

I sat down hard on a kitchen chair. It wasn't the answer I'd expected. "Good for you," I texted when I realized he was waiting for an answer. "Who is she? How'd you meet?"

"Actually, it's Ben's teacher. I've been picking him up at preschool and we started talking and really hit it off."

I closed my eyes. It wasn't that I didn't feel happy for Bryan...OK, I wasn't exactly thrilled for Bryan. I didn't want him to be miserable and alone, but for it to be that easy, meeting a preschool teacher?

"Hold on, I'll send you a pic," Bryan texted.

It took just seconds for the photo file to come through my phone. And there she was, possibly the most attractive teacher I'd ever seen in my life, wearing a yellow bikini, red sunglasses, and the cutest little brimmed hat to keep her skin from freckling. Bryan was beside her, toasting the camera with a can of Coors. He was deeply tanned, not quite as thin as he had been when he'd left, wearing swim shorts I'd never seen before.

"She's pretty," I texted back. "You make a nice couple."

"She's great, Jess. We're really happy."

"I'm glad."

The universe sent Bryan a potential swimsuit model to take to the beach. Big deal. The fact that I didn't have a sexy beach buddy, much less a beach, shouldn't make any difference in my happiness for Bryan.

I remembered Bryan on a summer day in our backyard, drinking Mike's Hard Lemonade with Ian while playing badminton, minus the net. Amazingly, the more they drank, the better they got at hitting the birdie back and forth. They were both shirtless and the blazing afternoon sun was doing a number on their shoulders, but despite my nagging, they hadn't bothered with sunscreen. I gave up and went inside to watch from the comfort of our air-conditioned house.

Exhausted and sweaty, Ian turned on the hose to take a drink and Bryan ducked his head under the nozzle and sprayed his head with water, splashing water on Ian until they were both drenched. Later that night, I made them both line up to spray Solarcaine on their sunburned shoulders.

Bryan had been his best self under the sun in the warm months, up for anything. But picturing him on the beach in NC with the model/teacher brought on a sharp pain in my temples, a beating drum of envy.

Act normal, I told myself. *Ask normal questions even though you don't want to know any more than he's already said.*

"So, what's her name?" I texted Bry.

"Sarah."

He then launched into a long list of what he liked about Sarah, each trait more endearing than the last. I carried my cell into the downstairs bathroom, rooting around in the medicine cabinet for Tylenol.

"Hey, I'm also starting my own business—well, not really a full-blown business, but I'm taking orders for these mini sculpted Jack-o-'lanterns I'm making. And so far, I've been swamped."

He had found it, I thought. The way to blend his love of Halloween with his artistry.

"So, they're clay?"

"Yes. Then I glaze them so they look like real pumpkins. Each one is different."

"That's so cool," I texted. "How do I get one?"

Bry gave me his website address and said I should order early because come October, he'd probably have so many orders he couldn't guarantee delivery by Halloween.

After we finished texting, I went out to the shed and brought in the green pail and beach shovel. In my room, I pulled out the Day of the Dead T-shirt he'd left behind, then sorted through my stacked Amazon shipping boxes until I found one that held everything. I tried to make my handwriting look upbeat, but aside from adding a smiley face, couldn't figure out a way to do that as I wrote his address. Then I put the box back in my car to mail at the post office after work the next day.

That night, climbing into bed, I wanted someone to be there with open arms, and a smile I recognized, and a voice I knew saying good night.

Adam was gone and Bryan had moved on. There was no getting around it.

I felt like I'd lost my best friend, someone I hadn't yet met. There was an open space in my life that needed to be filled, but I had no idea how to do that.

Eddie had told me I had to know what I wanted before I went looking. Was he right?

34

"SO LET'S TALK ABOUT YOUR HAIR," MADDY SAID, GRABBING AN APPLE AND settling herself on a high stool at the kitchen island.

"What's wrong with my hair?" I was attempting to wash Penny in the kitchen sink. So far, I was covered in more suds than she was.

"It looks—how do I put this?—a little fried."

"Fried?" I turned away from Penny for an instant and she scrambled out of the sink into the wooden dish rack. "That's nice, sweetheart. Come here, Pen-Pen." I tried to coax the dog back into the water, without luck. Oh well, at least she'd been wetted down. I grabbed the bath towel and wrapped her like a swaddled baby.

"I mean, how long have you been straightening it?" Madison said, her mouth full of apple.

"I don't know—a couple years?" I rubbed Penny's head with the towel as she squirmed.

"That's bad for your hair," Maddy said, getting up to help me dry the wiggling Penny. "And I suppose you don't use a good thermal conditioner?"

"What's that?"

"Geez, Mom, how can you not know anything about hair products?"

I shrugged. "I don't watch TV. Sue me."

I set Penny down and she bolted into the living room to roll around on the carpet to dry herself.

"What does your hair look like if you let it dry naturally?"

"A very fashionable frizzy mess," I said, rinsing out the sink.

"You can't keep wearing ponytails. It's just not sophisticated. I'm making you an appointment to get something done with it."

"I don't have time."

"And I'm going with you," Madison said, talking at the same time as me.

Three days later, Madison dragged me to Le Boutique, literally a pink house with a peppermint-striped awning.

"Jessica?" asked the receptionist, running her lacquered nails down an appointment book. I had to admit, her hair did not look fried. I could barely remember what healthy hair looked like, but hers was glossy.

"You're here for a makeover?" she said cheerily.

"What? No, haircut—"

"Yes, she's here for the works," Madd interrupted.

Over the next two hours, my eyebrows were threaded and dyed, my feet scrubbed and legs massaged (OK, that part I didn't mind), nails painted an orangey-red, lips outlined with a lip pencil that actually made them appear fuller. I tried my smile in the mirrors as I sat in the hair cutting chair. Eh, still too forced, like I was saying "cheese" for an unwanted photo.

"OK, well, we need to do some trimming," the blonde stylist said. She was wearing a leopard sheath dress and stilettos that looked like she was heading to a club the minute she got out of work.

"Just the ends," I said, slumped in the pink plastic cape she had draped over me. "I want to leave it long enough to put in a ponytail."

"Right, just the damaged hair then."

I closed my eyes and prayed I wouldn't leave the salon with a shoulder-length bob.

The stylist ran clippers through my wet hair so fast I couldn't tell what in hell she was doing to me, but it looked like an awful lot of hair on the floor. She spun my chair, clipped some more, then had me flip my head upside down while she sprayed something good-smelling from my scalp to my ends. Then there was lots of spraying, scrunching, and detangling. By the time she was done, my hair had air-dried.

"Voilà," she said, swinging the cape off me dramatically. "You look like a whole new woman!"

She swiveled me around so I could look in the mirror. My hair had always been straight, until I had the kids, when it turned wiry and frizzy. But the stylist had worked miracles. My curls were neat spirals, springing back in place when I pulled on them. Best of all, my hair was still below my shoulders.

"Oh my God, Mombo!" Madison dropped her magazine and ran to my side. "You look ten years younger!"

"Now, here's what you need to do this at home," the receptionist said as I cashed out and left with shampoo, pre-conditioner, conditioner, detangler, curling gel, shine spray, and a whole lot more self-esteem.

Despite liberal use of the products, I didn't achieve the same look as I had when I left the salon, but at least my hair no longer looked fried. After a few days, I mastered the lip pencil and when I practiced smiling in the mirror, I didn't quite recognize myself. It was as if I were becoming a new version of myself.

Was I getting to a better place? Maybe.

35

IT WAS A RAINY MONDAY AND EVERYONE AT THE OFFICE, EVEN JERKY, WAS in a bad mood. The rain left streaks on the windows and robbed the Three Stooges of their clear view of the downtown sidewalks. Jerky abandoned his post on the chair near the door and went to lie under the conference table. Wes had been sleeping most of the morning, snoring lightly, a sputtering sound followed by a whistle. We were all used to his sleeping sounds by then.

I was on my cell, shopping Amazon for compression socks. I'd read somewhere they helped tone calf muscles. Occasionally, I shuffled papers around on my desk, trying to look busy so Joe wouldn't pile more bills on me to reconcile. I had begun having recurring dreams about falling asleep at my desk, and some days this seemed plausible.

Joe was uncharacteristically quiet.

"For Pete's sake, someone tell a joke or something," Paulie said. "It's like a morgue in here."

"Knock-knock," said Sal.

"Who's there?" Paulie said, sitting up straighter.

"A little old lady."

"A little old lady who?"

"I had no idea you could yodel," Sal said, laughing. "Don't know where I heard that one...I crack myself up."

Paulie yawned.

"Good one, Sal," I said, putting my phone down.

"Thanks! Wanta hear another?"

"Sure."

"Knock-knock."

"Who's there?" I asked.

"Cash."

"Cash who?"

"No thanks," Sal said, laughing so hard he could barely finish his joke. "I'd rather have some peanuts."

I smiled at Sal. He had a good heart.

We sat in silence. I could actually hear the seconds on the wall clock tick by.

"Suppose we should start in on them tax reports," Joe said.

But when he made no effort to move, neither did I.

Wes snored so loudly he woke himself up. He wiped his mouth on the back of his hand and pulled his suspenders back up on his shoulders.

"Hey Joe, how's the missus? Haven't heard you say much about her in some time now," Wes said.

Joe put down the squeeze ball he'd been kneading and sighed heavily.

"Ellen's in Florida. Visiting her sister."

"Lucky her," Paulie said. "How long's she down there?"

Joe sighed again, then dug in his drawer for a mint, which he unwrapped, sniffed, and threw away.

"Don't know, really. She said a month, but now it's kinda open-ended."

Joe's wife Ellen stopped into the office from time to time. She reminded me of Mrs. Claus, pink-cheeked and buxom. They'd been married for more than thirty years. I knew all about the low-carb diet she was trying to get Joe to follow, that they had a cat named Noodles, but never any children. They'd been on so many cruises Joe had lost track, but on one seven-day trip he'd gained fifteen pounds, which was what precipitated the diet. If she knew about the almost daily Brew Coffee baked goods, Ellen would probably cry.

Joe stood up and walked around the counter to sit with the men. I picked up my cell to discreetly text Eddie to see if he wanted to go out for some bad karaoke Friday night. To everyone's surprise, Joe folded his arms on the table and put his head down. Wes, Sal, Paulie and I looked at each other, waiting for someone to say something to him. Jerky came out from under the table and laid a paw on his leg.

"Aw, what is it, buddy?" Sal asked.

"I think she's left me," Joe said, suppressing a sob. "She wants to stay with her sister."

Thunder rumbled outside and the sky darkened. It was Farmers' Market day, and it always rained on the vendors' tents.

"Well, shit,'course she wants to stay in Florida, the sunny state—who wouldn't wanta?" Paulie said.

Joe shrugged his shoulders but didn't pick up his head.

"I tell ya what," Sal said. "You hop on a flight and go down there and fetch her. Bring her back home."

"How am I gonna do that?" Joe looked up briefly. His eyes were rimmed in red.

Wes rubbed his hands together briskly. "Let's think on this. Between the five of us, we can come up with something."

I realized the men were including me in the conversation, so I stowed away my cell.

"How about you bring her flowers?" I said.

"I dunno."

"What kind does she like? Roses are always good."

"Daisies," Joe said glumly. "She carried them in her bouquet at our wedding."

"There ya go, that's the spirit," Sal said, patting Joe on the back. "What else you got?"

"How about a Hallmark card?"

"Or one of those edible arrangements? She likes fruit, doesn't she?" Paulie offered.

Joe sat back in his chair. "She does love her cantaloupe," he said thoughtfully. "And that fresh sliced pineapple, that's her favorite."

"You're a woman," Paulie said to me. "What would you do if your man flew down to surprise you with flowers and melon and asked you to come back home?"

Melt, I thought.

"Well, you can't make her come back, but if you tell her you love her, you miss her, and life isn't good without her, then she would have to listen," I said.

Joe pushed back his chair and stood up.

"Goddammit, I'll do it," he said resolutely. "There's gotta be an afternoon plane down to Fort Lauderdale. I'll buy her gifts when I get down there. She loves those key lime chocolates too."

"Don't forget about the diet," I warned him before he got carried away.

"Oh, hell, you're right—she isn't eating candy since the last cruise."

He clapped his hands together, grabbed his jacket and picked up his umbrella. Jerky was wagging his tail furiously.

"Hold down the fort, Jess?"

"Of course."

Joe stopped and turned back toward us.

"Thanks, guys. I owe you big time."

"Cinnamon buns!" Paulie yelled at him, but he was already gone.

Two days later, Joe and Ellen flew back home. She said the daisies had done the trick. She never knew her husband remembered her wedding bouquet. Within a month, they were planning their next cruise, this time on a ship offering healthy foods and plenty of activities on shore to keep Joe's weight gain under a pound a day.

36

"I want you to meet someone," Madd texted me while I was at the gym.

I hit the stop button on the treadmill and jumped off while it was still moving, stumbling a little, but I didn't think anyone around me noticed.

"Ohhhh," I texted back, already showing too much excitement. "Who is he?"

"His name is Cameron. He's a psych student at SUNY."

"I want all the details…how long have you known him?"

I walked to the locker room, taking a quick look at my ass in the full-length mirror. Was it getting smaller, or was I imagining it? Maybe it was just a flattering mirror. Whatever. I'd take it.

"We met two weeks ago."

"Two weeks?! And you haven't said anything?"

"I really like this one, Mombo."

A woman in the locker room got off the scale with a big smile on her face.

"Five pounds down," she told me happily.

"Congratulations!"

I knew the day was coming when I would be brave enough to weigh myself too. Soon.

When Maddy brought Cameron over the next night after dinner, I liked him instantly.

He was at least 6' tall and had a cute mop of dark curly hair. Best of all, he never took his eyes off Madison.

"Coffee?" I offered Cameron.

"Do you have tea?"

A tea drinker. I liked him even more.

"So, you guys met online?" I asked.

"Yeah, but we've been saying we need to make something up more interesting to tell people," Cameron said, reaching across the table to take Maddy's hand. "It's not very romantic to say you met on Bumble."

Madison laughed, the high, musical laugh she'd had as a kid. When she was turning seven, a friend let us hold her birthday party on a long dock on Campbell Lake. It had been a quintessential summer day, bright sunshine, made all the more perfect by a Barbie Doll cake I'd had made by the best bakery in town. There was a real doll in the center; the cake had pink buttercream frosting that looked like a flowing skirt.

The wind picked up out of nowhere, blowing fast across the water, and paper plates began flying off the dock like frisbees. Then a chair got knocked over, and to my horror, the table holding the cake began to wobble. It felt as if everything was moving in slow motion as I ran to grab it, narrowly missing it as the table crashed and the Barbie cake slid into the water, sinking.

Horrified, I turned to Maddy to tell her we'd get another cake. But she was laughing so hard she had to hold her stomach, pointing at the water where the Barbie doll had floated back up to the surface, a glob of pink frosting in her blonde hair.

We still joked about the capsized cake.

"So, Cameron, you're a psych major?"

"Yeah," he said, reluctantly taking his eyes off Madd to look at me. "Always wanted to be a school counselor."

"That's really great. So, you live on campus?"

"Nope, have a little apartment off Beacon Street."

"It's a really tiny place," Maddy said. "He calls it a safe house because it's so small and out of the way."

"You can barely find it," Cameron said. "I had to GPS it for a week just to get there."

"Cam has a chocolate lab named Ruby. He calls her 'Rhubarb.'"

"Cute."

"Cam also loves to cook."

"Grew up working in a Greek restaurant," he said. "I'll cook for you guys sometime. You like hummus?"

I smiled. The last time I'd had Greek food was the lunch special with Michael. Michael, in whom I'd apparently shown too much interest.

The company wasn't great, but the food was good. What had he said he needed to do to get away from me? Buy flowers? It didn't matter. All that mattered was seeing my daughter and her very charming boyfriend holding hands at my kitchen table.

37

Ian was in Keene camping with his father, Madison was with Cameron, and I was incredibly bored. After giving it some thought, I realized I'd gone more than six months without sex. It was true; I'd set a personal record.

Being horny was much different from being lonely. OK, yes, I was both, but somehow the urge for sex had taken precedence. I did what I always did when I was faced with a sexual predicament: I texted Eddie.

"I told you to invest in a good vibrator weeks ago," he replied.

"I wasn't that worked up then. But I am now."

Truth be told, I didn't really want to get it on with a rubber-coated dildo, most of them purple for some reason. Nor did I want to straddle one suction-cupped to a chair.

"I don't want one of those fake penis things," I texted.

"There are hundreds of sex toys out there. Google it."

I spent the next two hours scrolling through catalogs of every toy imaginable, in every size, shape and color (still predominately purple).

I wasn't crazy about the double dildo, butt plugs with racoon tails, or floggers for dominant women to use on submissive men. I'd always known if there was going to be a dom/sub episode in the bedroom, I'd be the one submitting. That had been my fantasy for years, but I'd never met anyone who wanted to play that particular game.

I became frustratingly aroused looking at pictures of nipple clamps with chains like necklaces on them to tug on and keep the nipples hard. Equally interesting was a series of harnesses and buckles designed to hold a woman down, face up or face down. I'd never seen a leg-spreader but found it very intriguing.

But I was flying solo. No leg-spreader for me. The wide array of vibrators surprised me, from the palm-sized butterflies to little pulsing ones to put over your finger, to the ones with attached dildos.

Then I found the toy that would change my life: the wand.

The one I liked best was an innocent-looking white one that ran on batteries, with a fat head to hold against any area you wanted. It had ten different speeds and a heating element.

I placed my wand order and on impulse added a lightweight whip made with soft suede strips that didn't look like it would actually hurt. It cost a ridiculous amount of money to expedite shipping, but I didn't care. I was in dire need of an orgasm, and I was tired of rubbing them out by hand several times a week.

My fantasies about submitting didn't include being hurt or left with strap marks all over my ass and thighs. But I had a particular fantasy about a man instructing me to undress, then inspecting me, then telling me to rub one out for him. The right man hadn't come along, so that fantasy stayed only in my mind. A dom/sub relationship didn't exactly fit in a long-term vanilla relationship.

I switched my cell screen to Tumblr, a pictorial site that let me choose how hardcore I wanted to go. I liked the images of public sex: a woman bent over on a hiking trail being taken from behind; a sex session in the back seat of a car, with the man pulling the woman's long ponytail. Another, which appealed to me greatly, was a woman lying on a coffee table with her legs open, and a man in a business suit on the couch, watching. Just looking at her.

When the wand arrived two days later, I locked myself in the bedroom to try all ten speeds. I quickly learned the continuous pressure setting was too much, the feather-light tickle was too light, but the pulsating speed, with its teasing up/down pulses, was just right. And the heat button helped enormously. Best of all, the wand was soundless. It quickly became my best friend several times a week, bringing on wrenching orgasms that made my entire body quake.

I was satisfied, for the time being.

Would there be lots of sex in my future? There'd better be.

38

"Let's just meet and get it over with," messaged BMyBuddy, whose photo showed a young-looking man in a black jacket and baseball cap with a NASCAR emblem.

I had to give Buddy credit for straightforwardness. It was a rainy Thursday night with nothing going on. Ian was bent over his books in the way I always told him would result in a weak neck.

"Sure," I messaged Buddy back. "Why not?"

We picked a bar right next to a mall with a brightly lit parking lot, so I knew I was safe. We decided on 8:00. I wrestled with the choice of mummy leggings or an army-green skirt, but the mummies glowed in the dark and might be too much for a dark bar.

The bar turned out to be way too brightly lit. Every stool was taken, but a sympathetic server told me to go ahead and take a booth. I got a spritzer and slid into the orange vinyl booth, trying not to look as foolish as I felt alone at the big table.

My cell chirped; it was Buddy, saying he was running late. I took a deep sip of the wine and club soda, pretending to study the menu.

"Can I take your order?" asked a server with a pierced eyebrow.

"I'm good. I'm waiting for someone."

"OK." The server turned away.

Ten minutes later, Buddy texted he would be there in five. At 8:40, just as I was getting out of the big orange booth to leave, he ran in—literally, running—with rain on his face. He was wearing the NASCAR baseball cap but looked at least ten years older than in his photo.

I shook his wet hand.

"Buddy?"

"Harold," he said, sitting down but not taking off his hat.

The server appeared and Harold ordered Captain and Coke.

"So."

"Yeah, so." Harold laughed weakly. "You new to the Fish site?"

"Relatively." I polished off the wine and considered a second one. "You?"

"Three years," Harold said, tossing the stirrer in his drink onto the table, then sloshing the ice in his glass around with his thumb in a way that made me think of monkeys.

"Really? That's a long time. And you haven't met anyone?"

Harold shrugged. "Well I was talking to a few gals, but then I got the cancer ...."

"Cancer?" I instantly felt awful for thinking he looked way older than his photo.

"Yeah, skin. Had this spot on my arm, thought it was a callous or something, you know. Never got it checked until it turned blue and started bleeding."

"Oh my God. I'm so sorry."

Harold went through three drinks as he told me in excruciating detail about the radiation and chemo and how his dog sniffed him and howled as if he knew about the cancer. I tried not to look at his long hair but couldn't help it. It was a bit stringy, but enough to cover his ears from underneath the baseball cap.

"You're wondering if I lost my hair, right?"

"I— I'm sorry," I stuttered.

"Well, have a look." Harold took off his hat and the lights reflected off his starkly bald head. The long strands of hair extended like sideburns.

"I'm sorry," I said for the third time.

Harold glanced at his watch. "Listen, doll, it's late and I gotta meet my brother at his house."

I waved to the server for the check.

He stood up and fished around in the pockets of his jeans. He turned them inside out.

"Geez, I left my wallet at home," he said.

"I've got it," I said, laying down $40.

It had stopped raining but billowing fog had set in, blanketing the parking lot. I stood uncertainly under the canopy.

"Good night," I said at last, holding out my hand to shake his.

"Aw, come here," Harold said, throwing his arms around me with such force he nearly knocked me over.

"Well. OK there," I said, steadying myself.

"Are we good?" he asked.

"We are good. Where's your car? Mine's this way," I pointed to the left.

"Oh, I don't drive. My brother's picking me up."

"OK, well, good night. I had a nice time," I said, searching for my car keys.

"Hey, thanks for the drinks, doll."

We both knew it was a one-time meeting.

I looked in the rearview mirror as I drove away, at Harold in the pools of fog, baseball cap tipped a little too far back, hands in his empty pockets, waiting for his brother.

You just never know. People have all kinds of private battles that no one else can see. I knew I was blessed, and I was thankful for the reminder.

39

I COULD SEE SOMETHING WAS WRONG THE MINUTE MADDY CAME through my front door, even though she was doing her best to hide her tear-streaked face.

"What is it?"

"It's Cam. It's over."

"What? Cameron? No."

"Yes, Mom."

"What happened?"

"He dumped me, out of the blue, just like that." She snapped her fingers.

"Sit down and tell me what happened."

Madd pulled out a chair and sat down heavily at the kitchen table, reaching down to scoop up Pen.

"First he didn't return my texts, then my phone calls."

"Is he OK? Maybe something's wrong." I was worried he'd fallen, gotten into an accident, left college and went home, wherever home was. I'd forgotten to ask him that.

"Nothing is wrong except he doesn't want to see me anymore. He dumped me," she said, pulling on her hair to look for split ends.

"OK, you said that—how do you know this?"

"I drove over to the safe house," she sobbed. "He was out on the driveway with Ruby and the look on his face when I pulled in—he treated me like a stranger, Mom, like he didn't even know—or care—who I was."

I put my arms around Madd and pulled her close until her sobbing calmed down to light sniffles and the occasional hiccup.

"So, what happened? What did he say?"

"He said I was pushing him for something he wasn't ready to give."

"What does that mean?"

"Oh, Mom, I made a huge mistake."

"He wasn't a mistake, sweetie. I thought he was a really nice guy."

"That's not it. I did push him." Madd buried her face in Penny's neck.

"How?"

"I asked if we were boyfriend/girlfriend or just hanging out."

Back in my junior high school days, it used to be called going steady. This usually meant holding hands in the hallway and kissing in the cafeteria in the lunch line, waiting for chicken and gravy on a bun. Also, walking to the school bus together for another kiss goodbye, followed by furtive phone calls before dinner. It was known by everyone which couples were boyfriend/girlfriend from day one.

"I'm sorry, but I don't see anything wrong with that, honey."

Maddy lifted her face, letting Penny lick her ear. "Mom, it was too early to define our relationship. I should have just let it grow organically."

I didn't exactly agree, but it wouldn't do any good to argue the point. "What can I do to help?"

"You can tell me what a shit bag he was."

"Total shit. He'll make a terrible school counselor."

"He will, right?" Maddy's voice had a bit of hopefulness.

"The worst."

"It shouldn't be this hard, should it?"

"Not for you, babe." I tousled her hair.

"Not for any of us," she sighed.

40

AFTER SEVEN MONTHS OF ONLINE DATING, I NO LONGER WATCHED Netflix and had cut back on my Amazon shopping considerably. I'd get home from work, make spinach salad with warm chicken, take Pen-Pen for a little walk, settle on the couch, and start looking.

But I wasn't even close to figuring it out.

My inbox wasn't filling up with messages from men making the first move. Maybe they were waiting for me to take initiative? But as I quickly discovered, most guys ignored my messages entirely. It was like messaging into an abyss.

Not for the first time, it occurred to me I might be doing it all wrong.

I'd started out with the casual, hopefully unintimidating approach: "Hey, how's it going tonight?"

It seemed like such an easy question to answer, but after sending it out to a dozen or so guys, I hadn't gotten a single response. I changed my tactic, reading their profiles and picking out little tidbits way down at the end to prove I'd studied everything they had to tell about themselves.

"Hey! I like Cold Play too…what's your fave song?" I asked MusicMan.

No response.

"Hey! I'm also a Halloween fanatic. What's your favorite horror movie?" I asked PumpkinGuy.

Come on, that was a simple question to answer and could have led to a lively conversation… if he'd replied.

"Hey! I see you have an iguana…that's an unusual pet…I feel ordinary just having a regular dog."

No response from iguana man? That was a downer. How many messages could he possibly get in a week from women interested in his reptile? Was it even a reptile?

I decided it was the exclamation marks that made me appear overly eager and therefore verging on desperate. *Take it down a notch*, I told myself.

"Hey. I also have two adult children and spend much of my spare time with them. Do you have sons or daughters?"

Blech! That had to be the world's most boring online dating message ever. I was putting myself to sleep.

"Never ask questions that require one-word answers!" Madison scolded. "You're supposed to sound flirty and energetic! And don't say hanging out with your kids is your social life!"

"It *is* my social life."

"I know, but never admit it, Mombo! Pretend you have an actual life!"

Penny, who had been dozing at my feet, stirred and looked up at me, giving me her all-knowing dog stare, making me believe she had me figured out. Maybe she did know me better than I knew myself. I wished she could share her wisdom with me.

Ian came into the room, opened the fridge, looked inside, and closed it again. "Dad's in town," he said, trying and failing to sound casual.

I didn't look up from my book.

"You think he might like to stop by the house for a couple minutes?"

I closed my book. "Ian, if you're trying to make your parents be friendly, it's not going to happen. He checked out of my life a long time ago, and I don't care to revisit that."

"I'm going to meet him at Roger's Rock for dinner. You wanta come, Madd?"

Madison hesitated. In the years since he'd been gone, she had seen him only a couple of times. She'd told me Adam texted her almost every day, but she didn't elaborate on whether she texted him back.

"Maybe next time," she said at last.

"He said tell you you're always invited," Ian said.

"Tell him thanks."

"Have fun," I said.

"OK, well, I'll tell him you said hi, Mom."

"Ian!" I tried to use my authoritative mom voice, but he was already out the door.

41

"WORST DATE EVER," MADDY SAID AS SHE LOADED JEANS INTO THE WASHER.

"Don't stuff so much in there; nothing will come out clean," I told her.

Ignoring me, she piled in hoodies until the washing machine was filled to the brim.

I sighed. She would never learn.

"Come sit; I'll make tea."

Madison settled at the kitchen table. "I need more than tea. This is a three-alarm call for chocolate."

"Oreos or ice cream? Oh, I've also got Kit Kat bars, those little snack size ones."

"Oreos," she said miserably. "Oh hell, give me the ice cream too."

I made her a bowl and set out a plate of Oreos, ready to eat them right along with her.

"He was on Bumble. We chatted for a day, then switched to texting, then we talked at night."

"Name?"

"Bruce," Maddy said, scooping up ice cream with half an Oreo. "We like the Cake song 'Love You Madly.'"

"Oh, I love that song," I broke in.

"Anyway," Madd continued patiently. "We both like scary movies, pesto pizza, The Walking Dead, he also has a younger brother...."

"Sounds promising."

"Yeah, it did, so we went to Nick's."

"Good choice." I twisted an Oreo in half and licked the center, remembering my first date at Nick's Tavern with Michael when he had seemed charming and attentive and not a selfish vain stoner.

"He was there first and was almost falling off the bar stool, he was so drunk."

"Maybe he was just nervous?"

"Mom, he had five beers in an hour."

"OK, so that's a lot of beer," I conceded.

"He kept talking without moving his lips, but when he finally smiled, he had teeth the color of corn kernels. OK, my teeth aren't exactly dazzling, but Bruce looked like he hasn't seen a dentist his entire adult life."

"You have excellent teeth!" I said, defending her pearly whites.

"I was so stupid," she groaned. "I broke the closed-lip smile rule."

"The what?"

"If they keep their teeth hidden in their profile pics, it's a good bet their teeth are a mess."

I made a mental note to add this tidbit to my online dating rule book.

"Then he ordered food—some sloppy bacon cheeseburger—and I felt compelled to order something."

"What'd you have?" I was always curious about food.

"Chopped salad," she said. "But the server forgot what kind of dressing I wanted and when she came back to check, Bruce yelled 'she said balsamic' loud enough for everyone at the bar to hear. People in the parking lot probably heard."

"OK, that's not good."

"Worst of all, it took forever to get his food because he ordered his burger well done. They brought it out charred and he sent it back to be cooked more. When it came out, it looked like black shoe leather."

"Yikes." I stood up, took her bowl, and loaded it into the dishwasher.

"There's more! He had some burger stuck in his nasty teeth. He took the stirrer right out of my drink and used it as a toothpick."

"OK, now that's just disgusting. Did you run?"

"I didn't want him paying for my salad, so I sat there until our bill came. He said he'd leave the tip if I paid the $58 bill, then he put $5 on the bar."

"He will never be able to show his face in there again," I said.

Madison put her head down on the kitchen table. Sensing despair, Penny came in and rubbed her back against Madd's legs.

"Why do we put ourselves through this?"

"Online dating is only for the strong-willed," I said, patting her head. "If we were weak, we'd have given up a long time ago."

Then we both laughed, because we were in the same boat. But the boats, both of ours, were still very much afloat.

42

As hard as it was to believe, my best friend Eddie was turning sixty. I'd known him all my adult life but knew the best days for us were still ahead.

I called Eddie's husband Donny, to say I wanted to throw a surprise party.

"I don't know, Jess," Donny said. "Eddie doesn't really like surprises."

"Of course he does! Remember when we said we were going to the beach, but we took him ziplining instead? And the time we got him those moose slippers?"

"OK, maybe you're right, but let's keep it small."

"I know. He doesn't like a big fuss made over him."

A week later, the guest list was up to twenty-five people, so many that I moved the event from my house to the party room at Nick's Tavern.

Amazon had so many "Over the Hill" gag gifts, I could hardly resist any of them.

It took two trips to the car to lug in all the decorations the Friday night of the party.

"Think you've gone a little over the top?" Madd asked, helping me blow up a life-sized inflatable walker for the elderly.

"Not really—do you?" I asked, tying black ribbons on helium balloons that said "Old as Shit."

"Of course not, Mombo."

"This looks fantastic," Donny said, coming into the room carrying a huge sheet cake with "Aged to Perfection," written in blue icing.

Ian was taping a poster up on the wall with photos showing Eddie from babyhood until his recent days, with a sign on top that said, "It Took 60 Years to Look This Good."

Over the next twenty minutes, the room filled with people ready to help Eddie celebrate. Despite the invitation requesting no gifts, everyone brought presents to put in the black cardboard mock coffin on the gift table. Someone brought a giant magnifying glass for him to read his birthday cards.

One of Eddie's neighbors brought an enormous cookie platter with messages piped in frosting that said "AARP," "RIP Youth," and "Old Geezer."

I went out to the parking lot to wait for Eddie, who was coming under the ruse of having a quiet dinner with Donny, me, and the kids.

He pulled in right on the dot of 7:00.

"You wore my favorite Poe leggings!" Eddie said. "Love those ravens."

"Happy birthday, honey." I kissed his cheek.

"Thanks, chicky. Where're the kids? Donny said he's running a little late."

"Inside getting a table," I said, not looking at him because I was a terrible liar. "It's crowded tonight; they're seating us in the side room."

"Starving," Eddie said, rubbing his hands together. "What's the special tonight? I could go for some good winey chicken."

I opened the door to the party room and we stepped into complete darkness. Then someone flipped the light switch and the guests all hollered "Surprise!"

It startled me as much as Eddie, and I had already known they were there.

"I should have been more suspicious," Eddie said, beaming nonetheless as he was swept into the crowd.

We toasted Eddie with champagne, then commenced with specialty cocktails. We all hooted while watching Eddie open his gifts, including emergency underpants, Senior Moments memory mints, a set of wind-up dentures, and a Potty Putter golf game. Madd and Ian put together a gift basket with Ben-Gay, a bag of prunes, Preparation H, and denture cleaner.

Eddie was a good sport all night long. He tried on the adult diapers, ate a prune, blew out the inferno of candles on his cake. By the end of the night, he looked a bit relieved as guests began to filter out and head home.

"Had enough being the man of the evening?" Ian asked, opening the tin of wintergreen Memory Mints and popping one into his mouth.

"It was great, but let's not do it again for another sixty years."

The song "Sea of Love" came over the sound system.

Donny held out his hand to Eddie, and they used the corner of the party room as a dance floor. Watching Donny and Eddie slow dancing made me believe there really was a match for everyone. And with the kids and friends like Eddie and Donny, it didn't seem such an emergency to have that person show up on my doorstep ASAP. I wasn't going to sit in my front porch rocking chair waiting. I was going to have a life.

A good life.

43

"HI, ARIESGURL. I LIKE YOUR PROFILE AND ALSO LIKE BEACHES AND bonfires," a message came across on a Thursday from Woodsman.

OK, so I'd never been on a beach at night with a fire. But I would love to.

I quickly pulled up Woodsman's profile. Thankfully, he had more than one photo. But he was, of course, an outdoor fanatic. His pics showed him rock climbing in summer, hiking in fall, and snow-shoeing in winter, all in a setting I didn't recognize. Adirondacks, maybe?

If I could walk on an incline on a treadmill, I could snow-shoe, I told myself proudly, even though his pics showed him traversing rather big hills. The shoes looked large and extremely stable, so the possibility of tipping over and face-planting in a snowbank seemed low.

Nature aside, Wood—real name Macon—and I had a few things in common. We both had two grown kids, liked Mexican food, and liked to travel. As the icing on the cake, he lived right outside Meredia and was my true age.

"Have you met nice men?" Macon messaged.

"Not exactly," I typed in, then deleted it. *Try to sound upbeat,* I told myself. "I just got on the site, so I haven't had a lot of experience."

Great. Now I sounded like a clueless newbie.

"There are crazy women out there. One woman I didn't know from her pictures."

Ahhh. So, catfishing happened at every age. Scary.

"Do you want to meet for a drink this weekend?" Macon messaged.

Did I? You bet I did. I liked that he was direct; it seemed confident.

We agreed to meet the next night, picking a pub about five minutes from my house and an equal distance from his.

This time I refused to get all worked up. I'd survived Michael. What could possibly be worse than being dumped by an angry pothead?

The pub was dim, but Macon was sitting at the bar close to the door and thankfully looked like his photos. He waved me over to him. I held out my hand to shake his, but when he didn't return the gesture, I had to turn it into a half-assed wave back to him.

"Hello!" I said, already sounding too giddy.

"Hi, Jessica. I's good to meet you."

Hold on. Had he said "I's?" And why was it so hard to hear him? The bar was mostly empty.

"You as well."

"Vould you like drink?" Macon asked.

I realized it wasn't that he was speaking quietly. It was his accent, so thick that he was almost impossible to understand.

"Where are you from?"

"Croatia."

"How long have you been in this country?" I asked, signaling the bartender wildly, because a glass of Pinot couldn't arrive soon enough.

"Tree months."

"Well." I began. "What do you do?"

"Fix medical equipment."

"That sounds interesting," I lied.

For the next forty minutes, Macon told me in excruciatingly precise detail how to repair ultrasound machines, including how to trouble-shoot problems, what tools to use, and how badly his lower back hurt afterwards.

Between the language barrier and his techie talk, I understood almost none of what he was saying.

"How old are your sons?" I asked, trying to steer things back to common ground.

"They twenty-four and twenty-five. Not used to being around people. Don't like go out. Stay inside."

"All day?"

"Ya, day and night."

"That's kind of sad. If they got out, they would get used to life here."

"Not veally," Macon said. "They don't go out muchly."

Macon pulled his buzzing cell phone out of his pocket.

Without a single word to excuse himself, he carried on a loud conversation in Croatian, at times gesturing to me as if describing what I looked like. Twice, I heard him say my name.

A full five minutes later, Macon finished his phone call. I polished off my wine and stood up, bumping our knees together in the process. Macon put out a hand to steady me and I tried not to recoil from his touch, managing to turn it into sort of a side step away from the barstool.

As luck would have it, Macon's car was right near mine. The short walk across the parking lot was agonizing.

When we got to my car, Macon pointed at my zombie leggings.

"I don't understand the pants," he said.

"No, I don't suppose you would."

"We do again?" Macon said, smiling.

"We won't do again," I said. "But good luck. Enjoy America!"

I'd tried to leave it on a high note but ended up sounding like Betsy Ross.

"No matter," Macon said, turning his back and walking away.

My jaw fell open. No matter? I had just nothing to say to that. No response. Nada.

But I gave myself credit for weeding out one more frog, and after all, it was a great story to share with Eddie and the kids.

44

"So, I was invited to have a viral drink last night," I told Ian while peeling potatoes in an attempt to make *Cathy Kitchen's* frittata for dinner.

"What's that?" Ian was at the kitchen table, slumped over his homework.

"You don't know? I thought it was a thing. It's when you sit at your house and drink, and they sit at their house drinking, and you go on WhatsApp."

"What the hell? That's completely stupid!"

"So it's not a thing?"

"No, it's not. And I'm not willing to sit and use an app while drinking beer in my living room, and if that means I'll be alone the rest of my life, that's fine," Ian said.

"Geez, and here I thought I was missing out on a trend."

"Don't waste your time with that one, Mom."

"Good to know," I said. "In other news, I'm thinking of trying speed dating."

"OK, this sounds interesting," Ian said, pushing aside his books.

"As you know, the last guys I went out with turned out to be something completely different than what I expected."

That was an understatement.

"I've lost track of your dates, to be honest."

"There was Harold, the sad guy with no money who lost his hair during chemo, and then Macon, that jerk who talked about me on the phone right in front of me then said it didn't matter that I didn't want another date...."

"Oh yeah, right! The one with the accent? You couldn't even understand him?"

"Exactly."

I'd given it some thought and realized if I'd met either of them in person, we would both have known we weren't a good match.

"The best way to meet a guy, I think, is to do it in person—you know, let it happen organically."

Ian was unsuccessfully trying to hide his laughter.

"Yeah, Mom, speed dating seems pretty grass roots. Doesn't sound artificial at all."

I threw a dishtowel at his head.

"Go ahead, let's hear it," he said.

"It's where you meet like twelve people in one night, talk for a few minutes, then discreetly decide if you want to see them again."

"OK, strange, but go on."

"It was popular years ago. I don't even know if they have it anymore, but it's all very discreet."

"Yeah, you said that."

I got out the grater to shred the block of sharp cheddar cheese. "How's urban planning?" It was Ian's least favorite class in his environmental studies courses for his four-year degree.

"Sucks."

"Teacher still talk about himself and not the actual class material?"

"Yeah. We know all about the birth of his first child."

"Well that's TMI," I said, sliding the veggies into a frying pan.

"OK," Ian said suddenly, making me jump. "They do still have it. It's called Flash Pre-dating. There are some right down in Ashton."

"Geez, you scared me. Let me see."

I leaned over his laptop at the cheerful logo: two entwined love birds texting one another.

The flash sessions ran two hours, during which I would meet up to ten men. At the end, I would choose the men I wanted to have an actual real-life date with.

"Yeah, but look at the age groups," I said, turning down the heat when the zucchini began to sizzle and pop on the stove.

"Well obviously you're in the over-fifty group," Ian chuckled.

"Stop it! Everyone takes a few years off their age, so if I was going to do it, I'd go to the 39-49 group."

"That's a stretch, Mom."

"Thank you for your support, Ian." I returned to the stove.

"There's one next Tuesday night in downtown Ashton. Give me your credit card. I'll sign you up now. And when's that quiche going to be done? Smells delish."

"It's technically a frittata, but I'm not sure how it's different from quiche, actually."

"Whatever," Ian said, getting out a plate and fork. "I'll take a big hunk."

I spent the weekend worrying about speed dating and what questions I would ask the ragingly cute, highly intelligent men.

Tuesday morning at my desk, I wrote practice questions on the back of some old invoices:

"Where did you grow up?

"What's your favorite color?"

"What do you do?"

"Like, what's your sign, man?"

I was so disgusted I crumpled the paper and tossed it. Then I started again:

"Italian food or Mexican?"

"Vanilla or chocolate?"

"Red or black licorice?"

"Raisinettes or M&M's?"

I realized every question was about food, and tried again.

"Betty or Veronica?"

"Mary Ann or Ginger?"

"Summer or fall?"

"Travel to Ireland, or to Cancun?"

"Mustard or ketchup on a hot dog? Relish?"

Whoops, I was back to food. I tucked the list in my purse for later.

Madison was working, so I made Ian my wardrobe consultant before he headed to the gym. I modelled Elvira leggings, a long skirt, and a shorter blue-and-white striped skirt, all topped with my oldest denim jacket.

"The jean jacket is to look a little casual, you know, laid back," I said, so nervous I considered pre-gaming for the pre-dating with a glass of wine. "I want to look young and thin. As if that's even possible."

"I like the jean jacket," Ian said. "Turn around. OK, definitely the striped skirt. It makes your butt look smaller."

"Thanks," I said, really wanting the wine.

"You know what I mean."

"Striped skirt it is," I said.

"And don't wear sneakers with it," Ian yelled on his way out the back door.

Shit. I was planning on sneakers, but I dug through my closet to find my one pair of walkable heels, ankle-strap with a cork wedge heel.

I didn't achieve the bouncy curls I'd left the salon with. I flipped my head upside down, then stood back up, a bit dizzy, and smiled in the mirror. My smile looked fake and my hair flat. Oh well. I'd done my best.

I was ready. I had to leave at 6:15. It was 5:45.

Penny followed me around, confused by all the activity. I knelt down in my wedge heels to stroke her chin and sing to her.

I texted Madison at work.

"I'm scared to death. I don't think I can do this."

"Mom, if you don't want to go, don't."

"Are you kidding? I paid $32 to register!"

"So go. Just try to have a good time. Even if it kills you."

On the drive to Ashton, I practiced smiling and saying a casual hello.

"How are you tonight?"

"How you doin'?"

"Nice to meet you."

"Hey, whassup?"

At red lights, I tried to arrange my face into a friendly, not desperate-looking, casual smile. I failed. Definitely not good in the pre-dating world.

"Oh, shit, just go with it," I told myself.

45

DOWNTOWN ASHTON WAS A NIGHTMARE WITH ITS UNFAMILIAR ONE-WAY streets. I circled three times before I found the restaurant, Ocean, then drove another four blocks looking for a parking lot.

I found a $25 lot, then searched until I saw one last spot at the end of a row.

"Hey, lady!"

A man rolled down his window and started yelling at me.

I left my window rolled up and pretended not to hear him, fiddling with my purse.

"Hey lady! That was my spot! I was just about to pull in when you cut me off!"

I opened my purse and pretended to intently be looking for something.

"Nice, lady, real nice. Have a good night!"

Well, that's a good start, I thought.

Ocean was down a cobblestoned street that made me walk in my wedge heels like a drunk person, which I wished I were—or at least buzzed. By the glass front door was a sign that read: "Closed for private party."

Inside, there was a ridiculously thin, bouncy young woman who greeted me before the door even shut behind me.

"Hi!" She thrust out her small hand. "I'm Laney!"

"Jessica Gabriel."

"Shush!!!! Don't use your last name!!!! Hahaha. First names only." She slapped a sticker on me with my name embellished with the love-bird logo.

The group of women clustered at the small u-shaped bar were all wearing jeans, khakis, jean skirts, or khaki skirts. I cursed myself for the heels; even sneakers would have made my striped skirt look less dressy.

I made a run for the bar, ordering a wine spritzer from a cute guy with an easy smile.

"Good luck," he said, and I swear I saw him wink.

I looked around the restaurant, trying to be casual.

There was a man wearing a bowling shirt with pigeons on it, talking to a guy wearing suspenders and very pointy shoes, and another guy with tattoo sleeves, still carrying his Harley helmet. Hmm.

"Excuse me, I don't mean to push."

I turned to find a tall guy wearing an untucked light-blue polo and black penny loafers.

"Sorry," I said.

"Not a problem. Thanks."

I stepped to the side to let him get up to the bar, stealing a look at his tag: Jack.

Two men by the registration table were talking loudly. "Yeah, so some bitch took the last space when I was clearly waiting for it. I had to drive six blocks to find another lot."

It was him! The yeller from the parking lot! I fought the urge to hide or run to the ladies' room. Squinting, I could see his nametag: Frank. Cross him off my list.

After a moment, Laney stood on a chair to be heard. "Good evening, singles!!! Who's as excited as I am to be here?"

Probably no one, I thought.

"Well, here's the update, hahaha, we're expecting more guys, but don't worry, ladies, there will be plenty to go around!! Hahaha." Laney said, nearly losing her balance on the chair. Luckily, she was wearing sneakers and not wedge heels. "Single ladies, have a seat at a table and the men will rotate to meet each of you."

It was like a bad game of musical chairs as the women darted to tables.

I was the last one standing.

"Are we having trouble, Jessica?" Laney pounced on me. "Let me help you find a table."

Yes, help the elderly, I thought.

She led me to the table farthest in the back of the room, in the shadows, basically halfway into the restaurant's kitchen. I kicked off my shoes underneath my lonely table and stretched out my toes.

"Okey-doke," Laney said. "Let's speed date!"

Pigeon-shirt man came to my table, sloshing his drink on the list of suggested questions.

"I'm Phil," he said, extending his sweaty hand.

"Jessica," I said, shaking it, then wiping my palm on my skirt.

"What brings you here tonight?" Phil asked too loudly. "Looking for a love match?"

"Not really. Just looking for friends, I guess."

"Yeah, ain't we all," Phil said morosely, staring into his drink. "Did you ever stop and think, there must be more out there than the life we're living?"

Startled, I sipped my spritzer. *Every day*, I thought. *Every. Freaking. Day.*

"So what do you do?" I changed the subject.

"Sell used cars." Phil dug into the pocket of his bowling shirt and fished out a card, handing it to me.

"I don't think we're supposed to give out our last names, or like, business cards. I think this is supposed to be anonymous."

"Eh, take it anyway. You might need a gently used car someday," Phil said sadly.

Ralph, wearing the suspenders, showed me pictures of his dogs on his cell phone.

"Oh, look at that little cutie," I said, pointing to a snow-white Maltese.

To my horror, he burst into tears. "Just found out she has failing kidneys," he wept. "Treatment's going to cost me thousands, but if I have to use up all my savings and sell my house, I will to keep her alive."

I nearly had tears springing to my eyes with sympathy for the man.

Parking Lot Crazy Man and I sat for the entire six minutes without speaking, both of us with our arms folded across our chests. I whistled a little to break the tension. He stared me down and I glared right back.

Next.

The Harley guy with full tat sleeves reached over the table and tried to hug me hello.

Well, that was ballsy, I thought. Maybe this would be the guy to try out my fantasies...he looked like the type that could be dominant but not hurtful. I liked the tats and the bad-boy image. I had an immediate picture in my mind of him standing in my room, jeans pulled down to his ankles, instructing me how he wanted to be sucked off.

I felt my face flush, so I shook my head to clear my thoughts.

"So, little lady," he growled. "You ride?"

"Motorcycles? I mean, cycles? I mean, bikes? Ride?" I was stuttering. I gulped my spritzer. "No," I finally said lamely.

"Then what do you do?"

This I had rehearsed since the debacle with Michael. "I'm rather impulsive. I love to take day trips, you know, unplanned little getaways to Lake Placid or Vermont."

I stopped talking. Harley guy didn't even notice. He was looking at the next table, where another single—a delicate, small-boned Asian woman—was laughing, tossing her head back to show off her tiny neck.

"Yes, and I also love to shark wrestle, make my own moccasins and do watercolor paintings with my teeth."

"Uh-huh," Harley guy said. "Good for you."

So much for a future adventurous sex partner. The six minutes couldn't end soon enough.

At last, Mr. Polo Shirt and penny loafers slid into the seat across from me.

"How're you holding up?" he smiled. "Need another drink?"

"Oh, no, thanks, I'm fine," I said.

"So this is quite a trip, huh?" Jack leaned back in his chair, his polo riding up a bit, revealing the button-down fly on his Levi's. OK! I forced myself to look back up at his face.

"Yeah, quite a trip." Goddammit, now I sounded like a parrot!

"So, tell me about you." Jack smiled.

"Well, I have two kids, a dog, a municipal job," I said, realizing I was making myself out to seem like the dullest woman in America.

"Where'd you go to school?"

"Oneonta State."

"No way!" Jack laughed. "Some of my closest friends went there. Great party school."

He looked at me a little more closely. "You a party girl, Jess?"

"You could say that...." I let my sentence trail off in a way I hoped was seductive and enticing.

"Oh yeah? What are you into?"

How to answer...how to answer?

"I'm up for pretty much anything," I said at last.

"I'm talking sexually," Jack leaned closer and whispered.

"I love to explore," I whispered back.

"Really? I love it when a woman who looks really buttoned-down is a bit of an animal inside."

I tried hard to focus on Jack to make a guess at his age. Late forties? Younger than me, for sure, but I still worried he was placing me in the cougar category.

Then Laney was ringing the damn bell to signal it was time for the men to rotate again.

"What's your last name, Jess? I want to friend you on Facebook."

"Gabriel."

"Got it," he said, writing it on the back of his hand with a pen. "Hey." He leaned in again. "You have really pretty hair."

Jack was my last six-minute pre-date. I was done.

"How'd we do?" Laney asked brightly as I was signing out. "So, which single men are you hoping to be matched with? All of them?"

"Um, one of them—Jack," I said quietly. "Actually, could I also be matched with the bartender?" I attempted a joke.

"Oh, no," Laney frowned. "He's not part of our group."

"Yeah, I know."

"Okey-dokey," Laney said, practically rolling her eyes at me. "Just one man on your list, then. I'll email you about your matches in a day or so. Until then, happy dating!!!"

"Well, it was a shit show," I texted Maddy when I got home. "A lot of very sad men out there. I made one of them cry!"

"Come on, Mom, it couldn't have been that bad!"

"One guy called me a bitch over a parking space."

"OK, that's mean...was there anyone you'd want to see again?"

"Yes, there was, this guy named Jack."

"Did he like you?"

"Well, I don't know." I felt a bit smug. "But he wrote my name down on his hand to friend me on Facebook."

"Does he know how old you are?"

"No, missy, I didn't tell him my age, and it would have been rude of him to ask, by the way."

"How old was he?"

"What's with you and age all of a sudden? I don't know, fifty? It was really hard to tell. It was a bar; it was dark in there."

"You must have some idea, Mombo."

"I don't want to just pull a number out of the air. Anyway, now we wait 24 hours for an email with our matches."

"How many matches can you get?"

"As many men as you like," I said. "But I only liked one."

I spent the next 24 hours planning a first date with Jack. Dinner up in Ashton, maybe some place with a view of downtown shops and sidewalks. Or a trip to the lake, where he would teach me wind-boarding, and I would somehow manage to look graceful even when I fell flat on my face. But no, that would involve wearing a bathing suit. Maybe a movie and late-night cocktail, ending up with a visit to his cool bachelor apartment. Followed by hours of sex in every position we could think of.

Laney's email came exactly 22 hours later, when I was at work. I took my cell into the bathroom so I could do a happy dance unnoticed.

Phew. OK, deep breath. I read the email.

Wait. There must be some mistake. All the single men, except angry parking lot guy, had chosen to be matched with me. Every man but Jack. I closed my eyes, opened them, and forced myself to read the email more slowly.

Jack had not chosen me. There would be no real date. Worse still, he hadn't friend requested me on Facebook, so I had no way to find him ever again.

There must be some mistake. I had to call Laney, and unfortunately, I had to make the call from the bathroom at work.

"Hello, potential lovebird!" she answered cheerfully. "How can I help you today?"

"Hi, Laney? It's Jessica Gabriel."

"Jess!" she squealed on the other end of the phone. "How are you, my single lady?"

"Good," I said, trying not to sound whiney. "I was just calling to ask, well, if there might have been a mistake in the matches...?"

"Mistake? What kind of mistake?" Laney trilled.

"Well, I was wondering, well, if someone was left off my match list by any chance?"

"Hmmm. I don't see how that could possibly have happened, but let me pull up your profile. One sec."

I heard her clicking on a keyboard.

"Well, aren't you the popular single lady! Nearly every one of our single men said they'd like to talk more with you! Lucky girl!"

Nearly every one. Except the one I wanted.

"I was wondering about, um, Jack?"

"Jack? Well, no, I'm sorry, Jack didn't check the 'talk more' box. He checked off 'no thanks.'"

I closed my eyes and pressed my fingers to my temples, exhaling.

"OK, well—thanks, Laney." I couldn't wait to get off the phone.

"Happy dating! Let us know if anything works out with any of our single men!! We like to keep in touch with our lovebirds!"

For the rest of the work day, my headache battled with my heartache over which felt worse.

When I got home, I put my purse down and then slumped at the kitchen table feeling sorry for myself. After a minor pity party, I got up and poured a glass of wine.

Penny was staring at me from the floor. I bent down to scratch behind her ear, and she yawned, then got up and padded off toward the living room.

"Hey, don't you know you're supposed to love me regardless of my dating life?" I said to her little rump as she walked away.

Clearly, speed dating was as random as online searches. I'd tried it, so I could check it off my list. Next.

I hadn't yet pinpointed exactly what I was looking for, and it looked like the universe wasn't going to send it my way anytime soon. But I was OK, I was good, and that missing part of me was shrinking, filled up with what I already had—a really great life, even without "The One."

46

"I'VE HAD IT," IAN ANNOUNCED ONE SATURDAY IN NOVEMBER AS HE CAME downstairs from his room. "I'm going off the grid."

"You're what?" I looked up from my book, *Excel For Dummies*, which I was studying to understand the monstrously daunting spreadsheets I faced every day at the office.

"I'm going off Tinder and Facebook. I haven't met anyone since the catfish, and I'm sick of Facebook."

"Yeah, Facebook sucks," I agreed, closing the manual, which hadn't taught me shit about Excel.

"It's all about how great people's lives are, how many beautiful people they have around them, how many promotions they've gotten. I am so sick of the photos of cute babies and dogs."

"We have a cute dog," I said, smiling at Penny as she wagged her tail at me.

"Yeah, but do you post pictures of her?"

"I did when she wore that snowman sweater for Christmas," I admitted, stroking her little rump with my toe.

"Don't even get me started on the selfies."

"You know it's all fake—right, Ian?"

"Yeah, Mom, but that doesn't make it any less aggravating."

I followed Ian, and Penny trotted after me to the living room, where he flopped on the couch.

"Truth is, I'm not going to meet women at school, because my classes are just guys." Penny jumped up onto the ottoman, then settled down next to Ian.

"Not a lot of women studying STEM? That's a shame." I shook my head. "There should be more women in math and science."

"Can we please stay focused here?" Ian said.

"What about the library?"

Ian rolled over and started scratching Penny on the head. "They're all with friends, and it's just stalkerish to keep staring."

"What about the gym?"

"They all wear headphones," Ian said. "What am I supposed to do, gesture for them to take them off?"

I'd run out of cheerful, motherly suggestions.

"How's the Excel going?" Ian said, changing the subject.

"Not good."

"Get the book out; I'll help you."

"You're the best, Ian."

"Yeah, yeah, yeah," he said, sitting up and putting Penny down on the carpet. "No offense, but I wish someone else would think that."

47

EVERY FEW YEARS, THE TOWN HAD A "HOUSEHOLD DEBRIS" CLEAN-UP DAY, which meant people could drag items out of their basements, garages, sheds, and God knows where else and leave them at the curb for the Department of Public Works guys to haul away.

The phones at work went crazy the week before clean-up day. I must have said a hundred times the town wouldn't take away major appliances like washers and dryers, computers, or large-screen TVs. Scarily, everything else was fair game.

A few days ahead of the pick-up, people started making piles at their curbs with paving bricks, mattresses, doors taken off their hinges, rolled-up carpets, artificial Christmas trees, and curtain rods. There were scuffed suitcases, broken umbrellas, rusty bikes, bent basketball hoops, and scratched-up cat towers.

But some of the curbside items were hidden treasures: wall clocks shaped like anchors, sets of dishes, coffee tables just waiting for a shabby-chic makeover, wicker chairs, pool toys, gardening tools, desk fans. Meredia became one big garage sale without any price stickers.

As good-quality items began to appear at curbs, a strange phenomenon began: people started shopping through their neighbors' piles and carting things away in their back seats or trunks. Most of the shopping happened at night when people could skulk away unseen. Some called it "junk-picking," others called it recycling.

There was an element of sneakiness to it, going stealthily into the night, and I didn't want to miss any of the fun.

Step one: put out my own toss-out pile. I still had Ian's baby clothes in storage bins in the basement. It was way beyond time to part with them; that third child had never come along. Friday after work, the night before clean-up day, I first dragged our old kitchen table, still smeared with red crayon, to the curb. Then I brought out two table lamps, an old orange vase, a set of coffee mugs I'd bought on Amazon and never used, a pair of skis Madd had used twice, and a bunch of hardcover books with dog-eared pages.

"Got anything good?" Lily rode up the sidewalk on her scooter to watch.

"I may find some doll clothes, if you're interested."

"Cool."

"You guys put anything out at the curb?" I asked.

I lined the lamps up on the coffee table and propped up the hard covers with a set of elephant bookends I'd dug out.

"My mom put out three octopus pillows, but someone already took them."

"You mean pillows for an octopus to use?"

"No, silly. Pillows shaped like an octopus," Lily said, furrowing her eyebrows.

"Thanks for the clarification. I would have nabbed them myself if I'd gotten there first," I laughed.

"Grandpa walked me around to look at stuff, but he said I could only get two things, and they had to be washable."

"Your grandpa's a smart guy."

"You said that already," she reminded me.

Lily helped me arrange some fabric daisies in the orange vase. We set out some old beaded necklaces and a few tarnished silver bracelets. By the time we were finished, it looked like a small curbside boutique.

"Yours is one of the best junk piles out there," Lily said admiringly.

After she scootered away, I texted Eddie to meet me at 9:00 that night, and to wear dark clothes. We were going junk-picking.

Eddie's CRV was black, so he drove. I fortified us with bags of ched-dar popcorn and Gatorade so we could make a night of it. We went immediately to the neighborhood with the biggest houses, the ones that gave the kids full-sized candy bars on Halloween. Eddie drove slowly so I could look out the window.

"Remind me again why we're sneaking around at night to do this?" Eddie said.

"Because it's a little embarrassing to pick through people's throw-aways in broad daylight," I said, craning my neck to peer into the dark and kicking myself for not bringing a flashlight. "Anyway, all the good stuff will be gone by morning."

The first house had a heaped pile of clothes and a washing machine. I sighed heavily. Hadn't the flyer explicitly stated no large household appliances? Did people not know how to read?

At the next house, several well-organized bins were set out, just ripe for the picking. I got out and closed the car door soundlessly. One bin had old vinyl records and Disney videos. Another had sheets and towels. But in the third, a shiny blue marbled bowling ball!

"What is it?" Eddie whispered over my shoulder.

"Holy shit, you scared the crap out of me. Don't do that!" I scolded.

"You said we had to be stealthy," he reminded me.

"Not with each other! If I scream, people will hear me and come out and catch us."

"So what?" Eddie said reasonably. "It's not like we're stealing."

We rolled the bowling ball onto his back seat and drove on.

I found a doll dress for Lily that looked like new and was 100% washable, a retro watch with an elastic band for Ian, and an antique school chair I knew I could easily refinish.

"Can you believe someone put out crutches?" Eddie asked me as we poked through one pile.

"Oh yeah? Well, check this out," I said, holding up a blonde flapper wig.

"Could be a Halloween costume," Eddie mused.

I considered for a moment, then the reality of putting a used wig on my own head hit me. I put it back down quickly.

We passed on 1980s clothing, plastic tableware, a broken picnic basket, a charred frying pan, a tattered green plaid ottoman. Eddie found a patriotic wooden birdhouse with a tiny American flag, and a set of Pilgrim salt and pepper shakers.

It was almost as good as Amazon shopping.

Another family had set out a dresser and placed smaller items inside. One of the drawers was stuck, so I tugged it hard, only to have it fall out and clatter to the driveway. A porch light went on and I heard someone opening the front door.

The back door of Eddie's car was halfway open and I literally dove, head first, into the car floor. "Go, go go!" I hollered.

Eddie gunned it, then slowed down several houses later.

"Again...not stealing," he said.

"Did you see me fly through that window? I can't believe it. I haven't moved like that since tenth-grade gymnastics."

"Impressive," Eddie agreed.

We wove through neighborhoods, munching popcorn and slowing down to take a look at curbside piles, bypassing anything in plastic bags or that looked as if it had already been pawed through.

When the kids were small, we went through the larger developments at Halloween for trick-or-treating. Adam would reluctantly join us, even though Halloween was never his thing. Maddy was always a Disney heroine, Snow White or Cinderella, and Ian was a policeman or vampire. I remember them running from lawn to lawn, Ian's black cape billowing out behind him, Madd's magic wand sparkling in the shadows, believing they would be young forever, knowing even then they were the best of times.

Every year, one of them would trip, spill their plastic pumpkin full of candy, and cry. The kids and I would get on our hands and knees to retrieve the Kit-Kats, bags of rainbow Skittles and mini Snickers from the damp grass.

We took baby Ian out in a stroller his first Halloween, dressed like a baseball player. For a few years, we pulled Madd and Ian in a wheelbarrow, which worked great until Ian stepped on the hem of her Belle dress and tore the lace.

Back then, families would leave their lights on past 9:00 and children traipsed the streets until they couldn't go any further and begged their parents to carry them home. Our kids always got a second wind when they got home to dump their candy on the living room floor. They traded chocolate bars like baseball cards, threw away the lollipops, and gave me my favorite: Three Musketeers.

Every night after dinner they were allowed to dig through their candy and pick out two things for dessert (me included, but Adam didn't like chocolate). After a week or so of this, all of us had enough sweets and I worried about their next dental exams.

"I miss the kids being little," I told Eddie as we wove through streets to look at curbside collections.

It wasn't the first time we'd had this conversation.

"I know, sweet pea, but like I've always said, you can't keep them little forever."

"Meh."

"What did you say?"

"I said 'meh.'" I slumped down in the passenger seat.

Eddie sighed. "Look, it's not like it's all over. You guys will have a chance to do it all again in the next life."

I sat up straight. "Really? You think so?"

"I do."

Eddie's reasoning was an enormous comfort to me. It made sense that I'd be with the kids in whatever came next. I couldn't imagine a life without them.

"Now quit being sappy and let's get on with the fun," Eddie said.

Junk-picking with Eddie under the half moon was exactly that: lots of fun.

I pointed excitedly down the street to an unmistakable glow of a Jack-o'-lantern. Without a word, Eddie drove up and pulled over. It was a plastic, battery-operated pumpkin with a toothy grin. I immediately put it into the back seat on top of the gingham tablecloth I'd picked up an hour before. I felt the feverish thrill of the hunt as I opened the cardboard box under the pumpkin.

"Anything good?" Eddie called from the front seat.

"How many times do I have to tell you to keep your voice down?" I scolded.

"WHAT DID YOU SAY?" Eddie bellowed out the open car window.

I shook my head, rifling through the boxes, using my cell as a flashlight to peer into them. I found a pair of red and yellow oversized clown shoes, a witch's hat, and a peacock-feather fan. Clearly, this family shared my good taste.

"If you find Halloween leggings, for god's sake, leave them behind," Eddie said. "You have more than enough already."

"Ha ha ha," I said.

At the bottom of the box, I hit the jackpot. It was an inflatable pirate skeleton on a Harley, still in its original packaging. It had to be four feet tall and six feet long. Triumphantly, I carried the box over to Eddie's window to show him.

"Well, let's go home and set it up," he said.

Eddie knew me inside and out.

When we got back to my house, every item from my curb was gone: the daisies in the vase, the elephant book ends, the baby clothes. All that was left was a bent Hula Hoop.

"Geez, thought someone would take this," I said.

"No one's in shape anymore; they can't Hula Hoop," Eddie said, trying to bend it back into a circle.

"Oh, there are people out there who've regained their fitness, believe me."

"Yeah, how's that gym thing going?"

"It's going. Just not great," I said, wrestling with the fabric skeleton.

"You'll get there, babe."

It took a while for the Harley skeleton to inflate, but once it did, it was a sight to behold, lit from within, flickering orange flames coming out the back, bony fingers poised on the handlebars, menacing grin on its face.

Even though it was nowhere near October, everything seemed deliciously Halloween.

We left the motorcycle guy up all night, then I packed it away for autumn.

By the time the DPW crews did their sweep of curbs to pick-up household items. All that was left was broken furniture, the ugly mattresses, some tires, and the goddamn washers and dryers.

48

I MADE IT A GOAL TO GO ONLINE ONLY DURING "RUSH HOUR," WHICH was after dinner to 11:00 p.m., because I didn't want to appear bored and needy, even though I was both. I tried to pace myself, but it was tough. I felt a strange sense of urgency getting back to the men who sent messages, winks, smiles, or the coveted emoji—the red heart.

I did rack up some winks: from the skinny man in a tree, to the profile pic of cows standing in a field (no man in view), the guy whose face was cut out of the picture ("Married," Madd said with conviction), and a man smashing a beer can against his forehead.

"I've actually seen two profile pictures of a man standing next to a casket," I told Eddie.

"No shit...who was in the casket, I wonder?"

"That's not the point. It's macabre."

"Could be a funeral director," Eddie said thoughtfully.

"Either way, it's a no-go for me."

"Aw, kid, thought you were a big fan of Halloween."

"Not that big."

One of the first questions guys asked was, "What are you looking for?"

How could that possibly be answered? I'm looking for someone to help pick out lettuce at the market? To go to the movies? To wake up with? To wash my dog?

"They want to know if you're looking for a LTR or if you're DTF," Madd explained patiently to her struggling mother.

"What if I'm somewhere in between?"

"Well, that means you're open to possibilities."

"And that's a good thing, right?"

"It's a very good thing, Mombo."

* * *

"This isn't working, Madd," I said over after-dinner coffee. "It's rush hour and I can't find anyone I haven't already messaged."

"Try not to be so picky. Are you still looking for tall men only?"

"I've messaged men who are my height. And I'm short."

"What about opening up the age range?"

"Overall, I'd guess guys take eight years off their true age. So, when I say I'll date a 55-year-old, I may get a geezer with none of his original teeth."

"You have a capped tooth, Mombo."

"Thanks for reminding me."

* * *

Another evening Maddy came over with a bag of plums, handing me one without even having to ask if I wanted it. We ate them silently.

"You're never going to meet anyone sitting on your front porch," she said at last.

"I'm waiting for a visit from Lily."

"She's a cutie, but she's not going to solve your dating dilemmas."

"Hey, I was out last Friday night."

"Talk to anyone?"

"There was a cute guy around my age with curly blond hair. He was chatting it up with the bartenders like he was a regular."

"Wedding ring?"

"Didn't see one."

"So did you talk to him?"

"Nope."

"Why the hell not?"

"Just when I was about to, he got a huge honking platter of wings. You know I won't talk to a man slobbering away at a plate of greasy wings."

"I don't like this no-wings rule," Madd said. "Bars have beer, and wings go with beer. Bars, beer, wings. You'll never get away from it."

"I think it's nasty."

"Mom, you'll never find a bar with just wine spritzers and salads."

"Hey, don't mock my spritzers!"

Madison was quick to point out the many mistakes I was making in my Fish connections.

"You can't keep checking to see if a guy has read your message! Every time you do that, it registers as you looking at his profile!"

Sweet Jesus. There were men I'd checked several times an hour, obsessively, to see if they'd read my messages. No wonder I'd never heard back, stalker that I was.

* * *

Another night, she caught me admiring a pic of a cute guy against a backdrop of puffy clouds that brought out his shiny white teeth.

"You're violating the rule here—how many times do I have to tell you, never message anyone with just one photo!" Maddy looked over my shoulder and scolded me.

"But it's such a nice picture."

"It looks airbrushed," she said suspiciously. "I'm going to do a reverse image search on it."

"What?"

It took her less than a minute to find the exact same photo on a site showing guys modeling trendy short hairstyles for men.

"I can't believe it," I sputtered in sheer disbelief.

"Believe it," she said wisely. "Lots of people do it. That's why you need to see at least two or three photos to prove it's the same person. One picture is never genuine."

"What a dickwad. I'm going to message him to take down that picture!"

"Yeah, like he cares what you think?" Madison was laughing at me again.

49

ONE MORNING, PENNY CAME RUNNING INTO THE BATHROOM CARRYING a small scrap of silver paper in her mouth.

"Give it here, honey." I coaxed it from her mouth.

It was an empty condom wrapper.

My first instinct was to chuckle and be glad Ian was being careful. My second was to text Eddie.

"Good for Ian," Eddie wrote. "Have you seen her?"

"No. It's noon, but no one has come downstairs, unless she's already gone."

"Don't ask a lot of questions if you see her!" Eddie warned.

"Of course I won't. When have I ever done that?" I was mildly insulted.

Two hours later, I heard Ian talking and knew he wasn't alone. I busied myself in the laundry room to give them space.

"Mom, this is Destini," Ian said a minute later from the kitchen.

"With an I," she said.

"An I?"

She was a tiny blonde, wild bedhead hair, blue eyes with remarkably unsmudged black eye liner and a pair of silver high-heeled strappy sandals dangling from her fingers.

"Nice meeting you," I said.

"You have a very cute house," she said. "I didn't see much of it when we came in last night—"

"It was late," Ian explained unnecessarily.

Penny nosed around Destini's perfect hot-pink toenails.

"So, can I get you something?" I looked at the clock, wondering if I should offer lunch.

"We're going out for waffles," Destini said. "With strawberries."

"At the diner," Ian said.

I realized he was glowing. "Well, have fun, kids!" I said, too brightly.

Ian smiled at me over his shoulder as they left.

I gave him the thumbs up, knowing afterward that it probably looked silly. It was just so great to see him happy.

I texted Maddy with the news.

"So where did he meet her?" Madd texted back.

"Must've been out. I think he went to see a band last night."

"And she stayed over? Does she look a little slutty?"

"Not at all," I texted, although I did wonder about the "I" in Destini and the way she made strawberries and waffles sound sexy.

Ian was gone all day. It had been nearly a 24-hour date.

"What did you think of her?" he asked when he got home that night.

"She seemed very nice. What does she do?"

"She's not in school right now, trying to figure out what she wants to do. For now, she's working at CVS."

"Nice. Does she live at home?"

"Just moved to a new apartment with two friends. She was with a really bad boyfriend and finally left him. That took a lot of guts to do."

"It did," I said.

"She's so small, but she's a really strong person inside."

I was proud of Ian for being attracted to that.

"How were the waffles?"

"Great, Mom. Everything was great."

"I'm glad."

"I'm going to call Madd," he said, taking the stairs two at a time.

Madison had always been the first person Ian went to for relationship advice. She could always be counted on for support, whether it was cheering him on or cheering him up. Ian had a serious girlfriend his senior year in high school. Maddy and I stood in Congress Park on prom night near a fountain and snapped at least fifty photos of them, Ian in a grey tux, Amber in a shimmering mermaid gown. But their first year in college, Amber met someone else and broke up with him by text.

Ian sent her roses and asked her to come back to him.

"You're pathetic," Amber had texted, her last message to him.

"I'm going to find her and break her legs," Maddy had said when she heard the news.

"Could you get someone to do that?" I'd asked hopefully.

Madd had come over with a bottle of tequila to spend the night with Ian, and by morning, he was cursing Amber and saying how lucky he was to have her out of his life.

It wasn't in the stars for Ian and Destini with an "I." She ghosted Ian after their night/day together. Ian texted, called and went back to the bar two nights in a row where they'd met, but didn't see or hear from her again.

"How is he?" Madd asked as she came through my kitchen door on the third day.

"He's sleeping."

"Told you she was a slut," Madd said. "Probably went back to the shitty boyfriend."

She went up to see if Ian was awake, then came down with a pink hairbrush full of blonde hair.

"This was on his dresser," Maddy said. "Not something he needs if he's going to get over her."

"Yeah, toss that in the trash."

"Or we could make some sort of voodoo doll," she said thoughtfully.

"Really?"

"No, Mom. Not really. You're so gullible."

I sighed. "Do you think he's OK?"

"Absolutely," Madison said with complete confidence. "No one keeps this family down."

"Not going to happen," I said, just as confidently.

50

RescueU had chosen an unfortunate name, in my book, because I didn't need to be rescued from anything. I didn't need to be saved from anything but the possibility of spending another Saturday night with a bag of Chex Mix and Netflix. I wanted to be intriguing, likeable, someone a guy would want to hang around with to see if anything developed, organically.

But Rescue was actually a firefighter/EMT with the local community emergency corps in town. I was impressed to know if we were out someplace, he could save the life of anyone who started choking, and also, he rushed into fires while everyone else ran out screaming.

Rescue, aka Curt, had a photo on his profile wearing firefighting gear, and another with his arms around someone who'd been photoshopped out of the pic. He was wearing a tux with a pleated shirt and dark-blue bow tie, maybe at a wedding, maybe one of his kids, which was a good sign because it meant they were all grown up. In the third pic he was wearing a knitted ski cap, but when I examined the photo closely, it looked like he was standing by a snowbank at the end of a driveway, not skiing down a scary icy slope. Not a semi-pro skier. Good sign.

Curt popped up on a search that had previously brought only a man with a flowing white Santa beard, a truck driver who badly needed a shower, and a guy peering at a bug under a microscope.

I passed the emergency corps building every single day going to and from work! What could be a better sign than Curt being so close that we could already have bumped into each other on the sidewalk? Maybe it was meant to be. Maybe.

Best of all, Curt messaged me first.

"Hey, neighbor," he messaged. "You work downtown?"

"Town hall. Behind the front desk."

"Yeah? I think we were in there a couple years ago, older man had symptoms of a heart attack and we were dispatched. Got there in under three minutes. Turned out it was anxiety."

"Probably paying his tax bill," I wrote. "People look like they're going to keel over when they come in."

"Yeah, I've had that feeling myself."

We asked the obligatory questions: Divorced five years, Curt had two grown kids and an apartment in the next town over. He had plans to build a house, but his work schedule barely gave him time to sleep, so that was on the back burner for now. He never watched TV and cooked once a week at the firehouse. His specialty was stuffed shells with homemade sauce.

We also exchanged horror stories about Fish.

"I've been ghosted more times than I can count," he wrote.

"Thought it was just me. Women do it too?"

"Oh yeah, especially after the first date. We have a good time, then they disappear and never answer texts again."

I couldn't imagine anyone ghosting fireman Curt. Hadn't they known a good thing when they saw it?

"Well, I met a fireman," I told Eddie the next day when we went for asiago cheese bagels at Brew Coffee.

"Ohhh," Eddie said, settling back in his chair. "Do tell."

"He's fifty, and 6 feet tall."

"So, he's already your type."

"Do I have a type?"

"Sweetie, you know you like them tall and younger."

"Yeah, if I can find them." I pulled a bit of cheese off my bagel to chew.

"So, when are you meeting?"

"Maybe dinner this weekend; he has to work an overnight Friday so he might sleep Saturday."

"Saving lives is draining." Eddie chuckled.

"I know, right?"

"Is that one of the old geezers coming up the street?" Eddie pointed out the window.

"Jesus, let's get out of here," I grabbed my purse and practically ran before Wes could see me and rope me into an extended conversation about town gossip.

"Caught up on sleep," Curt texted Saturday afternoon. "You pick a place and time and I'll be there."

There were too many restaurants to choose from, so I called on my best resource.

"Maddy, I can't find the right place to have dinner tonight," I texted.

"What are you looking for? Romantic? Pub with lots of people in case you run out of things to talk about? Candles on the tables?"

"None of those. Someplace with wine, and food that doesn't come in a spinach wrap."

We debated a while before deciding on Spice, a nice but not fussy restaurant in downtown Ashton. I pulled up the menu online and picked a meal—grilled chicken with roasted asparagus—to avoid the awkward moments of deciding what to order.

I texted Curt to meet at 7:30 at Spice.

"See you then," he replied. "Let's have a great time."

It was exactly what I wanted.

I wore ghost leggings with black boots and a long maroon sweater. Parking was always an issue in Ashton, so I left home at 7:00 for the fifteen-minute drive. Another good sign: a car was pulling out of the parking garage just as I drove in, giving me a premium spot. Spice was a short walk and I was inside with a wine spritzer by 7:15, trying to discreetly check my hair in the reflection of my phone.

Curt was ten minutes late, but that gave me time to drink half my spritzer, and when he came over to the table, he was wearing a long coat and the cute knit hat from his photo.

"Jessica?"

"Curt?"

He held out his hand and shook mine, that limp way some women do, then hung his coat on the back of the chair where it grazed the floor. Frowning, he folded the coat in half and placed it carefully over the chair so it didn't touch the ground. I'd tossed my wool jacket carelessly behind me and was actually sitting on part of it.

"What's good here?" Curt said, pulling off his hat to reveal a severely receding hairline.

Don't get me wrong; I had no problem with the follicley-challenged. But the tux photo was clearly more than a few years old.

"I hear the chicken is good—"

"Here we go, wings, wanta share a couple dozen?"

"Um, no thanks, not really a wing person."

Curt tipped his head to look at me. "How can you not be a wing person? That's un-American."

"Sorry," I said weakly.

When the server came over, Curt ordered a crab dip appetizer and wings, extra hot.

"You like crab?" he asked, handing his menu to the server without looking at her.

"I guess so."

But when it arrived it was a cheesy, milky mess with chunks of crab I could smell even before he scooped up a heap with a tortilla chip. It was possibly the worst thing to order on a first date. That, and the wings.

"I'm probably going to smell like seafood the rest of the night." Curt laughed.

"Probably."

He laughed again, as if it were actually funny.

"So, tell me more about your kids," I said, leaning back in my chair to get away from the pungent smell of cheesy crab.

Curt's face darkened. "They treat me like an asshole these days. Lived with their mother, my ex, since the divorce, and she's turned them against me with her lies."

"Wasn't your divorce, like, four years ago?" I polished off my spritzer and looked around for the server to order another.

"Five. But it dragged out in court for years. Worked three jobs to keep that bitch happy and all she did was complain."

"Wow," I said, signaling the server from another table and pointing to my wine glass for another.

When the food came, Curt asked for extra wet wipes. "I really get into my wings," he told the server. "Can get a bit messy. My date will have to tell me if I've got hot sauce on my face."

My grilled chicken was charred and the asparagus limp.

We'd covered all the small talk questions by text, so I was at a complete loss as to what to say. We ate in awkward silence.

"So, you never told me if you had pets," I came up with at last.

Curt put down a half-eaten wing and wiped his greasy face, leaving behind a smear of hot sauce on his chin that I didn't bother to point out.

"Had a beautiful Husky, Mandy, but she slowed down after eight years, dragging her back legs and then her eyes kind of glazed over. Wife had the kids convinced Mandy would get better but she got worse. Lost control of her bodily functions so she was shitting all over the house and had to sleep in the garage."

I closed my eyes, very sorry I'd brought the subject up.

"Told them it was time to put her down, but the kids kept saying I was going to kill their dog, so six months passed. One morning I got up and opened the garage door and blood was everywhere. Mandy had bitten through her own tail and bled out."

I gagged on my asparagus, then took a long drink of my water to keep my food down.

"Excuse me." I practically ran from the table to the ladies' room. It was an image I would never forget.

I splashed water on my face then used a paper towel to wipe off my smeared mascara, taking a deep breath before returning to the table. All I wanted was to pay my half of the bill and get the hell out.

"I paid," Curt said as if he'd done the most gallant thing in the world.

We put our coats on and left, pausing on the sidewalk while I fumbled in my purse for my car keys.

"Wanta come to my place for a few drinks?" Curt asked, leaning too close and breathing hot crab into my face.

"No thanks," I said, stepping away.

"Really?" He seemed genuinely perplexed. "Thought we hit it off."

"Really?" it was my turn to ask. "I don't think so."

Curt took a step toward me. "You know what your problem is? Women like you act one way when they text, then become a whole different person when we meet. Then you have to run because you can't keep up the charade."

What the fuck? I wondered.

I started to go, then turned back to Curt. "Here's some advice. Don't order hot crab dip and wings on a date. Don't rant about your divorce that was five years ago. And for god's sake, never tell that dog suicide story again."

"Bitch," he yelled as I hurried away.

I'd been emotionally catfished, thinking there was a connection that turned out to be a complete shit show. Then I squared my shoulders and marched to my car, quite proud of myself for knowing a loser when I had dinner with one. And for—almost—having the last word.

I was starting to learn how to recognize a really bad date when I was having one, and best of all, I learned how to get away with my dignity intact.

Something had changed in my months trying to successfully online date. I'd learned that people are extremely unpredictable and carried so much baggage it was a wonder they could stand up. I'd learned that every encounter carried a lesson. They were getting me one step closer to figuring out what I wanted, like Eddie had said when he'd sounded like an Oxygen channel movie. I'd learned to never give up.

But even if the universe didn't send me whatever I was looking for, I was OK; I was good.

51

WELL, GO FIGURE. ONE DAY, A GUY WALKED RIGHT INTO THE DOCTOR'S office where Madison worked.

"Tell me everything," I said as we settled at my kitchen table a week later.

I pushed my newest Amazon delivery box, a six-pack of florescent gym socks, under the table so she wouldn't razz me about it.

"Mom, he's so great," Maddy gushed. "He's twenty-four. Dark hair. Brown eyes. Really nice smile."

"Does he have a name?" I poured us iced tea.

"Billy. His name is Billy." Maddy stirred her tea. "Don't you love it when people use their nicknames instead of formal names?"

"I do. I love being called Jessie."

The back door slammed and Ian came in from the gym, tossing his backpack in the laundry room and going immediately to open the fridge.

We were silent.

"Sorry." Ian's head appeared above the fridge door to look at us. "Am I interrupting some mother-daughter thing?"

"Not at all, doodoo," Madison said. "Pull up a chair."

Ian grabbed a Chobani and settled down at the table.

"So Madison met someone," I said, eager to catch him up.

"Really? Good for you!" He high-fived his sister. "Is he The One?"

Maddy flushed and she looked down at her hands. "I don't even want to think about that. We just have a lot of fun together."

Over iced tea and grilled cheese sandwiches, Madd told us all about Billy. They both liked kayaking, classic movies, ice skating, autumn, white chocolate, seafood, and the color green. He was the older of two boys, had grown up in Rochester, and wanted to be a doctor.

He was healthy, just going to see the doc for a physical for a rugby team.

"He was so nervous when he came in, he stumbled over the carpet and almost fell." Maddy laughed. "He told me later it wasn't going to see the doctor that had him all worked up, it was seeing me behind the reception desk."

"Aww," Ian and I said in unison.

"Where does he live?" I asked, clearing off the sandwich plates.

"An apartment in downtown Ashton."

"You haven't been there yet, right?" Ian said, suddenly serious.

"What? Yeah, I've been there. We've been dating a week, dumbo."

"Oh no," Ian sighed. "Tell me you haven't had sex with him yet."

Madison stared at him blankly. "We've been together practically every night for a week, Ian. What do you think?"

I honestly couldn't tell either way what she meant, so I said nothing.

"God, Madd, you can't give it up that early in a relationship! Now he has the upper hand!"

"How does he have the upper hand?" Madison said incredulously.

"Yeah, how does he?" I chimed in.

"He got what he wanted; now he has the power," Ian said. "It's up to him where things go from here."

"I totally disagree," Madison said flatly.

"Yeah, me too," I said.

"Fine," Ian said, holding up his hands in surrender. "Just be careful."

"Ian, you were catfished, like, months ago. You need to let it go and stop being so cynical," Madison said.

"Are you still upset about that?" I asked Ian with genuine concern. "You know it was OK what you did, right?"

"And that little bitch Destini didn't deserve you—you know that too, right?" Madd said.

"Yeah, yeah, guys—don't let this turn into a conversation about me." Ian laughed. "I want to hear more from Madd so we can all jump on the happy train."

We talked another hour, and by the time we were done, we were all aboard Maddy's happy train.

52

I DREW THE LINE: I WAS DONE SPENDING MY WEEKENDS SCROLLING through the familiar line-up of men on Fish, staying home on my front porch, or cleaning my already sparkling kitchen. I decided to launch a new strategy. I made myself a promise to go out every Friday night during the month of December. People still met in bars, right?

Eddie and Don sometimes joined me, and Madison and Billy frequently showed up to keep me company, but the idea was to force myself to do things on my own, out of my comfort zone. It was my quest to become a confident, outgoing single woman who knew what she wanted. To grow organically, or "grass roots," as Ian succinctly stated.

Sometimes, I walked into a bar, found it nearly empty, looked around as if I were meeting friends, then left and tried someplace else. It could be exhausting and overwhelmingly intimidating, but hey, I was out of sweatpants and there was no Chex Mix being consumed.

As if it were a secret club, I never seemed to find the hang-out place for older singles, like myself. I had a roster of places I rotated through, following the bands that played music that didn't hurt my ears or remind me of my college years.

Friday night, as part of my pre-planning, I called On Tap Grill and asked the bartender who was playing.

"It's Street Junction," she told me.

"What kind of music do they play?"

"Kind of country rock with an edge."

"OK. Well, my girlfriends and I are looking for a place to go that's really, you know, hoppin'," I said, wincing for using such a ridiculous phrase.

"Right now, there aren't any seats at the bar, but it's really hit or miss."

I grabbed the jean jacket and rumpled Penny's furry back on my way out.

"Wish me luck."

When I got to On Tap, the lot was half empty. Not a good sign. When I went in, there was only a handful of people, all of them couples.

But it was only 10:00—early by some standards. The band was in full force. I took a seat at the bar on the far side and had to yell my order to the bartender, a blonde girl with a scoop-necked black top that showed way too much cleavage.

"Pinot and a glass of club soda with ice, please."

She nodded like maybe she remembered me, or at least my odd drink order.

I was the only person in the bar that wasn't part of a couple. But instead of running, I forced myself to stick it out. Street Junction played an hour-long set of cover songs, "Brown-Eyed Girl," "Take It to the Limit," and "Don't Stop Believing," among them. The bar gradually filled up with more couples and groups of friends.

"Is this seat taken?"

I turned to find a mid-fortyish man with a blue blazer and jeans, leaning in with blessedly wintergreen breath.

"No, please, go ahead."

The guy signaled to a pretty woman near the door, who came right over to sit in the bar stool. I sighed heavily. *That's it*, I thought. *Time to run.*

Salamander's was only a few miles up the road. The white lights draped in the trees and neon signs in the windows made it look like a restaurant you'd go to on vacation, even though summer was long past. I went in past the red booths full of couples digging into big ceramic bowls of jambalaya and pulled pork.

The band was an '80s cover band, absolutely nothing original. I settled into a black bar stool as far from the music as possible.

"Hey, haven't seen you in a while," said the bartender with the huge gauges in his earlobes. "Pinot and club, right?"

"Right!"

I sipped my drink.

A cute guy with salt-and-pepper hair across the bar smiled in my direction. I smiled back, but as he lifted his beer in a toast, I saw the glint of a gold wedding band on his left hand. I shook my head and looked away, pretending to love the music.

A few minutes later, Wedding Ring Guy got up to leave, and when he pushed his empty beer glass toward the bartender, I saw that the gold ring was a wider men's dress ring, and it wasn't even on his wedding ring finger.

Shit, shit, shit.

After a poor rendition of "Walk Like an Egyptian," and an even worse "Footloose," I noticed a guy in a baseball cap slumped over the bar, looking at me through half-closed eyes.

Must be tired, I thought.

The minute he saw me looking, he grabbed his drink and ran, I mean ran, to take the empty seat next to mine.

"Heyyyyy," he slurred. "Saw you lookin' and had to come over."

"How old are you?" I yelled over the music.

"Forty-eight." He tipped back his beer glass to get the last dregs of foam.

"Really? Forty-eight?"

He thought about it long and hard for a moment before telling me with beer breath, "No, thirty-eight."

Okaaaay.

"Want another drink?" the youngster asked.

"I'm fine—thanks, though."

He banged his glass on the bar to get the server's attention.

"So what do you do?" I hollered into his ear.

"Pipe fitter," he said, flipping his baseball cap backwards, which made him look more like twenty-eight. "Live right down the road."

"Uh-huh." I took a sip of my spritzer. "I hope you're walking, not driving."

I didn't ask his name and he didn't ask for mine, which I figured was just as well, since he wouldn't remember it the next day.

"Bartender!" the kid hollered. "A beer and another round for the lady."

I wasn't quite finished with my wine, but when another glass arrived, I paid with a $10 and left the $2 change on the bar.

Baseball Cap, however, was having trouble.

"Put it on my tab," he said.

"You don't have a tab," the bartender said patiently. She had a string of spiders tattooed across her throat.

"Yesh, I do."

"Look, I'll have to see a credit card. Or you gotta pay cash."

I slid carefully in my seat as far away as I could from Baseball Cap, hoping no one had seen him talking to me and think I was with him. He was still searching his empty wallet when the bartender came out from behind the bar and went to find the bouncer.

"You better go," I said. "They're going to throw you out of here."

Baseball Cap was chugging his beer, shaking his head. "I ain't leaving."

The bouncer came out of the back and strode over to us, tapping Baseball Cap's shoulder.

"Time to go, bud."

I nearly left the bar myself, but instead pretended to study the huge TV screen on the MMA channel. I watched a guy in a yellow leotard pick up his opponent and slam him onto the floor of the ring. The bouncer took Baseball Cap by the back of his shirt and hauled him up with one easy move. I think his feet were actually off the floor.

"He still owes me six bucks for the drink!" the spidery bartender yelled, then shook her head and swept the empty beer glass off the bar into the sudsy sink.

Meanwhile, I was watching MMA as if nothing unusual had happened in the seat directly next to mine.

I looked at my cell. It was only 11:15, but I felt like I'd been there for hours.

"Is anyone sitting here?" said a man with black hair and a puffy bomber jacket, startling me.

"No, go ahead." I waved my hand and looked away.

"Thanks. How's the music?"

I turned to Bomber Jacket Man and saw the second seat had been taken by a brown-eyed man with a neatly trimmed beard, who was smiling at me.

"Good, if you like '80s pop." I nodded my head to the cluster of twentysomethings jumping around to "Girls Just Want to Have Fun."

"I'm Al," Bomber Jacket said, "and this is Jeremy."

"Jessica." I shook their hands, which were a little cold. "Have you been outside?"

"Yeah, at a bonfire, at our age, believe it or not."

I tried to guess their ages. Al was gray at the temples and looked in his early fifties, but Jeremy could be anywhere from mid-forties to fifty.

But at least not thirty-eight, and he looked at me with fully functional eyes rather than droopy lids.

Blessedly, Al and Jeremy weren't drunk, and as they nursed their beers slowly, it was clear they weren't trying to get plastered.

"Got kids?" Al asked.

"Two. You?"

"Four daughters," Al said proudly, showing me pictures on his cell. "Two grandbabies already."

Jeremy was quieter, but when Al excused himself for the bathroom, he slid into the seat closer to me.

"I like your sneakers," he said.

"Thanks." I was nervous. I was also a bit buzzed from drinking three wine/club sodas over the course of the night.

"So, what do you do, Jess?" he asked, stroking his chin and watching me intently.

"Oh, I have a boring day job, but hey, it pays the bills," I said, laughing in a way that sounded giddy to my own ears. "But I write at night."

"Fiction?"

"Ad copy," I said, feeling apologetic. "What do you do?"

"Photography." He smiled. "You know, newborns, weddings, engagement parties, I'm working on a calendar...."

"Sounds awesome," I said, kicking myself for using that word. "Do you work out of your house?"

"I have a studio in a duplex I rent out on Campbell Lake."

"Cool," I said. Campbell Lake was known for its luxury homes.

"You have any pets?" Jeremy asked out of nowhere.

"A little dog, Penny—she's a little tomboy," I said. "You?"

"I rescue greyhounds. Right now, I have a brother and sister whose legs are in pretty rough shape. I brought them for X-rays yesterday and their femurs show tiny hairline fractures," he said, his brown eyes somber.

"That's so sad!"

"I try to carry them around as much as I can. I think they kinda like it, being lazy and relying on me."

Al came back and waited for Jeremy to get out of his seat, but he didn't budge. The bar stool on the other side was empty, so he sat down there, and suddenly, I was monkey-in-the-middle.

"So, where are your friends?" Al asked, looking around.

"Um, I'm here alone."

"Really? Why?" Al looked genuinely confused.

"It's actually easier to meet people this way," I said, as if I'd been successful at any attempts to mingle.

"Well, you know, it *is* hard to approach a bunch of women all in a circle," Al said, stretching his arms wide, stifling a yawn. "There's always that one that's married or something and she's always like, 'Let's go home,' as soon as you start talking to the cute one."

"Al doesn't have much luck with women, as you can tell," Jeremy laughed. "Can I buy you another drink?"

"I'm fine—thanks, though."

"C'mon, don't be one of those 'I'm fine' women," Al said. "What are you drinking, anyway? What is that, water?"

I looked at my glass of club soda, white wine, and melted ice. It was completely clear and looked more like water than water itself.

"She said she's fine," Jeremy interjected.

"Whatevs," Al said, looking around the room. "Oh, man, is that Ricky?" He got up and bounded away.

When I turned back to Jeremy, he was watching me closely. "Ignore him. He's a big kid in a man's body."

"How long have you known each other?"

"I used to date his sister, in another life," Jeremy said, tapping the beer glass with his long fingers. "He took me under his wing after she broke my heart. Kind of like an older brother."

"Sweet," I said, kicking myself. Why was I trying so hard to sound like I was younger?

"Yeah, I was a mess for a while, but I've found now that I'm in my forties, things don't seem so epic, you know? I can survive just about anything now."

I closed my eyes briefly. Forties.

"You've never been married?" I was wishing I'd taken Al up on that offer for another drink.

"Nope," Jeremy smiled. "Came close plenty of times, but it just wasn't meant to be."

From across the bar, which was starting to empty out now as

it neared 1:30 a.m., we heard Al whooping it up with a crowd of younger guys.

"Hey, are you on Facebook?" Jeremy asked suddenly.

I was instantly glad I'd changed my online status to single.

Al came back out to the bar for another beer, and Jeremy excused himself, sparing me an answer.

"So he used to date your sister?" I asked Al as he swigged his beer.

"Yeah, my little sister; they almost got married. They were young, though, too young. That was almost twenty years ago."

I tried to do the math but failed.

"How old is he now?"

"Jeremy? He just turned forty-three."

I shuddered visibly. My wine-filled stomach lurched. Fourteen years younger. I would have figured it out in fractions or percentages, but again, I hated math.

"I'm fifty-eight—you must be closer to my age. How old are you?" Al asked me pointedly.

"A woman never reveals her age," Jeremy said, sliding back into his seat.

"Hey man, you ready to pack it in?" Al said, draining his beer.

Jeremy looked reluctant. "You staying, Jess?"

I locked eyes with Jeremy and wished with all my heart he were a few years older.

"No, I'm ready to go too." I gathered up my purse and coat.

"Yeah, I'd better get home to check my dogs," Jeremy said, shrugging on his jacket.

We hurried through the parking lot in the cold, our breath seeming to freeze in the air as we exhaled. Our cars were in the same row.

"Nice meeting you." Al threw his arms around me, nearly knocking me off balance.

"OK, OK, well, you too," I said, clapping the back of his shoulder awkwardly.

Jeremy waited until Al climbed into his SUV, then said quietly, "So you going to tell me your last name?"

"Gabriel," I said, not able to come up with any reason not to tell him.

"Great to meet you, Jessica Gabriel," he said, pulling me into his arms.

I closed my eyes for a moment.

"Hey, what are you doing tomorrow afternoon?" Jeremy asked, looking down at my face. "Maybe you can come over and meet my grays."

"Maybe."

"OK, well, I'm going to friend you on Facebook."

"Sure," I said weakly, watching him go.

Jeremy friend requested me before I even got home. I accepted his request, figuring it would be a good way to let him know my approximate age, and who knew? Maybe he had a Mrs. Robinson complex.

I washed my face and stared in the mirror. Under the bright lights, it was clear I was not in my forties, but maybe I didn't quite look fifty-seven. Maybe.

"I love your dimples and long hair," Jeremy messaged me minutes later on Facebook. "I can't wait to see you again and talk more. I'd really like to get to know you better."

I sighed, climbing into bed. Penny launched herself at the bed like she'd been catapulted, trying to make it to the top, scrabbling at the side of the bed like a rock climber before dropping back down to the floor.

"Come here," I said, lifting her up with me and sighing.

Where had all the single men (my age) gone?

53

JEREMY SENT PHOTOS OF HIS GREYHOUNDS, WITH THEIR NARROW BODIES, alert eyes and impossibly long, spindly legs.

"Come visit me," he messaged, late Saturday afternoon.

I was mightily tempted. To distract myself, I cleaned the shower. I scrubbed down the kitchen counters. Then checked for more messages. None.

I vacuumed my room while Penny barked at it like it was an intruder. Checked my messages again.

"Here's my address," Jeremy wrote. "You might want to GPS it because it's hard to find with all the bends in the lake."

Google Maps said it would take me only seventeen minutes to get to Jeremy's address. Aw hell, why not? The kids weren't around, my house was sparkling clean, and Penny was passed out asleep.

It took me almost an hour to get ready.

"I hope you're still coming to see me," Jeremy messaged.

"Can I bring anything?" I asked.

"Just yourself, Jess."

Goddammit, were all forty-somethings as sexy as he was? I wouldn't know.

It didn't take seventeen minutes to drive to Jeremy's. It took thirty minutes to find the house, because I circled the lake twice, straining my neck to look at numbers on mailboxes. It was dark outside, making it even more of a challenge.

At last, I pulled off the snaking, narrow road that wound around the lake, and into an unpaved driveway that had his house number on it. Shutting off the engine, I looked in the rearview mirror, fixed my lipstick and attempted to fluff my flat hair, without much success.

"Hey, Jess!"

Jeremy's house had a wide front balcony overlooking the lake. He was standing out there looking down at me.

"Hey, Jeremy. I found your place, no problem at all."

"Actually, you found my neighbor's place. My driveway's over here."

"Oh, sorry," I said, dropping my keys down the side of my car door.

Lights went on inside the neighbor's house, then on the porch, and a man in an undershirt stepped outside.

"Who's there?"

"Just my girlfriend. She'll be out of your driveway in a sec," Jeremy said.

I was glad it was dark and my head was down as I fished around for my keys. Girlfriend?

I almost hit a car backing out of the wrong driveway and swerving into Jeremy's, while he watched. He must have been laughing, but he hid it well.

"Did you find the place OK?" he laughed.

"Yeah, I'm fine, I mean, I got here fine. Sorry I disturbed your neighbor."

"He's usually outside with a twelve-pack anyway weekend nights. He was just being nosy. Come on in."

"Gorgeous house," I said.

"Yeah, wish it were mine. Landlord lets me fix the place up. I tore down the flowered wallpaper when I first moved in. I'm working on the floors right now."

The greyhounds bounded to me, a flurry of motion, as soon as I went inside.

"Sit." Jeremy held out his hands, palms down. To my amazement, both dogs settled down on their haunches, still panting, but calming down.

"Drink?"

"Sure, whatever you're having," I said, looking for a place to put my coat and purse. There wasn't much furniture in the big, open space that was a living room-dining room-kitchen. But up a split-log staircase was a wide loft with a skylight framing a dark sky scattered with stars.

Jeremy came out and handed me a Miller Lite Tall Boy, more beer than I'd ever be able to finish. Gamely, I took a long chug, spilling it on my T-shirt in the process.

"Wanta sit down?"

I looked around again. The only furniture was a round brown suede chair so deep it looked like I'd have to crawl into it. Jeremy folded himself into the chair and held out his hands to me. I awkwardly climbed across the cushions, slipped, and landed with my face squarely in his lap.

"Come up here," he said, reaching under my shoulders and pulling me into a sitting position right next to him. Jeremy kept his arm draped over my back as I tried, without success, to compose myself.

"So how're you doing?" he asked, his fingers grazing my neck.

My mind went blank. "I'm good. You?"

"Great, now that you're here. Tell you the truth, I didn't think you'd come."

"No? Why's that?" I looked around for my beer, which I'd put down on the ledge near the kitchen, completely out of reach. So much for getting a little buzz on to help break the ice.

"You seemed to be completely undecided. Either that, or you don't like me."

"Oh, I like you," I blurted out.

"Good." His hand dropped to the front of my shoulder and I instantly regretted the push-up bra, so heavily padded he wouldn't be able to find my breasts no matter how hard he went looking. If he were even planning to look. At least it was black, not the beige bra I'd considered.

I prayed I didn't smell like the spilled Miller Lite.

"We can do whatever you want," he said. "We can sit here and hold hands and watch Netflix, we can have sex, you can spend the night, whatever."

Ah, so many options. The only one I ruled out immediately was spending the night.

"Yeah, we can have sex," I said, finding my confidence. "That would be fine."

Fine? That made it sound like he'd invited me for tea.

"Come on up," he said, standing up and heading to the stairs.

The dogs were sprawled out on the bed, sleeping soundly. But instead of shooing them off, Jeremy pulled a comforter from the end of the bed and spread it on the floor. He sat down and patted the space next to him, pulling off his shirt to reveal a sculpted, suntanned chest.

I had a sudden image of Jeremy directing me to lie down while he calmly spread my legs and harnessed them open so he could see and explore every part of me. Of course, in this fantasy, we were lying on the actual bed, not the floor.

Feeling like I should take something off, I bent down to untie my sneaks, trying to balance, then giving up and sitting down to kick them off. Jeremy had stretched out on the blanket lazily. I lay down next to him, feeling the hard floor under my back.

Would it be too much to ask that he move the dogs off the bed so we could use it?

Rolling on his side toward me, he put his hands on my face and kissed me deeply, winding his tongue across my teeth and into my mouth. I tried to reciprocate but ended up biting his lower lip.

"I'm not very good at this," I said.

"You're fine. Relax."

In one smooth move, Jeremy lifted my T-shirt over my head and began stroking the area around my push-up bra.

"Very pretty," he said, dropping his face and kissing my skin.

Suddenly impatient, I unclasped the bra and shook it off. I cursed the fact that I was lying down and my boobs would no doubt be sagging sideways.

A moment later, it didn't matter.

Jeremy put his mouth on one nipple while toying with the other, making them both stand up with exquisite sensitivity. I squirmed and tried not to moan. When had I last been touched like this? The vibrator wand was good, but didn't come close to a real-life lover.

He took my hand and brought it down to the crotch of his jeans, where I felt a bulge so hard, I started fumbling at his zipper right away. After a moment, he unzipped and slid easily out of his Levi's.

I sat up and tried to slip seductively out of my jeans, but they wouldn't budge. I had to lie down to get them on, and apparently would have to do the same to get them off, all while Jeremy was sitting over me, watching. My jeans were tight at my hips and I was suddenly completely stuck in them. Smiling, he reached down and yanked, peeling off my panties at the same time.

Well there I was. Naked, fighting the urge to cover up with whatever edge of the blanket I could manage to reach.

"Nice," he said running the palm of his hand across my stomach, which I was sucking in with all my might, hoping it looked flatter than it actually was. I fought the urge to giggle as he went lower with his fingers, finding places that were more ticklish than erogenous.

Then he found all the right places.

"You want to keep going, right?" Jeremy said, his hands hovering between my thighs.

I nodded my head, having trouble forming words at that moment.

Jeremy slid his fingers inside me and I gasped, arching my back right off the floor. "Yes, I guess you do," he said, smiling. Then he brought his fingers to his mouth to taste me. "Yum," he said.

I was almost embarrassed by how wet I was, by the slurping noises we both heard as he moved his fingers inside me. Those thoughts washed away as he pulled the top of my slit firmly upward. I felt my clit pop out from under its sheath. No one had ever done that. Then he lowered his face and started swirling his tongue all around it.

"Ahhh," I groaned, unable to contain myself.

I reached down to stroke his ears. I didn't want to just lie there enjoying myself, but when I started to sit up, he gently pushed me back down.

"Shhhh," he said, his lips pressing into me, tongue still moving.

Two long dog noses poked out over the edge of the bed, then two sets of eyes were staring at us as if they knew exactly what we were doing.

"Go back to sleep," Jeremy said, and the doggie faces disappeared.

Using his fingers and his tongue, he stroked me and lapped at me until I was bucking my hips all over, the comforter rippling beneath my back. Jeremy put his hands under my ass and pulled me even closer, until his face was buried in me. Just as I felt the waves building up to orgasm, he sat up and moved away from me.

"Um," I sputtered, worried that he was done.

Thank God he wasn't done. He reached into a drawer and pulled out a thick roll of condoms in silver packages.

"You don't need—" I stopped, trying to think of a casual way to tell him I'd gone through menopause without sounding too much older than he was. But it was always smart to use a condom.

"You're on the pill? I'm going to use one anyway, babe," he said, expertly rolling it down his erection.

He lay back down and pulled me over and on top of him in one easy move, pushing on my hips down until he was inside me, sliding in, incredibly snug and warm. We both moaned out loud.

"Wow, you're tight," he breathed into my neck.

Yeah, especially for someone who's had two kids, I thought.

My thoughts were erased as we found our rhythm, Jeremy lifting his hips and me grinding mine down on him.

"Nice sweet pussy," he whispered.

We started out slowly but couldn't help but speed up the pace, at last slamming into each other, thrashing, Jeremy biting into my neck and me riding him, not giving a shit what my paunchy stomach looked like. It was exquisite; I'd forgotten how great sex could be.

And then it began in my mind: The Great Orgasm Debate.

Could I get off? Was I even close? How close was he?

I didn't want him to think he had failed me. Especially at his young age.

I also didn't want it to look like I wasn't sexually responsive enough to reach orgasm. Or worse, too old to enjoy it. Could I get off? Was it time to fake it then go home and take care of myself later? Would it be insulting to him if I started rubbing my own clit to come?

Faking it was easy enough, but certainly not the best option. What if—

"Come for me," Jeremy whispered. "Give it to me. I want it."

Then he pulled me down by the shoulders so he could bite at my nipples, still hard, and that was it. I forgot to debate, I forgot everything and went. Right. Over. The. Edge. We came almost simultaneously, crashing orgasms that shook our bodies and left us drenched, my head lowered to his chest, both of us gasping for breath.

"Good lord," I said into his shoulder blade.

"Ditto," he said, kissing me on the top of my head.

I tried to gracefully roll off him, but ended up half-falling on my side of the blanket. I propped my head up on my arm and hoped I still looked seductive and that my hair wasn't a rat's nest. Jeremy got up and went into the bathroom. I heard water running and was glad we had used a condom, because I hadn't been left with the sticky mess.

Still magnificently naked, Jeremy came back to the bedroom, opened the dresser and took out a tie-dyed pouch. He pulled out a small, dark pipe and started tamping down inside it with his finger.

"You smoke?" he asked, lighting up and drawing heavily on the pipe, exhaling the unmistakable smell of weed.

What the hell was it with men and pot-smoking these days? I was ready to say yes, but remembered I'd have to make my way home on the winding road around the lake, which I'd probably have to circle twice again to find my way.

"Thanks, maybe next time," I said.

Jeremy's eyes had gone dreamy. "You're really something, Jess."

I lay back down on the rumpled blanket and stared through the skylight at the stars.

"So are you," I said a moment later.

He opened my legs one more time and planted soft kisses between my thighs, gently, as if he were kissing me good night.

* * *

I waited until Sunday afternoon to text Jeremy, even though it took all the willpower I had to not begin the day with, "Good morning, lover!"

"Hey, had a great time last night...you?" I texted at exactly noon. *Good*, I thought to myself, *nice and casual but still referencing the incredible sex.*

I waited at the kitchen table. And waited.

Penny padded in and nudged her nose at my foot. Then she put her little chin up in the air and started barking loud enough to be heard down the street. She had heard Lily's arrival before the doorbell even rang.

I threw open the front door and Lily bustled in, snow in her hair, on her eyelashes, and falling off the top of her boots.

"Hey sweetie, haven't seen you in a while!"

"How much did you miss me?"

"This much," I said, stretching out my arms.

Lily sat down and patted her lap for Penny, who ran to her.

"So, what are you doing, just sitting around?" she asked.

"Yeah, hanging around."

"I'll stay and hang with you. My parents said it was ok."

"Thanks, kid."

"You're welcome."

Then she launched into a story about her best friend in first grade who she called a sister because neither of them had one, and after all, they both liked everything purple and playing badminton in gym. They'd exchanged braided friendship rings, sat together at lunch, and even liked the same boy, which Lily didn't think would be a problem.

I glanced discreetly at my watch so I wouldn't interrupt her story.

"Whoops, what time is it?" Lily asked.

"Quarter after five."

"Gotta go, my grandpa's coming for dinner and he always brings cupcakes for dessert. With pink frosting and sprinkles that look like real glitter."

She struggled back into her winter gear, barely resembling her graceful self.

"Mwuh!" she blew me a kiss.

Lily would one day give the world a run for its money.

Hearing about the cupcakes made me hungry. Maybe I could walk down after dinner and see if they had an extra cupcake and tell them what a sweetie they had for a little girl, maybe meet the lucky grandfather.

My cell phone buzzed—an incoming message.

Thank God! I wanted to be sitting down to feel the full effect of what I imagined would be a sexy text from Jeremy. Instead, he had texted this: "Hey. Lisa, stop busting my balls. Sorry I cancelled last night, but I was out shooting film for the calendar. I'll make it up to you with my tongue later, babe."

I read the message three times, trying to make sense of it.

For starters, clearly, I was not Lisa. Secondly, he'd been with me Saturday night, not out taking photos. And last, but certainly not least, he was going to use his tongue—his magic tongue!—to make her forget she was mad at him.

WTF??

I didn't text Jeremy again, which essentially meant I was the one ghosting him, which made me feel less let down. I gotta say I missed that magic tongue.

Back to the vibrator wand it was.

54

IN DECEMBER, WE PUT UP A LITTLE CHRISTMAS TREE IN THE WINDOW AT work. I should say, I put up the tree, and the guys asked when I was bringing in holiday cookies. Me? Bake? I didn't think so.

I was working my way through an enormous stack of tax bills at the office when I heard the building's front door slam. I glanced at Joe, who was texting, then looked up to see who it was.

"Can I help—"

It was Michael, smiling at me as he walked across the lobby. He was wearing a navy ski jacket, a striped scarf, and the aviator sunglasses he wore when we went out for falafel. It wasn't even sunny outside.

Jesus. Maddy had been right. Someone had walked right into my office, but instead of being someone wonderful, it was my worst nightmare. Then the front door banged again and a slim, young blonde woman came in, rubbing her bare hands together to warm them.

"Mikey, it's too cold to wait in the car," she whined.

"Sorry," Michael asked, not even glancing her way. "How are ya, Jessie?"

I blinked my eyes, hoping he would disappear. No luck.

"How can I help you?"

"Here to pay the taxman," he said, taking his time pulling out his checkbook.

The blonde went over to the radiator near Jerky's chair and turned around to warm her ridiculously cute ass. The men's jaws dropped in unison. Even Jerky was entranced.

"All right, I'll take your payment," I said, looking squarely at his right shoulder.

"Don't spend it all in one place," Michael said, ripping out his check with a flourish.

"OK," I said, wondering how he could think he was the first one to make that dumb joke.

"So," he said, leaning closer over the counter. "How are you, Jess?"

"Good, fine," I said, painfully aware that Joe had stopped texting and was watching me with interest.

"You know what? I should apologize," he said.

"No need for that!" I said, wishing he would leave.

"It's just, you texted me a lot and I felt like it was getting too intense," he whispered, making Joe swivel his chair closer. "I hadn't been with someone who liked me as much as you did, at least, not until Lacey." He gestured at the blonde with his thumb.

"Good luck with that," I said, rustling papers and trying to stay calm under Joe's open stare.

After an excruciatingly long pause, Michael finally turned away from the counter, holding out his hand to pull Lacey close to him.

"See ya," he said over his shoulder before letting the door slam behind him on his way out.

I burned with fury. Liked him as much as I did? I was checking out the waiter at the Greek restaurant! I was back on Fish that night.

But he was right, I realized with a sinking heart. I had texted him and asked to see him a lot. I had pictured us having dinner in a nice restaurant, holding hands in a movie theater, even introducing him to Maddy and Ian. I had, for that short amount of time we dated, pictured him as my boyfriend, even when I wasn't sure that was what I really wanted, or what we had the potential to be. And it had been way too early. I'd learned a lot since I'd known Michael about rushing things and getting carried away.

I hadn't genuinely wanted Michael, but I wanted what he represented. I liked the idea of Michael more than I liked him in real life.

"Soooo," said Wes, who had of course woken up in time to watch the entire exchange. "What was that about?"

"Nothing."

"Didn't seem like nothing," Joe snorted.

"That's Michael Warner—a real pothead, that one," Wes said, pulling a baloney sub out of his lunch bag. "Know him?"

"Not at all," I said, straightening my shoulders and reaching for another stack of bills to reconcile.

I was remarkably unfazed.

Paulie got up and went to the window to watch Michael and Lacey hurry to their car across the street, then turned quickly, startling his friends.

"Look sharp, gents, we're about to get a visitor," Paulie said. "And for god's sake, someone wake up Wes."

They whistled to Beef Jerky, who was near the window drooling over pigeons on the rooftops nearby. As if he knew what was coming, Jerky dashed under the table and didn't come out.

Joe took his feet off his desk and grabbed some loose papers, squinting down at them as if he were actually working.

The change in the men was remarkable. I barely recognized them.

The front door opened and in came Linda, the friendly trustee who'd interviewed me with Joe. She was wearing a red coat with a furry white hood.

"Well, hi everyone."

The men at the table who were hunched together, all studying the same newspaper, looked up as if they hadn't panicked when they saw her approaching the building.

Joe scrambled to his feet.

"Linda! Nice surprise. Is it cold enough for you out there?"

"It's freezing—the wind goes right through me!"

"That wind chill's what gets ya," Sal said, clearly unable to stop himself from joining in any conversation whether he was included or not. "Heard we're in for a deep freeze end of the week. Only getting worse."

"Ouch," Sal said, rubbing his shin where Paulie had clearly kicked him to shut up.

"Actually, I came to see Jessica," Linda said, leaning on the counter. Her lipstick was just a little too coral for the red coat, but otherwise she was the best-dressed person ever to come into the office. "How're things going?"

"Ah, good, great," I said, watching Joe continue to look busy when I knew he was just leafing through a pile of invoices he would be putting on my desk the minute Linda left.

"Everyone helping you out?" Linda looked around the room and nodded to the trio at the table. It was an acknowledgment without actually saying a word. They continued their close scrutiny of the same page of the newspaper.

"So, everything's copacetic?"

"Yes. Everything's fine, thanks."

"All righty, well let me know if there's anything at all you need," Linda said, turning around. "You know, you really should turn the heat up in here. I don't know how you can work without gloves on."

I didn't offer up the fact that a warm office made Wes sleepier, so the men kept it chilly. I'd started wearing wool turtlenecks, and when the men made their daily donut run, I turned the thermostat up.

"Come anytime!" I called out to her before the heavy door shut.

"OK, men, at ease," Paulie said.

Jerky came out from under the table and bounded back to his chair by the window.

"Whew, that was a close one," Wes said, yawning.

"Prosthetic, is that what she said?" Sal asked. "Like someone's fake leg?"

"No, copacetic," Paulie said thoughtfully. "I think it might be French."

"I think it means the room is clean," Wes offered.

"No, no, it means it's crowded in here," Joe said. "Hope she isn't gonna tell you guys to stop hanging around here again."

Again? Had the Three Stooges been asked to leave? And what about the dog?

I thought about telling them copacetic meant everything was fine, but didn't want to make them feel bad. Their definitions of the word were much more fun.

55

It was my nine-month anniversary of joining the Y, and things were getting moderately better. I still hadn't even approached the scale, but my endurance was definitely up. I could carry a huge laundry basket upstairs without losing my breath. I'd graduated from old sweats and Ian's marathon T-shirt to spandex leggings from Amazon and a hip-length Tencel top that wicked away moisture, which was good because after twenty minutes on the treadmill, I was a sweaty mess. I started rowing for fifteen minutes after the treadmill. The rhythm relaxed me and I got lulled into the zone.

Some days I closed my eyes and thought about going on vacation to a pet-friendly beachside resort, maybe with the kids or Eddie and Donny, maybe by myself. I'd earned a week's vaca-time at the office.

One day I was blissing out and heard someone say my name. I opened my eyes and rubbed the sweat out of them. It was Twin T-shirt Man, Brant.

"Hey, Jessica, right?"

"Yeah," I said, refusing to slow my pace this time.

"How're you doing? You look good."

Brant looked even better.

"Oh, thanks." I chugged on, wondering if he would notice my wicking shirt was not doing its job.

"How've you been?" he asked, leaning his arm casually on the hand rail of my treadmill.

"Good. You?"

"Really good," he said, the smile lines around his eyes crinkling.

"How're those fig trees?"

Brant laughed and I realized I'd revealed how many times I replayed our first meeting in my head, trying to figure out when it crashed and burned.

"They're coming along nicely. I'll bring some for you to try sometime."

Huh. It had been three months since I last saw him at the gym. Unless he was planning on carrying figs in his gym bag for weeks, it was unlikely I would ever have any. I looked up at the TV screen, where Cathy was grating fresh fruit for lemon bars.

"I'll let you go," Brant said. "Listen, we could go for that coffee if you still want to."

It was my turn to hesitate, surprising both of us.

"Thanks, I appreciate the offer, but I'm really busy these days," I said at last. "You know, crowded social calendar, no free time." Leave it to me to overexplain.

Brant paused, looking momentarily confused. "Well, then, I guess I'll see you around."

"Good luck with the figs!" I called after him in a voice so loud I swore it echoed. He waved his hand without turning back around. I picked up my pace, deciding I was going for my personal best, or at least a heart rate stronger than a desert animal's.

Had I made the right choice by turning him down? I had made the decision without over-analyzing, and that made it certain it was the right move.

56

METROMAN LOOKED PROMISING WHEN I CAME ACROSS HIS PROFILE AFTER the holidays. His pics showed him wearing a dark suit in front of a Lamborghini, making a toast with a glass of champagne.

Classy, I thought.

Plus, he replied within a few hours after my boring message: "Hey, I like your car...a bit nicer than my Honda SUV. What are you toasting?"

"Wrapped up a huge deal in Manhattan," Metro, real name Richard, messaged back. He owned his realty company.

"That's great. What property did you sell?"

"Uptown condo. Half a mil."

Half a million? What was his commission? 15%? I had no idea.

We agreed to meet at Hamlet's Study in Ashton, a new place known for trendy custom cocktails. I wore black dress pants, the wedge heels, and a red-and-black blouse with buttons down the back. Richard was already at the bar, wearing a navy pinstriped suit different from the one in his photos, and a thin paisley tie with a monogrammed clip.

"Hi, Richard." I held out my hand. "I'm Jessica."

He took my hand and held it up to his mouth, brushing it with a kiss.

"Well, OK there, thank you." I slid into the silver filigree bar chair that couldn't even be called a bar stool because it was so fancy.

"What would you like?" he asked.

There was a four-page menu just for cocktails. I scanned it quickly, looking for something that wouldn't knock me off my feet after the first sip.

"Vesper Martini, please," Richard told the bartender. "Grey Goose, hold the lemon twist."

"A Tom Collins?" I said, defaulting to a drink whose name I could remember. "And no lemon, please."

Actually I liked fruit in my drinks, but didn't want to look childish. Maybe holding the lemon was trendy. Richard looked pointedly at my unpainted nails. His own were glossy and better manicured than mine had ever been in my entire life.

"Do you get down to the city often? Which clubs do you like?"

"My daughter and I have a tradition of going to see the Radio City Music Hall Christmas Show with the Rockettes," I said. "We like Carnegie Deli; their Reubens are out of this world."

"Ah," Richard said.

We sipped our drinks in silence.

"You have really nice skin," I blurted out.

It was true. His skin was perfect, his pores practically invisible.

"Clinique for Men," he said nodding, agreeing with me about his complexion. "SPF 30 all year around, charcoal purifying mask weekly, and a monthly facial, of course."

Of course.

"So," I began. "Have you met a lot of women on Fish?"

Richard frowned. "I find most of them to be unsophisticated. I'm thinking of dating older women because they may have more class."

"Excuse me," I said, making a run for the ladies' room.

"It's going terribly," I texted Maddy. "He's a snob and I look like a country bumpkin."

"Then run," she texted back. "Ian did it, and you can too!"

"I can't run. He's sitting right by the door."

"Is there a back exit?"

"Yeah, probably with an alarm that would go off if I tried to get out."

"Well, just end it gracefully."

Richard was texting when I got back to the bar. He took his time finishing his message before looking up at me.

"I have to go now," I stammered. "My dog puked."

"All right." Richard was clearly not disappointed. "I'll get the tab—you go on ahead."

"Good luck in your search."

"Same to you," he said, frowning again. "Toodles."

And with that, I ran.

57

IAN CAME DOWNSTAIRS WEARING A BUTTON-DOWN OXFORD SHIRT, ONE step up from his usual T-shirt with a band and its tour schedule on it.

"What's with the fancy shirt?"

"Got a date," Ian said, smoothing the front of the shirt over his chest. "How do I look?"

"Amazing."

"Thanks." He smiled, and I still recognized the fourth-grader who came home with first prize in a spelling bee. He was still an exceptional speller, come to think of it.

"So where are you going?"

"To a play at the Westin Theater."

"Really?" I was mildly surprised and wished I'd had a date to see a live performance. That was a classy idea; if I ever found someone with class, I'd keep that in mind.

"Met on Tinder?"

"Actually, she's from my bio class at school. We were lab partners."

"Wow—she's smart and has good taste?"

"Why do you say that?" Ian grinned.

"Because she's going out with you."

It was quiet in the house after Ian left. Pen-Pen was dozing in her doggy bed that looked like a little blue couch. I made myself French toast and scrambled eggs for dinner and thought about calling Eddie and Donny to come over to play cards. Maybe a drinking game, since it was Friday night.

I walked around picking up Penny's dog toys: the cow that mooed and always surprised her, the lone red sock, a rubber duck, a hippo wearing earmuffs. Then I went into my room and foraged around in the closet for an Amazon box that held a photo album from my wedding to Adam. The box was lightly coated with dust, and inside, the edges of the album were starting to fray.

When Maddy was eight or nine, she and I used to look through the album and plan her future wedding. There was always a fancy church with pink roses in every aisle, a gown with a train so long it had to be carried by her maid of honor, and a blond man in a white tux waiting for her at the altar. I was always surprised by this, because Adam had dark hair, but Madd was adamant about the light-colored hair.

"I want babies that look like Ian when he was born," she finally told me, something so heartwarming I never forgot it.

If Adam and I had stayed married, we'd have been together twenty-eight years. For a long time, my wedding day was my happy place. Later, it would be beach vacations with the kids, a song Maddy made up to soothe baby Ian when he was fussy, the time Ian caught a sunfish and cried because it had to go back into the lake because he wanted to keep it as a pet, the white patent-leather Mary Janes I always got Madison for Easter, putting out cookies for Santa, watching the kids play soccer under a sun so hot I was worried about heat stroke. It was baby teeth under pillows, the math homework I always left to Adam to help with, and all those popsicles and playgrounds and pirouettes in Madison's ballet class, which she took only because she wanted to wear the pink tutu.

Did Adam have his own collection of memories? Not for the first time, it hurt to know there wasn't any other person I could reminisce with about the kids' births, when Adam ate three packets of Saltine crackers during my long labor with Maddy because he didn't want to leave my side and go to the cafeteria, how he'd snuck me ice chips when the nurses said no liquids, when Ian eased into the world with a smile on his face, the flowers that arrived from my sister in a blue vase shaped like baby booties.

Where had they gone, those years when I was so busy, I hadn't realized they were the best of times? I once thought I would give anything now to go back to those days and have the kids, my best friends, by my side.

But I believed what Eddie had said that night while we were junk-picking, that we would all be together in the next life to do it over again. And I realized I wouldn't take back my married days to Adam or Bryan. The years had been good ones, most of the time, but

I was a different version of myself now. Still loving, hopefully funny, but strong in a way I hadn't been before. Maybe there wasn't a missing piece. Maybe I'd been whole and complete all along. OK, that might be overdoing it, but still. I had changed.

I was on my way to regaining my fitness, for god's sake.

I scooped up Penny for bed and was just dozing off when Ian came in and turned on the hall light.

"How was the play?"

"It was good," he said, stroking Penny's belly. "It was a musical."

"You don't like musicals."

"This one I did, because there wasn't a lot of dancing."

"So, when are you guys going back out?"

Ian stood up. "I don't think we are meant to be anything more than friends. She's great, but there wasn't that spark. And that's OK."

"So, what's your plan now?"

Ian grinned. "I'm just going to see what comes along and go with it. Try to stop looking so hard. There's a girl out there somewhere looking for me—and who knows, she may just find me first."

When he took the stairs two at a time to go up to his room, I could hear him humming.

58

I HAD HIGH HOPES IN FEBRUARY FOR LAUGHINGLARRY, THE MAPLE SYRUP mogul. His profile picture showed a smiling guy in front of an enormous vat bubbling with sugary syrup. He was holding a huge wooden spoon as if ready to give it all a stir, and he had such muscular arms he probably could do it, too.

"So, you make maple syrup?" I asked Larry, who had carefully clipped salt-and-pepper hair and an unfortunate cologne choice. We were having chicken Caesar salad and iced tea in an Ashton bistro.

"Family business," he said. "Oh, I have something for you," he said and searched his blazer pocket and produced a glass bottle shaped like a maple leaf, filled with amber liquid. "Our best seller. We're in specialty stores across the Northeast, expanding soon down the coast."

"Thank you," I said, tucking the bottle into my purse.

Larry had pulled up in front of the restaurant in a Mercedes, talked about his barn and horses, and I realized he'd made his fortune in syrup.

I pictured myself at Laughing Larry's syrup production barn, lining up glass bottles, putting on the amber labels, then retiring up to the big house for a bottle of good wine and some grilled salmon, maybe prepared by a house chef.

"I like your earrings," he said as we ate our salads. He looked far wearier and more worn-out than his online photo, but made up for this with sincerity.

"So, how long have you been on Fish?" I asked Larry.

"About three months this time. I keep quitting, then signing back up."

I laughed. "Yeah, I've been ready to throw in the towel lots of times. Lots of desperate men on there."

"And women," Larry said, stirring sugar into his iced tea. "They should come with warning signs."

"Yeah, ha-ha."

"So you're divorced?" Larry said, dabbing his mouth with his napkin.

"Yup." I poked at my salad, shaking my head a little to make my feather earrings move in a way I hoped was seductive. "You?"

"I'm still married."

I choked on a crouton. "Excuse me?"

To my horror, Larry's eyes welled up with tears. "Well, my wife, she left me."

"I'm so sorry. How long ago?

"Thirty weeks," Larry said. "That's not the worst of it."

"No?"

Laughing Larry was a misnomer. He put down his fork and sat back in a way I knew meant he was going to tell me the whole story. I looked around for the waiter, hoping he'd arrive with the check.

Larry produced a handkerchief from his pocket and wiped his eyes. "Left me for our son's best friend. Just up and left."

"How old is your son?"

"Twenty-four." He began to sob.

"I'm so sorry," I said weakly.

"I think they went to Long Island," Larry said. "Some days I can't even get out of bed; syrup production slowed down drastically these last six months. One of these days, I'm going down there to look for her."

"I am really sorry," I said, coming up blank with anything else to offer in the way of sympathy.

The waiter zoomed in with the check and Larry sat back up to pay with a gold Visa card.

On the sidewalk after lunch, he leaned in—probably for a peck on the cheek, but I wasn't prepared and didn't have time to turn my face, so his lips landed on mine.

"Oh," I said awkwardly. "OK, well there, now. There you go."

"Thanks for being a good listener," Larry said, the crumpled handkerchief still sticking out of the lapel pocket on his blazer.

"I hope you find what you're looking for," I said, feeling like that wasn't quite the right thing to say, but again, I came up empty. "And good luck with that syrup production!"

We parted ways, and when I looked back, Larry had the posture of someone exhausted and beaten down. Poor guy.

The kids and I doused pancakes with the amber syrup for days. It was overly sweet and delicious.

"He had a Mercedes and horses?" Ian asked, chewing and pouring more syrup on his pancakes. "Geez, you kind of struck out there."

* * *

GoodSoul's photo on Fish showed a cute, buttoned-up type with scholarly-looking glasses. His profile paragraph had flawless grammar and spelling, a major plus in my book.

"Let's go feed the ducks at Kelly Park on Saturday," Mr.GoodSoul messaged me. "I'll bring the bread."

It was mid-February, but the cold had given us a reprieve. Temps were in the mid-40s and winds had lost their ferocity. We met at a park bench. I liked Mr.GoodSoul's bookish vibe, sort of college prof mixed with lab scientist. His real name was Gordon, and he brought gluten-free, organic Ancient Grains bread that he tore into small, perfectly square pieces before dropping them at the ducks' feet. It looked as if he'd been doing it all his life. I imagined him meeting a different woman every weekend, tossing pumpernickel with PleasantlyPlump, seedless rye with TinyandTrim, baguette with BigandBeautiful.

"I used to take my kids here when they were young," I said, remembering them chasing and trying to catch the ducks.

"Kids? You have kids?"

"Yeah, well, they're adults now. Madison's twenty-four and Ian is twenty-one."

"Hm. I don't have children." Gordon frowned at his handful of bread. "I don't recall seeing that detail in your profile."

"Well, you must have nieces and nephews that you spoil," I said, blowing on my hands because I'd been optimistic about the weather and hadn't brought my gloves.

"None, actually. Kids were never a priority."

The conversation pretty much went flat after that, and soon the bread was reduced to tiny crumbs. The ducks were pissed. They started squawking, waddling their way out of the pond toward us. They looked aggressive and determined, as if we were deliberately withholding bread scraps. I was laughing, but Gordon turned and started striding quickly away.

The angry ducks chased us, right on our heels, using their crazy flapping wings as weapons. You never know the wrath of a duck until you've been flapped by one. I started laughing so hard I almost peed, but Gordon wasn't pleased.

"It was nice meeting you, Jessica," he said, holding out his hand stiffly.

"You too, Gordy," I said, just to see how he'd react to not being called his formal name.

He shuddered, then put on sunglasses. "Right-oh," he said before turning away, not even bothering to walk me to my car.

* * *

StarPlayer's photo on the dating site was so fuzzy I could only tell he was wearing hockey skates and waving at someone. With my expectations as low as they could get, I agreed to meet Mr. Star for morning bagels. When I got to the coffee shop, a short man I didn't recognize stood up and waved his arms to catch my attention.

StarPlayer, real name Eric, was at least ten years older than the Fish hockey photo (if the photo was even him), and the hair he'd described as "thinning" was bald on the top, long and stringy in the back. I'll take a good shaved head any day. This guy hadn't seen shampoo in a week.

We stood in line silently to order coffee. I got a plain bagel and a small chai tea. Eric ordered basically everything in the display case: an oversized cinnamon bun, a huge chunk of coffee cake, a cheese Danish, and a bran muffin.

"Hungry?" I asked him.

"Yeah, a little," he said, counting out exact change at the register. "I'm going running later and I need my carbs. Training for a marathon, actually."

"Really? Which one?"

"Ah, not sure yet," Eric's face reddened visibly. "Gotta start small."

"Oh yeah, sure."

We carried our tray to a small round table and pulled up wicker chairs. Then I felt something brush up against my ankle. Through the glass-topped table, I could see that Eric had slipped off his moccasin (no running shoes for him), and was stroking me with his foot, wearing white tube socks that had seen better days. I jerked my leg away, spilling my tea.

"Whoa there, clumsy," Eric said, patting at the table with his napkin. "Don't get too excited; there's no rush."

"What?" I choked a little.

"I mean don't be so antsy. We've got plenty of time. Let me dig into my food and then we can get outta here."

"Are you thinking I liked your little game of footsie?"

"I know women like you," Eric said calmly, bits of cheese Danish stuck to the sides of his mouth. "You haven't been touched in a very, very long time, so when a man makes a move, you really dig it."

"Have a nice day," I said, standing quickly and moving to the door.

"Hey, what about your bagel?" Eric called after me.

"Help yourself!"

As I ran by the window outside, I saw him lean over and take the bagel off my plate.

"This isn't going well," I texted Eddie. "I feel like an idiot."

"Give it some time."

"I've given it lots of time! Enough for me to see how random this all is. Some of the profiles sound great, but when you see them in person, no thank you. Worse, the ghosting makes me feel ridiculous and rejected."

"How can they reject you when they don't even know you?"

"Yeah, that's what Ian says, but when you message for a week then he drops off the face of the earth, it's not exactly a confidence-builder."

"Ya gotta just keep trying."

"I don't think you understand how awful it is, Eddie. One guy messaged me sixteen times in two hours! Another one said he wanted to name his cat after me. Another guy asked if he could bring his ex-wife to meet me, because he values her opinion!"

"OK, so you're getting some of the frogs out of the way. Keep your chin up."

"I'll try. Gotta go now. I have an important date with my vibrator."

"Have you set a personal record yet?"

"Still working on that," I texted. "Night."

59

It was time for the late winter continuing ed classes at the high school, and Eddie signed us up for a doozie: "Cascade of Color: Aura Drawing."

"Geez, Eddie, I was never good at art—you know that. You always got straight A's," I protested. "I couldn't even make a square paperweight in ceramics, remember? The teacher thought it was supposed to be a donut?"

"Yeah," Eddie said thoughtfully. "It did look a lot like a chocolate glazed."

I threw a dish towel at him. Penny looked up, then settled her chin on her front paws to snooze again.

Tuesday night's aura class was in the same high school art room where I met Eddie and he took an artistically challenged freshman under his wing. I'd been worried we were expected to draw auras with crayons, but the room's largest table was covered with sticks of pastel chalk, from subtle pink to shocking chartreuse.

One of the smallest women I'd ever seen was standing with her back to us, humming and swaying her hips, when we walked in.

"Hello?" I said.

"Oh sweet Jesus, you scared me," the tiny woman said, fanning herself with a sheet of construction paper. "It's not nice to sneak up on people like that."

"Sorry," I said, trying to judge the woman's height compared to mine. She was easily under five feet tall. "We're here for the aura class?"

"Of course you are! I'm Giovanna—call me Gigi." She held out a hand covered in turquoise rings and bracelets, some of them silver, some beaded, all of them making her wrist look fragile. But her grip was like steel when she shook my hand. I tried not to wince. When she let go, my fingers felt numb.

"Brenda!" Gigi called. "Come over and meet two new friendly faces!"

A sullen teenager looked up blankly from her cell phone, made no eye contact whatsoever, and went back to texting.

"Yours?" Eddie asked.

Gigi sighed. "My youngest. Your aura's looking mighty dark," she yelled to her daughter. "We're expecting another student, but it's almost 7:00, so let's dig in," Gigi said, unwinding an orange gauze scarf from her neck to reveal a third-eye pendant.

Eddie and I sat down on stools next to each other.

"No, no—don't sit so close; you must give your auras room to breathe!" Gigi was scolding us now.

Obediently, because we were, after all, in school, we sat a few seats apart. My stool was tippy, but I was afraid complaining would make my aura darken.

"When you go deep into yourself and face who you truly are, colors will reveal themselves," Gigi whispered.

Eddie and I leaned in to hear better.

"What colors do you think you see?" We waited, thinking the question was rhetorical. "What do you see??" Gigi sounded impatient.

"Ah…rainbows?" I guessed.

"No," she said sternly. "That's what amateurs see. Try harder."

Across the room, Gigi's daughter was making circling motions around her head and pointing to her mom.

"Let's try something else to break this glacier that's getting in the way," Gigi said. "Close your eyes and pick up a pastel stick. Pick the one that calls to you."

I reached as far as I could, and when I opened my eyes, I was holding dark gray chalk. Eddie had a bright, sunny yellow.

"And so, we begin," Gigi whispered. "We see the light, and we see the dark."

I wished I saw an easy exit so I could make a run for the parking lot.

Gigi swept aside the chalk and rolled out an enormous swath of butcher paper, covering the art table from end to end. "See where your color takes you," she instructed.

Eddie immediately began drawing stark geometrics, shading with his one chalk stick as if he had the whole box. I drew a smiley face.

"Sorry I'm late." A woman with a blonde ponytail and a fringed leather purse rushed in. "Traffic."

"Yes, well, how do you think we got here?" Gigi asked in a voice so loud it echoed around the art room. "There's always traffic, but your classmates made it here on time. You must be Nadine. Take a seat."

All three of us sat up straight on our art stools. Gigi clearly meant business.

"Pick up a mirror and gaze into it," Gigi whispered. "Look beyond your own face and watch for rolling hills of color."

There were small hand mirrors on the table. When I gazed into mine, all I saw was a zit cropping up on my chin, and that my waterproof mascara hadn't lived up to its claim to last 24 hours.

Across the table from me, Nadine was using her mirror to touch up her burgundy matte lipstick. Luckily, Gigi was focusing on Eddie.

"You have gorgeous light around you, Edward," she whispered. "Can you see it?"

Eddie's face turned pink, but he nodded gravely into his mirror. "Well, the lighting in here must be kind; no fluorescents."

"OK," Gigi said, using her outside voice. "Edward is getting it, but you two—" She looked sternly over the tops of her leopard cat-eye glasses. "You two need to open yourselves up to the nuances of color."

Nadine and I looked at each other. I tapped my front tooth to let her know her lipstick was smeared. She smiled, and I hoped I had cleared my own dark aura by being nice.

"Let's pair up," Gigi said briskly. "You ladies work together."

I always hated when teachers told us to choose partners in gym class, because I was frequently the odd person out and had to do the drill with the teacher as a partner. Aside from a brief burst of potential in gymnastics, I'd never been a high achiever in anything athletic.

Ignoring us completely, Gigi turned Eddie's stool to face her and began scribbling furiously on the white butcher paper with deep gold chalk.

"I guess it's up to us to figure this out," I said quietly to Nadine.

"No whispering!" Gigi snapped, still drawing.

Nadine and I giggled.

"And no laughing! If you can't be serious, I will ask you to leave!" And send us…where? Detention? The principal's office?

"So, we're supposed to draw each other's auras?" Nadine said. "I'm not much of an artist. Is it supposed to look like a rainbow?"

"That's what I thought!" I said, dangerously close to eliciting the wrath of Gigi. "But she said no. The colors are supposed to call out to us."

"Hmm," Nadine said, pursing her burgundy lips. "Did I miss the part where she gave instructions?"

"That's the thing about these night classes…the teachers don't actually teach. They make us figure it out ourselves."

Nadine looked thoroughly confused.

"Let me take a stab at this," I said with more confidence than I felt.

"Do you need to see my eyes, or can I close them?" she asked nervously.

"Eh, close them."

I heard Gigi say softly to Eddie, "Your colors are alive; they're calling me closer."

I glanced at Eddie and he shrugged, still faintly blushing.

For the next twenty minutes, I chose chalk sticks randomly and scribbled on the white paper, forming deep purple circles, red waves, stripes of forest green, and in one corner, a small square of brown. When it felt complete, I stopped and sprayed my work with a bottle of hairspray Gigi had brought to keep the colors from smearing.

"Ohh, that looks great," Nadine said, leaning over to look. "What does it mean?"

"I have no idea!"

Across the table, Gigi gave a dramatic sigh and put down her chalk. "All right, let's see what you've come up with."

She looked closely at my drawing, then at me, then at Nadine. We were both too intimidated to laugh.

"This is marvelous work, very intuitive," Gigi said, running her fingers around the edges of the paper. "You've told quite a story about Nadine."

"I have?"

Even Gigi's daughter got up and came over to look, showing interest for the first time that night.

"Have her translate it for you," Brenda said, slipping off her earbuds.

"Well," Gigi said, clasping her hands over her heart. "The dark purple represents an energy blockage, restricting your spiritual connections.

But the deep red here is strength, showing you're a survivor. This green shows a change coming, or some new growth. Excellent work, Jessica!"

"Cool," Brenda said.

It was my turn to blush.

"What about that brown in the corner?" Eddie asked.

"That, my dear, is all the crap she has been through," Gigi said.

"All of that's true, for sure," Nadine said, brushing her hair away from her face." I just separated from my husband and it's unbelievably hard."

"I understand," I said.

"The worst part is it's been really rough on our son Tristan," Nadine said, looking down at her hands. But we're still a family, and who knows what the future will bring, right?"

"Right!"

"But can't just stand still—gotta gather my wits about me and forge on," she said, rubbing her palms on her jeans, then looking up and smiling. "Didn't kill me, so I must be stronger."

"Can I take this home?" Nadine asked, pointing to the drawing.

"It's all yours," I said, helping her roll it up.

Gigi's drawing of Eddie's aura was all swirls of yellow and gold. "Edward and I are very psychically attuned," she raved. "We're both lovers of exquisite beauty and have deep artistic abilities. Gold auras mean we have many friends and admirers."

She had gotten right to the very core of him.

"Do you have any hidden jewelry?" Gigi asked, putting her hand on Eddie's chest. "Yellow aura people like to adorn themselves."

Eddie took a step backwards and was, for once, utterly speechless.

"He's married," I blurted out. "Just doesn't wear a ring. But boy, is he ever married!"

"I thought he looked married," Nadine added.

Brenda laughed so hard she had to bend over to catch her breath.

"That's enough from you, missy," Gigi said. "You know your aura darkens when you sass your mother."

Brenda plugged back in and started cleaning up the chalk table.

"You didn't have your turn, Jess," Eddie said.

"It's fine. I think I know my colors."

"You have that little pile of shit too?" Nadine said.

"Oh, I've got that."

Before we left, Nadine and I exchanged cell numbers. Gigi actually offered her number to Eddie, but he pretended not to hear her.

"Well, Edward," I said in the overly lit parking lot. "Aren't you something, man with the golden aura."

"You too, chicky. Who knew you were psychic?"

"Not me, that's for sure."

"Sorry you never had your aura drawn," Eddie said.

"Eh, I don't care."

"Tell you what—order some colored chalk on your favorite shopping site and we'll do it with the kids."

"Sounds like a plan."

60

THE NEXT WEEKEND, I CALLED MADISON.

"Are you ready for this week's rundown?"

"Hold on, let me get a drink."

"It's four o'clock in the afternoon!"

"It's freaking iced tea, Mom!"

"You know I hate it when you curse," I said. "Well, by far my best date in a month was with my new friend Nadine from the aura class."

"Cool. Maybe you can go lesbo and have a happy life together."

"Madison!"

"Every day you tell me the guys from Tinder are a mess, but there must be some good ones out there," Maddy said, sipping audibly. "Otherwise we'd stop doing it, right?"

"I think we've all just lost our minds. At least, my matches on Fish seem to have."

"OK, let's hear it."

"Well, there's the guy, TaurusBull, who wants to call me his sister during sex and say, 'I hope Dad doesn't catch us.'"

"Oh, God, Mom, tell me you didn't—"

"Of course I did not; what are you thinking? He told me this ahead of time, you know, like a script."

"Sweet Jesus."

"And some other guy wanted to know if I wore silk or lace panties!"

"What did you tell him?"

"Cotton."

"Oh, Mombo. Well, at least you were honest. Did you hear back from him?"

"Never. Then there's a man, StraightArrow, whose hobbies include knife-throwing."

I heard Madison start to choke into her cell. "Are you kidding me? Geez, if he wants to throw something sharp, why not try darts?"

"Good suggestion. Do you want his number?"

"I mean, is that his job, like knife-thrower in a circus? Sideshow act? Or is he just an amateur thrower?"

"Maddy, I didn't interview him. I unmatched him in like two seconds."

Madison's choking dissolved into giggles. "Tell me more, Mom. You can't make this shit up."

"Well, there's the green-eyed, 6'3" musician, LuvNotes, who told me right off the bat he doesn't drive, because he had to sell his Subaru to get his guitar fixed."

"Oooh, Subarus are nice," Madd said.

"Can you stay focused, please?" I nudged Penny with my foot, then felt bad, so I bent down to scratch her ears. "I asked him how he gets to work, and he says he was mugged and the robbers hurt his shoulder, so he lost his job."

"Oh, that's so sad! But, hey, if his shoulder is hurt, how does he hold his guitar?"

"EXACTLY!" I yelled into my phone. "My question, exactly. I've hit rock bottom. Fish sucks, man."

"Maybe you should widen your search area," she said kindly to her old, lonely mother.

How far out are you going?"

"I think up to 60 miles away."

"Go 90. If he's worth it, he'll drive to see you."

"Yeah, well, maybe—if he has a car."

We both went quiet.

"How's Billy?"

"He's amazing," Madison said. "We're taking a ride up to Lake Placid next weekend."

"That's so great! I'm happy for you."

"Yeah, so guess I'm proving Ian wrong about the whole having sex too early thing."

"It's always good to put Ian in his place," I said.

"K. Text me later."

"Love you."

"Love you too, Mombo."

61

"WE HAVE A LOT IN COMMON, ARIESGURL," MESSAGED YOURROMEO. "WE both have small dogs and drink tea and don't watch TV. If you're interested in talking, you can reply anytime. I'll be around."

Hmm. It was the politest message I'd received. I quickly scrolled through his pics. One was a distant pic of him in front of what looked like an adobe hut. Another was of him holding a newborn, pride written all over his face. The last was of trees on a hiking path in spring.

So he was a hiker—so what? Most of the guys were.

I deliberated for a couple of minutes about ordering hiking boots on Amazon and trying to break them in and dirty them up before any kind of outdoor date. Too much work, I decided immediately.

I messaged Romeo back after waiting a few hours to downplay my interest. He was fifty-seven, had three sons, the one granddaughter, and a little terrier named Chloe. He was a fitness buff, and owned a company that designed and built custom staircases. His name was Hudson. He lived about ten minutes from me.

"I keep myself healthy—no fast food or Cheetos for me—and always end up hanging out with younger people," he messaged. "People say I'm youthful and don't look or act my age."

Why was he making such a big deal about being young at heart?

Shit. I had registered for Fish as a 49-year old. That posed a serious problem, but I put off figuring that one out so I could ride the high of getting to know Hudson. I liked his genuine, personable messages. Maybe he was put in my path because he lived so close to me. Maybe I would read his aura and it would be all gold and yellow. Maybe we would travel to New Mexico and take selfies by an adobe hut.

Over the next four days, Hudson and I were in constant contact, through the site, then texting, then talking by phone. He'd been divorced fourteen years and dating ever since.

"Just haven't met The One," he texted. "But I won't settle. I'll keep looking till I find her."

Being the boss hadn't been easy, he told me. One office manager, Shelley, had so much trouble doing her job that Hudson basically did it for her.

"Why did you keep her?"

"She was really nice, she walked Chloe, and she made this really great carrot cake every week for us."

Hudson made me laugh the way I did with my kids.

He was passionate about his work, especially custom jobs using wood other than ordinary oak. He loved mahogany and cypress on curved railings with fancy newel posts.

"We did an open spiral staircase this week," he texted, and I could almost hear the excitement behind his words. "Gorgeous, curved railings, inlaid box newel posts, you name it."

"Did it look like 'Stairway to Heaven?'"

"Pretty much."

"Guess you hear that joke all the time," I texted.

"Yeah, but that's OK, Jess."

We made a date for dinner Wednesday. Hudson said he would pick me up at my house after work.

"He's picking you up here?" Madison said incredulously. "You never give a guy your address, much less get into his car!"

"Relax. We've been talking for a week. I know where his stair company is, the names of his kids, what kind of chow his dog Chloe eats—"

"OK, OK, but give me his cell number just in case."

"Fine," I said, writing it down and handing it to her.

"Don't go casual," Maddy advised as I was pulling on mummy leggings. "Wear your black skirt and that red blouse with the buttons. And for god's sake, go a little crazy and leave the top two open."

I would have felt more at ease with the Halloween leggings, but she knew things about dating etiquette that I did not. Red blouse it was.

Hudson texted me ten minutes before his arrival.

"I'm on my way. It's not too late to run."

I couldn't get my breath fresh enough, so I brought toothpaste into the kitchen and scrubbed my teeth with my fingers. When he pulled into our driveway in a really clean red Jeep, I dabbed toothpaste on my tongue, which made my breath overly fresh.

I peeked out the front door when he got to my porch.

Hudson looked even better than his photos. He seemed very young, with a full head of sandy-colored hair, bright blue eyes with those dark rings around the irises, and broken-in straight-leg jeans. He smiled through the window even before I opened the door to usher him in.

Penny immediately bounded to him, tail wagging furiously. Hudson got on his knees to rub her neck. Then he stood up and leaned in to kiss me.

I kissed him right back, standing there in my kitchen.

"You taste good," he said, brushing my hair off my shoulder.

"Just brushed my teeth," I said, feeling foolish. What kind of ice-breaker was that?

We hurried down the porch in the winter wind. Hudson opened the Jeep door for me as I attempted to climb in gracefully, wearing a fitted skirt.

"Is it warm enough in here for you?" Hudson said, sounding worried.

"It's great."

Hudson drove to one of those ridiculously romantic restaurants with votive candles on glass-top tables and a brick fireplace with orange and blue flames. We rushed in from the cold.

He came over to pull out my chair and I pretended I'd known he was going to, even though it was the first time in my life any man had done that. The server had placed a menu in front of a seat across the table, but Hudson slid into the chair directly next to mine.

"I don't want to be too far away from you," he said, briefly squeezing my hand, which I prayed wasn't sweaty.

Over shrimp scampi, light on the garlic, I told Hudson about Madison and Ian and their dating experiences, and he told me about his family. Two of his sons were single, the oldest married with the new baby.

"She's incredible," he said about baby Emma. "Every time I see her, she's a new person."

"Do you see her a lot?"

"Not as much as I'd like, but I'm hoping to get babysitting duty when she's a bit older," he said, smiling.

I cleared my throat. "Speaking of a bit older, I'm, well I'm actually a couple years older than I listed on my profile."

Hudson wiped his mouth with his cloth napkin.

"OK. How much older?"

"Ah, eight years."

"OK. So that makes you—"

"Fifty-seven," I said, my face burning.

"Huh."

I drank a sip of my water, waiting.

"All right," he said at last. "Anything else you want to tell me?"

"I sometimes eat Cheetos," I blurted out.

Thankfully, he laughed. The awful moment was over. "So, do you like this restaurant?"

"I love it," I said, and he slid his hand over to squeeze mine.

Our server stayed discreetly away from our table except to refill our Pinot Grigio.

I'd promised Madison I would text from the ladies' room, but couldn't bear to leave the table and miss a chance that he might hold my hand again. Two hours later, we walked through the dark parking lot to his Jeep. Hudson opened the door for me. I got in ungracefully and reflexively put on my seatbelt.

Hudson got in the driver's side, started up the engine. and turned on the heat. Then, smiling, he reached over decisively to unclasp my seatbelt and pull me to him. His kisses were maddeningly slow, making me lean into him as if I'd never been kissed in a Jeep before after three glasses of Pinot. OK, so I hadn't. Then he turned his face, angling his mouth firmly on mine, and I pressed hard against him. My hands found their way into his wild swath of hair—no sticky products, so the waves were natural. YAY!

Hudson gathered up a handful of my hair, pulling it gently to expose my neck, which he covered with kisses, nibbling at my skin. I felt a moan forming in my throat, but managed to turn it into a sigh at the last minute. He toyed with the edge of my skirt, and I fought the urge to open my knees. I also fought the need to pee, wishing frantically I'd made that trip to the restaurant bathroom. The top buttons on his polo shirt were open just enough for me to slide in one hand and brush his chest with my fingers.

"I don't have sex on the first date," I said, breathing in the clean smell of his neck.

"Neither do I," he laughed. "And I don't have sex in cars, either."

"Or in parking lots."

"Agreed," he said, kissing me again.

But when he gently pushed my legs open and slipped fingers inside my panties to my very wet place, I rethought that rule and considered asking him back to my house. His teasing fingers didn't stay in me long enough. It would be a vibrator night when I got home.

62

Two days later, Friday night, Hudson picked me up at my house in an equally clean red Ford truck.

"I missed you," he said, pulling me into his arms and kissing me, even though it had only been 48 hours. We drove silently the ten minutes to his house. I tried not to fidget.

When we turned left onto his property, I sat up straight in disbelief. It was incredible. He had a restored farmhouse on grassy fields as far as I could see. There was an orange plow at the end of the winding driveway, and a shed that exactly matched the house. Parked behind it was a tractor.

His little terrier Chloe sprang up to greet us when we went in Hudson's house. I openly gaped at the enormous kitchen, spotlessly clean, the high ceiling over the living room with its stone fireplace, the cherrywood end tables and curved couch that looked like tapestry. Even the travel magazines on his coffee table were fanned out to perfection. There were two graceful elephants carved out of some kind of fancy wood standing in one corner, and a waist-high sculpture of a seashell in the entry to the kitchen.

"Sorry if it's a mess," Hudson said, plumping a gold-tasseled pillow.

Through another set of archways, I could see a cozy den with another fireplace. On the far wall was a formal oil painting of Chloe, looking very regal, especially for a dog. I tried to guess in my mind the cost of a portrait that size and came up blank. Hmm. But no family photos?

The only thing that made the room look remotely lived-in was a fleece blanket on the black leather chair, but a moment later, Chloe took a running jump and settled herself into the blanket.

"Her chair," Hudson explained.

I thought about my kitchen table littered with a few days' worth of mail, coupons, an old soup can filled with pencils, spare change, the empty paper towel holder, and maybe even Penny's leash. There were no carved shells in the entryway and my kitchen had counters—not an island. I still had candid photos of the kids on my walls; Adam's talent for photography had become a lifelong hobby. None of us had portraits done.

My house has character, I reminded myself, straightening my shoulders. It looked like people actually lived there. Hudson's place looked like he had a cleaning service go in two or three times a week.

"I haven't dusted lately," he said.

I looked around for dust and saw none. Not even a stray dog hair.

"This can be your bathroom to use," Hudson said, leading me through a gorgeous guest room with a bed covered in pristine white blankets and a lace coverlet.

I wasn't sure I'd heard him right. My bathroom?

The marble countertops were as clean as if the room had never been used. On the far side of the room was a deep garden tub, sparkling white, with huge silver claw feet. Everything matched: the creamy shower curtain, the scallop-edged fingertip towels, the perfectly pleated curtains. The bath towels, also folded and looking brand-new, were monogrammed in silver with his initials.

"Nice." I tried not to sound as overwhelmed as I felt.

"Thanks. I designed the house myself."

There was one thing strikingly missing in Hudson's one-floor home: a staircase.

"Yeah, didn't want to bring my work home with me," he joked.

Hudson led me back through the guestroom. In the hallway, I looked over my shoulder to see another bathroom, this one in shades of sea-foam blue.

"How many bathrooms do you have?"

"Three," Hudson said casually. "All of them full baths."

Hudson pulled out a bottle of red wine and a type of cork opener I'd never seen before—was it electric? It unscrewed the cork without him even having to turn it. He expertly swirled the wine into delicate long-stemmed glasses, leaving them drip-free with a practiced flourish.

"You're good at that," I said.

"Yeah, well—I practice when I'm alone."

"Really?"

"Not really, Jess." He held out his wineglass for a toast.

"To our second date," I said, clinking his glass and causing my wine to splash.

"You know what happens on a second date, right?" Hudson said, deliciously teasing.

Pulling out a remote control, he switched on music that came from nowhere I could see.

It was a song I loved.

"No one ever likes my music," he said as I started singing along.

We looked each other in the eyes and I thought of the saying, or was it lyrics, that you could get lost in someone's eyes. His were somber, as if he were very serious about something.

"Come here," he said, taking me by the hand and leading me to his bedroom.

His enormous bed was straight out of a home fashion magazine, complete with matching shams, bed skirt, and those little pillows with the buttons in the middle that make everything look elegant.

Hudson saw me looking. Laughing, he scooped up the pillow collection and carried them over to a small loveseat by the bay window, where he set them down carefully. He came slowly back across the room and took me by the hand.

"Jess."

I thanked god I was wearing a shirt without buttons. He pulled it over my head and off me in one easy motion.

"Undress me," he said.

I fumbled nervously with the buttons of his shirt. His chest had a smooth cover of fuzz the same sandy color as his wild head of hair. He helped me with the zipper of his jeans as I struggled to slip mine off without falling over.

"Beautiful," Hudson said, tracing the edges of my bra with the tips of his fingers. He pulled me up into his arms and set me down on the bed, hovering over me to kiss my mouth, ears, and neck, biting gently in a way that made me start moving my hips toward him. He held out his hands to pull me up to unclasp my bra, drawing in a breath as he saw my nipples harden.

"Jess," he said again.

I kept my eyes open as he lay down on top of me, nuzzling my breasts, and I could feel a bulge against my thighs. I moved my leg closer to press against it.

"How much further do you want to go?" he asked, pulling away from me in a way that was agonizing.

"Just a little more."

What I meant was, "Have your way with me, sweetheart."

I realized I was supposed to be participating, so I slid down and tugged at his boxers, releasing his penis, which sprang to attention.

It was perfect, I thought as I put my mouth over it.

"Oh, honey," he sighed.

He didn't do that annoying thing some men do and push my face onto his penis, pumping away. He let me lick as I wanted, swirling motions along the head, then deeper to the back of my throat. I liked it as much as he did.

"I need to get inside you," he groaned.

He rolled me over and used his fingers to find my entrance, pushing into me in one smooth motion. We both made the same noise.

And then, suddenly, I couldn't feel him anymore.

"Sorry," he said, pulling out his flaccid penis. "Sometimes the plumbing doesn't work the way it should."

"It's OK," I lied, shocked by the sudden end to our sex.

Then Hudson used his head to move my legs open and buried his face between them, licking any reservations right out of me. He stroked me with his tongue, working my clit in one delicious motion as I rocked my hips, fighting the urge to grind on his face. He pulled away, his face slick with my wetness.

I waited uncertainly. He came up to the top of the bed and lay next to me.

Well, that's that, I thought.

But Hudson wasn't done with me yet. "Come up here," he said. "Sit on my face."

He didn't have to ask twice. I was only too willing to comply.

It wasn't the most graceful sex position, straddling his face, but I closed my eyes and grasped the carved wooden headboard for support.

He lifted his head up until even the tip of his nose was in me, moving his tongue from side to side and in circular motions, pulling me squarely down on him until I was afraid I'd suffocate him. After a while, I didn't care about anything other than the tremors running up and down my legs, the exquisite sensation of him tonguing my engorged clit as I rode the waves.

But it seemed the longer he licked, the harder it was to even approach orgasm. I would get to the edge of the cliff, right there, ready to jump off, then all of a sudden, I was all the way back from the ledge...the female equivalent of performance anxiety.

"I have trouble getting off," I said apologetically, moving carefully, reluctantly off him and lying back down.

Hudson laughed. "All women have trouble reaching orgasm." He wiped his chin. "You taste good."

Give and receive, I thought. It was time to concentrate on him again.

I was pretty confident in my ability to get him off orally, or at least put on a good show trying. I ran my hands all over his chest and ridiculously flat stomach (he wasn't kidding about being a hiker/biker/runner) and down to his thighs, deliberately avoiding his pelvis.

He moved his hips to one side to try to reach my fingers, but I stayed away until he pressed his erection against my shoulder, and then neither of us could wait. I took him in my mouth, pumping slowly at first, then steadily, as he held my hair out of the way to watch closely.

This time, thankfully, he stayed hard the whole time.

"God, you're good," he said, his breath catching in his throat.

I didn't even have time to wonder if he would finish; his whole body spasmed as he came, a warm stream down my throat, and all I had to do was take one big gulp and swallow.

"Here." He sat up. "Let me get you a washcloth. You don't have to—"

I pushed him back down on the bed. "I already did, honey."

"Was it too much?" Hudson looked worried.

It wasn't the first time a man had ever asked me about the volume of his ejaculation. What was it with volume? The more the better? Not really.

"It was fine."

"Good, because it's been a while."

I crawled up the bed to him.

"Do you want to spend the night?" he asked, pulling me into his arms, tucking my head against his chest. I couldn't think of any reason not to.

He eased off the bed, giving me a chance to take in the full glory of his muscular butt, with those round concaves at the hips you get when you're really fit. I'd never had them and had rarely seen them.

At his dresser, Hudson pulled out a laundry-fresh white T-shirt, all soft and silky. "Is this all right?"

It was so nice that I wondered how I could manage to sneak it home and keep it.

I waited until he was pulling on his own shirt to bolt for the bathroom, hoping fervently he wasn't checking out my ass. In his bathroom, I tried to wipe off my horrendously smeared mascara with water and Kleenex.

Hudson came in with a new toothbrush. "For you."

It was a fancy angled toothbrush with a neon handle, not one of those crappy ones they give you for free at the dentist.

"I'm sorry—I'll be just a minute. I have to take Chloe out. Be right back."

I leaped into the oversized bed before Hudson could get back inside, pulling the sheet up but leaving my shoulders showing and fluffing my hair against the pillow in a way I hoped looked seductive and youthful.

Hudson came back in with a bottle of water for my nightstand. "Anything else you need? What can I get you? Is it too warm in here?"

There was a slight breeze from the ceiling fan over the bed, making the temperature about as close to perfect as it could get.

He eased into the bed as if he were afraid of jostling me. I settled my face on his pillow.

"Good night, honey," he said, already half asleep.

"Night, Hudson."

I tried hard to fall asleep in the crook of his arm, but my forehead started to sweat, making my hair stick to my neck, so I had to move carefully away. Hudson slept as silently as my kids had when they were little, so deeply I used to shake them to make sure they were still breathing.

In the middle of night I got up to pee, feeling for the light switch in the dark bathroom. His toilet was in a little room of its own. Private. When I got back into bed, Hudson was turned on his side away from me. I touched his back then leaned in and covered his shoulders with kisses.

Sometime later, Hudson got out a remote control and turned the ceiling fan off. "Your arms felt cold," he said, tucking the blanket carefully over me, smoothing out the folds.

At last, we both slept.

I rolled over at the sound of the front door opening, feeling for Hudson on his side of the bed. It was empty, but still warm.

"Hi, baby," Hudson said in the doorway as he unleashed Chloe. "Did we wake you?"

"No. What time is it?"

"Just after 8:00. How'd you sleep?"

"Really good," I said. It had been a deep, dreamless sleep and I'd forgotten where I was.

"Did I snore?"

"Not at all."

Hudson leaned into the bed to give me a big squeeze. I turned my head away, hoping he couldn't smell my morning breath, patting him awkwardly on the back.

"Shower time?"

"It is."

"I put some shampoo in the guest bathroom for you. I hope it's OK. It's some extras of mine. I think I have too many hair products for a guy," he said sheepishly.

Taking a left at the kitchen, I got lost looking for the luxe bathroom he'd called mine. I had to call Hudson to show me the way. I smiled at the bottles lined up in neat rows on the countertop. There was an amazing array of shampoos and conditioners and spray leave-in frizz tamers. No wonder his hair was always so soft.

After turning on the shower, I went to stare at myself in the mirror. I looked like someone who'd been having sex all night without sleep. As the mirror steamed, I couldn't help myself. I started poking around the drawers.

In the back was a half-full bottle of nail polish remover sealed in a plastic ziplock bag. A small blue comb that looked brand new was in the second drawer. In the bottom drawer was a powder compact I didn't bother to open. The items looked old, almost dusty, as if they'd been there for years.

By the time I emerged from the bathroom, delicious smells of breakfast were coming from the kitchen.

"What can I do to help?" I asked, tousling my hair while his back was turned. I'd put on too much leave-in conditioner and my curls had gone flat.

"Not a thing. Just relax and drink your mimosa."

Hudson was wearing a black T-shirt with the word GENUINE across the chest, his hair still wet from the shower. A slender champagne flute was on the countertop, and I slid into the barstool without complaint.

"You like your eggs any certain way?"

"However you make them."

Hudson expertly chopped yellow peppers, cherry tomatoes, and zucchini on a cutting board and slid them into a copper-bottomed skillet to simmer.

"Remind me to give you some tomatoes before you leave."

"You have a garden?" I asked incredulously.

"Yeah, I like to grow my own veggies. Part of being healthy."

Over plates of the best omelet I'd ever tasted, I caught Hudson looking intently at me. I hoped there wasn't Swiss cheese on my face.

"I can't figure you out, Jess. Usually I know by the first couple of dates if we're a match."

"Fish said we were a match," I said, trying to discreetly wipe my chin. And I agreed wholeheartedly.

"We'll see," he said, taking my empty plate.

Hudson wiped down the counter with a dish towel, then folded it carefully in thirds and hung it in the center of the oven door rack. A minute later, he reached for it again, refolding exactly the same way after he'd used it.

No wonder his house looked so perfect.

"Thing is, I don't like to invest a lot of time into something I don't think will go the distance."

I wondered what that meant, but I was too busy enjoying the bubbles in the mimosa.

"I've just recently become aware of my own mortality," he said, looking very serious.

"Don't be silly. You're a very young grandfather."

"No, I mean I want someone to spend the next twenty-five years with. I'm starting to feel like I'm running out of time. In ten years, I'll be almost seventy," he said, turning away to soap up the egg pan.

"We have all the time in the world, sweetie," I said, draining my champagne flute.

63

"ONE WORD," EDDIE SAID DECISIVELY. "VIAGRA."

It was Sunday and I'd told Eddie all the details, including my surprise at the sudden loss of Hudson's erection.

"I can't talk to him about that."

"If not you, who will?"

I thought for a moment. The owner of the comb in the bathroom had to have dealt with the same situation. Was Viagra discussed then?

"Anyway, it doesn't matter," I said. "He rallied and came through beautifully. Get it? He came through?"

"Ha ha. I get it. Men age badly in that department," Eddie said, pulling a grape out of the fruit bowl. "I've always thought they should have Viagra vending machines, you know, like the ones for condoms?"

"Great idea! Let's do it before someone else thinks of it."

"Or maybe just send him some Viagra free trial coupons in the mail, anonymously."

I swatted Eddie with a dish towel, knowing I couldn't bring up the subject with Hudson so early in the relationship. Maybe down the line. I was surprised he hadn't talked to a doctor about it. Didn't he know it was very common?

Honestly, I didn't care about the temporary lapse in Hudson's potency. We'd done just fine, the two of us. There was more to sex than just thrusting.

"Oh good lord, Jess, you're practically glowing," Eddie said, shaking his head.

64

"Good morning, beautiful," Hudson texted me Monday before I even got out of bed.

Hudson was an amazing texter. He began every sentence with "hon" or "sweetie" or "baby." I locked most of his messages to save forever.

"You make me feel very special."

"You are special, Jess."

I began to lean in on his praise and affection for me, something I relied on even as I felt a nagging sense of disbelief that someone so sweet had come into my life—through a dating site, no less!

We joked about the toothpaste I'd wiped on my teeth in my kitchen just before he'd arrived. About the way he folded his dishtowels. Even about his spotless house.

"I'm a little OCD," Hudson said.

I didn't care. I just thought of him as amazing.

"Turn over so I can kiss your back," he told me in bed.

"You're tickling me."

"I'm loving you, my sexy kitty," he said.

Even our dogs were crazy about each other.

Penny and Chloe were close enough in age and size to be great companions. We started taking them for walks after Hudson closed up his shop, covering blocks of Meredia until all four of us were tired. I always ended up carrying Pen-Pen because she got winded even before I did.

We walked downtown and I showed him my work neighborhood, pointing out the deli where I sometimes got a turkey wrap, Brew Coffee where Joe and his buds had standing orders for danish, Stone Soup Antiques, and the barber shop that gave Ian a great, precise clean-edge cut.

"I should go there," Hudson said. "I could use a new barber."

"But your hair is perfect!"

"Aw, you're biased," he said, pulling me close to kiss my neck.

We were all thirsty, so I unlocked the town hall to get us drinks from the water cooler.

Under the glow of the street lights, without the fluorescent overhead lights, ringing phones, nonstop chatter of the men, and the buzzing fax machine, the office was quiet, quaint, and almost charming, like someone's Victorian sitting room—except with desks instead of Queen Anne chairs.

"Here, let me get the full effect," Hudson said, pulling out my desk chair and ushering me into it, then going back to stand in front of the counter, as if he had just walked in.

"Do I look professional?" I pursed my lips at him.

"Very much so."

"Do I look like I won't take any excuses for not paying your water bill?"

"Honey, you look like you won't take shit from anyone," he said, coming back to stand behind me.

"Good, because I won't," I said, as he spun my chair around to face him.

The tired dogs had settled down, side-by-side, on the carpet by the vault. The only sound was the gentle click of the time clock and the hum of the radiator.

"Start up your computer, baby," Hudson said.

"I can't go on porn sites," I laughed. "Joe checks my Google history. I swear, he does."

"Joe barely knows how to open the vault. But it's not porn I'm after. It's you I want."

Hudson found a jazz Pandora station and turned it on softly. Smiling, he reached down and gathered up my hair, tousling it first, then pulling it up and off my face.

"Lovely."

"Not really!"

"Shhhhh," he said, pulling me up into his arms and kissing me with a fierceness that no longer surprised me. It was just his way.

"The police station is just across the street, you know."

"I know. I'm not planning on committing any crimes. Not crimes against society, anyway."

He pulled my hoodie gently away from my waist, running his hands around the edge of my jeans. Without a word, I held up my arms for him to take the hoodie off me. Before he could ask, I slid out of my jeans, standing in only my undies by my desk chair. I did a quick spin to show him all of me. My modesty had long before gone out the window.

"You little tease," he said, stroking my legs, using the tips of his fingers to find me already wet and ready.

"Um," I said, already unable to form words. Having Hudson at the office at night was an incredible turn-on. How many times had I fantasized about having sex with him at work? Too many to count.

"Do you want it, honey?"

"I do," I breathed, swaying into him slightly.

"How do you want it?" There were too many choices, all of them delicious. "Take me in your mouth, sweetie," he said. "Please."

I got on my knees in front of him, praying his zipper would open easily, because my hands were shaky. I slid him into my mouth, licking the head the way he said he liked it best, then using my hand to stroke while I sucked.

"Stop, stop," he said, moving slightly away. "I want to come inside you."

I wiped drool from my chin. "How do you want me?"

Without a word, Hudson pulled me to my feet and turned me toward my desk, holding his penis so he would stay hard. He pressed slowly on my shoulders until I was leaning over, then pushed into me in one smooth motion.

Our noises woke the dogs, but we didn't care. I bent over my desk, crumpling papers with my damp elbows, thrashing my hips back toward him, slamming really, opening my legs wider so he could press harder.

"My juicy little puss," he breathed into my back, licking the salt off my neck. "You're mine."

"I'm yours."

Groaning and shuddering, Hudson came, heaving, falling out of me as our juices dribbled down my thighs. I grabbed a handful of Kleenex from the box on my desk.

"I'm so sorry," he panted. "I didn't mean to make a mess."

"Completely worth it," I said, wiping myself. "Now I have something to think about at work."

Chloe was raring to go, but Pen was sleeping, so I cuddled her in my arms and carried her home. It was late by the time we walked back to my house.

Hudson turned to me after he settled Chloe in the Jeep. "I'm loving everything about you."

And that meant—what?!?

I was definitely on the happy train, doing a little dance in the kitchen. Penny tipped her head sideways, as if she were trying to figure me out.

65

"SOMETHING'S WRONG," I TEXTED EDDIE TWO WEEKS LATER.

"Trouble in Erection Land?"

"No, jerk, and stop calling it Erection Land. But it is about Hudson. He doesn't call me honey or sweetie anymore, and he isn't putting xxxooo at the end of his texts."

"That's a real first-world problem."

"I'm serious! And when he texted me good morning, he said, 'Have a nice day.'"

"What the hell's wrong with that?"

"He usually texts all the time, all day. Why would he say have a nice day?"

"Jess, you're letting yourself get too far ahead. He's probably busy at the shop."

"I don't know."

"So, he didn't call you sweetheart—what did he call you?"

"Jessica."

"News flash. That's your name."

"I feel like I'm in grade school when people call me by my full name."

"What do you call him?"

"OK. Hudson. Or sometimes Huddy."

"Well I'm sure he isn't insulted by you using his name."

Damn Eddie for being so logical. Still, I couldn't ignore the nagging worry that gave me a stress headache that only got worse as the day wore on.

That night, Hudson called around 5:00, which was unusual because he didn't ever close the shop before 8:30. He must still have been at work.

"Did you have a crazy day?"

"Yeah, some custom balusters weren't up to spec," he said, sounding tired.

"So they won't pass inspection?"

"Nope. So I took over the job myself."

"Why don't you have one of the other guys do the job?" I asked, looking inside the fridge for something easy to make for dinner and wishing I hadn't eaten the last quinoa burger.

"I don't trust anyone else."

This was true. Hudson had a team of designers and builders, but often said he had to oversee them to make sure they were doing things the right way. It was his company, and everything had to be done to perfection.

"I'm sorry." I pulled out leftover pasta, hoping Ian hadn't eaten the last meatball. "Well, I had quite a day. This old lady called to complain about someone throwing garbage over her side of the fence, but it turned out no one lived there! So, she has some kids tossing garbage, which is really too bad. Dumb Wes thought maybe she was littering her own backyard. Who would do that?"

I was still laughing at the incident.

"Uh-huh," Hudson's voice sounded far away.

"So, what are you doing later?" I opened some Tupperware and prodded the spaghetti with a fork, looking for meatballs. "Do you want to take the dogs for a walk? Or we could —"

"Listen, we have to talk," he interrupted.

I was startled by the serious tone of his voice.

"I should probably do this in person, but—"

"Do what? I'm not following you."

"Here's the thing," he started, stopped, then started again. "I just don't think we're a match. I don't see us together in the future."

"What are you talking about?" I asked, dropping the container of dinner food into the sink.

The phone went quiet.

"Are you still there?" I asked, my voice cracking.

"I am," he said, his voice eerily calm. "There's a little voice in my head that keeps saying it's not right, and I've got to listen to it."

I felt the sickness in my stomach rising to my throat.

"What's not right? I don't understand."

"You and me. We aren't meant for each other."

"I don't understand," I said again.

"All right. When I look into the future, say five years down the line, I don't see myself with you."

"But no one can predict the future; there's no crystal ball," I said, wiping my eyes with the back of my sleeve. "And who would want one? We just need to take it as it comes. See what happens."

"I can't do that, Jessica. You're not the one for me. There really isn't anything else to say."

I slid down to my knees on my kitchen floor.

There was dead silence on the phone. From out the open window, I could hear cars going by and kids laughing and even Penny scratching at the front door to come in. I couldn't move.

"You still have a hoodie at my house. I'll leave it on your porch."

"Don't come here," I said, pressing my forehead against the wall.

I didn't get up off the floor until Eddie got there twenty minutes later.

"He couldn't get it up anyway," Eddie said later, apparently trying to be helpful.

"That only happened a couple of times," I yelled at him, furious at myself for having shared that with Eddie. I still felt protective of Hudson.

"And he was obsessive about his perfect house. Didn't he, like, vacuum up every last dog hair?"

Thinking of Chloe made me cry even harder.

Nothing Eddie said helped. Neither did the sobbing I did into his shoulder.

"Shush," he said, rocking me like a child.

"This one could break me," I said, leaning on his shoulder.

"Never," Eddie said, pulling me closer into his arms. "Not in this lifetime, Jess."

66

MONDAY, I WANTED SO BADLY TO CALL IN SICK, BUT JUDGING BY THE WAY I felt when I took to my bed after Bryan left, it would be even worse to stay home. I hadn't slept more than thirty minutes at a time. I cried so hard my pillowcase was damp. Penny, my little life-saver, stayed awake with me all night while I wailed, kicked my feet, and punched at the blankets, finally throwing them all on the floor.

I pictured Hudson in his king's bed, sleeping like a baby now that he'd tossed me to the curb.

What the fuck had happened?

He didn't see me in his future? We'd never even talked about the future! I hadn't asked him for anything! Had I pictured myself in his beautiful house, writing at the dining room table while Pen and Chloe had puppy play time and Hudson made dinner? Sure, I had. Absolutely. But I had never told him this fantasy. Not a single word.

He had called me juicy! Kissed the small of my back. Said he was loving every part of me.

Things made no more sense at dawn than they had at midnight. I pulled on the same clothes I'd worn to work the day before, as if doing that would take back the day and Hudson's terrible words.

When I got there, Wes and Joe were already arguing. This morning's inane subject: what type of clouds were gathering over Brew Coffee on the corner.

"Those fluffy ones, cornelius, they don't mean rain," Wes said, scratching his ear then looking at his finger.

"Cumulus, you idiot," said Joe, who abandoned his desk and sat at the conference table with his friends. "It's them voracious clouds you need to worry about."

"I think you mean cirrus," I said, immediately regretting it because it might have drawn me into the conversation, and I just wasn't in the mood to be cheered up by their silliness.

The men switched topics entirely, launching into a detailed conversation about how many fire trucks were in last year's Memorial Day parade.

I pulled out my cell. Madison had deleted all Hudson's messages, even those I'd locked, and his cell number from my directory, but what she hadn't thought of was deleting his incoming calls from my dial log. It made my stomach lurch to see how frequently he'd called me: first thing in the morning, during my lunch half-hour, at bedtime.

I worked on auto-pilot while the guys' discussion branched out to historic facts, or rather, their lack of ability to distinguish fact from fiction. I skipped lunch and ate a handful of almonds for dinner, thinking maybe I could go on some sort of grief diet. I pictured myself running into Hudson at the grocery store weeks from now wearing leggings so loose they were hanging off me. My cart would be full of fresh produce and his with boxed mac and cheese because his garden had been consumed by worms.

It was agony not to text him.

I felt like if I could find the right words, I could make him understand I wasn't wrong for him. That we were right for each other. Who looked ahead five years down the line? I went back and forth between disbelief and shock and a mind-numbing sense of loss all the long hours of the day.

I got immediately into pajamas when I got home. Already on the grief diet, I had Cheerios for supper. I had to text him, to appeal to him. Maybe he would say he'd given it some thought and regretted his words. He'd had a lousy day at the shop. He hadn't been thinking clearly.

He must have realized by now that he loved me too.

I held out until 8 p.m. when I knew Hudson would be leaving the shop to go home.

"I miss you," I texted.

Disgusted with myself, I picked Penny up and carried her to the tub, washing her with my hydrating shampoo and thinking about the bathroom at Hudson's that he'd said was mine. Who does that?

I'd turned up the volume on my cell, and when it beeped with an incoming message, I let go of Pen to grab my phone. She immediately jumped from the tub and ran into my bedroom to dry herself on my comforter.

It was an email from Groupon for a night's stay in Vermont, with a fruit basket and complimentary red wine.

"Do you miss me?" I hit send before I had the good sense to delete my text.

Hudson's reply came back a few minutes later. "Most of what I'm feeling is relief."

I was stunned, then I was furious. No, I was beyond furious. But this time, I wouldn't let myself sink to the floor. At that moment, I knew we weren't ever meant to be together, because he was a complete dick. A limp one, at that.

Penny came to my side and nudged my leg. She was a ball of static fluff, with shampoo suds still on her nose.

"Come on, let's get you rinsed off," I said. "And if you have any advice for getting over an asshole guy, please share it."

67

"Maybe don't fall in love so fast," Maddy said. "That tends to freak guys out."

"I was so happy," I wailed. "Now I feel so foolish. I'm mad at myself. I'm mad at him. I'm just plain mad!"

"I know. It's OK."

She stood up and opened the pantry door. "What do you have to eat in here? What are these?" she asked, pulling out my package of Fig Newtons. "Something new?"

"I had a craving," I said miserably. "In fact, hand them over."

We ate in silence for a minute.

"It's not OK! He was supposed to be The One! I thought he was The One! I thought I was his One!"

"You said you didn't believe in The One," Madd said calmly. "But it wasn't him. I thought he was kind of fake."

"You met him only once!" I wailed some more, leaning down to scoop up Penny for sympathy.

"Well, first impressions count."

"I had to sit there at work, where we had sex at my desk, knowing he doesn't care anymore, he just cut me off—"

"Whoa, whoa, whoa," Madison held up her hand. "You had sex at work? When was this?"

"I don't know, a few weeks ago," I said, avoiding eye contact.

"Ohhh, bad idea right there. Isn't the police station, like, right across the street?"

"I don't care," I said. "I don't care about anything but getting him back."

"Why would you want him, anyway? He said he felt relieved it was over! Dickwad."

I had to agree; he was a dick. But I remembered the weekend at his house, when everything had seemed so great. Perfect, even. Had I been seeing just what I wanted to see? Was he pretending to be someone he wasn't? I had no answers. I did, however, have a headache.

"What's your plan now? You always have a plan," Maddy said.

"I have no plan," I said, trying not to sound completely self-pitying.

"Amazon shopping spree?"

"Maybe," I said, my mood lightening for an instant.

"Going back on Fish?"

"Yeah, 'cause that's worked well for me so far," I said morosely.

I drank deeply from my glass of room-temp tap water, remembering how Hudson always gave me bottled water in a fancy glass, with a fresh slice of lemon. I'd taken my Fish profile down after the first date with Hudson, and he'd done the same. Most likely, his was already back up on Fish looking for The One.

"Well, good. Maybe it's time to take a little break," Madison said, looking very serious. "When's the last time you were by yourself?"

"I've been alone!" I cried. "After Bryan left and before I dated that shithead Michael."

"That was months, Mombo," Madd said patiently. "That barely counts."

Truth be told, I hadn't been alone since I'd met Adam in college. I'd moved from my mother's house straight into my first apartment with Adam, and when that marriage failed, I'd met Bryan very quickly afterward. Too soon? Maybe.

"Don't tell me to read books on being my own best friend and draw smiley faces on Post-Its to stick all over the house," I said, wishing I didn't sound so shrill.

Madison sighed. "It seems to me you're afraid of being alone."

"Well, I'm not. Not at all."

"Just an observation," Madd said, opening the fridge and pulling a peach from the fruit drawer.

Later, with Penny dozing on my feet in bed, after ordering peanut butter dog chews, chandelier earrings, and black-and-orange striped tights on Amazon, I heard the question over and over in my head. Was I afraid to be alone?

What was I afraid of?

It came to me hours later, when Pen was snoring but I was wide awake. I was afraid. I had many fears, but they all boiled down to this: I was afraid I had become unlovable. That no man would ever love me the way I loved him.

That, and spinsterhood.

When the kids were small, there was a farm up the road with a makeshift wooden produce stand where we could buy berries and corn and zucchini. We called the farmer Mr. Zucchini because he grew the most enormous squash we had ever seen—not just then, but even to this day. We couldn't figure out when he stocked his farm stand. We never saw him outside, so we decided he only went out at night. He was a mystery man. All the neighborhood parents liked to tease the kids that on Halloween, Mr. Zucchini gave away dried squash chips and flattened blueberries, something that made them avoid the farmhouse altogether.

One summer several years later, the veggie stand stayed empty. Another mom in the neighborhood said Mr. Zucchini had passed away. None of us had ever known the elusive farmer, but at the end of that summer, Mrs. Zucchini started sitting by the empty produce stand in a little red folding chair, holding a rain umbrella over her head to keep the sun off her face.

She always had a tabby cat dozing on her lap. I came to think of her as the lonely cat lady. I waved at her from my air-conditioned car while she sat in the sweltering heat. I didn't even know her real name, but without produce in the stand, there was no reason to stop.

One day when I slowed down to wave, I saw her dabbing her eyes with a handkerchief. I knew she was lonely and missed her husband, but I was busy with the kids and back-to-school time. The next summer, Mrs. Zucchini stayed inside, and a few years later, she died. The farmhouse was sold, the produce stand dismantled.

I didn't want to become Mrs. Zucchini with a cat and an umbrella in the summer and no one stopping to visit. I'd tried not to think about the passage of time, but here I was, almost twenty years later, and I didn't have young children to take care of any longer.

Most of all, I didn't want Ian and Madison to feel responsible for keeping me company. I wanted them to live their lives independently from me, maybe have dinner with me sometimes, or lounge around on a Saturday and tell me about their week. Bring the grandkids to visit.

But there was something more. What else was I afraid to face?

And then I knew. I was worried that maybe the best years of my life had come and gone. The kids had been my whole life for two decades.

I'd been completely immersed in being a mom. I loved every second of it and would do it all again in a heartbeat. Maybe in the afterlife.

But there wasn't any going back, just moving forward, and I needed to square my shoulders and keep my chin up and take whatever was coming my way. Maybe even embrace it. I was stronger than I'd been in my marriages, I realized, no longer trying to fill an empty space. Maybe I'd been whole all along.

I'd slept with my arm hanging off the bed after Bryan left, leaving Penny with plenty of room to herself. But the next morning, I woke up in the middle, my arms flung out, stretched out on my back, taking up most of the bed, actually crowding my little dog.

I was an unmarried adult woman, feeling, for the first time, something close to exhilaration.

68

"How are things?" I texted Bryan before I went to work one morning in February. It was nearly the one-year anniversary of his move south.

I didn't get a reply until I was at my desk wrestling with the purchase order software. Wes, Sal, and Paulie gathered around the conference table, already getting excited about the 17th annual strawberry fest, which wasn't until June. They were in a heated debate over whose wife would make the best shortcake.

Joe was feeding Jerky some of the peanut butter dog snacks I'd brought in.

"We have news," Bry texted back.

I snuck my phone into my pocket, feeling ridiculous, and went into the bathroom, turning on the water so they'd think I was washing my hands, as if I were doing something wrong texting in there.

"We?"

"Sarah and me...I asked her to marry me, and she said yes. We're engaged!"

I had been examining my gray roots in the bathroom mirror, trying to remember when I had last visited the salon to have them colored.

Engaged? What?

I put down the toilet seat, cursing the damn unisex bathroom, and sat down, my knees actually shaking.

"That's great," I texted back. "So great."

"I know. I never thought she'd say yes, but she told me she knew I was The One the first time she laid eyes on me."

I closed my eyes. There it was again. The One. The Fucking One. Had I ever been anybody's One? Had I been Adam's? Bryan's? I shook my head. None of that mattered now. Adam had his RV life, and now Bryan had the new love of his life. In less than a year. I tried to remember when he'd told me he met Sarah but came up blank. Three months before? Anyway, it was within a few months of leaving New York.

I had a sudden, vivid image of Bryan's face at our small, unfussy wedding ceremony, calm and peaceful as if it weren't even a big step for him to marry me, as if it was meant to be. Later, we'd toasted each other with sangria and fed each other meatballs at the Italian restaurant, and he'd leaned over to whisper something in my ear.

"Thank you for having me," he'd said.

"My pleasure," I'd whispered back.

I was grateful for all the good years with Bryan. I wanted him to be happy, and I knew it wasn't with me. But to fall in love so quickly—out of nowhere, really—with a swimsuit model/teacher? How had that happened?

Was it fate? Dumb luck? Did that mean, by contrast, I was cursed with bad luck? I knew it made no sense comparing myself to Bryan, but we had been husband and wife, and now he would be with swimsuit-model-worthy Sarah. And I couldn't even find a steady boyfriend.

Great—now I was a melodramatic spinster on a pity train. I put my phone on my lap to rub my throbbing temples.

"How are the kids?" Bryan texted when I picked up my phone again.

"Good. Really good. Madd loves her job and met someone she really likes. Ian is doing great at school and has decided to let nature take its course and meet someone organically, as he says."

"Tell them I said hi," Bryan texted.

"Sure will."

"How's that cutie pie Ben, and Cassie?"

"Ben is a real handful, such a personality, and Cassie's going to night school to be an X-ray technician."

"Cool," I texted.

"Hey Jess? I wanted to thank you."

"For what?"

"For letting me go. For knowing it was the right thing."

It was suddenly ragingly hot in the bathroom, and I stood up to pace, as much as I could pace from the toilet to the sink to the paper towel dispenser.

What to say? What to say? You're welcome? It was my pleasure letting you go? Neither of these was true. It had been wrenching. I'd felt like I had taken a direct hit to the back of my knees when Bryan had left. More than once, I'd wanted to get in the car and drive all night to North Carolina to find him and beg him to come back.

But I hadn't. I hadn't, because I knew both of us needed—deserved—more than what our marriage had become. We had stopped bringing out the best in each other. The laughter had gone silent. We had to separate to even be friends again. I had never regretted meeting, being with, and marrying Bryan. He had been in my path. He was part of my story. He always would be.

I had grown stronger during my single life after Bryan, and if he was grateful, so was I.

"I'm glad it all worked out," I texted.

It was meant to be. He was meant to be happy. He was meant to be free.

"Keep in touch," was his last text.

I went to the sink to wash my hands. The soap dispenser held nothing but a few watery bubbles at the bottom. Did no one else but me notice these things?

"Geez, did you fall in?" Wes asked, guffawing, when I emerged from the bathroom.

"Here's a new batch," Joe said, adding to the pile of invoices on my desk.

"The secret is how much lard you use," Sal said, speaking way too loud for the office.

Use your indoor voice, I wanted to tell him.

"No, it's the sugar that's the thing," Paulie rallied back. "Use too much, and the berries bleed all over."

"It's neither," Wes said. "It's the ripeness of the berries. You pick them even a day too early, you'll end up with sour strawberries. Too late, and they're soft."

"None of your wives won best shortcake last year," Joe yelled over the counter. "It was Marla Stokes, remember? The newcomer."

I'd heard them mention Marla before because it was rumored she was sleeping with the planning board chairman. As for being a newcomer, she'd lived in Meredia eight years.

"Yeah, well, she was probably screwing the judge," Sal said, wiping his nose on his sleeve.

"Probably," Wes grunted, chortling.

I was happy for Bryan, I realized. Fully happy. Happy enough to let the town comedians jabber on down another nonsensical tangent, entertaining one another and even me.

Whatever was next, I decided I would be open to possibility. Every day carried the potential to bring something new and unexpected. And that was a good way to live, working very hard to trust the universe.

69

Online, BoldMan was wearing a ski hat, about to take a run down a steep cliff-like hill, looking like an excited kid. So what if I didn't ski—I could wait in the lodge by the fireplace, right?

He was fifty-nine, which was great, but unfortunately, lived more than two hours away, which could pose a significant logistical challenge.

His profile left much to the imagination: he only said he liked to ski, hike (of course), swim, and hang out with his kids.

It was worth a shot.

"You don't give much away in your profile," I messaged Bold. "Are you waiting for someone to ask the right questions?"

"Ask away." His response came within minutes.

"What's your name?"

"Daniel. Yours?"

"Jessica. How old are your kids?"

"Twenty-nine and thirty-two. Yours?"

"Twenty-one and twenty-five. So you ski?"

"Love it. You?"

"I'm more of a ski fan, like, I watch the winter Olympics. Winter your favorite season?"

"Summer," Daniel replied. "Yours?"

"Fall. Orange leaves, a snap in the air, no humidity."

"Yeah, humidity does terrible things to my hair." Which was a joke, because his head was shaved in all his photos.

I defaulted to my speed dating questions, which he returned with some of his own.

"So, would you take a trip to a beach or to mountains?"

"Beach, hands down," Daniel replied. "Morning person or night owl?"

"Mornings suck."

"You've got it there. Everything good happens at night. Dogs or cats?"

"Definitely dogs. I have a little one sleeping on my feet right now. Literally, on my feet."

"Small dogs for sure. I have four that rule the house!" Daniel wrote. "Long hair or short?"

"On a dog?"

"No, yours," he replied. "I'm looking at your profile pictures right now, Jess. Is your hair still long?"

"Got it trimmed recently, just the ends."

"It's very pretty," Daniel wrote. "I like it long."

"Thank you."

"Hey, I hate messaging through this site, I'd much rather text. Sound good to you?"

"Absolutely," I replied, sending him my cell number.

That was the first step in online dating intimacy—switching from using the site to message to actual texting, which involved sharing phone numbers. My kids, of course, told me to never give out my cell number, because if things didn't work out with a guy, it would be easier for him to stalk me.

Daniel didn't seem like the stalker type.

His first text came across. "Will you send me some photos of yourself? I'm a very visual person."

"There are four photos on Fish," I reminded him.

"I want close-ups."

Hmm. I wasn't really a selfie person. I always looked uncomfortable and never knew whether to smile with teeth or closed lips. Whichever I chose looked unnatural.

"Will you do it for me?" Daniel texted.

I got out of bed and looked at myself in the mirror. Not exactly camera ready, my hair was tousled, eyeliner faded, and lipstick nonexistent.

"I look like shit," I told him.

"I doubt that. Send some."

So I made funny faces, sticking out my tongue and scrunching up my face, sending him the silliest ones.

"You're something else, Jess."

"I'll take that as a compliment."

"That's how it's meant," he said.

"Where were we in our conversation?"

"Do you wear sundresses or shorts?"

"Shorts and sneakers. Swimming or kayaking?" I was trying to come up with questions that might make me look somewhat athletic.

"Depends. Is it skinny dipping?"

Hm. I thought about that one. I couldn't remember the last time I'd shed my clothes for a swim.

"Do you skinny dip?" I was too curious to pass up the chance to find out.

"All the time. My mother has a lake house and I go in after dark. It's very quiet and secluded."

"Alone?"

"Sometimes yes, other times no."

I was oddly jealous of the women he'd taken a swim with, which made no sense, because I didn't even know him.

And so, since we were both night people, we spent the next two hours texting. He told me about his idyllic childhood, raised with two sisters who argued over who would take care of him when his parents were out, how his dogs once ate an entire coconut cream pie, how much he'd missed his daughter when she moved out and went to Michigan for a job.

"Yeah, I'm really lucky to have both my kids around," I texted. "Don't know what I'd do without them."

Turned out that both of us were language and grammar snobs. We compared notes on the worst offenses.

"I could care less," I texted.

"Supposably," he replied.

"I ain't got none."

"You don't need to water it or nothing."

"There, their, and they're."

"Your a good writter," Daniel texted. "Im impressed by you're spelling."

"LOL. Your pretty amazing to."

"We could do this all day," he texted.

Soon we were debating whether it was lonely being single.

"I'm happy being alone," Daniel texted. "I have a lot of things that keep me busy."

"Such as?"

"I have a lot of projects going at my house, and I have a home gym and work out every day."

Oh geez, I thought. Another fitness nut, probably in better shape than me. Probably? Definitely.

"Tell me something personal, Jess," he texted next.

I came up blank. "You go first."

"OK. I have Lyme Disease."

"OMG, I'm so sorry. Was it a tick?"

"Yes. Eight years ago, after a hike. On my shoulder."

"Did it stick on you a long time?"

"It dug right in. Then I took some bad advice and tried all the ways I shouldn't have to get it out."

"Like what?"

"Scratching at it with a credit card, rubbing alcohol, burning it. And all the time I was torturing it, it was seeping poison into my bloodstream. It was a mess by the time I went to the hospital."

I wiped my sweaty forehead, feeling sick at the image. Fucking tick. "Did you get sick right away?"

"I had partial paralysis. For two months I couldn't use that side of my body. I lost thirty pounds."

OK, the weight loss doesn't sound so bad, I thought, then I kicked myself for thinking that. Of course it was awful, and from his pictures, he looked slender to begin with.

"Are you all right now?"

"Comes and goes," Daniel texted. "There are days I have trouble getting out of bed, but I push myself. I get tired a lot, but hate taking it easy. I never miss a day at the gym."

Good for him, I thought. I was still trying to regain my fitness.

"I'm sorry," I texted, not sure what else to say.

"Don't be. It's just something I deal with. Everyone has things going on that people can't see. This is just my thing."

"That's true. I'm glad you're OK."

"Now it's your turn," he texted.

"My turn for what?"

"Something personal, Jess. Make it a good one."

Geez. I couldn't come up with anything. I had nothing.

"Come on," Daniel texted. "Tell me what you like."

"Chocolate. Wine spritzers. White pizza. Horror movies."

I was embarrassed to see three of the four things I listed were food and drink. Couldn't I have come up with something that made me seem athletic, or at least like I got off the couch on weekends?

"I'll tell you what I like. I'm a very physical person. I love to explore."

Now he had my full attention.

"I'm also very oral." Daniel texted. "You?"

"Physical?"

"No, oral."

"I think so," I texted Daniel. "I'm not sure I know what you're saying," I lied.

"Do you like being licked?"

Well, there was a question. There it was. I read it three times. How to answer, how to answer?

"I'd love to lick you all over," Daniel texted, sparing me an answer.

My stomach lurched and I knew, at that moment, I was in deep trouble. I'd wished for adventure, and sure enough, it had found me.

"Really? We haven't even met in person yet."

"I have a really good feeling about this."

"Good night," I texted.

"Good knight, deer one," he texted back.

All that, and a sense of humor too. I was officially smitten.

70

WITHIN A DAY, DANIEL AND I WERE TEXTING CONSTANTLY, JOE GLOWER-
ing at me and jamming more files into my inbox. This, while he spent
about 6 ½ hours of his 8-hour workday shooting the shit with the
Three Stooges.

But I had plenty of work to do, so I limited my texting to lunchtime
and after work. The best texting was at night, when I stretched out on
my bed and turned on quiet music, making him seem not so far away.

We had tentative plans to meet over the coming weekend, but it
was only Tuesday.

"Tell me your dreams," Daniel texted.

"You mean like flying, or all my teeth falling out?"

"Not your nighttime dreams—what do you daydream about?"

"I don't know. I guess I think about my kids and hope they'll be
happy adults."

"I'm talking about fantasies, Jessica."

That stopped me cold.

"I fantasize about winning the lottery. LOL."

"Physically. What are your physical fantasies?"

I thought for a minute. Slimmer thighs didn't seem to be the kind
of answer he was looking for.

I took the bait. "I think about feeling so good I lose control. Like an
out-of-body experience. I don't know how to explain it."

"Ah," Daniel texted. "You want to hand over control?"

Hmmm. Did I want to?

"I guess maybe. But I'm not exactly passive or anything like that."

"Women who want to submit are usually confident, high achievers,
very much in charge of their lives. They just want someone to take
over during sex."

Submit? I had thought about it more than once.

I had an image in my mind of a woman kneeling naked before a man,
kissing his feet. Nope, that wasn't my thing. But a woman kneeling and

giving an exquisite blow job? That could work. I realized I had no idea where the line between conventional sex and erotic submissiveness was drawn. Maybe it was time to find out.

"I don't know," I texted Daniel.

"Maybe give it some thought, then. See how you feel."

I gave it some thought. I didn't know yet what he was talking about, but whatever it was, I was intrigued. Daniel seemed very confident, and I liked that about him. He was, indeed, a bold man.

71

"I MADE BROWNIES. MY HAIR SMELLS LIKE CHOCOLATE AND SUGAR," I texted Daniel.

Moments later, "My favorite things: your pretty hair and dessert."

Smiling, I sniffed my hair. "If only I could bottle this."

"I'm getting hard just thinking about you."

"Really?"

"Really. Do you want me to send you a picture?"

"Yes?"

"Only if you want me to."

"I do want it," I texted.

And Daniel sent it, and it was amazing.

"Is this sexting?" I asked.

"It is, deer. Now it's your turn," Daniel texted. "Start with your tits. Make sure your nipples are hard."

Tits? I hadn't heard that word in a long time. But it was better than calling them boobs. Take pictures of them? It was thrilling and daunting at the same time.

"Wouldn't you rather wait and see them in person?"

"I want to see what color your nipples are."

"Pink, I guess?"

"Show me."

Well, it *was* my turn, after what he'd sent me. To hell with locker-room modesty. It was about time for things to change, dramatically.

I was the only one home, but I went into the bathroom and locked the door anyway. Breathing faster, I pulled up my shirt and bra and saw I didn't even need to pinch my nipples to make them stand up. It was a new kind of selfie, I thought, my body instead of my face. My breasts looked good, as it turned out, actually quite perky and firm.

"Nice," Daniel texted after I sent it. "Now I want you to spread your legs and take a picture for me. A close-up."

"Why?"

"That's what I want. But don't do anything you don't want to do."

I felt my face flush. "It's Tuesday night," I texted back. "Do you think this is the right time for this?"

"It's always the right time, sweetie."

I realized I did want to show Daniel. Tingling all over, I went into my bathroom and closed the door.

Goddamn, it was bright with all the lights on. It was like a stage. I knew I would need soft lighting, to say the least. I peeled off my spider leggings, tangling my panties in the process.

I struggled to find the right angle, trying not to think about a visit to the gyno and putting my feet in the stirrups.

Penny, who had followed me into the bathroom, tipped her head to the side as if asking what the hell I was doing. I had no answer for her, or for myself. I shooed her out of the bathroom.

For the first six tries, I took pics of the bathroom floor tiles. Then all I caught with the cell camera was my thighs, which made me shudder until I convinced myself photos always make you look bigger than life. Finally, I had a clear close-up inside my thighs, all pink and swollen and ready for Daniel.

I didn't even hesitate before sending the photo.

"You look wet and lovely," he texted back. "Your wings are open like you're ready."

I smiled, reading the message over and over again.

72

"I HAVE SOME SIMPLE TASKS FOR YOU," DANIEL SAID THURSDAY NIGHT
after I'd settled down in bed to talk.

"I'm not going to wear a skimpy maid get-up and wash your floors
by hand."

"Damn. Really? You won't?"

"Nope."

"Well, cross that one off the list. No, seriously, I want you to start
stretching."

"Stretching?"

"Yes. I want you to limber up."

"What for?"

"So I can put you in various positions."

Positions? Like what, reverse cowgirl? Or something even more physically demanding? I tried to picture it in my mind and came up empty.

"I want you to be nice and flexible," he said, his voice calm, light,
and teasing.

"We'll be doing all these positions when we see each other this weekend?"

"Not all of them," he laughed. "We'll start out slow."

"OK. I'm not sure I'll ever be what you'd call flexible, but I can try."

I couldn't sleep, so I thought back to ninth-grade gymnastics when
the gym teacher told us to "limber up." I stood up and put my hands
down to the floor, barely grazing it with my fingertips. Bent at the waist
a few times. Rolled my arms in circles. Then I got serious, doing runner's
squats until moisture beaded up around my ears, deep lunges, lying
side lifts, standing and lifting my calves off the floor. I threw in some
stomach crunches and a couple push-ups for good measure.

I hoped it counted as going to the gym.

Then I went into the kitchen for water and some Cheetos, telling
myself the healthy no-cal water balanced out the salty Cheetos. I didn't
care. I was on my way to becoming limber, and maybe regaining my
fitness along the way.

73

"I've mailed you something I think you will like," Daniel texted.

My mind immediately leapt to Godiva chocolate, and after that, diamond jewelry, neither of which seemed plausible but made for great daydream fodder.

"What is it?"

"Patience, honey. You need to learn that, too, as one of your lessons."

I had to wait an exasperating three days until a box was sitting on my front porch. It was breezy outside, so I called Penny and sat down on the rocking chair, plumping the red anchor pillow up behind my back and settling in for something that would hopefully be a token of Daniel's feelings for me. Oh hell, just something artsy or pretty.

Inside the package was a smaller box, gossamer black, tied with a perfect black satin ribbon. Whatever it was, it was already lovely.

I tugged at the bow and carefully opened the box.

Inside, lined up in perfect rows, were twelve wooden clothespins.

A squirrel ran up the driveway, but Penny made no attempt to chase it. From down the street, I could hear the tinny sound of a bicycle bell, and wondered if it might be Lily heading my way. Instinctively, I shut the box. She might ask what was inside, and I would be unable to explain it, because I had absolutely no idea myself. Clothespins. Was I opening a laundry business?

"Come on, Pen," I said, opening the door. Penny nudged a stray leaf with her nose before following me inside.

I pulled out my cell to text Daniel. "So, I got the package."

No reply.

Clothespins. When Madison was little, she hung Barbie doll dresses on a twine clothesline across the length of her bedroom. Those clothespins were plastic and had little pink hearts on them. I had a photo of the Barbie laundry line, someplace.

"Hey, babe," Daniel texted at last.

"Hey, so yeah, I got the box."

"Did you open it?"

"Of course I opened it. I mean, I was supposed to, right?" Maybe this was one of his teasing games where he wanted me to wait. Screw that.

"So, what do you think?"

What did I think? I had no idea what to think.

"You don't want me to do your laundry, right? Because I would never do that in a million years…" I texted quickly.

"No, dear, I wouldn't ask you to do my laundry. I have something more interesting in mind. Can you guess?"

"Bedsheets? You want the sheets hung outside to dry?"

When my sister and I were young, we had a good-sized blue aluminum pool in our backyard. We spent most summer days submerged, splashing and trying to do water aerobics, staying in until our fingers wrinkled and we began shivering. We had a tattered clothes tree that always seemed shaded and never dried our swimsuits and beach towels, but I don't remember there being clothespins. We tossed the towels on the line and hoped for the best.

"It's nothing to do with laundry, silly."

"What is this, a riddle?" I kicked off my sneakers and opened the fridge for a bottle of grapefruit seltzer.

"No, dear, it's not a riddle, it's not a joke. It's serious."

"OK. Tell me."

"I want you to clamp one on your nipple and take a picture for me."

I sat down, sloshing my seltzer on the table. "You want me to do what with them?"

"Just clip them on gently. It doesn't have to hurt."

"Yeah, well, it doesn't exactly sound comfortable. Why don't you clamp your own nipples?"

"Because that wouldn't be a turn-on."

He was right about that. It wouldn't be sexy at all. There was absolutely nothing provocative about men's nipples. Nope.

I opened the box and picked one up, clipping it on my thumb. It was tight. The end of my thumb started turning purple almost immediately.

"What do you think?" Daniel texted.

"I don't know what to think." I took the clothespin off my thumb, which had started to throb. It had left small marks like little teeth in my skin.

"I know you, and you're going to try it, so just let me know later. Gotta go."

He said it didn't have to hurt. That wasn't what he was looking for. How long would I have to leave them on to take a picture? A couple of seconds?

Suddenly, the kitchen was way too warm.

I looked down at Pen, watching me closely.

"Of course I'm not going to do it," I told her, and myself.

I put the cover on the box and carried it to my room, where I put it on the floor and kicked it under my bed. Clamp my nipples. Who was he kidding?

I was less resolute when I woke around 3 a.m. Goddammit, I was intrigued. Digging under my bed, I pulled a clothespin out of the box and toyed with it. I flicked on the nightstand light and stood in front of the full-length mirror, pulling my T-shirt over my head. In the shadows, my stomach looked almost flat, as long as I didn't turn sideways. Even my face seemed more hollowed out. Night lighting was kind.

My nipples were already hard as I eased the clothespin onto my right breast.

"Holy shit!" I said out loud. It stung like hell. I pulled it off and rubbed the sore nipple.

But the left nipple was far less sensitive. Who knew?

It dangled at a strange angle, but I wasn't going to try to get it on straight. I picked up my phone and took six quick pictures. Then I eased it off. It was something I'd never seen, or ever imagined I'd do, but it was a turn-on for me to be his visual sex toy. And he said it didn't have to hurt.

I felt victorious. I felt light-headed. I felt provocative.

The only thing I didn't feel was ashamed.

All of the pictures came out clear, but some showed my whole breast and some just the clamped nipple. I sent them all to Daniel. I didn't know which he would like most.

I liked all of them.

"Did it hurt?" Daniel texted the next morning.

"No. They pinched."

Like he'd said, they hadn't hurt, but they did hold my nipples erect and left little pink marks when they came off.

"Now you're getting the hang of it, honey."

His praise was sweet like rain.

"Another thing I need to know. Do you look at porn?"

Hmm. Should I tell him about my interest in Tumblr, and in particular, the elegant black and white photos involving a woman's mouth and a penis?

"I'm sure you do," Daniel chided. "Admit it."

"OK, I'll admit it."

"Tumblr?"

"How did you know?" I was worried that, among other things, he'd become able to read my mind.

"I doubt you watch bondage videos or anything hard-core. I see you more as a Tumblr woman."

I lay down on my bed, waiting for what he would say next.

"So here's what I want: send me links to the images that get you going."

"LOL. Get me going?"

"The ones that make you wet."

Well there it was, right out on the table. He couldn't be clearer.

"What gets you hard?"

"You," he texted simply, seconds later.

It was exactly the answer I was looking for.

74

By Friday, we needed to see each other as soon as possible, which meant one of us would drive to see the other Saturday.

Daniel volunteered.

"Do you want to have dinner together?" I asked Daniel.

"I was thinking more like breakfast."

"What time are you planning to leave your house?"

"6:00 a.m."

I laughed. "Ian is going camping with his father for the weekend, and I don't think he's leaving till 9:00. Can you hold off until then?"

Saturday morning, I helped Ian pack up his gear.

"You trying to rush me out, Mom?" Ian said as he shouldered his backpack.

"Why would you say that?" I asked, my voice sounding a bit too high in pitch.

"No reason," he said, kissing my forehead. "Do something fun this weekend."

I planned to.

Twenty minutes later, Daniel pulled up to the sidewalk in a silver Cadillac Escalade.

Thankfully, he looked exactly like his photos, although his face wasn't stern, because he was clearly so pleased to see me. He had dark-brown eyes and very fine features that reminded me of someone in a painting, because the lines of his nose and chin were so elegantly sculpted. He was about 5' 11", very fit of course, with strong, broad shoulders and lean muscles in his arms. His hands were long-fingered, with the same fine bone structure as his face.

To me, he was amazing.

I'd made coffee and gone for a quick trip to Brew Coffee for fresh pastries.

"I can't believe you're really here, in my house," I said nervously as we sat down in the kitchen.

"So what do you think?" He drummed his long fingers on the table.

I tipped my head to one side the way Penny does when she's thinking.

"Not too shabby. Nice, actually." Daniel smiled. "You don't look like someone who bosses women around."

"You just never know, do you?"

"Do you ever get nervous?" I asked nervously.

"No. Are you ready to take me to your bedroom?"

"So much for small talk."

"Are you ready?" he asked again.

"Oh, I'm ready."

"This is cute," he said, looking around my room. "Now take your clothes off for me."

"Are you undressing too?"

"No. Not yet."

I tried to hide my disappointment.

"Where are they?" he asked.

"Where are what?"

"You know what I'm asking about."

I did know. I reached into my nightstand drawer and took out a fabric pouch holding the dozen wooden clothespins. "Here they are."

Daniel's smile deepened "Did you try them more than once?"

"Yes."

"Take your clothes off for me."

I debated a slow strip dance, but in truth I was out of my clothes in less than a minute, throwing everything in a heap on the floor.

"Good girl. Now lie down," he said, holding out his hands.

I stretched out on my back and handed him the clothespins. "Be gentle," I said.

"Is that how you want me to be?"

"Yes. You need to be careful with me."

Daniel ran his hands over my neck and chest, almost tickling, until my nipples were hard, then carefully clamped each one. He looked very serious.

"I'm going to hold you down now," Daniel said calmly. "And as much as you struggle, you won't get away, because I'm far more powerful than you."

He held my arms over my head, pushing me down. I closed my eyes. Daniel grazed my neck with his mouth, then used his teeth to bite gently on my skin in a way that might leave a small mark.

"I'm going to let you go, but keep your hands over your head," he directed. "And don't move, or I'll stop what I'm doing."

I did as he said. It was thrilling.

"These are so pretty," he said, touching the clothespins on my nipples.

"Thank you," I said, eyes still closed.

He grazed the tips of his fingers up and down the insides of my arms, then bent his head and used his teeth to tug at one of the clothespins, making my nipple twist a bit.

"Ouch," I whispered, opening my eyes.

"You can handle it," he said, running his hands across my waist and down.

My eyes were still closed, but I could feel Daniel pulling at one of the clothespins with his teeth, opening the clamps, then the release of pressure as he pulled it off. The nipple stung a bit and was swollen and sore, as if it had been lightly bitten. I felt him move down the bed and all in one movement pushing my knees wider apart and up, so I was completely open to him, which could be awkward but wasn't.

"Hold still," he told me, and I did.

I felt his warm breath between my legs and fought the urge to squirm, waiting for his tongue to touch me. Instead, I felt a sudden, firm pressure directly on my clit, and it wasn't the sensation of being sucked, stroked or licked; it was a tight, snug squeeze that didn't release.

"Open your eyes."

Daniel had pulled my hips up onto his lap so my pelvis was elevated and open, my legs spread so I had a clear vision of my engorged pink clit, clamped by the clothespin. It was throbbing, a hot little pulse mimicking the rolling waves of orgasm. The sensation was exquisite. I even loved the way it looked, the odd contrast of a practical, hard object on my soft, tender skin.

"Like it?" he asked, bemused.

"I do." I leaned back to wait for what would happen next.

I didn't think about what would come next. I didn't need to know. I turned my rational brain off to leave my mind open to what we would do, which heightened all my senses. I trusted him to not hurt me or make me look or feel foolish. It was my own form of submission, and to me, it was exhilaration at its very best.

Daniel sat up, his hands on my knees, pulling my legs apart to look at me. Just look. I fought the urge to close my legs, because it felt strange to have someone staring at my private places, but after a moment, it felt utterly powerful to hold someone's fascination that way, just by being a woman. After a moment, he eased off the clothespin and put it on the bed. Then he turned his attention back to me.

I watched Daniel's face as he looked in wonder, as if it was the loveliest thing he'd ever seen, the first one he'd seen (ha, like that would be true!). At last, he ran his fingers down the inside of my legs and lightly touched me. I let out a groan, which I worried sounded weird, but it was too late to care. He used his middle finger to press my clit, without moving; the pressure was unbearable. I fought the urge to buck my hips and start a rhythm. He moved his fingers down to my very wet place, grazing it, then held his fingers up and licked them.

I let out another moan. I couldn't help but lift my hips up, trying to get to his face if he wasn't going to bring it down to me.

"Stop," Daniel leaned away, sitting back on his heels on the bed. "What did I say about moving?"

"You said don't."

"That's right," he sighed, looking down at me in a way I could only describe as amused. "You're going to have to do better than that."

"I'll try."

"Shush," he said, running his hand down my forehead to close my eyes. "Relax."

That was impossible. My whole body felt on edge, tingling, with all the sensations centered on my pulsating, clamped clit.

He took out his phone and took pictures of my spread-open legs. I wanted to be on display for him. It excited me that Daniel might look at the photos and get turned on by my intimate places. He might have control, but I felt powerful.

"They're private, just for us," he said when I opened my eyes.

"OK."

So now we had another secret.

Then he bent down and used his teeth to ease the clothespin off my skin, releasing the blood flow, bringing in a rush of heat, the sensation washing so fully over my body that I knew if I touched myself, I would immediately orgasm.

Daniel made me wait. And wait. And wait. I felt myself becoming more wet under his steady gaze.

I wanted his tongue, but instead, he used his fingers to stroke just inside the lips of my very wet entryway, the spot that throbs under the friction of a thrusting penis. Instead of rubbing the spot, he flicked it with his fingers, flicking, flicking.

"You have a really big squirter," Daniel said, clearly admiring it.

I knew what squirting was, but honestly thought it wasn't something that could happen to me. Wasn't it just pee that shot out? But as Daniel kept flicking the nub of nerves, it became harder and hot and as sensitive as my clit.

My breathing became heavy and I began to pant. I wanted to move my hips toward his fingers but didn't dare move, because that might make him stop. After a glorious few minutes, I pulled my own knees frantically open and warm liquid sprayed out of me, a small gush, an arc right into the air.

Daniel gave a light, satisfied laugh.

"Good girl."

"Holy crap," I said. "What was that?"

"That was squirting, honey, and you did it very well for a first-timer."

"Did I pee on you?"

Daniel laughed harder. "No, I didn't make you pee. I made you come."

"I thought coming only happened with my clit."

"Well now you know," Daniel looked down at me, clearly amused. "I'll make you come many ways, over and over, until you don't know where the orgasms are coming from."

I closed my eyes and shuddered. No one had ever said anything like that before; no one had been that confident. I loved that he never hesitated. He knew exactly what he was doing. No fumbling around like guys often do, uncertain and nervous. I felt more relaxed, knowing he was in charge.

He placed the two clothespins down on my nightstand.

"You're such a newbie, my Jess," Daniel said. "What did you do when you were married? Missionary?"

I chose not to answer that. I had been in two consecutive marriages in which the sex had fizzled out. Then I had some mishaps along the way. I'd had plenty of sex with Hudson before he broke my heart. But I hadn't been ready for this kind of adventure until Daniel found me. Now it seemed I would be open to just about anything.

"Next time I'm going to tether your wrists to keep your hands over your head, and tie your legs open," Daniel said. "You're going to like it, a lot, my sweet AriesGurl."

I knew he was right. I believed him. I trusted him. It was my pleasure to hand over control.

75

"WHAT'S UP WITH YOU LATELY?" EDDIE ASKED A WEEK LATER, OVER AN early sushi dinner.

"What do you mean?" I asked, blowing on my green tea.

"For one thing, you never call anymore, and when I call you, you're always busy."

"Work has been busy, and I'm trying to hit the gym more often."

"Right, work and gym. Then why do you seem different?" I dribbled a bit of cold rice down my chin. "What's going on?"

"Nothing." I shrugged. "Same old."

Eddie narrowed his eyes at me. I prayed I wasn't blushing.

"You hiding something? Or maybe someone?"

I felt my entire nasal system burn as I ate too much wasabi. Choking, I emptied my water glass. My secret life with Daniel had to stay just that. If Eddie found out—or, God forbid, the kids—it would horrify them, make them think I had lost my shit altogether. It was the kind of secret best kept that way. That was part of my fixation with Daniel. Only he and I knew.

I excused myself from the table and went to the ladies' room. A text came in from Daniel, this time a selfie of him blowing me a kiss. In return, I opened my knees and sent a quick shot of my navy-blue panties.

"Well, now I'm hard at my desk," he texted back

I smiled. The more photos I sent Daniel, the freer I felt. I felt a connection with my own body and a sense of pride that someone wanted to see every feminine part, that it turned him on just to look. That made me feel gloriously sexy in a way I'd never felt before. Something to be admired, maybe drooled over.

"Gotta go," I texted.

"Talk later, Jessica."

Eddie was still shaking his head when I got back to the table. "There's something going on, and you may as well tell me now, because I'll find out eventually," he said, finishing his tea.

I just smiled and shook my head.

76

WHOLE DAYS WENT BY WHEN I DIDN'T HEAR FROM DANIEL, AND I TRIED not to read into it. Just when I'd begin to agonize, a message would come through from him.

"What else are you interested in? Tell me something you've never done," Daniel texted one night as I sprawled on my bed with Pen.

The list of what I hadn't done was too long to even begin. It would be easier to list the short number of things I had done, although that tally had grown considerably since meeting Daniel.

"I don't know," I texted. "What do you want to do?"

"I don't think you're ready for my list."

My heart leapt. He knew how to capture my full attention.

"Try me."

"Hold on," Daniel texted. "I have a call from my son coming in."

I didn't hear back from Daniel that night or the next day, and I tried to keep busy and not panic. The second night, a text came through as I was at my dining room table, trying to come up with an enticing blog topic for a company that made backpacks from recycled plastic water bottles.

"Threesome?"

I shut down my computer. No one was home, but when I got this text from Daniel, I shielded my cell and looked around to make sure no one was reading over my shoulder.

"Well hello, Daniel. Nice hearing from you. How've you been?"

"Good, you?"

"Also good."

"So, threesome?"

"What about it?" I texted.

"Ever had one? Ever wanted one?"

I held my thumbs over the letters on my cell, but found myself unable to form a response.

"Jess?"

"I don't know what to say."

"When in doubt, default to the truth."

Truth be told, I had thought about being with another woman and a man, but my fantasies were very selfish: in them, the woman, unusually beautiful, was playing with my nipples while the man, spectacularly built, was stroking himself, watching us. If anyone got into oral, it was the woman licking me, not the other way around.

And there was always alcohol involved.

"Yes. I have thought about it."

"You and two men?"

God no. It was enough to work out the logistics of having sex with one man, much less adding another penis to the equation.

"No. Another woman and a man." Then I began to picture being with Daniel and a second woman, and I knew I would want to slap her if she tried to kiss him or touch him anywhere. Share Daniel? No thanks.

"Would you ever do it? Would you want another woman to join us?"

"No," I texted back immediately. "It's not something I'd like."

"Why not?"

"I wouldn't want to share a man with another woman."

"Ah," Daniel texted. "Are you a jealous girl?"

I hesitated, then typed, "I guess so."

"Hmmm. What if you made the rules about what would be done? How the man could touch the woman?"

"Or not at all?"

"Or not at all," Daniel said. "That would be up to you."

"I wouldn't be able to make the rules."

"Why not?"

"Because you set the rules," I said.

"Good girl."

"You know, I kissed my roommate in college." I wanted to sound like I'd at least pushed the envelope.

"Every woman kisses another woman in college, sweetie."

Damn. So much for sounding more unconventional then I'd already shown him. Clearly, he was far more experienced. I was the eager student.

"I'd like you to give it some thought," he texted.

"Think about what? Kissing a woman?"

"I'd like to see you doing more than just kiss her."

I didn't know what to say, so I said nothing. Where did he fit in his threesome scenario? Would he be the director, telling us what to do? The center of attention? The cameraman?

"Just let these ideas sit, Jess. See if they resonate. Play with them."

77

FOUR DAYS WENT BY WITHOUT DANIEL ANSWERING MY TEXTS, SO I TRIED calling, but it went right to voicemail.

I rehashed everything I'd said and done to try and figure out what was wrong. Was it because I balked at the idea of a threesome? Worst of all, I hadn't told anyone about Daniel, so I had to fret alone over his silence. The whole thing was way too complicated, and secretive, to share. But it didn't go unnoticed.

"Why are you moping around?" Ian asked, packing his gym clothes to head out.

"I'm not moping around. Why do you ask that?"

"Geez, Mom, you've moped on and off for a year. Do you really think I don't know a mope when I see one?" He gave me a hug before heading out the back door. "Stop moping," he called out before the door shut.

I spent the rest of the night flat-out moping.

"I'm so worried about you," I texted Daniel on day four.

"Don't be," he answered.

"My god, you're there? I thought you'd fallen off the face of the earth!"

"I've been under the weather."

"Under the weather? Sick?" I picked up Penny and started to pace.

"The Lyme flared up. I was in the hospital a few days."

My stomach lurched at the thought of Daniel in a hospital bed, maybe even wearing a paper-thin, undignified hospital gown tied wrong in the back.

"Why didn't you tell me?" I texted quickly.

"I didn't think it was something you needed to know."

Tears sprang to my eyes. I didn't have to know? What was I, a casual friend? I looked around for Kleenex but settled on a dinner napkin.

"I was so worried," I said again, wiping my eyes.

"No need. I'm fine."

I sat back down, hard, at the table. The playing cards were still out from the heated game of Crazy 8s the night before. I picked them up and shuffled them, on auto-pilot.

"I'm glad you're better," I texted a moment later.

Daniel didn't reply. Not that day, or the next, but three days later, he texted while I was walking Penny toward Lily's house, just in case she was outside. It was still chilly, so I'd put a little sweater on Pen that said "When all else fails, hug your dog."

"How's it going, doll?"

Pen sniffed around then lifted her leg to pee. I swear, sometimes she thought she was a boy dog.

I took the high road. "I'm really good. You?"

There was no sign of Lily, so we turned back home.

"Busy, busy. But hey, I'm getting that thing set up for you."

"What thing?"

"The threesome. I have an old friend who said she might be willing."

An old friend? What the hell did that mean? A former girlfriend? Lover?

An image came to my mind of Daniel stroking the other woman to orgasm, while I sat at the foot of the bed watching. All I could picture was a younger, more fit woman with perkier tits than mine stripping for Daniel as he got the world's biggest hard-on. Or both of us sucking him. Was he setting this up for me? Or for himself?

"You still have those clothespins?"

Thoughts of a threesome left my mind immediately.

"Yes."

"I want to show you something. Hold on."

My breathing sped up, and a few seconds later, an image came across my phone.

It was a woman bound to a bench, hands over her head and legs splayed apart. Surrounding each nipple was a circle of clothespins pinching the skin; there was a trail of them leading down her stomach, then a row clamped inside her thighs. In the corner, sitting in a leather desk chair, was a man in a dark business suit drinking a martini. Just watching her.

There were dozens of clothespins on the woman.

It was an assault on my senses. I closed my eyes.

"So, what's your sched like next week?" he texted a moment later, and I could almost hear the impatience behind his words.

"What? For what?"

"For some play time with another woman."

"I'll have to get back to you," I texted. It was the first time I'd stopped messaging him first.

The image of the clothespinned woman and the man casually watching her stayed with me all night. She was no more than sexual entertainment for him, an object that wasn't beautiful or artistic or daring. It was more of a mockery, knowing he was enjoying watching what he had done to her with the tight clamps along the length of her skin.

I tried to keep my mind occupied the next day, and then the day after that. By the third day, Daniel and I hadn't texted a single time, which wasn't rare, but the thing was—I realized I had nothing to say.

* * *

"Hey," he texted after four days.

"Hey back," I answered after several minutes. I had to tell him how I felt about the clothespins.

"How've you been?"

"Good. Busy."

I cleared my throat. I had the texting equivalent of speechlessness.

"Listen," Daniel texted. "If it's the threesome thing, we can back off for now. I have other things to work on with you."

"Like the clothespins?"

"Hahaha," he texted with the devil's face emoji. "So, you did like that."

"No, actually, I didn't."

There was a long pause.

"She wasn't being hurt," he texted.

"Looked to me like she was." I rubbed my eyes with the back of my hands.

"You tried the clothespins. You liked it."

"I tried two."

"And?"

"There's a difference. She was clearly in pain, and he enjoyed it. The clothespins on me didn't hurt."

"She was putting on a show. That's all."

"He was making a show of her. She was helpless."

"Listen, maybe we should talk later."

Maybe. Maybe not, I thought.

I opened a kitchen cabinet to get out a mug for tea, then put my phone inside the cupboard and shut it. I sat down and pulled my knees up to my chest as if folding myself up to stay safe.

I'd loved the thrill of secrecy, but the stakes got higher with every request he made. The clothespinned woman had been visually shocking, far beyond my sense of eroticism. He had shown his true self, and I didn't like what I saw.

What would be next?

I realized I'd given up a very big part of myself in my time with Daniel. I'd let go of my inherent sense of boundaries and handed over my hard-earned independence. And I had worked too hard over the last ten months to feel whole again.

A week later, a text came through from Daniel.

"Hey babe. What's new and exciting?"

I debated answering, deleted his message, and threw my cell on my bed.

But it had to be done. I couldn't have him texting me at all hours of the day and night with his sexual suggestions, some of which might still captivate me. He could reach me at a vulnerable time and I'd give in to his wishes. Then I thought about the clothespinned woman and I felt resolute again.

I wasn't ashamed about what I'd done with Daniel. We were two consenting adults. I wasn't ashamed. But I was finished. Done.

I picked up my cell.

"I don't want you to contact me anymore," I texted Daniel. "I don't want to hear from you again."

"Catch you at a bad time?"

"No, this is a good time. Don't call or text. I'm serious. I can't do this anymore. I don't want to. I'm done."

There was a long pause and I thought he'd gone away from his phone.

"You're too vanilla for me anyway. You don't have it in you to explore new things."

He was angry. And he was right. I'd pushed my boundaries as far as they went. His went further into sadism than I'd ever expected. Maybe I was vanilla. But I was strong and true to myself, and in the end, that was better than exploring any sexual fantasies I could dream up.

I got the box of clothespins out from my top closet shelf, carried them to the kitchen, and dumped them, one by one, into the trash, on top of broken eggshells, granola-bar wrappers, and crumpled paper towels. I thought about taking a pic of the buried clothespins and sending it to Daniel, but that would open myself up to him again, and I couldn't take that risk. I didn't even want them in my house, so I tied the bag and carried it out to the trash, letting the lid close with a crash.

I blocked Daniel, then deleted our entire conversation history, his name in my contact list, his phone number in my call log. There was no way for us to reach each other anymore.

Thankfully, Ian was out. I texted Eddie.

"I need you," I said simply.

"Be over in twenty."

Over tall glasses of wine, I told Eddie everything, right down to the last detail.

"Are you kidding me about this?" he asked incredulously. "You did clothespins?"

I nodded my head miserably.

"Aw chicky," Eddie said, reaching across the table to hold my hands. "What's a sweet woman like you doing with a dom with an attitude?"

"I didn't know what I was getting into," I gulped at the wine. "I liked having a secret life, not the same old dull life I had with a stupid job. My best friends are my kids and a little dog...and I liked Daniel. I really liked him."

"Geez, you didn't see any of this coming? Did you try to read his aura?"

"I didn't think of it...a lot of it was over the phone." I finished my wine and reached for the bottle to pour another glass.

"Yeah, phone sex—that's a dangerous game to play."

"It was fun at first...until it wasn't."

"Well, you tried something new. Good for you. Now we gotta get you back on track. And your life isn't stupid. I'd be the first one to tell you if it was."

"Thanks."

"Good thing the April classes are starting soon," Eddie said decisively. "Whaddya say we venture into the world of coin collecting and tarot card reading?"

"Anything you want, sweetie. I'm in."

"I'd rather see you rolling coins than on these roller-coaster relationships."

"Agreed," I said.

I picked Penny up and we both looked out the kitchen window at the bare trees. It felt like March would never come to an end. If spring was a time for fresh starts, I needed it, badly.

78

A WEEK LATER, IT WAS A STRESSFUL AS USUAL DAY AT WORK. WES AND Paulie were arguing over the name of the grocer whose store had closed in 1975, and whether Sal's old sump pump would keep his basement dry when the rainy season came along. No mindless topic was off limits.

My cell vibrated on my desk. It was a call from Maddy, which was strange because she couldn't use her phone at the doctor's office, and she couldn't be at lunch: it was only 10:30 a.m.

I took my phone into the bathroom.

"Mom?" Madison sounded frantic, and I sat down hard on the toilet seat.

"What's wrong? What is it?"

"I stopped at your house to throw in some laundry." Madison was hard to understand, and I realized she was trying to catch her breath.

"Are you all right?" I felt my own panic rising in my throat.

"It's Penny, Mom."

"Penny?"

It had been chilly in the house, so I put a little orange fleece doggie jacket on her. Then I left for work as I always did, telling her I'd be right back and I loved her. She had settled down on the kitchen floor to wait for me.

"What about Penny? Is she hurt?" I had an immediate image of little Penny with one of her spindly legs in a cast, dragging it around behind her, and felt a tug at my heart.

"Mom," Madison sobbed. "She's gone."

"You mean she got out?" I pictured Madison opening the door and Penny, always full of energy, bounding out and racing down the street.

"Mom, she's gone. She died."

Nothing she said made any sense. I felt a copper taste in the back of my mouth even as my mind rejected what she had said.

"That can't be true. She may be hiding somewhere, sleeping."

"Mom, I'm looking at her right now. She looks like she's sleeping, she looks peaceful, but she's—she's," Madison was unable to get the word out. "She's cold, Mom."

My ears began to ring. I tried to stand up, but my knees gave out and I sank to the green linoleum bathroom floor. I felt a scream forming but when it came out, it was a low moan.

I wiped my sweaty forehead on the sleeve of my sweater. Shivering, I struggled to get off the floor, using the sink to balance myself and open the door. The ringing in my ears was so loud I couldn't hear my own voice. I somehow managed to open the bathroom door and step out.

"I need to—to go," I said to Joe.

Surprise registered on all the men's faces.

"You OK?" Joe said. "You look like you should sit down."

"You're pale as a ghost," Wes agreed. "Want some water?"

I made my way to the main door, using my shoulder to push it open. Outside, the wind whipped my hair into my face, blinding me. I used the railing to feel my way down the stairs and went two blocks in the wrong direction of my car. I had to backtrack, taking an agonizing amount of time.

My screaming began as soon as I shut my car door, a terrible wailing without any words except "no, no, no." I pounded my palms on the steering wheel. I grabbed handfuls of my hair and pulled hard, not even registering pain. It couldn't possibly be true. Penny had been by my side during all the rough patches. She had never been sick. She would live to be fifteen.

I put my car into gear and backed carefully out of the parking lot, signaling to take a right. I drove slowly, scrubbing at my eyes with the back of my hand. It was a four-minute commute. When I got home, Madison was waiting for me on the front porch, looking very much like she had on the first day of kindergarten: lost in disbelief.

I stumbled up the porch stairs toward the front door.

Maddy pulled on my arm to stop me.

"Mom—I don't know if—I don't know if you want to see her."

But I was already at the window and saw Penny stretched out on her side, little legs crossed gracefully, the way she always slept. The little fleece jacket was still on, covering her small back. Her eyes were open.

I bolted across the porch and leaned down into the bushes, retching up the fruit salad I'd had just a couple hours before at breakfast. Madison came over and smoothed back my matted hair.

"I need to see her," I said at last, wiping my mouth.

Penny was lying right by the door where she always sat waiting for me. But when I opened the door, she didn't bound to me with excitement, barking to welcome me home. She didn't stir.

I collapsed onto the floor, looking at the back of her neck where the fleece didn't cover her. I had just gotten her groomed and her fur was perfectly clipped at the back of her neck. She always looked so tiny after getting groomed, fragile almost, so pretty, so much a little princess.

"She's a really good girl," the groomer had said. "She's such a cuddle bunny, always wanting to be held."

I touched her head. She was so cold I imagined she'd caught a chill, some kind of bronchitis and couldn't breathe—or something—because it made no sense that I had left her two hours before, all wagging and bright-eyed, and now she wasn't even Penny anymore; she was like a doll, empty and cold.

"Mom—" Ian came in and knelt down next to me. He bowed his head and started to cry.

"It's OK, honey," I said, sounding like a robot, knowing I was telling him something that wasn't true. It wasn't OK. It would never be OK.

Maddy came out of the bedroom with the fuzzy pink blanket I used to cover Penny in the middle of the night when her nose didn't feel warm.

She draped it carefully over Penny, covering her cold nose.

We stayed on the floor for what felt like a very long time, arms around one another, leaning in for support because alone, we knew we would fall apart.

"What do we do now?" Ian asked, touching the edge of the blanket.

"I don't know what to do," Madison said shakily.

I was on auto-pilot. We couldn't keep Penny where she was on the floor, but it seemed insurmountable to move her. I called Eddie.

"Jesus," he said. "I can't believe it. Not Penny!"

"It happened and we're all here and I don't know what to do next."

"I'll be there in twenty."

We waited for Eddie in silence. I couldn't say if he got there quickly or if it took a while, because it felt like time had stopped. All I wanted was to go back to the morning, when I told Penny I'd be home soon. If I could go back, I would have stayed with her. I would never have left her side. I tried to remember what I'd said to her the night before, certain I'd told her she saved my life, every single day.

Eddie came rushing in, coming to a halt when he saw us on the floor.

"Hey," he said to all of us. He leaned down and felt the blanket draped over Penny. "She's cold," he said, which infuriated me.

"We know that," I snapped at him.

"How—how did this happen? Did she choke?" Eddie had tears in his eyes and was clearly having trouble forming words.

"We don't—I don't know—we couldn't tell."

Then it was the four of us sitting in silence next to Penny.

"We should call the vet," Eddie said at last, pulling out his cell phone.

When Eddie reached the vet's office, they said to bring Penny in. The office was just north of town.

None of us made a move to touch Penny.

"I'll get her," Eddie said finally.

"Please don't touch her," I shrieked, finding my voice again.

Eddie pulled back as if he'd touched something hot.

I eased Penny onto my lap, where she'd sat a thousand times before while I was writing at the dining room table. I'd imagined her being very light, but like a small statue, Penny was immobilized, frozen, and heavier than I remembered. The soul is weightless, I thought, trying hard to distance myself from emotions. Her soul had been gone when I had gotten home. She'd left before I had a chance to say goodbye.

I held her close in my arms as we all walked to the car, as if to keep her warm.

"Did she choke on something?" our kindly old veterinarian said after we'd carried her into the office and placed her carefully on an exam table, still wrapped up.

"We weren't there. She was alone," I said.

"How old?"

"Six," Madison answered quickly.

I held on to the edge of the table to steady myself. "She was just in two months ago for a check-up and everything was fine."

"These things happen, and we often don't know why," the vet said gently. "But given her breed, it was possibly heart failure. Did she pant a lot? Have difficulty walking distances?"

I felt my stomach turn over and thought I might be sick.

"Yes—she did pant, but we always thought she just didn't like warm weather," I said shakily.

"When dogs aren't getting enough oxygen, they will frequently pant," the vet said, as if it were consoling information.

I thought of all the times I'd carried Pen home when she'd grown tired on a walk, but in a million years, it never came into my mind that she had a weak heart. Not Pen, who was always there, my strength, my rock. Not Penny, who had my heart, who carried it with her now and forever.

I tried to find words to ask the questions I would one day need answered.

"Was there something we could have done for her?" I said, my ears ringing so loudly I could barely hear my own words.

"Well, there are heart medicines, but I can't say they would have significantly prolonged her life. It's likely she lived as long as she could until her heart failed."

My hands were clammy, and when I clasped them hard, digging my nails into my palms, I had no sensation. "Would that be quick?"

"Oh, yes, split second. Like going to sleep, lights on, lights off, just like that," he said sympathetically. "She probably didn't feel a thing."

Lights on. Lights off. Lights on. Lights off. Lights off.

"If you want to know exactly what happened, I can—"

"No," I interrupted. "I don't want her touched."

The doctor looked startled.

"I'm sorry, I—" I began to say.

"No need to apologize, but do you need to sit down? Or some water?"

"What do we do now?" I asked, knowing I would puke up even water.

"If you want her ashes, we will give her a private ceremony," he said, sounding professional again.

"I—yes, I want her ashes."

"What does that mean, a private ceremony?" Eddie asked, speaking up for the first time in the exam room.

"It means she will be cremated alone, not with other pets."

I closed my eyes and felt my stomach turn over. When I opened them, Eddie was handing me a wet paper towel.

"Thank you," I said, wiping my face.

"Would you like to take the blanket?" the doctor asked.

"No!" I said too sharply. "I mean, no, I want it to keep her warm. I want it to stay with her."

"I'll give you time to say your goodbyes," the vet said, leaving us.

Ian and Maddy moved toward the table together, each of them placing their hands on Pen's back.

"We love you, little one," Madison choked out. "We love you, Pen-Pen." They were both crying as they left the room to wait in the car.

"I can't do it," I said desperately to Eddie. "I can't—I can't say it. I can't say goodbye. I can't do it."

"Then don't," he said, putting his arms around me. "You don't have to say it."

"I don't want to leave her," I said desperately, crying into his shoulder.

"Sweetie, she's already gone. This isn't Penny anymore. It's just her shell."

She's already gone, I thought, and that was the most terrible of all truths. She was gone. I didn't know if she had a choice, or if the choice was made for her, I didn't know anything about how the universe worked—all I knew was that she would never have willingly left me. She had been taken from me. I was enraged. I felt robbed of something most precious to me. I would have given anything I could to have her back, to cuddle her even one last time, to look into her wise, dark eyes and thank her for saving my life every day.

I felt dizzy when I lifted my head from Eddie's chest. He steadied me as I leaned down to Penny and pulled the blanket a little away from the back of her neck. I touched her smooth hair where it was neatly groomed in layers like I'd worn my own hair in high school. When her hair grew out, we'd always called her a sheep dog, but now it would never grow out again.

"You're my baby," I whispered. "You will always be my baby girl. I will always love you. You will be in my heart forever."

I tucked the blanket carefully back around her the way I used to swaddle the kids when they were infants.

"I don't want to leave her," I said shakily.

"Honey, Ian and Maddy need you now," Eddie said. "They need their mother."

Being their mother was the only thing that got me out of that room and away from Penny. It was the only thing keeping me breathing. It felt like the only thing left.

When I got to the car, I saw Ian and Maddy in the back seat. Ian had his arm around his sister and she was crying hard into his chest. Eddie got out of the car to hug me when he dropped us off. The kids stumbled up the stairs of the front porch and went inside.

"You're going to be OK—not right now, but soon," Eddie said, breathing into my hair. "It will get better with time."

"I don't want time to pass!" I said angrily, pulling away from him. "I don't want to forget what she was like, what we did together, how much I love her. I saw her this morning! I don't want to think about time going by until I haven't seen her for months. I can't handle that. I can't."

Eddie took my hands in his. "I'm so sorry, honey. So sorry. Wherever she is now, her heart is strong and she is running in the sun. She would hate to see you suffer like this."

"All right," I said before turning away and going inside my house.

It was unthinkable that I would sleep in my bed without Penny. Madison made up the living room couch with sheets and blankets and pillows.

"I'm staying over," Maddy said.

"Thank you," I said, my voice cracking. "But I only have one couch."

"Ian's got it all figured out."

Ian lugged over the air mattress he used for camping, from his room upstairs. I watched dully as he used a small pump to inflate the double bed mattress on the living room floor for Madison and him to sleep.

"Voilà," he said, waving his hand. I was grateful he was distracted for a few minutes in the house of grief.

"You guys must be hungry," I said, realizing it was long past dinner time. "Can I make you something?"

"Mom, we should be making you dinner," Maddy said.

"I'm sorry, I'm just not hungry."

"Tea, then?"

"Tea would be good."

But when she brought the steaming cup to me, I couldn't take a single sip because my stomach was still churning, twisted as if I wouldn't even be able to swallow without it all coming back up.

We didn't know what else to do, so I crawled under the blankets on the couch and the kids got into sleeping bags on the air mattress. It was unbearably quiet.

"Wow, Madd, I haven't slept in the same room as you in forever," Ian said.

"Feels kinda nice," Madison replied.

"I remember when you were six, Maddy, and had your own room and Ian was so desperate to be with you—he would wait until you were sleeping, then sneak in his blanket and pillow and sleep on the floor next to your bed."

"No!" Ian said. "I left my warm bed to sleep on her floor?"

"I kinda remember that," Maddy said.

"Another time you had a sleepover with your friends, and everyone was in sleeping bags in the living room, and you wouldn't let Ian sleep down there with you. But in the middle of the night, he brought down his blankets and slept on the kitchen floor, just to feel like he was part of things."

"OK, even worse! You let me sleep on the cold, hard kitchen floor?"

"I knew you were there, but I didn't kick you out. Doesn't that count for something?"

"When you were a baby, Ian, your sister used to climb into your crib to sleep with you. I have pictures of you two somewhere."

I hadn't known how uncomfortable the couch was until I was lying down on it. I reached behind my pillow to plump it up and heard something squeak. When I pulled it out, it was one of Penny's favorite chew toys, a green alligator that squeaked when you pinched its tail. I held the toy to my face and sobbed into it until Madison took it away from me.

"I want it—I want to keep it!"

"I'll put it someplace safe," she said, leaving the room.

"I'm so sorry, Mom." Ian was crying quietly, his shoulders shaking.

"Come down with us, Mom," Maddy said when she came back to the living room.

So all of us, just the three of us now, lay side by side on the air mattress, holding on to each other for dear life, until the sun went down and darkness set in, obliterating everything but our shared grief.

79

Ian and Maddy were still sleeping early the next morning, so I rolled carefully off the air mattress and stumbled to my feet. I was so light-headed I had to hold on to the wall and make my way into the kitchen. I opened the cabinet and pulled out a mug, but my stomach turned over when I thought of making coffee or brewing tea.

It was a twenty-minute drive to the salon, but when I got there, I realized it wouldn't be open for another hour. I reclined the seat of my car and closed my eyes, but all I could picture was Pen wearing the little "hug a dog" shirt to stay warm. When I took it off, her fur was always matted down and she shook herself like dogs do after a bath, until her hair stood up, all frizzed out. Then she would look at me as if I'd done her a great indignity by messing her up. She was always such a girly-girl, just like Maddy.

When Madison was in elementary school, she wore her hair long and down her back. She liked it braided, but first I had to work a comb through the snarls. I'd sprayed on detangler until her strands were damp. She'd always complained and pulled away from the comb, making it even more difficult.

"Maddy, all over the world right now there are little girls getting their hair combed by their mothers, and all of them hate it," I told her. "But when it's over, their hair looks pretty all day long."

She'd accepted that, and all too soon, she was doing her own hair. I missed those mornings helping her get ready for school.

I may have dozed a bit in the car. When I opened my eyes, the mall lights were on and I could go in.

"I want it short," I told the stylist.

It was the same young woman who'd worked miracles on me just a couple of months earlier. Back when I wanted to look fabulous to go out and start dating. I felt so angry at myself now—I'd wasted time on my appearance instead of spending it with Pen. I'd spent hours waiting for replies to my online messages, as if that mattered. I'd cried over men.

Over men! My grief now was crushing. This was loss. This was anger at the universe. Everything else was infinitesimal and far, far away.

"How short?" the stylist asked.

"Short short."

"You have such pretty hair—I hate to see it all go," she said, pursing her plum-colored lips. "Let's start off with shoulder-length."

Still dizzy, I closed my eyes and listened to the shears clipping away. My mind was stuck on replay; all I could picture was Penny waiting for me on the kitchen floor.

When the kids were little, they were both scared at night, even after bedtime stories and checking for monsters in the closet and under beds. I used to rub their backs and sing, but as they grew older and their lives became more complicated, their worries became larger than what was under the bed. I'd always told them their thoughts were like a tape recording playing over and over again, until the worries were engrained in their minds.

"Replace it with something good," I'd told them. "Instead of fretting over the math test tomorrow, picture yourself somewhere safe and peaceful where you feel relaxed and happy."

For both of them, their happy place was the beach at low tide.

Adam and I had taken the kids every August to Maine for a week, even when Ian was a baby and we had to lug in a pop-up tent to screen him from the sun, change diapers on a towel, feed him baby peaches and carrots from tiny jars with a rubber-tipped spoon. By the following summer, Ian had been on the go, crawling away from us toward the crashing waves of the ocean, or following flocks of seagulls ready to bite his little toes.

Madison had thrown a handful of Cheetos once to feed the birds and they descended in alarming numbers on our beach towels, scaring the hell out of her. But Ian held up his baby fists, shaking them at the birds as if to defend her, her little hero. I remember getting annoyed with Adam for taking pictures with his cell instead of rushing to scare off the birds.

My thoughts were already stuck on the image of Penny lying on her side near the kitchen door, her legs crossed so prettily at her ankles. I tried to distract myself with images of the beach, the birth of my kids, a particularly amazing Christmas. Then I thought about the day we got Pen from a friend whose Yorkies had puppies.

The puppies were loud and raucous, trying desperately to reach us to be picked up and held. They had formed a dog pyramid, each standing on another's shoulders. Down at the very bottom was a tiny girl dog waiting for the other dogs to calm down. When they did, she looked up at us, wagging her little tail excitedly, not barking at all, just staring up at us, and that was it. We all knew we belonged together.

In four years, Penny had seen me through my divorce from Bryan, watching the kids grow up and need me less and less, several thwarted relationships, a new job, days in the sun and rain, nights when she licked my tears and settled herself against my legs to tell me I wasn't alone.

"You save my life every day," I used to tell her before we fell asleep. Now it was up to me to save myself, something I was completely unprepared to do.

"A little shorter," I told the stylist.

I didn't know why it was so urgent to get my hair cut off. All I could think of was having it be as low maintenance as possible. No more tons of product. No more fuss. Without Pen, nothing else mattered, least of all my own appearance. I left the salon with a short bob that I could wash and air-dry and never think about, which was exactly what I was looking for. The world felt like a different place, and I was a different person.

80

Maddy called my office and told them I was taking a few sick days.

"Joe said to tell you they're all very sorry," she said when she got off the phone.

I knew it was time to call Bryan. I wanted to wait until I could tell him without sobbing, because we had promised one another long ago to not break down in front of each other. But that could take months, and he needed to know now.

It was around bedtime, but I dialed his number. This wasn't something I could text him about.

"Jess? What's wrong?" Bry sounded alarmed already.

"Hey," was all I could manage. "How are you?"

"I'm OK, but what's wrong?"

"It's Penny," I said, trying hard to hold back the tears. "She's gone."

"You mean lost? Run away? It's not like her to leave your side."

I started flat-out crying. "No Bry, she passed away. She died."

There was a long pause from the other end of the line. I could hear Bryan taking deep breaths. I could picture him pacing, taking long strides across the room, then back again.

"Jesus," he said at last. "Not Penny."

I had no response because he was right. Not Penny.

"Are you guys OK?" I could hear a break in his voice and knew he was trying not to cry. He and Penny had always been close, wrestling on the floor, playing tug-of-war with her chew toys, running around the backyard.

"We're all right. Just trying to get through the days." I lay down in bed next to the pillow that still smelled like Penny.

"What can I do to help?"

Nothing, I thought. No one could do anything to help.

"Tell you what," Bryan said, his voice a little less shaky. "I can come up there. If I leave in the morning, I'll be there tomorrow, middle of the night."

I closed my eyes. It was just like Bryan to want to make things easier on the kids and me. But I thought if I saw him, and went into his arms, I would break down even more by leaning on him. I had to try and get through this, the kids and me, even though nothing would ever be the same again. Nothing.

"Thank you for saying that, but you shouldn't do that."

"I want to help."

"You do help, just by knowing how much we love her—all of us, including you—and by remembering all the good times we had with her."

"I don't think I have a picture of her," Bryan said, his voice shaky again. "Can you send me one?"

"Sure."

"Promise you'll call if you need anything?"

"Promise."

I'd avoided looking through the photo gallery on my cell, because I knew it was full of pictures of Pen: Penny in a little Santa suit, in a glow-in-the-dark skeleton Halloween costume, Penny on her birthday eating a doggie treat shaped like a cupcake, rolling over for someone to rub her tummy. Sleeping at the edge of my bed.

Down at the end of my gallery, I found pictures of Penny and Bryan on the front porch, sitting side by side, both squinting in the sun as I called their names to take a photo. After that she had crawled on his lap and licked his nose, a slobbery dog kiss, and he'd wiped his face on his sleeve. But she kept kissing, and he never pushed her away.

81

THREE DAYS MELTED AWAY, THREE NIGHTS SPENT WIDE AWAKE. I WAS still sleeping on the couch. I spent a long time sitting on the kitchen floor in the spot where Penny had lain waiting for me.

I realized staying home brought no relief, and work might be a distraction. That, and I was using up all my sick time.

I got dressed and drove in to work on auto-pilot.

The men were talking when I went into the office, but quickly fell silent.

"Good morning, Jess," Sal said, standing up to greet me.

Wes, Paulie, and Joe also stood up and for a terrible moment I worried they were going to hug me, and that would send me right back out the door.

"Morning," I said, not meeting anyone's eyes.

I went behind the counter to hang up my coat.

On my desk was a small bag from the bakery. Inside was a fresh cinnamon bun. "Your favorite," Joe said.

It was true, cinnamon buns were the one thing I couldn't resist when the guys made a run to Brew Coffee. Next to the bakery bag was a card in a pink envelope. There was a pawprint with angel wings on the cover. Inside the card was the message: *Your dog is wagging its tail in your heart—that's why it hurts so much. Please accept our deepest sympathies.* It was signed by Joe, Wes, Paulie, and Sal.

It was the most touching card I'd received since the kids were little and brought home Valentines for me made with doilies and construction paper hearts cut with safety scissors.

Tears sprang to my eyes and I tried to choke out a thank you to the men.

"It's OK, missy." Wes waved away my attempts to talk.

I noticed a member of the group was missing.

"Where's Beef Jerky today?"

Wes looked uncomfortable. "Thought I'd leave him home for a while. Didn't want to upset you."

"It wouldn't upset me. It would make me happy to see him."

"Then I'll bring him tomorrow," he said, smiling widely.

I went into the back office to find the birth certificate folder, which Joe always misfiled, banging my elbow on the cabinet as I slid the drawer open. It was suddenly too much effort to stay composed. I leaned my head into the musty genealogy books, pulling my cardigan closely around my chest where my broken heart was.

"Hey, girl, you OK?" Sal asked from the doorway, peering inside.

"I'm good," I said, trying to steady my voice.

"Okaaaay," Sal drew out the word. "Can we do anything at all to help?" He gestured out toward the table, where the other men were staring intently at us.

"No, thanks. I just need a minute."

"You need to talk? We're good listeners."

"Maybe later."

"OK, you just take your time."

I didn't get much paperwork done, but just making it to 5:00 felt like a big step, and the men were actually a welcome distraction. But as soon as I got inside my car, the rage spilled over again and I pounded the steering wheel with my fists, screaming and yelling at the universe.

Was I going to make it without my girl? I had no idea how.

82

EDDIE WENT ONLINE AND FOUND A PET BEREAVEMENT SUPPORT GROUP. It met twice a month at the animal shelter in Ashton, the largest ASPCA in the area.

"I can go with you," Eddie said as I got ready to go on Wednesday night.

"It's OK," I said, putting on my coat. "I've gotta do this alone. I feel like I should."

The shelter was a long, low brick building, mostly dark at night, but one room was brightly lit, so I headed there. There was a large circle of metal chairs in the room, pictures of pets all over the walls, and the floor was tiled with white squares and purple paw prints. A tall woman with crazy curly hair clapped her hands to get our attention.

"Please take seats, everyone," she said. "I'm Sandra, and I'll be facilitating the group tonight."

I took a chair and settled in. The chair was cold, so I sat on my coat. When I looked around, I saw people of all ages—mostly couples, but a few singles like me. I squinted at Sandra to see if I could decipher her aura, but everything looked gray.

"I see a few new faces in the group, so I want to welcome you," Sandra said. "For starters, I want to review the way our time together works. You can talk or just listen. I'm an MSW specializing in grief issues. I'll do my best to address your questions and concerns. Most importantly, trust that this is a place to share anything you choose to about your pet, because we've all experienced loss."

I was grateful we didn't have to go around the circle and say our name. I wasn't ready to do any talking yet.

"When our pets pass over the rainbow bridge, they join the animal spirit of the universe," Sandra said. "There, they meet the Divine and are fully renewed. The animal spirit is everywhere, across the land and oceans and sky."

I never liked that "rainbow bridge" metaphor, but the possibility of becoming a part of a larger spirit was a comfort to me.

Most of us in the small circle of chairs had been crying when we walked into the community room at the shelter. Most of us still were.

Sandra had brought along her dog, a black lab she named Mr. Leprechaun, because he liked to dance. The lab padded around from chair to chair for neck scratches, but when he came to me, I couldn't touch him. I didn't want any dog but my Penny.

"If you're still suffering in three months, as if the death had just happened, you may be having a major depressive episode, and you should get professional help," Sandra said.

OK. So, should I mark my calendar for July and hope the despair would just drop away? Like magic?

"Does anyone have something they'd like to share?" Sandra said. "Remember, you don't have to speak if you aren't able to."

A middle-aged man across the circle from me spoke up. "My dog Louie got out of the house and disappeared. He hadn't been acting like himself for the days before, but he'd never run away before. He just never came back. I didn't know what to tell my kids. I didn't know if Louie had passed away that night."

The man began to sob. "I didn't know if he was out there alone, trying to get back home."

He took a moment to regain his composure. "We put up posters all over town with his picture. We put together a reward, even. But it's been a month now. I don't think Louie's coming home."

I cried openly then, lowering my head, trying hard not to sob. Sandra passed around a box of Kleenex.

"We feel your pain," Sandra said gently.

I swore after all the crying I'd done over the past year, I would start carrying a handkerchief. Maybe something embroidered with my initials. With lace on the bottom.

"My cat Paisley went out one night and didn't come back like she always did in the morning," an older woman said, clinging to the handle of her straw pocketbook. "I left food out for her, but I had to go volunteer that morning at the food pantry. When I came home that afternoon—it was just a few hours later—Paisley was at the back door, already...already passed away. She had tried to come home to me to say goodbye, but she was too weak to make it up the back steps. She was all curled up in a ball, looking more like a doll, or something else, not my Paisley anymore."

I closed my eyes, feeling her pain. We were all connected by grief.

"I watched my little pug Gracie get hit by a motorcycle," said a man wearing a fly-fishing baseball cap. "Middle of the day; the douchebag never even stopped to see what he ran over. My little girl landed on the curb and was gone before I even got to her."

"Can we talk about the stupid things people say after we lose our dogs and cats?" the man with the baseball cap asked. "Like, 'Time to get a new one to replace it.'"

"Or 'Someone needed a new pet in heaven,'" spoke up a woman wearing a long gauze skirt. "Or 'It was just their time.'"

It was quiet in the room for a moment. I looked at the pet posters on the wall.

A young woman smoothed her hair with shaky hands before she spoke. "I got home and found my black lab Toddy lying with his sister's body. He refused to move away. He growled at us when we tried to touch her. My husband had to pry him off her. We cried, all three of us, all night long."

"Animals can sense even before we can that a member of their pack is ill," Sandra said. "They frequently sit and wait with them to bear witness as they pass away."

"I'm not sorry her brother stayed with her, because I never wanted her to die alone," the young woman said. "But now Toddy is mourning right along with us, and we want him to feel better."

"Are his sister's things still around—her toys, blankets, dog bed?" Sandra asked. "It might be easier on Toddy if you put those things away for now, because they all smell like his sister, and he may be still waiting for her to come back home."

"I kept my dog's ashes in the car for a year, because he always loved going for a ride," said a woman who had been silent until now. "I don't know if I'll ever be able to get another dog."

"You may need to wait years before you can love another pet, and welcome it into your home," Sandra said. "Remember, every pet is unique; you will never replace your lost pet with an identical new one."

We all nodded in agreement.

"I have the ashes of many pets I've had during my life," Sandra said. "I've told my kids when I die, mix our ashes all together and scatter us in the ocean."

The young couple holding hands, both of them openly crying, said they started their cat Sassy on chemo after finding a lump on her belly. She was from a feral litter. Their mail carrier had seen a hawk swoop down and take one of the kittens. But their kitten had been rescued.

"Feral cats have shorter lives," Sandra said. "You gave Sassy the best possible life she could ever wish for. She would never have had a family on the streets."

The hour-long meeting ended after Sandra invited all of us to the next meeting two weeks later. I gathered up my coat and walked out with some of the others.

"See you next time?" the woman who'd had the feral cat asked me.

"See you then," I answered.

I started the engine in my car and put on my seatbelt but left it in park. I watched through the window as Sandra finished stacking the chairs in a utility closet and turned out the lights in the rec room.

Lights on. Lights off. Lights off.

"I miss you," I said out loud, quietly at first but then my voice swelled into a wail. "I MISS YOU!" I screamed at the top of my lungs over and over, tears running down my face until my voice became a whimper.

"I miss my girl," I whispered into the night.

83

O NE WEEK LATER, E DDIE, THE KIDS AND I PICKED UP A SMALL PAPER BAG
with a handle tied with raffia. It wasn't at all heavy. We carried it into
the kitchen and set it on the floor where Penny had lain. Wordlessly,
the four of us sank to the floor.

Inside the bag was a small scroll wrapped with black ribbon. We
set it aside without taking off the ribbon and unrolling it. Next was a
little pink bag with something round inside. Shakily, I opened the bag
then felt wild sobbing beginning in my chest. It was a circle of white
clay with a perfect impression of Penny's little paw, so tiny it looked
like a puppy's. But then again, she had always been a puppy, in size
and in spirit.

All of us were crying hard. Madison took out the next tiny envelope
and looked inside. It was a lock of her hair, golden brown, and I knew
it had come from the back of her neck. By the time we got to the tiny
mahogany box at the bottom of the bag, we were all sobbing so hard
none of us could take it out, so Madison gently repacked the bag with
the scroll and the clay and the envelope holding the tiny scruff of hair.

It was impossible to believe my Penny, such a bundle, was reduced
to a tiny bag like the kind you might use to carry a gift for someone's
birthday or anniversary.

All that mattered was this: Penny was home again.

84

Two weeks later, at the end of March, we had an unexpected early burst of spring.

We wore cardigans instead of parkas; I got out my sneakers after the dregs of dirty snow melted in one warm afternoon.

With the unseasonably warm temps and painfully brilliant sunshine, blossoms sprang up everywhere: yellow and white daffodils, pink and deep-purple tulips, blankets of light-blue forget-me-nots. Skeletal, dry gnarled branches were suddenly forsythia bushes, ground cover greenery gave us clutches of violets, a rhododendron bush came out of nowhere.

I hated the flowers and everything beautiful that reminded me of Penny. But being outside and working until every muscle in my body ached helped clear my mind. Ian and I raked up nearly ten bags of leaves and dry vines, tied loose branches together with twine and left them at the curb to be collected by the DPW. Ian cut down a scraggly pine tree near the front steps with snaking roots cracking our driveway. When he thought I wasn't looking, he wiped tears from his face. I worked until my arms were so sore, I could barely lift my coffee mug.

I knew very little about gardening. In a nutshell, I knew perennials came up every year, start seedlings indoors, move them outside to acclimate them, transplant them, and wait for blooms. I spent so many hours outside that my knees were embedded with grime, I had half-moons of soil under my nails and smudged dirt all over my face.

I planted what I liked—deep-orange poppies in an old metal watering can, a bright-red azalea in a silver bucket slightly green with age, purple coneflowers whose centers matched the ledge I painted on the porch.

I dug, weeded, and pruned every weekend in the spring. I uprooted squares of sod and put them down in a patchwork pattern in the mud beneath our picnic table. My yard had been in a constant state of disarray since I'd moved in, I realized, and although I didn't really care what it looked like, tending to it kept my tears at bay, at least for a little while.

I found a bag of bulbs I'd brought years before still in their original paper bag. The bulbs had slender green stalks, the earliest beginnings of leaves, exposing its vast root systems and bulky bulbs entwined forming a mass like small potatoes. I gathered them up and dug a few inches into the soil to the dirt to plant them, not knowing what might blossom and not caring, either. I unearthed so many fat worms, I considered opening a bait shop.

My work was frenetic, I went for hours hacking out crabgrass and weeds, digging up soil and turning over sod, grooming the edges of flower beds, trying to identify flowers by their leaves. I carried my trowel in my back pocket in case I saw a stray dandelion or clump of crab grass. I bent over the ground not even trying to hide my ass from the world, ripping out the knees on all my jeans, splattering bits of wet dirt in my hair and ears.

Everywhere I looked, I saw Penny. I saw her traipsing happily around the backyard like a sheep in open pasture. I saw her nosing through the pile of twigs and grass. I saw her lying in the sun. I was grateful, so grateful, that Penny had been by my side through the divorce. I was still burning with fury that she was taken away without warning, without any signs, without any logic. Out of nowhere.

Penny had gone on her own terms. She didn't have to grow old and slow down and get rheumy eyes and diminished hearing. Maybe she was sparing us that. I thought that was incredibly brave. And one day I would be thankful, grateful to her for making that choice all alone. My Pen-Pen.

I couldn't turn away from the fact that I still had mothering to do. Ian had told me seeing Penny's body was the biggest shock of his life, and I wanted to show him that nothing in life, not even staggering loss, was insurmountable. Maddy asked me to get matching tattoos inside our wrists, Penny's name with a heart at the end. I was giving it serious thought. Nothing could possibly make me happier than looking at her name every day.

Change was inevitable and out of my control.

I was working hard to trust the universe, even when it made no sense to me.

I was alone that spring, by choice. I didn't want anyone around who would try to talk me out of my grief or try to make it all better. I didn't expect to be alone forever, but to a great degree, I didn't care. I cancelled my membership on Fish. I was done with online dating. I would wait to see what the universe had planned. I had to believe better times were ahead.

When the branches of a wilted shrub in the far corner of the yard burst with lilac blooms, the scent was so strong I could smell them from the kitchen sink. I pulled the plastic covers off the rocking chairs on the front porch and sat there in the late afternoons after work. Not long ago, Penny was on my lap, and I rocked us both. I knew I had to move away from the grief, a little bit each day. But I didn't want to leave behind the last time I saw her, all springy and sweet and full of life.

I was in a strange place of limbo, not planning the future, trying not to live in the past. Just getting through the days and bracing myself for whatever would happen next, hoping I'd be strong enough to get through. And once I got through it, I knew I would be able to face anything, because nothing would ever be as hard as losing Pen.

I was surviving the immense loss. I didn't really expect to. But I was surviving. Somehow, I was surviving.

85

A FEW WEEKS LATER, AN EMAIL CAME FROM SANDRA THAT THE ANIMAL shelter was looking for volunteers for all kinds of activities, from walking dogs to playing with cats to helping with the gardens.

I signed up for yard work. I liked being out in the sun with my hands busy. I was always thinking about Penny, but my crying jags were more manageable when I was outside working.

Clouds were gathering the Saturday I was volunteering, and by the time I got to the shelter, it had turned into a downpour. I got out of my car and opened my hatch to search for an umbrella, coming up empty. I tried to run and avoid the puddles in the parking lot, but by the time I got to the front door, I was soaked.

Sandra met me in the lobby and handed me a towel to wipe my face.

"Hold on to it," she told me. "One of our indoor chores today is laundry."

The other volunteers had cancelled, so I spent the morning washing and folding pet blankets and towels. Most of them had seen better days, but there were many cozy fleece blankets like the ones my kids used to sleep with, because both of them had been too warm at night for a comforter.

"These are nice," I said, folding a fleece. "Do they keep the dogs comfortable?"

Sandra looked at me over the rims of her red-framed glasses.

"Comfortable? Have you ever been inside the shelter before?" Aside from our meeting in the rec room, I hadn't.

"Come on," Sandra said, straightening up and stretching her back. "You can help me with what's next on the list: chow time."

We loaded up two wagons with huge bins of dry food and water, and Sandra hit numbers on a keypad to let us into the animal units. As soon as we got inside, I heard the sounds of barking, so loud the noise bounced off the walls and spiraled back into the middle of the room, a roaring cacophony of sound.

I looked around and immediately felt ashamed for thinking the animals had comfortable quarters. It was warm and dry, yes, and the dogs were each in their own walled-off space, but that was all that could be said. Their spaces were barren—no stuffed toys, rubber balls or rawhide chews anywhere. All the dogs I saw down the row of tiny spaced-off pens were large dogs, all of them on their feet, all of them barking loudly and continuously. Many were pacing or circling, a few were spinning as if they were puppies chasing their tails, but this wasn't a game, it was some kind of fixation. Their eyes were dilated and bulging.

"What's wrong?"

"What's wrong?" Sandra gave a short laugh. "Kennel sickness is starting to set in. They spend too much time alone with nothing to do; they're constantly under stress from the noise and chaos in these unnatural surroundings. This isn't like home. Hard as we try, we can't make this place comfortable and loving. We do the best we can, but the dogs get strung out."

My heart sank. That's just how they looked: strung out.

"What's worse, the more overstimulated they become, the less chance they have of being adopted because they appear mean to people, even when they're the sweetest dogs in the world, just scared out of their minds after being here so long."

"How long?"

"Jess, we see dogs start experiencing negative effects of being here after two weeks. Some of them stay for months."

At the end of the first row of pens, a small white dog with gray ears was sleeping in a perfect circle on a threadbare towel. It was the tiniest of spaces in the row, and her food had been tipped over.

The note card posted on the door said she had been there three weeks, she was shy around children, and that her name was Lucy. I hesitated outside the door, not wanting to wake her, but I did want to sweep up her food and fill her bowl with fresh kibble. As I stood watching her, Lucy lifted her head sleepily, one drowsy eye still closed, and looked at me.

I blinked hard and looked away.

When I turned back, Lucy was at the door, two front paws up, trying to make herself look much taller than she actually was. I didn't know how she could possibly have moved that fast, so I nudged the door open slowly and slid in quickly in case she tried to run.

She didn't run.

She lay down and rolled onto her back to show me her tummy. I stroked her soft belly gently and she pretended to nip at my fingers, her own little game. After a while, she got back onto her little paws and looked up at me. She was panting.

I backed out the door and shut it, then slid with my back to Lucy down to the floor. I stayed there until I heard Sandra calling my name.

"I'm down here," I called back.

Sandra's wagon was empty as she rolled it down to where I sat. Instead of asking what I was doing, she sank down to the floor and sat with me. We were both quiet.

"Something spook you?" she said at last.

"The little dog—" I pointed behind me.

"Lucy. She's a cutie, isn't she?"

"Cutie," I echoed. "But what's wrong with her?"

"What do you mean?"

"I mean, I think someone should look at her, the vet here or someone," I said shakily. "She's panting a lot."

Sandra turned around to see Lucy, still looking at us, waiting patiently.

"Jess, all dogs pant. She's happy to see us, that's all. Maybe needs more water. Maybe she got a little warm in this weather. There's nothing wrong, aside from her being in this kennel, which is the last place she wants to be."

"Where does she want to be?"

"Home." Sandra said simply. "She wants to be home."

Lucy wasn't shy around children, I thought. She had just been waiting for a family with older kids that wouldn't pull her tail or pick her up and drop her.

I think she had been waiting for us.

And we were waiting for her.

It took just one day to adopt Lucy. Ian and Madd went with me to pick her up, arguing over who got to hold her in the car.

She'd had all her shots, but I took her to the vet the next day. I asked him to listen to her heart three times.

"She's fine," the vet assured me. "Take her home."

86

My work situation was improving. Wes was finally on medication and didn't fall asleep in the middle of a sentence. But some things never change. Beef Jerky still barked at the birds outside. Talk of the Spring Fling Festival, gossip about who was dating whom (all unconfirmed) and nonsensical discussions about weather took up most of the day for Joe and his cronies.

Everyone had their own interpretation of the fair weather.

"Farmer's Almanac predicted it," said Sal.

"El Niño is bringing crazy climate changes," argued Wes.

"It's not spring, it's just a warm spell," said Paulie. "It'll snow again before the month ends."

Turned out, he was wrong.

In my back garden, purple and pink tulips and yellow daffodils nosed their way up through the hard soil and I was able to lay down a dark, earthy mulch earlier than usual. The kids and I went to the garden shop and picked out a beautiful cherry tree sapling that would burst into bloom with cascading pink flowers each spring. We found a place in the sun and took turns digging a deep hole to plant the roots that already looked strong and healthy.

Then I got down on my knees and carefully placed the tiny mahogany box with Penny's ashes into the soil. On top of the little box, I set her favorite chew toy, the green squeaky alligator.

We stood in silence for a moment and I knew we were all talking to Pen, and to the universe. I held the tree and the kids filled in the hole until the sapling stood straight upright. Ian attached a small rope to make sure it didn't bend in the wind. But I knew it would grow to be the strongest tree in my yard, the most resilient. The most precious, because it came from Penny.

We had been her whole life. Start to finish. Our home was her home. It was a life cut far too short and that would always be very difficult to accept. But we had loved her, all of us, we would love her forever, and wherever she was, in the wind, or the grass or the sky, she would also love us forever, all of us imprinted permanently on each other's hearts.

"This is for you Mom," Ian said, holding out a small jewelry box. Inside was a silver locket with simple filigree around the edges.

"Open it," Maddy said.

I pried it open with my fingernails. Inside, tucked behind a bit of glass, was a tiny lock of brown hair, unmistakably Penny's.

Madison helped me put it on and then we all cried some more, this time not completely overwhelmed with sorrow—this time with memories, this time with love.

87

"Postcard from Dad," Ian announced a few weeks later as I was having tea. "You may want to read this one."

On the cover was a photo of an old-fashioned airplane. Adam was in Kitty Hawk, North Carolina, where the Wright brothers were first in flight.

It wasn't a place I'd have had any interest at all in visiting. I was glad he was there himself. Or with someone else by now, I thought, realizing I'd let go of the raging resentment plaguing me for months after he'd left.

It was addressed to Ian.

"Read the message," Ian said.

"Please tell your mom it was a shock to hear about Penny, and I can only imagine how awful it must be for her. Penny had a personality all her own, feisty, loving, intuitive, and smart, very much like your mother. Take care of her, Ian, and tell Madison to do the same. I will always remember Pen as the little fluffball who never left Mom's side, her constant companion."

Ian put his arms around me as I wiped away tears.

We put the postcard on the fridge for Madison to see.

April marked the one-year anniversary of Bryan's move south. He and Sarah were living together, and he was working for a chain of retail stores, designing their sets and window displays, traveling from store to store which gave him a good sense of freedom. His Jack-o'-lantern business was booming; he had enough orders to be busy all the way through till Halloween.

They took Ben to the ocean every Saturday and Sunday; Bry was teaching him to body surf, even though he was only five.

Madison and Billy celebrated their six-month anniversary with a wild rapids raft trip in the Adirondacks.

Ian, permanently off Tinder as he'd always threatened, was focusing more on his studies and waiting for the right woman to find him. He brought his books to the Starbucks in Ashton to study, just to get out of the house. When he took a break and looked up, there was often a girl or two smiling at him. He'd found the more he ignored them, the more women showed interest in him.

"Had I known, I would've done this all along," Ian said thoughtfully.

I was delighted for both of my kids. They deserved it.

One Sunday afternoon in the late-April sun, Lucy and I were sitting out front watching cars go by—not waiting for anything, just sitting—when I heard Lily singing before she even came around the corner on her scooter. She was wearing a blue dress and had a dandelion tucked behind her ear.

"Hi Jessie!" called out a taller, lankier Lily. "I missed you."

It had been a long winter with only a couple of visits from Lily.

"You got another dog!" Lily said happily. "Wait, where's Penny?"

"Honey, Penny went to heaven a little while ago," I said gently.

"I'm so sorry for your loss," said a tall man standing a couple of steps behind Lily. "If this is a bad time, we can—"

"Not at all," I said, feeling my heart thud faster. I tried to stop myself from flat-out staring. He had wild blond hair and was wearing a broken-in pair of Levi's. He had deep green eyes with flecks of gold like the inside of marbles, as if the sun was shining behind them.

"I'm Sawyer," he said. "Sawyer Canton, Lily's grandfather."

I regained some of my composure. "You look too young to be—"

"Yeah, I get that a lot," he said lazily. He took a step toward me and held out his hand. "And you are?"

"Jessica—" I got up out of the chair so fast it fell over backwards. "Jessica Gabriel."

I took his hand, and his eyes crinkled with deep smile lines at me.

"Good to meet you, Jessie."

I've always liked it when people call me Jessie right away. It's a good sign.

Lucy had bounded off my lap and into Lily's arms, and then they were both squealing and rolling around on the grass near the sidewalk.

"Looks like they're going to be a while," I said to Sawyer. "Would you like to sit down for a bit?"

I cursed myself for sounding so formal, but his hand had been warm and he'd had that firm grip that meant he was confident and he was still staring at me, his head slightly tilted as if trying to remember whether we'd met before.

I tried to look graceful as I upended my tipped-over chair.

"I'd love that, Jessie."

And so we sat and rocked, almost in unison, for what I felt could be a very long time.

Share Your Opinion

Did you enjoy *A Girl Like You*? Then please consider leaving a review on Goodreads, your personal blog, or wherever readers can be found. At Circuit Breaker Books, we value your opinion and appreciate when you share our books with others.

Go to circuitbreakerbooks.com for news and giveaways.

CARI SCRIBNER of Ballston Spa, New York, has been a journalist and a freelance feature writer for more than twenty years. With topics ranging from travel to trends and from breaking news to family life, her work has been published in many outlets, including *The Daily Gazette, The Saratogian, Times Union,* and more. Her short/flash fiction has appeared in *Bartleby Snopes, Brilliant Flash Fiction, Corium, Drunk Monkeys Fiction Southeast, Fiction Southeast, Flash Frontier, Gravel, Litro, New World Writing, Nottingham Review,* and *Vending Machine Press.* She lives with her two dogs, Lucy and Miloh, while her three grown children live nearby. *A Girl Like You* is Scribner's first novel.

CPSIA information can be obtained
at www.ICGtesting.com
Printed in the USA
FSHW010938250421

9 781953 639004